REA NOLAN MARTIN

SUNNYSIDE
UP

Cover & Interior Layout Design: VMC Art & Design, LLC

ISBN: 978-0-9910322-4-2

WIAWAKA
PRESS

For Johnny,
My editor-in-the-sky
who slipped quietly into the ether
as I was writing this story.
Your presence abounds, brother,
and is deeply felt always.

"And where we had thought to find an abomination, we shall find a god; where we had thought to slay another, we shall slay ourselves; where we had thought to travel outward, we shall come to the center of our own existence; where we had thought to be alone, we shall be with all the world."

—Joseph Campbell

ONE

ADELAIDE

A delaide Somers awakens with a jolt from an awkward sitting position on the marble bench, her neck in a twist, a line of indelicate spittle sliding from the corner of her otherwise parched mouth. It takes her a moment to notice that she's in the vestibule of the family funeral chapel, although she can't recall why. As far as she knows, no funerals were scheduled for this afternoon. Oh, wait, she thinks. *Oh no!* Her brain scans the details of the past few days. *Oh God.* It's a funeral, all right, she remembers. And not just anyone's. Not the memorial service of 99-year-old five-time Bingo champion, Candace Jeffries from

1

Hazardville, or 101-year-old vaudeville veteran, Babs Gibbons from the Actor's Home. Those were last week.

Weren't they?

She drops her head in her hands. This can't be happening. *Again.*

Stricken, Adelaide rises from the bench, dabbing the corner of her mouth with her grandmother's blue lace handkerchief. The one with the worn corners she'd been saving for her wedding, as if that would ever happen. She secures the wiry hairs of the steel gray chignon at the nape of her neck, and nobly raises her sagging chin. Courage in the face of tragedy, always. Stiff upper lip, *always*. No matter what toll this death has taken and continues to take on all involved, she will persevere with dignity. What choice does she have? The Somers family has anchored the remains of every decent citizen in the township of Outskirt, Kentucky since well before Adelaide came along. Since the dang war, for pity sake. And not just any war. The War Between the States. *The Civil War.* Or whatever folks are calling it these days. *That* war.

And just because it's… She clutches her chest. *Just because this time, it's…*

Good grief, she thinks, how will I do it? How will I…? Well, she just will, that's all. She understands her job. She buries the dead; that's what she does. Afterwards, she personalizes their gravestones with the trivial minutia that once decorated their lives. She'll do this until she herself joins the underground party. If there is such a party, that is. She's not convinced. And if there isn't, well. She'll just lie right there and enjoy the silence. What else can a body do? Until then she'll honor the dead and console the bereaved like the professional she is. Although technically, this time, she is the bereaved. Is she not? Or at least one of the bereaved. She gulps the humid air.

Be still my shattered heart.

Not generally given to self-pity, Adelaide shakes the pleats of her snug black woolen skirt from the static grip of her black tights, and strides across the slate floor with a conviction she doesn't feel. The heels of her polished ebony pumps punctuate the silence, echoing off the stone walls, the cast iron arches and empty wooden pews like a warning. *Click clack. Beware! Click clack. Beware!* Where are the mourners? she wonders. Why aren't they here yet? Even her family.

Even his.

Did his family disapprove of her engagement to Julian so vigorously that they would boycott their only child's funeral? Well, the hell with them, she thinks. She'll bury him directly after the service in her own family graveyard right behind the chapel. In spite of his rogue ways and irreverent manner, she'll celebrate his infidel life with a Christian service anyway. After all, he was hardly an atheist. Not that they discussed religion even once. There was no time! But given a few more years, he would surely have embraced faith of some kind. Wouldn't he? One certainly can't be penalized for dying prematurely, she reasons. At least Julian can't. Adelaide will see to it. After all, she's the one in charge of this funeral parlor. No one else even bothers to show up for work! Except her younger sister, Felicity, that is. But who can count on Felicity?

Crossing the transom briskly, she picks up the pace as she goes. *Clickity click click clack.* She must first retrieve Felicity from whatever nonsensical task she's currently engaged in. A séance this time, no doubt, a tea leaf reading, or an out-and-out alien abduction complete with time travel hallucinations. Could be anything. More advice from the *Purple People* or her invisible friend, Celeste—who knows? Good grief, at this point, nothing about Felicity would surprise her.

If need be Adelaide will grab her sister by the back of her delicate ivory neck. She'll extract her from the fantasies that seduce her and drag her back into the harsh realities of the real world. After all, why should Felicity be allowed to check out? To burden Adelaide with all her fantasmagorical unreliability? They're supposed to be partners, are they not? Wasn't that the arrangement? Not that Felicity has ever been a true partner, at least not for a while. For one thing, she hasn't been herself since the accident. But then neither has Adelaide. And who can blame them?

Every time they turn around, they're burying Julian.

TWO

ADELAIDE

Adelaide sneaks up to the community room on tiptoes. The heavy oak door is cracked open just far enough to reveal Felicity in all her solitary glory. Their mother's Belgian lace cloth is draped carelessly in the center of the mahogany banquet table as if dropped from the sky by Felicity's imagination. A porcelain teapot in her younger sister's right hand is tipped and pouring who knows what—100-proof granny apple moonshine for all Adelaide knows. Moonshine would be a relief. A welcome explanation for Felicity in general, not to mention her recent behavior.

Unlike Adelaide's sober attire, Felicity

is dressed for an Easter parade in a silk dress decorated neck to ankle in a spray of wildflowers. A vintage dress once belonging to their Aunt Lillian, its age advertised in cracked buttons and loose seams that billow around Felicity's near skeletal frame. Skeletal, at least, in comparison to Adelaide's buxom rotundity. Nevertheless, it's Felicity's favorite dress, the one she requested to be buried in when the time comes. Not that Felicity has a date with death. She doesn't. And not that it's likely Adelaide will be there to inter her anyway. Felicity is half a decade younger than Adelaide with a fair amount more vitality, in spite of her loose grip on reality.

Unaware of Adelaide's hovering presence, Felicity continues. "Ah," she says gaily to the empty room. "Finish those eggs, Sadie Mae. Perfectly cooked sunnyside up, just the way we learned from Grandmother Somers. Don't leave a single bite; there are children starving in the Congo." At that, she throws back her head and laughs ruefully, silver curls floating down her back like ribbons. "Remember when our mamas used to tell us that, y'all?" she says. "As if the remains of our eggs had the slightest chance of making it to the Congo!" She leans in, wide-eyed. "You ask me, they should have threatened to send our leftovers to the kids in the holler where they could have fattened up some of those underfed bellies, poor babies. Why, I would have delivered them myself!"

Just when Adelaide is about to scream with frustration—*how can you indulge your fantasies at a time like this!*—it occurs to her that Felicity may not remember what happened. That her sister's fractured psyche may still be jarred from the accident. It's possible. Even likely. After all, they were both with Julian when the car...*when the car...uhhhh.*

Lest Adelaide wander any further into the ruins of that long-buried memory, she leans into the heavy door and flings it wide open.

The sudden movement startles Felicity, whose reflective cat eyes solidify in her head like marbles. "Adelaide Frances Somers," she says breathlessly. "Why, y'all scared the living daylights out of me!" She lifts a doily from the table and fans her face. "Mercy me!"

Adelaide's first instinct is to knock Felicity right off her selfish little planet. After all, it was Adelaide, not Felicity, who was engaged to be married to Julian. Was it not? And isn't Adelaide the one who should be indulging herself? But no, Adelaide is the practical one of the pair, so for the sake of time she will postpone her well-deserved breakdown, or better yet, cancel it altogether. Instead she takes a seat in the wicker chair beside Felicity and clasps her sister's clammy hands. Using a childhood nickname, she says, "Flitty, he didn't make it, girl. I know it's hard to believe. I barely believe it myself, but…he's gone." She stares into Felicity's glassy green eyes. "Julian's… gone. And we just have to accept it."

As Adelaide delivers this news, a fat tear forms unbidden in the corner of her right eye, trailing slowly down her plump cheek. *Julian's gone!* Hearing these words uttered from her own mouth, she is crushed by an avalanche of grief. *It can't be true! What am I saying? It's all a lie!* And instead of comforting Felicity, she collapses helplessly onto Felicity's bony lap.

"There, there, sugar," Felicity whispers, stroking Adelaide's head in a repetitive, irritating manner that Adelaide tolerates because it's the only human touch she can remember since the accident. It's as if she's felt nothing at all since that day, whenever it was. Time is a junk drawer.

"I was there, Addie, remember?" Felicity says distantly. "It was such a long drop. It went on…," she continues in a hollow, nearly disembodied voice, "…forever. Why, I thought it would never end."

Adelaide wiggles out of Felicity's hold and sits up straight. *Long drop?* Felicity's story is an abomination in no way compatible with what actually occurred, at least according to Adelaide's memory. But that conversation will have to wait. "You remember?" she asks, dumbfounded.

Felicity nods blankly. "Sometimes."

"And still, you..." Adelaide points to the tea cups and empty chairs. "You engage in this... escapism?"

Felicity smiles serenely, her full lips bleeding fuchsia lipstick into the folds of her alabaster complexion. For an alarming moment, her face morphs into a young woman's, and Adelaide sees her as she once was—a fragile, absent-minded sylph with tantalizing beauty. Beauty that, however unwittingly, affected every male who crossed her path. Including Julian. Facing this, Adelaide's tight cord of compassion snaps. "Listen here, Felicity Jane, instead of throwing tea parties with y'all's invisible friends, how about getting a grip on reality? How about not leaving it all up to me? Hmmm? How about doing your dang job? And while you're at it, helping me do mine?" She stomps her foot. "Doesn't this enterprise belong to both of us? We've got a business to run, for cripe sake. Carry your goldarn load."

Adelaide's harsh throaty words wash over them both like an ice bath. To Adelaide it feels fresh, cleansing. Sane. What she needs right now is a cold sober partner she can rely on. "Can you do that, Flitty?" she says. "Can you carry y'all's load, so I don't have to do it for the both of us?" Truth be told, Adelaide is sick to death of doing everything for everybody every dang day.

"What is it you need from me, Addie?" Felicity says, wide-eyed.

Adelaide isn't falling for the innocent routine this time. Felicity knows exactly what's expected of her; she just doesn't do it. "What do you think?" Adelaide says. "I need you to play PaPaw's Hammond. Distribute the prayer cards. Contact our lazy cousins to carry the coffin." She locks eyes with her sister. "I haven't seen them in I don't know when. Have you?" She scans Felicity's get-up. "And I would also appreciate it if you would dress in something sober and suitable to the tragic occasion."

"I'll see what I can come up with, Addie."

"And don't be surprised if Julian's family doesn't attend," Adelaide continues. "In fact, don't expect them at all. They don't care a whit about their son. He's dead to them." At this, her eyes nearly pop out of her head. "Oh, my God, Felicity," she moans, "he's dead to me, too. Isn't he? And you!" Her voice drops two octaves. "He's dead to us all."

Felicity shakes her head sympathetically. "Oh Addie, who cares about Julian's family. Right? And anyway, they've been late every time."

"They never did like me," Adelaide whimpers, rummaging through the left side of her oversized Sears & Roebuck brassiere for Granny's handkerchief. Retrieving it, she blots her milky eyes. "They think I'm too uppity for their rugged cowboy. Too...too..."

"Snobbish?" Felicity offers.

Adelaide blinks. "Snobbish?" she repeats, aghast.

"Or just rigid?" says Felicity. "Close-minded?" She shrugs. "I don't know."

"You think I'm close-minded?" Adelaide exclaims.

Felicity turns her back, collecting the cups and saucers from the table. "If the Italian leather shoe fits, Addie."

"What?!" says Adelaide. "For your information, I've never owned an Italian leather shoe in my life."

"I believe y'all are wearing one now," says Felicity. "In fact, I believe you're wearing two."

"Lawdy, Felicity Jane, these pumps are twenty years old if they're a day!"

Felicity places the unused cups and saucers in the sink. "Still," she says. "How many people can afford shoes that last over twenty years?"

"Are you saying I'm a snob? The idea is preposterous!"

Felicity stares ahead thoughtfully. "More like...an inflexible force," she says absently, glimpsing her pink plastic watch. "Does that sound more accurate?" She adds in a panic, "Mercy, Addie, I've got to get going, I really do, and so do y'all. I don't have a thing to wear to this funeral. I wonder if Mother has anything in her closet." She rushes past Adelaide and up the back stairs to their apartment.

"Don't show up in anything striped or neon!" Adelaide calls after her. "And none of those wacky pop-beads, or whatever you were wearing last week. We've got a family reputation to uphold!"

Dearly beloved.

THREE

ADELAIDE

The sign at the front of the stone chapel is cockeyed, having shifted in the recent spring rains. It seems like it's been raining for months, if you ask Adelaide. Years! Or maybe not raining so much as drizzling in a muddy, gray, suicidal sort of way. All the days, however many there are or have ever been, seem to converge into one big never-ending day that wraps itself around Adelaide like a python. A big bossy day that owns her, or thinks it does. But unlike Felicity, Adelaide's too practical to escape into crazy town, as tempting as it is. She kicks the lower corner of the sign to loosen it, then lifts

11

it up, straightening it with her white-gloved hands. *There.* She steps back to admire her work, clapping her gloves to release the dirt.

"*Sunnyside Up Funeral Home and Chicken Farm,*" she reads aloud with a nostalgic sigh.

The chicken farm came first, followed by a few hogs. Ever since childhood, Adelaide heard the stories. Money was plenty tight after the war, they'd said, so the family received the odd overnight travelers on their way to Lexington. Word spread, and the Somers homestead became a popular stop. Of course, the guests had to eat, so every morning Great-grandmother Somers cooked up a delectable pile of freshly laid eggs the only way she'd ever allow them to be served—sunnyside up with sausage and gravy.

"Sunnyside up isn't just an egg," she'd said. "It's an attitude."

And a business was born.

Great-grandmother developed a reputation in the region, and eventually Great-grandfather Otis, imitating the lines of the main house, built a separate stone guest house where the chapel now stands. Two years in, one of their guests up and died in his room. Since no one claimed him, Otis took pity and buried the man right there, adjacent to the family graveyard. After that, he found his calling as a sort-of preacher, and the rest is history.

Adelaide steps back, observing the lower hanging portion of the sign with its chalk scrawl that reads: *Deceased of the Day: Julian T. Buck*

There it is, right there in front of her. Swallowing a lump, she forces herself to read it unembellished by her usual grief-inspired hysteria. She will not cave in. Not today. Julian deserves a dignified departure, and in spite of everything, she will provide exactly that. And anyway, how will Felicity ever recover her sanity if neither one of them is ever able to bury Julian? Somebody has to do it, and no one else seems to so much as remember the man is dead. Not that it's easy for Adelaide of all people. But she's the only one strong enough to keep trying. To reinforce the message, she forces herself to say aloud in her deepest, most credible voice, "Julian T. Buck is no longer among the living. He is a goner. He is D-E-A-D dead." She raises her chin resolutely. "Extinct."

There. The foul thought is out of her head, fully formed and spoken. In so doing, its sharp raggedy edges have lost their power and can no longer tear apart her hypertensive heart. She has faced the thought down, twisted its wrist, and forced it to drop its weapon. Trembling from the struggle, she lumbers up the three slate steps to the chapel, releases the cast iron latch, and enters the innermost circle of her personal hell.

From the balcony, Felicity strikes the opening chords of her original tune, "*When the Sweet Hereafter Claims Your Ungodly Bones*" on Great-grandfather's creaky old organ. Down below in the vestibule, Adelaide gathers the spray of sickeningly sweet Easter lilies, her white gloves stained instantly orange from the shedding pollen. She surrenders to a series of wildly robust sneezes, and halts to wipe her nose with the sleeve of her slick black rayon blouse. She is a mess of mucus. "Damn lilies," she mutters at the same time she reminds herself that lilies are Julian's favorite. Or were. *Were his favorite.* Because now he's dead.

Julian is dead.

In spite of this setback, Adelaide progresses stoically to the foot of the raised altar, where she bows reverently before laying the lilies across the closed pine box. She would like to have upgraded the package to a varnished mahogany casket with brass fittings, but no one in Julian's family would acknowledge the request, never mind pay for the upgrade. In fact, no one in Julian's family, except his decrepit Cousin Thaddeus, showed up at all. There sits Thaddeus in the front pew, bent like a comma, dressed in an ill-fitted brown tweed suit, a derby cocked to one side of his shiny, oversized head. His beady coal-black eyes glare at Adelaide, as if she's not entitled to bereavement. *Because she and Julian weren't married.* As if bereavement were a competition, and he, a blood relative, the front runner. If Thaddeus really is a blood relative at all. Who knows where he came from? In all the time since Adelaide met Julian, she was never introduced to Thaddeus even once. It might have made her think twice about the wedding. Just look at him. Anyone can see what an oddball he is.

While Felicity's hymn drones on interminably, Adelaide reconsiders Thaddeus, thinking perhaps he has a purpose after all. Perhaps he knows something the others don't. Maybe he's an attorney of some kind, here to execute Julian's last will and testament. As if Julian had a will. But you never know. Maybe he wrote up a simple document bequeathing his rusty old classic Chrysler convertible, broken-down Wurlitzer, and wormy trunk of beaver skins circa Lewis & Clark to his next of kin. A status Adelaide never managed to achieve. Or maybe it was more than that. Maybe Julian's brief career pitching manure at Churchill Downs led to an inside bet that accumulated millions. Why not? Luck is luck. All you technically have to do is show up.

In her heart, Adelaide knows this is nonsense—her little story about Cousin Thaddeus, not to mention Julian's imaginary millions. Her head is crammed with it though; she can't help herself. It's as if the rest of her life will involve nothing more than filling-in the blanks of Julian's life. All the things he could have been, but wasn't. Could have done, but didn't. All the achievements and betrayals of a lifetime, squeezed into the confines of Adelaide's tight little crowded attic of a cobwebbed brain. She, the author of Julian's life as it might have been.

Had he lived.

Felicity strikes the final chord, holding it dramatically along with her trilling soprano, "Aaaaa-meeeeeen." Afterwards, she winds her way noisily down the narrow spiral staircase to distribute memorial cards and programs. She is dressed in a red plaid jumpsuit. Her mass of silver curls is bound at the neck with a black velvet ribbon, her wink to solemnity. She offers a card and leaflet to Thaddeus, who is clearly transfixed by her. Who wouldn't be? She's dressed like a package of scotch tape.

Felicity retreats gracefully from Thaddeus, serving up her fare to Mr. Barrows, their faithful groundskeeper, and his wife, Inis, their drive-by housecleaner. She moves on to a gallery of elderly women in the middle pews, all dressed in brightly colored spring suits—lavender, daffodil, and mint. Feathered hats top their blue-gray bubble-cut hairdo's. Where did they come from? she wonders. Adelaide has spent her entire lifetime in Outskirt and never seen a single one of these wide-open potato-faced women since she was a child. And since Adelaide herself is now technically an elder, she would surely have run into them at some point. Not that Adelaide considers herself elder-ly. At least she didn't before Julian...*before he...*

Unable to complete the thought, she steps behind the podium, tapping the microphone to make sure it's on. "Testing, testing," she says. Satisfied, she bows her head. "Dearly beloved..." She blots her eyes with the corner of her gloved pinky, and inhales deeply. The words fill her mouth like gumballs.

"Julian Buck..." She clears her throat. "is...dead."

The odd menagerie of mourners blink in unison, staring blankly back.

"Did anyone hear me?" she says, exasperated. "Is anyone listening? Julian T. Buck! Is! Gone!" A sob bubbles up from the soles of her 20-year-old Italian black leather pumps. When her misery is barely acknowledged in the pews, never mind returned with the appropriate fervor, she practically spits, "What's wrong with you people?! Why did you bother to come! Don't any of you care at all?" She shakes the podium. "He's dead, did you hear me? And he's not...*he isn't...*"

She loses her grip on herself as well as the podium, which rocks back and forth precariously before tumbling down the steps—*thump thump thump*—careening this way and that. She watches, paralyzed, as it strikes the unlocked wheels of the bier, rolling the casket recklessly down the aisle, pew after pew, like an unhinged caboose.

From her station at the back of the chapel, Felicity rushes up the aisle to block it broadside with her slight body, stabilizing it, and securing the wheels. Afterwards she glides up the aisle to the altar where she embraces her sister, arresting Adelaide's runaway emotions as surely as she arrested the bier.

"Addie," she says, "why don't we finish this later? There's no need to do everything now. You said yourself nobody cares."

"If not now...then...when?" Adelaide pants.

"Tomorrow," Felicity says. "How's that, Addie? How about we finish tomorrow?"

"But the body..."

"The body will be fine," Felicity says. "We'll pop it right inside the walk-in. Keep it good and cold until you're ready. No reason to worry at all, I promise. About anything. Not one single thing."

Adelaide sees the sense in this, since she can't go on anyway, and after all, the family isn't even here. Hers or his. And come to think of it, maybe she's been hasty. Maybe their families needed more time all along. They could be on their way right now, slowed down by their swollen grief-stricken eyes and bleeding hearts. After all, who wouldn't be slowed down by the death of Julian?

Felicity takes her by the elbow. "Come on now, Addie," she urges gently.

And Addie concedes, allowing Felicity to lead her down the aisle like the inconsolable widow she would have been had she gotten the bastard to marry her in the first place.

Only the dimwitted make it out alive.

FOUR

ADELAIDE

The next morning Adelaide sips her brewed chicory while flipping through the damp pages of the *Bluegrass Bugle*. Why the paper is so wet she has no idea. It practically disintegrates in her hands. Delivery is not what it used to be. Halfway through she scans the scant obits, muttering, "No one's dying anymore is the problem. This planet will run out of air any day now, but not before Felicity and I go broke."

She reaches into the paper bag Mr. Barrows placed on her back step earlier this morning. He's a weird dude, Barrows, she thinks. Not to mention his wife, Inis. But they mean well, and they never forget her donuts, so what the hell. She selects a crème-filled pastry, and devours it handily. To be honest, she can't stop eating. Grief does that, she supposes. Consume or be consumed. In Adelaide's experience, there's no in-between, so she may as well accept her plight. She has certainly consoled enough customers to know that much. Some wither away like Felicity. Others, such as Adelaide, expand like the Hindenburg. She just hopes she doesn't explode mid-air.

Just as she licks the last of her gooey fingers, the great disappearing Felicity shuffles into the kitchen, lost in her voluminous sunflower housecoat. Her bony feet are wrapped in the mink slippers she constructed out of Mother's old stole. The beady snout on the left slipper bites its own tail. Adelaide shivers involuntarily. She's always had an aversion to Mother's stole, and the hand-fashioned slippers are even creepier.

To be honest, Felicity's whole look this morning is a freak show. The harsh morning light streaming through the eyebrow window above the back door ages her. There is something garish about the light today, it's true. Adelaide's glad she can't see herself. If she had to put a name to the light, she'd call it burnt emerald. As if they'd landed in Oz after the tornado. A gaggle of chirping munchkins at the back door wouldn't surprise her in the least. This thought makes her anxious, and she hovers over the donuts for a minute before selecting a chocolate-glazed cruller to distract herself.

"Googisoejrpso," mumbles Felicity as she shuffles sleepily to the percolator.

Adelaide screws her fingers into her ears to make a point. "Good gravy, Felicity, ENUNCIATE, will you? What the hell does *googisoejrpso* mean? What do I look like, a Russian spy?" She pulls her hair out on both sides of her head. "A Romanian gypsy?"

Felicity turns, surprised, and with great exaggeration says, "Good. Mor. Ning."

Noting Felicity's lush silver hair swept up in a bedazzled headwrap made of something incomprehensible, Adelaide barks, "And what in the Sam Hill is on your head?" While she waits for an answer, she flips *The Bugle* to the crime section, because you never know where your next customer might come from. They don't have to actually bury the criminals at *Sunnyside Up*. They can do all the expensive prep work and ship them to the prison cemeteries where they belong. The money is the same. And anyway, she reminds herself, not everyone convicted of a crime is guilty. It pays to be open-minded.

"What's on your head?" Addie repeats at a higher pitch since the hat covers Felicity's nearly deaf ears.

Patting her head forgetfully, Felicity says, "Oh that. I caught a chill last night, and Granny suggested I wear a ski cap to keep my ears warm. It felt too confining, so I cut a hole in the crown to let my hair out." She pours coffee into the chipped demitasse, adds a cube of sugar and stirs.

"Granny?!"

"That's right," says Felicity. She selects a package of digestive crackers from the overhead cabinet. "I know y'all aren't on speaking terms with her right now, but that's not my problem." She inspects a cracker and nibbles the edges like a squirrel.

Confused by all the things she wants to say, Adelaide's brain jams and she bites her tongue. She has to choose her battles. "Instead of wearing a hat, Felicity, maybe y'all should turn up the heat in your room. We could store bodies in there. It's arctic."

Felicity ignores the comment, or maybe she didn't hear it. She turns from the counter with her coffee just as a calico cat Adelaide has never laid eyes on leaps onto a chair. Felicity leans over, nonchalantly running her fingers down its sleek, curved back with satisfaction. "Hey, y'all," she coos. "How's little Izzy? How's my boy?"

"Izzy? Your *boy*?" Adelaide says, incredulous. "Where did that cat come from? What do you mean, *your boy!*"

"I don't know where he came from," says Felicity. "From my room, I guess. I don't keep tabs on him, Addie. He's a cat."

"I can see he's a cat. When did you get him?!"

Felicity cocks her head, thinking. "I don't know. When did Mother die? Around then."

Even though Adelaide knows that's impossible, she says, "So, at least you know Mother died?"

Felicity sits at the table with her tiny cup and saucer. "Oh, Addie, Addie, Addie. What am I going to do with you?"

Adelaide pushes her chair back from the table. If there's one thing she's not in the mood for right now, it's this conversation. "I need a break," she says. "I haven't slept in weeks. You're the only one who sleeps anymore, Felicity. You sleep like y'all bit the poison apple, while I'm up all hours cleaning up the mess the dwarfs left behind." In her rush to get the hell out of here, her right thigh gets stuck between the chair and the table. She fights her way through, muttering under her breath, "Only the dimwitted make it out alive."

"Dwarfs?" says Felicity, pinkie extended, demitasse at her lips. The cat jumps onto her lap, purring.

"Never mind," Adelaide says flatly as she finally breaks free of the chair. "And don't let that cat on the table while I'm gone. Cats are vile little germ factories."

"Where y'all headed?" says Felicity.

"Out for a walk," Adelaide snaps as she tugs the legs of her sweatpants. She pushes one foot then the other into her black rubber boots and grabs the gray slicker from the hook. "I'll try to be back before your class. If I don't make it, just go on alone this time. It won't kill you."

"But where are you going?"

"Insane, like everybody else around here," she says. "Just in case you need someone who understands you."

"But Dr. Joy says we're both supposed to attend class."

"Phooey, Felicity Jane, you hear me? Phoo. Phoo. Phooey. Did you hear that, or do I need to repeat it?"

"Are you cross with me, Addie?"

Adelaide huffs. "I go to that class to support you, and that's the only reason," she says. "To be blunt, I don't buy the nonsense they're selling, and I never will." She shakes her head. "The light and the dark and the way thought amplifies times seven from one thinker to the next and another seven times back without a word exchanged." She wags her finger. "Utter hogwash. As if your imagination needs the slightest encouragement to fall right off its rocker."

"Well, maybe we should just try it, Addie. Hmmm? Let's experiment right now." Felicity places her cup in the saucer and closes her eyes. "Think of something and send me the thought."

Disgusted, Adelaide closes her eyes and imagines two hundred pounds of puckered fat flying directly at her emaciated sister. "Okay, there," she says. "I've sent you something." She raises her fist victoriously. "Enjoy it."

"Okay," says Felicity. "I hope it was good, because now I'm sending it back to you times seven." She opens her eyes wide. "What was it, Addie?"

Adelaide blinks. "Never mind."

"But what was it?"

"I will not give it credence."

Felicity shrugs. "So, y'all don't think I should go to the classes?" she says.

Waving her hand dismissively, Adelaide says, "Do what you want."

"Dr. Joy buys the hogwash," Felicity says, nodding. "Oh, yes she does."

"Maybe she does and maybe she doesn't. Maybe she just thinks it will help you out of your current…dotage. Or whatever it is you're disappearing into."

"It won't hurt y'all to learn a thing or two, either, Addie. I mean, everything's changed if you haven't noticed."

Adelaide struggles with the zipper on her slicker, which in turn catches on her sweatshirt. She has to admit things have changed, but she doesn't have to admit it to Felicity, since Felicity's the one who changed things. And Julian, of course. Julian changed things the most. Her heart stops.

Oh my God.

Hand to chest, she sinks in despair. "Julian!" she utters on exhale.

Felicity leans over and clasps Adelaide's hand. "Not to worry," she says. "The time will come."

"But…hasn't it been…"

Felicity shakes her head emphatically. "This is not the time, Addie. Trust me."

Adelaide knows Felicity isn't to be trusted, especially with such an important task as Julian's burial. But she just can't think about it right now, and anyway it will get her nowhere.

Just then a horn honks out front. Adelaide jumps back a step while Felicity spills the remains of her coffee on the cat who dives under the table, screeching. Adelaide parts the café curtains, but can't see the vehicle for the ancient budding magnolia that hugs the back of the house.

How odd, she thinks. Other than Inis and Barrows there hasn't been a soul on this property in ages. Inis doesn't drive, and Barrows makes his way around in a dilapidated milk truck. She turns to Felicity, frowning. "My word, Felicity, do you think we have a caller?"

FIVE

ADELAIDE

By the time Adelaide lumbers down the back stairs, circles the massive magnolia, and arrives at the turnaround, the car is slowly making its way back up the driveway. Not just any car, Adelaide notes. Julian's car. His unmistakable 1940 buttercream Chrysler convertible to be exact. She rubs her itchy old eyes with her fists so hard they squeak in their sockets. *Is she seeing things?* No, she can't be. The thing is right there in front of her. Taunting her! But when was the last time that old thing wasn't rusting in a ditch? The last time it was all shined-up and roadworthy like that? Good lawd, she can't remember if it ever looked so good. Jules always intended to restore it, it's true. But he never got around to actually doing it like he never got around to a lot of things. Like marrying Adelaide.

As it pulls away from the house and up the driveway, she can make out the driver's round head and prominent ears topped with a black bowler hat. A head and hat that look suspiciously like Cousin Thaddeus'. But what is that old coot doing here? she wonders. And why is he driving with the top down in all this drizzle? Most of all, if he came to give her the car, why is he exiting the driveway?

As he barrels down the long winding drive, Adelaide can only conclude that he had no intention of giving her the car. That he came to show it off. To rub his inheritance in her face, just as Mother once rubbed her almighty social status, however questionable, in his. The fallacy in that retribution is that Adelaide is not her mother, far from it. And who knows if Thaddeus is Julian's real cousin either? The jury is hung out to dry in a steam bath; it doesn't have a chance. He could be an imposter, an escapee from the federal prison convicted of robbery and fraud. A mass murderer for all she knows. As he waves from behind, Adelaide's middle finger pops up without her full consent in a gesture unworthy of her upbringing. Well, who cares, she thinks, balling-up her fist and shaking it in the air. Who the hell cares about your dang car!

She does.

The car disappears into a vanishing point on the horizon, and Adelaide, defeated, wanders over to the hammock amidst the pines. Even though the hammock is damp, she drops down, *uummph*, and steadies herself with one boot on the ground, swinging. Just back and forth, swinging. Swinging and gazing up through the clearing in the tall pines where the infernally dreary sky threatens. She remembers the time Jules picked her up for their first date. *Remember that?* She grins. *Oh yes, indeed I do remember that.* How he couldn't apologize enough for arriving in his cousin Rasmus' decrepit old truck? If he'd arrived on the back of a three-legged pygmy hippopotamus she wouldn't have cared. She remembers that evening, alright. How young they were. How nimble. How fresh.

Thinking on that day, *dreaming on it,* she sees herself in all her youthful glory. Not the rapidly-spreading matron she has regrettably become, no. Back then her best feature was a pair of sapphire blues with long black lashes that she embellished with her magical Maybelline wand every time her mother turned her back. Then there were her long limbs and elegant hands, in spite of all the graveyard pruning. Not to mention dense, shiny raven hair that swung to her waist. *Her tiny waist.* Her twenty-two-inch waist. Yes, indeed.

Back then her waistbands weren't all stretched and twisted like they are now, and her blue eyes didn't look like jaundiced ping pong balls squeezed right out of her head from hypertension. Oh, Adelaide knows what she's become all right. And she blames it all on Julian. Not that Felicity gets a pass, no. Felicity's bizarre behavior is responsible for at least half of Adelaide's obsessive eating. Just the thought of all this misery causes Adelaide to squirm on the hammock. She lifts her midriff, reaching behind to yank down her bunched-up slicker. While she's at it, she lowers her waistband for air. A woman's got to breathe.

Off to her right, she notices the tulip shoots pushing through the soil, not quite as high as they were that evening so many years back. Adelaide remembers clearly how Julian came to the door armed with a fistful of bright yellow jonquils, not for her, but for her mother. One of his many attempts to win her over. Not that Mother appreciated the flowers, no way. He may as well have served up a platter of desiccated dung beetles stuffed with spider meat. Mother had it all in for Julian from the get-go, just as Julian's family had it in for her. Doomed lovers they were. So doomed.

"Doomed," she says aloud just to hear the tragic sound of it. "Double-doomed." He from a rough-cut coal mining family in the holler and she from refined morticians in the foothills. A regular Romeo and Juliet, minus the costumes and castles. Minus the good parts. And let's not forget the sonnets, she thinks. How in the world folks spoke to each other back then without cracking each other up is beyond her. Just thinking about it, she breaks into a long, deep throaty chuckle that ends in a hacking cough.

Swinging in the hammock, reminiscing for who knows how long, Adelaide recalls meeting Julian in the 1950's. For the life of her, she can't pin down the exact date, or even the year. In fact, her memory couldn't be blurrier after all those donuts. And also, time is becoming less and less relevant, it seems. Less meaningful. Less real. It could have been yesterday that she met him. Or today. It could be happening right here, right now. Right in front of her. Or not at all.

What she remembers is that she was at least eighteen and finished with school. Her days then were spent working as a trainee at *Sunnyside Up* under the tutelage of her great-uncle, the Right Reverend Bertram Somers. Earlier that spring, Julian's youthful Aunt Petunia dropped dead of a ghastly disease. Word got to Adelaide's father whose cousin served with Julian's father in the Battle of Normandy. Their service created a bond between the families, he said, even though they'd never directly met. Julian's clan had lived in the holler for over a hundred years, and no one from the holler had ever been serviced at *Sunnyside Up*. But that was about to change. Exceptions were made. Invitations extended. Not that it wasn't awkward. It was.

Mother, all pumped-up with her own bloated pedigree,

was not on board with this arrangement one bit. She did not buy into all the class equality that tried to poke its opportunistic head up in the years following the war. Such efforts did not serve people like her, she said. It served the underdogs in search of a free pass. She did not care a gopher hole who served in what war and where or who survived, if anyone. She was the granddaughter-in-law of the original minister of the chapel that eventually became a funeral parlor when folks started seeking a decent and dignified departure for their loved ones. Her husband's family, and hers by marriage, shoveled its way to social acceptance six feet at a time. She was not about to give up an inch of it for any coal miner's family. Ordinary humans were owed no favors by the privileged. According to Mother, privilege needed no defense.

The hard-earned struggle of her social climb pumped its way through Mother's veins like clotted blood. She had made something of herself. And no one, *but no one,* had the right to wiggle in and make room for themselves at her mahogany claw-footed table. Especially some good-for-nothing from the holler, which included Julian and the entire Buck family. Needless to say, after the services, Petunia was buried elsewhere. Adelaide's daddy was only willing to push his socialist tendencies so far when it came to Regina.

Back then Adelaide was too in love to see how dead-set against Julian her mother really was. Not that she would have cared, but she might have been more careful. For instance, had she realized how desperate Mother was, Adelaide might have covered her tracks the night she and Julian cavorted behind the miner's shack on the abandoned lot behind the graveyard. Who would possibly be looking for anyone there? They had to cross three gully-washed culverts and a temperamental electric fence to get there. Not to mention the wild pigs.

Right now, Adelaide has no trouble tuning into that scene with high-fidelity. "Mercy!" she says aloud, just thinking about it. *"Mercy! Mercy! Mercy!"*

There was the bristle of Julian's dark beard. That and the fullness of his tobacco-scented lips. How delicate his kisses were, especially considering the lumberjack quality of his steel-gauged body. The scratch of his hands on her bare shoulders cracked her like thunder. *Even now!* Her eyelids shut right down from the force of it.

Ka-boom!

They didn't have relations that night. Adelaide wouldn't have allowed it. Or maybe Julian didn't try, she can't remember. What she does remember is smoking cigarettes for the first time. *Winstons.* One after the other between swallows of the rock gut whiskey pilfered from his cousin's still. Of course, these unwholesome activities were strictly forbidden by Mother and God, in that order. Not to mention Daddy and the Right Reverend. Well, at least she had her clothes on, for cripe sake. Most of them, or some of them. Didn't that count for anything? Apparently not, because Adelaide was grounded for a month. Not that she didn't escape once in a while. She did. And it was ever the more thrilling for the risk.

Drunk on the memory of that first sultry night and the secretive ones that followed makes Adelaide crave a Winston right this minute. *Mmmhmm.* The jingle pops in her head, and she sings it aloud in her husky, offkey contralto, "Win-stons taste good like a cig-a-rette should." She lifts her right arm dramatically above her head, then slowly carries an invisible cigarette down to her lips like Marlena Dietrich, speaking of smoke. If Adelaide had a pack in her pocket right now, she'd smoke them all right down to her cuticles. To be honest, she can't remember why she ever quit in the first place. Dying from smoke beats the hell out of exploding from donuts. If anyone would know that, she would.

The hammock rope presses into her soft flesh. She tries to push herself up, and fails. What was she thinking lying on this soggy hunk of string? And when did it get so moldy? Tiny little bugs march across her neck, and she freaks out, brushing them everywhere in an ineffective, spastic defense. She's got to get out of this thing! After several attempts to push herself forward, she tries just relaxing her body and rolling off sideways, which eventually works. She drops onto her tummy on the bed of damp pine needles, and catches her breath. Just melt into the earth and close her eyes until the Second Coming, whenever that is. *Take your time, Jesus!* She could just lie right here and avoid all the dastardly issues that demand her constant attention. Issues like Julian and Felicity.

And just sleep.

As she thinks about raising herself up on all fours in preparation for the heroic effort of standing, Felicity comes running across the driveway screaming, "Addie! Addie! Oh, my God! What's happened! Are you dead? Oh, Addie dear, please don't be dead!"

Adelaide can't help thinking how much easier life would be if she were.

Felicity arrives breathless, her daisy housecoat stuffed haphazardly into a pair of old dungarees and topped with a faded red jersey. The bedazzled ski cap remains on her head, ears exposed now, silver hair still cascading through the hole in the crown. "Are you alright?!" she gasps, hand to chest.

"I'm fine, Felicity," says Adelaide. "Stop being so melodramatic. What all's in that basket of yours, anyhow?"

"I've been told it's time to groom the graveyard," she says, wide-eyed. "Our dearly departed are feeling neglected. Their resting place is overrun, so they say. And don't think they don't notice just because they're underground, Addie. They most certainly do notice. Six feet of dirt is no obstacle to the deceased. In time, they learn to see beyond it."

Adelaide sighs. *Uh huh.*

"Uncle Pothead told me it's no wonder nobody's signing up for funerals with us these days," Felicity continues. "Aside from the obvious disrespect to the family, he warned me that the condition of the yard is a disaster for business."

Pothead was their Grand-uncle Stewart, thusly named because his head was the shape of Mother's cast iron chili pot and just as cavernous.

"I dunno," Adelaide grunts as she drags herself upright on the trunk of a pine. *Oh, the knees!!!* "I'm not up for working the yard today, Felicity. And anyway, it's drizzling." Her right cheek is a pin cushion of pine needles that drop off one by one.

"It's always drizzling these days," says Felicity. "Our loved ones can't suffer just because it's raining all the time. And anyway, Pothead won't leave me alone about it." She turns to her right. "Okay, okay, Uncle!" she scolds the air. "You made your point."

Adelaide stares at her sister, drinking her in—the wacky clothes, the hat hair, the fuchsia lipstick bleeding into the corners of her once perfect little bow of a Shirley Temple mouth. Felicity's crazy, Adelaide knows, but maybe that's what you get when you compress all that kinetic energy into one tight little filament of a body. Adelaide wishes she could poke a hole in each of her sister's ankles to release some of the pressure.

"Pleeeaassse, Addie!" Felicity pleads. "Will you help me? Pothead's gone mad and he won't drop the subject."

In the end, Adelaide concedes because it's a miracle Felicity wants to engage in anything other than pop-up tea parties with spooks. Not that Pothead isn't a spook; he is. But at least he's got her doing something productive. And anyway, who else is going to do it? Their cousins, Edgar and Samuel, haven't seen fit to show up in however long. Adelaide can barely remember what they look like. If there wasn't straight up physical evidence of their gravedigging over the decades, she'd be wondering if she'd made them up altogether. But then, imaginary people are Felicity's department, not hers.

Obituary for Release to:
Bluegrass Bugle &
The Louisville Gazette
Saturday, September 1, 1945

Miss Annabelle A. Jackson, 75, Goes 'Sunnyside Up'
Born: May 5, 1870
Passed into eternal life: August 30, 1945

Miss Annabelle A. Jackson of Outskirt, Kentucky, bid
final farewell to her Sunnyside Up family on Sunday
following a pot roast supper with her elder sister,
Gertrude, at their home. Regarding her sister's passing,
Gertrude commented, "I'll tell you what; it was a dang
pity. Belle was really enjoying that delicious roast, which
was not her recipe or we'd both be dead." When further
queried about the circumstances, Gertrude explained
that she'd just excused herself from the table to walk
their whiny, one-eyed beagle, Felix, out the back to do
his business. "And when I returned, there was Belle
all laid out on the floor face-up with a bent fork in her
right hand. She was a left-hander, so I knew right away
something was wrong."

Among other administrative duties at the *Sunnyside
Up Funeral Home and Chicken Farm*, Miss Jackson was
the self-appointed Supervisor of Thematic Funeral
Services. As the Outskirt Fire Department will not likely
forget, she directed Junior Roger's memorable Viking
Funeral down at Wankakee Lake involving a row boat,
a gallon of gasoline, and a blowtorch. And who could

forget Georgette Mikelson's Cinderella Farewell in which the deceased was dressed in the old pink ball gown that finally fit her after sixty years and a bout with consumption. Mrs. Mikelson was carried in a buggy attended by six children dressed as mice, and led by the Mikelson's old mule, Hedwig.

According to Annabelle's niece, Mrs. Regina McManis Somers, wife and business associate of the esteemed Jasper Somers, proprietor of *Sunnyside Up Enterprises*, "Annabelle's position will not be refilled since the entire idea of thematic funerals was absurd from inception."

Annabelle is survived by her sisters, Abigail, Lillian, Trudie, Cassie, Lucille, and Miranda Mae, and is predeceased by her baby brother and Purple Heart recipient, PFC Stewart Jackson, USMC, known affectionately as Pothead. Her extensive collection of ceramic doll heads will be glued to her tombstone, as declared in her Last Will and Testament.

Sunnyside Up invites mourners to join them in wishing Annabelle a distinguished farewell with balloons and clappers on Friday from 10-2 and 7-9. Services will be held Friday at 9:00 a.m. in the chapel, followed by a yodeling competition in the barn.

When asked for a comment, Mrs. Regina Somers stated, "Sunnyside Up isn't just an egg, it's an attitude."

SIX

ADELAIDE

Adelaide follows Felicity over the gravel drive past the giant spreading magnolia to the one-acre fenced-in family plot at the back of their ten-acre parcel. The rambling fence is a broken-down atrocity, it's true, and she makes a note to berate Barrows about his reckless disregard for detail. You can't even pay folks to do a job anymore, she thinks, disgusted. Although, come to think of it, she can't remember when she last wrote a check to him or really, anybody. Maybe she owes him money. But if that's the case, why does he keep mowing the lawn and delivering groceries? Why does Inis keep cleaning the house and preparing meals? Good grief, if she owes them money, let them send a goldarn bill. Doesn't she have enough to worry about? Last she noticed, they'd each had two hands and a pair of corneas. Although the way the house and yard have been looking, their cataracts are probably thicker than the crabgrass.

Felicity offers Adelaide her wicker basket filled with gardening tools, a feather duster, and a half-dozen polishing rags. "Choose your weapon," she says.

Adelaide grabs the rags and duster. "I'll do the mementos," she says. With all this rain, the mementos should be well-rinsed and a lot less work than the gushy flower beds. She flips the hood of her slicker overhead and drags herself to the graves of Granny McManis' maiden siblings in the Jackson cluster at the far northeast corner near the woods. This is where, among others, her Grand-aunts Trudie, Annabelle, and Lillian are long buried, not to mention Cassie, Lucille and Miranda Mae. Best to begin with people she actually cared about when they walked the earth. If only her mother had been like her aunts, Adelaide thinks, childhood might have been bearable.

Bent at the waist to protect her screaming knees, she starts by polishing the red and black poker chips glued to Trudie's stone. Oh how her aunt loved a good game of cards, Adelaide thinks, chuckling. A regular gamester, she was, and damn good at it! Not to mention how she became the town bookie. Adelaide has a vague girlhood memory of the first whiskey-soaked night that Trudie beat the men at their own game. What a ruckus, yes indeed. Trudie didn't give a damn about sparing those grizzly old men an ounce of their overgrown egos. Even though she was reportedly a real looker in her youth, she wouldn't marry a one of 'em out of pure spite. Or maybe they just weren't smart enough for her.

Onto Annabelle's porcelain doll head collection, Adelaide

notices how ratty the hair is on the heads glued to the north end of the stone. She hopes Pothead doesn't complain about it to Felicity. As if Pothead really complains to Felicity. *Ha!* Either way, Adelaide is certainly not up to washing the ratty doll hair of twenty creepy cracked doll heads, that's for sure, even for Annabelle. Not to mention combing it out with tiny hair picks and drying it. She'd rather tie little rain bonnets on their heads one by one, which will happen right after she rises from the dead in a burst of glory.

An hour later, following slow progress on the Jackson corner, she grits her teeth and starts on her mother's stone. Not that she remembers much about her mother's death. She doesn't. Or her father's either when she thinks about it. She can't even recollect seeing his grave. Where is it? Nowhere near her mother's is all she knows. But how can she keep track of everyone? She loved her father, but life can be so overwhelming, not to mention death.

One at a time, she polishes the 49 salt & pepper shakers affixed to her mother's fifty-plus-year-old hunk of engraved granite. Like her mother before them, the circus elephants mock Adelaide, as does the parade of scary clowns, Mardi Gras masks, and ridiculous rhinoceros ballerina shakers glued at 90 degrees to all sides of the headstone. The tumbling pink elephants are last. Rain drains from their trunks like a fatal infection.

"Adios, Madre," she mutters dismissively as she moves on to the next row of graves.

She wishes she felt an ounce of sentiment for her mother, but she doesn't. Even if she did, she wouldn't give her mother the satisfaction of showing it. Mother, known to the universe as Regina McManis Somers, was a frosty and unforgiving force with an ice pick for a tongue. Felicity doesn't harbor the same harsh maternal memories, but if you ask Adelaide, that's because Felicity's too darn forgiving for her own good. Maybe if she'd cultivated some boundaries she wouldn't dress like a starved minstrel and talk to spooks all day long.

Adelaide walks right past Granny McManis' taxidermy collection to Great-uncle Chuck's army of tin soldiers. How Chuck's trinkets were allowed, she'll never know. Someone must've forgotten to tell him that Kentucky, a critical border state, turned infamously Union, not that everyone was on board. Adelaide considers knocking them all off, but in the end, he was what he was, and what's the sense in pretending otherwise? Dishonesty has its own price. It's not like he can do any more damage at this point. But just in case, she plucks a four-star general off the side and tosses it into the woods.

Burdened by the weight of her unwieldy memories as well as the immoveable force of her spreading body, Adelaide is just plain wrung out. Add to that the water torture of the constant drizzling rain against the hood of her slicker, and she's hit her limit. She fishes through her brassiere for her hanky, and dabs her face. In addition to the memories and the weather, Adelaide is overwhelmed, as she always is, by the absurdity of the bric-a-brac that surrounds her. Just look at it! *You can't take it with you, people!* And even if you could, why would you?

Not that Adelaide is unaware of the tradition. Past generations of the Jackson and McManis clans were obsessed with any kind of collection—penguins or pigs; lipstick or arrowheads. It was a constant competition. Back in the day, they made sure the youngsters knew exactly how to memorialize them. Made them sign promissory notes with drops of pinkie-pricked hemoglobin. It's as if they'd been thinking about death since birth. "How will I be remembered?!" is all that mattered. It's probably why they had kids in the first place. Every action calculated to enhance their counterfeit memory.

They managed to pass this tradition on to Adelaide's generation, too. To everyone but Adelaide, that is. Adelaide doesn't want any of this crap near her gravesite. She wants a clean, polished stone of lily-white marble. She collects nothing, and is spare in all endeavors. Simplicity is a virtue; clutter a cloven hoof. A clean stone is the only thing that would ever stand out in this bloody five and dime of a graveyard anyway.

All this work has stimulated Adelaide's appetite something fierce. She rummages through her slicker for fuel, landing on a sticky cough drop at the bottom of her right pocket. She picks it off and pops it in her mouth. Dwelling on death is a hazard of the trade, she thinks, as she prods the cough drop from the roof of her mouth with her tongue. Sooner or later every living thing will die, including her and Felicity.

And...oh no. *Lawd no.* Here it comes.

Julian.

This time the thought is a surprise attack. A nuclear missile launched from a distant base, entering her brain seventy times seven. Exploding it. Where did it come from? Who sent it? *What happens next?* Julian T. Buck is dead. As in—no longer walks the earth. As in—no longer drives a rundown old 1940 buttercream Chrysler convertible. No longer hays horses. Digs graves. Plucks the fiddle. Mingles with her in rapture. Where did he go? *Oh, my God. Where?*

Almost on cue, the wind picks up, the willow branches whip back and forth, and a lump the size of a Kentucky coal mine lodges in her throat. Or maybe it's the cough drop. She calls out to Felicity on the other end of the yard. "F-F-Fl-itty!" She inhales her screech like a donkey in distress, *'heeee'*, exhaling, *'haaaaw!'* "Come quick! Oh Flitty! *Fl-it-ty!* You won't believe what's happened!"

Felicity cocks her head and turns. How Felicity hears her

over the rustling branches, Adelaide has no idea. But she does. She hears her. They are twin souls. Two sides of a damaged coin. How did she not realize this before? She should not be so hard on Felicity. What would she do without her?

"Did you need me, Addie?" Felicity calls out eerily, her voice trailing in the wind.

Adelaide nods, her chin trembling, waterworks sprinkling.

"Be right there," Felicity calls back, rushing across the yard past the swinging branches of the wind-swept willow and the tall pin oak to Adelaide's side. Wrapping her bony arm around her sister, she says, "Let's get back then, shall we, Addie?"

Adelaide hands her the cloth and duster, and together they turn toward the house. She tries to calm herself down. Get a hold of yourself, Adelaide, she tells herself firmly. You can't fall apart now. You're the only sane one left.

Obituary for Release to:
Bluegrass Bugle &
The Louisville Gazette
Monday, January 11, 1955

Death of Granny McManis Stuns Friends and
Enemies Alike
Born: February 6, 1878
Passed into eternal life: January 8, 1955

At 77, Abigail Loretta Jackson McManis looked older
than Peabody Mountain where she was raised by
impoverished parents and a herd of bossy sisters.
At the age of fourteen, when her youngest brother,
Stewart, was born, Abigail packed a rucksack and fled
on foot as far away as she could get. To hear her tell
it, she traveled holler to holler till nightfall, when she
passed out in a dry gully just outside Outskirt Hollow,
where she was eagerly taken in and cleaned-up by the
nearby McManis family. Less than a week later she was
married off to their delinquent son, Bosworth, known to
most as Moon. Abigail and Moon stuck it out some forty
years till he died of a buckshot wound cleaning his own
rifle behind the family still. When asked about Moon's
drunken mess of a demise, Abigail was known to wag
her bent old finger and say, "I am a relation of General
Andrew Jackson, 7th President of the United States 1829-
1837, who fought like a weasel for his country. So don't
be asking me how Moon done hisself in. Anybody could
see that man was beneath me from the get go."

This past Saturday Granny McManis, as she came to be known throughout Outskirt, climbed into the family pickup which she was forbidden to drive for too many reasons to name. She got as far as the post office before she ran that vehicle straight into a cast iron lamp pole, and that was that.

In addition to her husband, Bosworth, Mrs. McManis is predeceased by her maiden sisters, Annabelle, Lillian, Trudie, Cassie, Lucille, and Miranda Mae Jackson, as well as her baby brother and Purple Heart recipient, PFC Stewart Jackson USMC.

She is survived by her only child, Regina McManis Somers, wife and business associate of the esteemed Jasper Somers of Sunnyside Up Enterprises, as well as her granddaughters, Adelaide Frances and Felicity Jane. She leaves behind her taxidermy collection of squirrels, snakes, and possum, which will be glued to her tombstone, as stated in her Last Will and Testament.

Sunnyside Up invites mourners to celebrate Granny's passing in the chapel this Friday at 3 p.m., followed by a catfish supper in the community room. Sparklers and bottle rockets will be lit in the graveyard at dusk.

When asked for a comment about her mother's passing, Mrs. Regina Somers stated, "Sunnyside Up isn't just an egg, it's an attitude."

SEVEN

ADELAIDE

Seated at the small enamel table in the kitchen corner, her back to the wall, Adelaide leans down to slide the baked clay jug of PaPaw McManis' reserve hooch from underneath the table then hauls it up, grunting. *Uuuuhhhh.* What an effort, but totally worth it. She stands to get some leverage then pours a jigger or so, which becomes a gusher, into a large mug of sweet tea, adding an extra tablespoon of sugar, and stirs.

Just the act of stirring it all together like this causes relief to course through her veins. Working in that graveyard is not for her. Never was, never will be. Give her a funeral service to orchestrate, and she's your girl. Not that she's orchestrated any recently, but whose fault is that? It's not as if she can conduct a funeral without a dead body. Without a life well-lived. Or even half-lived, like Pothead's and some of her other goony kin. Although to be honest, not all of them were goons. Most notably there was her second cousin once removed, the Honorable Cecil McManis, judge of the tenth district court, who led a lucrative life before losing it all at the derby. But that's a McManis male for you. Waving one crooked hand at everybody else while betting on a loser with the other.

Adelaide cranes her neck, scanning the room. Somewhere around here is the 3-ring binder containing every *Sunnyside Up* obituary ever written, and there were some humdingers. First there were the bright-eyed obits about how flawless everyone was that were approved by Mother for public consumption. These were fashioned from interviews with each family member before death. "Make sure you tell them how I loved the bunny rabbits," mumbled drunken Uncle Bert before collapsing from syphilis. And then there was cousin Renfro's last request to "add in the part about how I coulda shot that two-timin' skunk, Elliott Ward, but I let him scoot back into the grease bucket whar he belongs," when all along Ren was three-timing in three different states. But no one knew about that till the three wives showed up at the funeral with an assortment of look-alike kids.

Then there was *Sunnyside Up's* secret stash of real-life obits, the true grit. *The Drafts.* Adelaide makes a mental note to look for the book in the parlor files tomorrow. She wrote a few of them herself, but Mother turned the task over to crazy cousin, Becky, when she graduated from the junior college with a degree in typing. Why Mother did that, Adelaide can't remember. Just to show Adelaide who's boss, probably. But maybe somewhere in those drafts is a clue that will help solve the mystery of what happened to this town. Where everybody went. How most of Outskirt got sucked down a sewer hole leaving her and Felicity in the catch-all to fend for themselves. Not that she'd admit any of that to Felicity, of course. Why, Felicity can barely cope with seeing and breathing at the same time. The last thing Adelaide wants to do is shine a spotlight on the family's genetic insanity. Best forgotten for now, or at least overlooked.

She shuts her eyes and slowly inhales the fumes from the mug. Alcohol is so medicinal. So deeply healing! Whoever invented bourbon should win a Nobel Peace Prize, she thinks. Or just a bunch of money from somewhere, who cares where? There's enough pretense in the world. One whiff of bourbon and she collects her fugitive emotions so expertly as to have nearly forgotten why or how they escaped in the first place. A little sweet tea, a little bourbon, and twenty minutes without Felicity, and her brain slips right back into her skull. She takes a long hot sip, swishes it around in her mouth like dental rinse, and down the hatch. *La de da.* Life is a carousel.

What created her anxiety in the first place, of course, was Felicity's insistence that they spend the day at the cemetery. Because of Pothead, of all people! How's a gal to maintain her composure in a place where disturbing memories are constantly crouched like thieves, ready to pounce? And not just her own memories, but the not-so-buried memories of all the underground scalawags.

She dunks a chunk of Inis' peppery gingerbread into her tea then directly onto her tongue before the cake has a chance to fall apart. *Mmmmmm.* She's got to learn to say no to Felicity, is the problem. To be more protective of herself and less protective of her unbalanced sister. After all, not protecting herself does zilch to protect Felicity anyway. Felicity's just *out there*, whether Adelaide comes to her rescue or not. There's no drawing her back in at this point.

"No," she practices with half a mouthful of cake. Then more forcefully, "No, I said. No!"

Felicity's footsteps in the hallway proclaim her arrival, and Adelaide slips the jug of bourbon under the table. No point broadcasting the booze to Felicity, who definitely doesn't need to add liquor to her naturally intoxicated bloodstream. The girl barely finishes a cracker the entire day, not to mention a real meal. A shot of whiskey could easily land her in a hospital. If she could even get to one. After all, who would drive her? Neither one of them has driven in years. Barrows, she supposes. In his milk truck! She shakes her head slowly. That'll be the day she rides around in that clown car.

Felicity crosses the threshold cuddling her squirmy new cat, what's-its-name. Adelaide can't remember the critter's name, and anyway, Felicity's probably changed it five times since this morning. They might as well name it *Whoziwatz,* since that's what they'll end up calling it, like everything else. Either that or *Thingamajig.* What was its name this morning? she thinks. Oh yes, Izzy. A boy named Izzy, for pity sake. This is the same cat Felicity claims to have had all along. Adelaide knows that's pure collywobble, but what can she do about anything anymore? Nothing. Not a single thing.

Still decked-out in her wacky housecoat and topless ski cap minus the dungarees, Felicity doesn't get past the refrigerator before Whoziwatz jettisons from her arms like a demon projectile, landing all the way across the room on the counter. Adelaide's mouth is too full of cake to protest without gagging, so she bugs her already protruding eyes so far out they practically dangle. Taking note, Felicity gently nudges the cat off the counter and onto the floor, wiping the counter with the sleeve of her housecoat.

Adelaide swallows her cake in a hurry, developing an inconvenient throat bubble. "You better use some ammonia on that counter, Felicity Jane," she warns. "If you don't want to get cat scratch, that is." She wags her finger. "And also, if you want to keep the cat."

"What's that, Addie?" says Felicity. "I can't understand you. You have a bubble."

Adelaide clears her throat several times, followed by a quick swallow of the spiked tea. "Clean the dang counter with ammonia, I said!"

"Oh, Jelly's perfectly clean," says Felicity. "Trust me, I just bathed him in the sink."

"You bathed the cat? You're not supposed to bathe cats, Felicity. It might even be against the law. Cats are supposed to bathe themselves."

"Oh Addie," Felicity sighs, "how can I possibly trust him to take a bath by himself? He's a cat!" She reaches under the sink and grabs a sponge. "And anyway, it was his idea. He jumped into the sink while I was rinsing my nylons." She wipes the counter absently. "My nylons are absolutely ruined," she adds. "But when do I wear them anyway? I don't even know why I was cleaning them."

She tosses the sponge into the sink, fetches some tea for herself, and slips onto the chair beside Adelaide. "Jelly's an unusual cat, Addie. A spirit guide, I think. Just leave him to me, and everything will be fine. You'll see."

Adelaide dunks her cake, wishing she'd had the sense to add an extra jigger of bourbon to the tea before her sister arrived. Or just filled the whole dang mug with hooch. Who needs tea? The only thing it's good for is disguising hooch.

Grabbing the seed catalogue at the center of the table, Felicity absently turns the pages as she sips. "Lilacs," she says, pointing to a picture. "We could use some new lilac bushes. They're my absolute favorite!" A few more pages in and she looks up in earnest. "Come with me to the class tonight, Addie? Please? I don't want to go by myself, and anyway, it'll do you good."

Adelaide says, "No," with emphasis, pleased with the follow-through on her previous plan. *She did it!* No explanation, just, *"No!"*

"Pleeaaaase?" Felicity pleads. "Pretty please?"

Adelaide stares ahead as if she's actually considering the request, which she emphatically is not. Not for a single second. *The answer is No!* She gets caught up in Felicity's appearance again, however, and irritated beyond measure, reaches up and yanks the cockamamie ski cap from her sister's head. Felicity's silver curls cascade to her shoulders in a youthful, fluid manner. How her hair keeps growing robustly while the rest of her languishes in decline, Adelaide finds odd. Not to mention the fact that Adelaide's own hair falls out in handfuls. "And don't ask me again," she says petulantly. "I'm too tired after all that wretched work in the dang graveyard. I told you I didn't want to do it in the first place. It's not for me. Next time, call Barrows. Or your cousins. Remember them?"

"But Pothead…"

"The hell with Pothead!"

"Oh Addie," Felicity scolds.

"Oh Addie, yourself."

Felicity shakes her head. "And not just Pothead, Addie, if I'm being honest. It was more than Pothead, believe me. You remember the purple people…"

Adelaide pounds her fist. "Don't, Felicity. Just. Don't."

"But, Addie…"

Adelaide points her finger at her sister in warning. "I can't hear about the damn purple man again, Felicity, not one more time."

"There's more than one…"

"We had an agreement."

"There's a ring of them…"

Adelaide cranes her neck forward, her eyes bleeding into Felicity's gaze. "Listen to me, Felicity. They are. In. Your. Head."

Felicity stares down at her folded hands. Her right eyelash is half unglued, hanging off the lid like a centipede. Her neck and cheeks are splotched with cemetery dirt. "You just have to come to the class with me," she tells Adelaide. "I'm not giving up. Plus, it'll be good to be with people who are just as confused as we are, don't you think?" She shakes her head. "You can't deny how confusing it all is, Addie."

"What the hell are you talking about?" says Adelaide. "Confused about what?"

Though to be honest, every conversation with Felicity leaves Adelaide a little more confused. In fact, right now her mental health feels at genuine risk and her feet are sweating. She's got to get these boots off! She turns sideways, trying to loosen her rubber wellies toe-to-heel to avoid bending over. As if she were the least bit capable of bending over.

"I'm talking about the times," Felicity continues, wide-eyed. "About what's happening around here. Where everybody went, including Edgar and Samuel. Where are they?" She frowns. "I haven't even heard the phone ring; have you? I haven't heard it in ages." Her voice trails off like smoke. "Do we still have phones, Addie?"

Felicity watches Adelaide struggle with her boots, and finally kneels down and tugs one from her sister's right leg, and then the left. She hesitates for a minute then ducks under the table and drags out the jug of bourbon. "Why, would you look at this," she says. "Mother's been drinking again." Sliding the bourbon over to the lower cabinet while still on her knees, Felicity asks Adelaide, "Have you heard the phone ring lately, Addie?"

To be honest, Adelaide had forgotten about phones altogether, or frankly, that they'd ever owned one or talked to anyone besides each other and the skeletal housekeeping staff. "Maybe the phone's broken," she says. "I hope it is. I can't think of a single person I want to talk to anyway, except..." she blinks, arrested by the thought, afraid to say it aloud. *Julian,* she says to herself. *Julian.* She swipes her forehead three times, muttering, *"Cancel! Cancel! Cancel!"* under her breath, as her Scottish Granny taught her. Best to banish that omnivorous whale of a thought before it swallows her whole.

Felicity drops the telephone reference, but continues to nag mercilessly about the class. "It'll be so good for y'all, Addie! You'll learn so much!" *Blah blah blah. Meow meow. Oink oink.*

"Why don't you just take off with the purple man?" says Adelaide, smugly, though she instantly regrets it.

"But Addie, I thought we agreed..."

"We did," she says. "Sorry."

But it's too late. All her stupid comment buys Adelaide is another half-hour of relentless persuasion, at the end of which she blurts, "Fine, I'll go to the goldang class!"

Adelaide knows she should have resisted, but in the end, she caves into Felicity because of her sister's crying need for company. Adelaide's company. The truth is, Felicity needs help just living and breathing in the real world, never mind dressing herself and getting on a bloody bus. *And actually going somewhere!* She needs help bridging the growing sinkhole of an eroding mind that's taking her down by the minute. And this is her way of asking for it. *"Take me to my class! I can't go on my own!"* It could be a class on rockets or rocks, it wouldn't matter. She can't go anywhere alone.

If you ask Adelaide, what Felicity really needs is to get the hell away from the damn graveyard. To talk to real people instead of spooks. Sometimes Adelaide thinks of kidnapping Felicity and moving them both far from *Sunnyside Up*. But the thought doesn't linger. She hasn't got the stamina for a move that big, and she knows it. From their ancestral property, no less! Where would they live? A condominium in Louisville? A retirement home in Franklin? She just can't picture them anywhere but here. Besides, if they moved from Outskirt, who would bury the dead?

In preparation for tonight's class, they retreat to their respective bathrooms to rinse off the graveyard grime. As a condition of Adelaide's surrender, Felicity also agrees to pin her hair at the nape of her neck in an age-appropriate chignon. Enough of her hapless appearance, Adelaide had demanded. If they're going to be seen together in public, Felicity had better resemble an adult.

Upstairs, drying off her baggy old beanbag of a body, Adelaide takes note of her tired surroundings. Her bedroom hasn't changed much in all these years, she has to admit. In fact, not at all. She never seems to have the appetite to refresh the peeling floral paper or the faded bed linens. Every day she walks past the chipped walnut nightstands and matching dresser without a thought of replacing them. Or even refinishing them. The water stains are unsightly, not to mention the frayed basketweave rug that covers much of the scuffed wide-plank floorboards.

In truth, there's something comforting about all this disrepair and the memories it suggests. Memories of climbing out that window, for instance. *Oh yes!* On a bedsheet fastened to the ten-ton dresser! Remember that? *Oh yes, I do. I do, indeed.* Memories of climbing up the trellis after midnight, missing the window ledge, and nearly landing on her head. She chuckles heartily, breaking helplessly into a good belly laugh. What a sight she was that time, all covered in loam and smelling like a flock of chickens. *Mercy!* And why in the world would she do anything to alter all those memories at this point? Is she really going to spruce up her room like a *Ladies Home Journal* centerfold for pity sake? Hardly. At least not at this age. Face it, she's got one foot in the grave and the other on a banana peel. Wherever she lands, decorating will be the least of her concerns.

Adelaide rummages through her sparsely equipped closet, and struggles into a freshly ironed paisley shirtwaist dress. She has to loosen the snug belt a couple of notches for comfort. There. It feels rather good to get dressed though, she has to admit. Not to be slouching around in a pair of sweatpants. If only they were dining at a fine restaurant instead of falling asleep in a meditation class, or whatever woo-woo she's about to be subjected to, life would be tolerable. Adelaide hasn't been to a dining establishment of any kind in so long, she can't remember when. Not for pizza or barbecue, or even a decent Salisbury steak. Or how about her favorite *Supercalifragilistic Black Cherry Ice Cream Sundae Jamboree* at the downtown Outskirt soda fountain! *Remember that?* Oh my, yes, she does remember that. How could she forget! She smacks her lips. Now that was an excursion worth repeating.

She sits all spread-out at the dressing table, powdering her wrinkly old prune face in the mirror and sliding a loose hair back into her bun. *There.* Best she can do with such scant raw material, and anyway, it's hard to look at herself. Harder and harder to imagine herself in her feminine prime. You ask her, she looks more like a man every day. Before descending the back stairs to the kitchen, she selects a clean hanky from her linen drawer, and slides it deftly into the corner of her jumbo-sized engineering marvel of a brassiere.

Ten minutes later, Felicity shows up in the kitchen wearing a pair of grass green ski pants that loop under her feet, beneath a scarlet mohair tunic. Her chignon already hangs by a pin. She looks like a Christmas elf, but what can Adelaide say? She's running out of comments. And anyway, it'll be dark by the time they get there.

First thing Felicity does is root through the storage closet and emerge with a big white tufted jacket, puffy as a cloud, that Adelaide's never seen before.

"Look at this, Addie," she exclaims. "I didn't even know this was in there. It's exactly what I dreamed of before opening the door! I'm getting very good at conjuring things."

Adelaide has no idea what's in that closet, and judging by what comes out of it, is perfectly content with her dearth of knowledge. Felicity's wardrobe is a costume trunk. Where she gets this stuff is her own beeswax. If she ever asks Adelaide to help her clean out that closet, the only tool she'll need is a match.

As they walk out the door, Adelaide grabs her knitting satchel behind the umbrella stand so she'll have something to do in class besides listening to a bunch of BS. After all, she's a doer. She does things. Her life is filled with concrete tasks, like consuming Inis' food and burying bodies. She has to keep her hands busy. Right now, she's knitting the start of a coaster or a bedspread. She hasn't decided. She's been knitting it for years, but things always get in the way. Things like death, insanity, and a bunch of graveyard rabble-rousers who refuse to stay buried. Or in the case of Julian, to be buried at all.

The changes are coming.

EIGHT

ADELAIDE

Down the stairs and out the driveway, the sisters hold onto each other for balance, teetering slowly to Outskirt Corner across from the old Dollar Store that was condemned after the incident. What incident, Adelaide can't remember, just that people were desperate. But who cares about that now? They've all moved out anyway. Outskirt is a ghost town.

Adelaide's lumbago is acting up from all the damn stooping in the cemetery. Felicity's got a lighter step, but not by much. They inch up the driveway like tiny little wind-up farm animals. A skinny old hen and a worn-out sow. Adelaide curses the fashionably steep half-inch heels she chose. She should have worn her oxfords with the orthotics. Her vanity will be the death of her.

Even after all the inching along and other delays involving a rut, a sewer grate, and a menacing plaid snake, they arrive at the corner right on time, her dress shoes all scuffed at the toes. You would think the crazy psychedelic bus had been lying in wait just for them. It pulls up exactly as they round the corner, making Adelaide wish she'd moved more slowly or better yet, backwards. How will she ever get through this evening? *How?*

From the looks of it, this bus might be the same vehicle that took them to the last class, but who can be sure? It's so much to take in. Neon scribble covers the outside. Inside, rubbery seats sparkle with shimmery upholstery. Random bottles of who knows what along with groceries and cleaning products slide back and forth willy nilly. Because of this blatant vulgarity, Adelaide can't pretend she's on a cultural excursion to the Smithsonian, as she'd like to. Not that she's been to the Smithsonian, but that's not the point. The point is she once thought of going to the Smithsonian, and even becoming a member. A lifelong member at that. She's the type of person who considers belonging to museums for life. That's who she is. A cultural sophisticate. This bus isn't going to a museum. It's going to Uranus on an acid trip.

Settling into the first row so she can exit as quickly as possible, Adelaide is transfixed by the chubby teenage driver with buck teeth and coke bottle glasses.

"I hope you can see in those things," she snaps.

Felicity elbows her, but seriously, the child is about ten years old and, as far as Adelaide can tell, half-blind. Or maybe she hasn't seen a young person in so long she doesn't know what they look like anymore. Anyone under thirty looks like a toddler. The glasses are a separate issue, and they're a half-inch thick at least.

The bus drops them off twenty miles away at the huge dilapidated red barn behind Rockland Rodeo. A rodeo seems appropriate to Adelaide, considering all the bullshit that's tossed around in these meetings. But anyway, they're alive and safe, arriving just as the sun sets, so no one can see Felicity in her elf costume. So far so good.

First thing Felicity predictably does is plant herself in the metal folding chair directly in front of the podium.

"No way," says Adelaide. "No how. I'm not sitting here. Y'all can find me in the back with the sane people."

"Oh, come on, Addie," Felicity whines, patting the seat beside her. "Sit right here. You might learn something if you stop wandering around per usual. If you really focus." She bats her centipede lashes. "Stay with me, Addie."

"No," Adelaide repeats, pleased with her self-resolve. "No."

Felicity bows her head and sighs. "I didn't come all this way for myself," she says softly. "I have true conviction that this is the only way out of our confusion."

"*Your* confusion," Adelaide snorts, "let's be honest." But the vulnerable way Felicity hangs her head cracks her resolve.

"I don't know how I'll do it without y'all," Felicity moans.

Adelaide traces circles on the dirt floor with her tarnished pumps. "Oh, for cripe sake, Felicity, fine," she says. "But don't expect me to stay up here for long. I'm no teacher's pet. In fact, you can count on me *not* staying up here. How's that? When you see me collect my things and head to the back, don't you dare try to stop me." She glares at her sister. "I will not be stopped, do you hear?"

"Just give it a chance," says Felicity.

Adelaide plops down, turning right, left, and all the way

behind her to see who the other suckers are. To see if she recognizes any of them from the last time she came to one of these Ouija festivals, whenever that was. Or if some of them managed to escape. It's hard to remember everything. Or anything at all sometimes, when she thinks about it. Time is so distorted—all drawn out and at the same time squeezed together, popping out like hernias here and there, all out of sequence. It's as if Wednesdays are suddenly Sundays but only the third week of every other month. Impossible to track. Like someone locked-up Father Time and swapped his calendar for a roulette wheel.

Or maybe it's her. Adelaide makes a note to get a calendar for the house so she can cross days off and try to make sense of things. She remembers her PaPaw complaining about how time sped up in his later years, so that could be it, too. The simple scourge of age.

Standing at the podium dressed in an inappropriately diaphanous white gown, the instructor, Mrs. Phipps, claps her hands. "Take your seats," she rasps into the microphone. "We've got a lot to cover tonight."

Even though they're seated right up front, Adelaide can barely see leathery old Phipps the way she blends right into the columns of the old barn, not to mention the dirt floor. Adelaide should have brought a pair of binoculars, but that might have been excessive since she has no plans to watch or listen to a word the old bat says. Not that she's that old, either, just leathery, like she spent every summer of her entire life sunbathing on the summit of Black Mountain slathered in baby oil mixed with iodine behind a reflector. Adelaide knew girls like that back in the day. Girls who had no respect for the tenuous lifespan of their fair Scottish skin. Girls whose skin died decades before their bodies did. That's Phipps. The Coppertone ghoul.

Although it could be the shitty lighting. It's even darker

than usual tonight. And weirder. Five of the ten bulbs hanging on cords from the pitched ceiling are burned out. Even the moonlight that sometimes leaks through the wide cracks in the old barnwood is obscured by clouds. Will it ever clear up? All Adelaide wants to do is click her heels and land in the ratty recliner in front of her fireplace. Well, not so much ratty as nicely broken-in. She reaches for her red yarn and knitting needles, and spreads them across her lap. Purl one, slipstitch, and she's off, determined to finish whatever the hell she's knitting, no matter what. It's bound to turn into something.

Phipps takes attendance counting each occupied seat, then leans into the microphone and proclaims, "The changes are coming," in her ominous lisp. "Mark my wordth," she says. Her blank eyes widen to an unnatural size, and she taps her pointer on the dirt floor like a blind woman locating a curb. Her spiked orange hair adds a creepy accent to the whole picture. "You have to learn to recognithe the changeth if you're going to get anywhere," she says.

Adelaide squirms in her seat and tries to bolt, but Felicity grips her hand. "Not yet, Addie," she whispers. "Please."

"The thame thing will hold every one of you back," says Phipps through her whistling dentures. She picks up her stick and points to various people, "You and you and you." She steps out from behind the podium. "And you," she says, pointing her stick directly at Adelaide.

"I knew it, Addie," whispers Felicity. "She's got a message just for you!"

Adelaide drops her knitting right back into the satchel, and makes a break for the back.

"You can walk away from me," says Phipps, ratcheting up her volume. "But you can't walk away from your attachments, can you, hmmm?"

Adelaide can barely hear her for all the windblown sound effects screeching through the walls and roof beams. *Get me the hell out of here,* is all she's thinking.

"Attachments are what will keep us all from progressing," she says. "But for those who manage to put away desires, progress will reveal itself in what may feel like scary ways. Scary, that is, until you recognize its source."

Adelaide hears, *"Progreth will reveal it-thelf in thcary wayth,"* and suppresses a giggle, though she doesn't know why she bothers to suppress anything. She's the only one here who's right in the head.

Nearly at the back of the barn now, she leans against a sturdy post to catch her breath. Upfront she sees Felicity's arm shoot up like an eager third grader's. "How will we recognize the changes?" she asks.

Leave it to *'Felithity'* to dive headfirst into this hogwash, thinks Adelaide.

"Your behavior will alter," says Phipps. "The editor within you that censors your language and body movement will slowly fade until all that remains is the real you. The permanent you. The unshakable, *eternal* you." She takes a deep breath. "This is the stripping of the false self, the temporary personality that animates our earthly personas."

"Perthona," Adelaide repeats under her breath. *"Your* earthly perthona." She chuckles. "Your earthly freak show *perthona,"* she says louder, emboldened.

"Ha ha!" chuckles someone behind her, which startles her.

She whips around to her right where a tall lean young fellow stands grinning. His skin is so tattooed he looks like a walking totem pole. Not to mention his shaved head covered in chartreuse fuzz like baby blades of spring grass. He strikes a rakish pose. Adelaide wishes Mother had met this kid. She would have begged Adelaide to marry Julian. *"Hurry up and marry him!"* she'd say. *"We'll pay for everything! Throw in a Tudor mansion and a Cadillac!"* Compared to this kid, Julian looked like royalty.

"This class is a bunch of bullshit," says the fellow, which charms her.

"Oh?" she guffaws. "Is it now? And who might you be?"

"Dulles," he says. "I'm just here cuz it's the only show in this whole stinking phantom town, and somebody told me to come here." He pulls out a plastic stick and inserts it in his mouth. When he puffs on it, smoke comes out.

She narrows her eyes inquisitively. "What's that?"

He removes the stick in a tantalizing manner, exhaling little clouds. "What? You've never seen one of these?" He leans in closer as if to assure himself of her ignorance. "It's an e-cigarette," he says wide-eyed. "You putting me on?"

"In my day, we smoked natural cigarettes," she replied with a teasing dollop of benign indignance. After all, why be harsh? She doesn't want to come on too strong. There's something about him she likes. "Healthy tobacco grown right in the earth." She points down for emphasis.

"Oh yeah? Well, these here are healthier," he says. "Although that news keeps changing, so stay-tuned. At least it's better than the crack I was smoking day and night." He rubs the mouthpiece against his shirt to clean it off, and offers it to her. "Go ahead, try."

She hesitates, but feeling devilish, accepts.

"Just puff," he says, and she does.

She's astonished to find that it tastes like marshmallow perfume, if ever there were such a thing. She inhales again. It doesn't burn her throat at all. Exhaling, she says, "So this is good for me?"

"Maybe. Who cares?" He grins, shrugging. "Anyway, keep it."

"Oh, I couldn't..." But he pulls out another from his back pocket, so she does.

What a delightful turn of events, thinks Adelaide. If only he had a shot of whiskey.

Much to her astonishment, he pulls a flask from his back pocket, untwists it and chugs.

She steps back, standing side to side with the boy. Obviously, this is the place to be. Right here in the back of a dark, cavernous abandoned barn on the outskirts of Outskirt. She hasn't had this much fun in eons. When he hands her the flask, she says, "Don't mind if I do."

Phipps walks up and down the center aisle, tapping her pointer on the packed dirt floor as she walks. "At this stage, the most obvious change, and yet in some ways the most subtle, is the change in energy," she says, then pauses. "The most sensitive among you will notice it first."

In the front row, Felicity's long bony arm shoots up again. Adelaide is pretty sure her sister is the only one in the entire barn who's tuned into this malarkey. But what the hell, Adelaide's having fun, so who cares about anybody else. *Stay as long as you like!*

Phipps turns around as if she knew Felicity would raise her hand again. "Yeth, Felithity," she says.

"What does it feel like?" Felicity asks earnestly. "I mean, the intense colors, yes, but the sense of shifting energy also seems real."

"Did everyone hear that?" shouts Phipps. "Felithity feelth a shift."

Adelaide surveys the scattered audience. By their blank stares, she can tell that no one gives a dang about whatever shift Felithity feels in the frigging energy field. What does that even mean? She checks out the guy halfway up on the right dressed in a full 3-piece striped suit, complete with clown tie and fright wig. It's a miracle Felicity hasn't married him yet. This thought concerns Adelaide, because what if Felicity were to fall for him? Or what if she fell for the guy two rows up dressed in ballet tights and a tuxedo jacket? What then? Any number of these freaks would be a more suitable companion for Felicity than Adelaide is. Yet Felicity is all Adelaide's got. What if Felicity married and moved out, leaving Adelaide completely alone? The idea terrifies her enough to pay the slightest bit of attention to Phipps. An absolute minimum of focus so she can pretend to converse about the evening when they get home.

Way up front, Phipps raises her voice, "When you begin to pay attention, everything changes," she says.

"Oh yeah, right," Adelaide mumbles. "I've been listening to you for weeks now, and nothing's changed."

"Got that right," says the young fellow. He's not even looking up front. He's staring down at some little rectangle gadget he pulled out of his pocket, pressing buttons all over the place.

"What's that?" Adelaide says.

He looks up, "For real?"

"Yes, for real. What is it? And why are you staring at it like that?"

"Um, it's a phone?" he says. "But I don't know why my friends aren't answering me. Must be a bad signal."

Adelaide shakes her head, amused. Kids are so dumb. Heads full of helium. "Try plugging it in," she says chortling. "You might get a call."

A laugh bubbles up and out of his throat. He can barely contain it. "You're funny," he says.

From the front, Phipps says, "When you do the work, your vibration is raised. Your frequency changes. In turn, your energy becomes visible outside of this realm, and your ability to communicate is enhanced both here and there."

"Who the hell wants to communicate with 'people outside of this realm'," says Dulles in a cloud of marshmallow vapor.

"Did I hear a question from the rear?" Phipps asks.

"Yeah, why am I here?" Adelaide mutters sideways.

At this, Dulles offers her his knuckles in some sort of victorious adolescent gesture, so she makes a fist too. What the hell. *Be young!* Then he bumps his fist against hers, which tickles her, starting a flirtatious chemical reaction in her belly that she hadn't anticipated. When was the last time she felt this way about anyone? Or anything? Suddenly she feels young! *Is* young! Life is on rewind.

In the front, Felicity rises in all her elfin glory. "Can you tell us why the new energies are here?" she asks as if anyone cares.

"Of courthe," says Phipps, "and thank you for athking, Felithity. Did everyone hear the quethtion?"

The ones who aren't snoring, nod lamely.

Phipps points up to the rafters. "Transformative energies are entering the atmosphere," she says. "To help us. I cannot emphasize enough what a gift this is." She strikes her chest dramatically, as if the gift is more than she can bear. "What a merciful gift! With these eternal energies we can grow faster than ever before. We can expand our hearts and minds to join the loved ones who have advanced before us. And we can do all this in a much shorter period of time. In that way, our losses are minimized, and our suffering is contracted. But first..." She paces across the stage, tapping the pointer as she goes. "... first we have to run through the field of attachments and learn to eliminate them." She wags her finger ominously. "And that, of course, is the personal impediment that each of us must face alone. No one can do it for us."

Adelaide barely hears what's going on for all the resurrected hormonal distraction going on in her body. Why, if she were sixteen, she'd shanghai Dulles for a reckless night behind the shed. *Without a care!* But maybe she is sixteen. She feels sixteen! After all, age is a hall of mirrors. And maybe the energies really have transformed her. Maybe that's what all this means! *Why didn't you just say so?!*

Risking everything, she turns to the boy and says, "You remind me of someone. Someone very dear to me." This causes her to blush so deeply, she feels feverish. She retrieves her hanky and fans her face. *What will he say?* She hasn't had a flirtation in so long, it makes her woozy.

"Oh yeah?" he says easily, checking her out. "You remind me of someone, too." He shifts positions and points his cigarette stick at her. "In fact, you reminded me of her the second I saw you."

Giggles rise uncontrollably up Adelaide's throat like champagne bubbles. "Is that right?" She can't even look at him. Instead she looks at her scuffed shoes, which she all at once wishes were three-inch strappy red sandals. "And who might that be?" she says.

"Emmaline," he says grinning.

"What a lovely name," she says. "Is Emmaline your girlfriend?" *Or maybe an ex-girlfriend,* she thinks hopefully.

"What? No. My granny," he says. "My pop's mom. She was one cool old lady. I was her favorite, but she croaked the day I turned ten."

Adelaide feels like she was punched in the gut with a bag of wet cement. What a fool she is! Just as she's about to burst into tears of humiliation, Dulles says, "Hey look at that!"

"Look at what?" she says, as if she could possibly look at him right now. Or anyone.

"Well, just...the whole color of the place," he says. "The lighting..."

Something about his voice seems so familiar it spooks her. Just the tone of it, and the way it drifts off in a vapor trail. She forces herself to raise her head. To look up and into his blue-eyed tattooed face, and she does.

But he's gone.

Obituary for Release to:
Blue Grass Bugle &
The Louisville Gazette
Saturday, July 5, 1940

PFC Stewart Gustave Jackson Drives His Tractor
into the Quarry
Born: February 1, 1892
Passed into eternal life: July 4, 1940

Forty-eight-year-old Outskirt resident, PFC Stewart
Jackson, formerly of Peabody Mountain in Outskirt
Hollow, snapped his neck after driving his tractor up
Turkey Bend some twenty miles to Daniel Boone Quarry
and right the hell off the east ridge. "He drove up and
looked around for a minute," said a confused laborer.
"Like he were takin' it all in. Then I seen that crazed look
in his good eye, and I ran for him, but it were too late."

PFC Jackson, a Purple Heart recipient, was wounded
in June of 1918 while performing his duties as a gunner
for the USMC at the Battle of Belleau Wood near Marne
River, France. He was released from the military hospital
two months later to his sister, Abigail Jackson McManis
of Outskirt, Kentucky who hadn't seen or heard from
him since the day she ran away from home at the age
of fourteen. In response to his collect phone call from
USMC headquarters in Washington D.C., she replied
"Y'all are friggin' kiddin' me, right? No #%*$^@ way."
She had a change of heart when they informed her of his
Purple Heart and pension.

PFC Jackson, affectionately known as Uncle Pothead, was proud of his experience in the Marine Corps. He could recite his version of the Battle of Belleau Wood by heart. "We saw 'em comin', yes sir," he said to anyone who would listen. "We got into position 'n gunned the crap out of the bastards, oh yeahhhhh." Over time, the folks in Outskirt swallowed the urge to run for the hills whenever Jackson showed up, but they mostly stood in place out of respect for his service since no citizen of Outskirt Hollow had ever received a medal of any kind. Jackson overcame his limitations and went on to become a bell ringer at the Outskirt Elementary School. There the usual delinquents made fun of his odd-shaped head and the one eye. "Y'all listen to me, you rotten punks!" he'd scold. "Ye'll amount to nothin' if y'all don't learn to hold yer tongues. I'm a marine, dangit! Show some respect!" Following all such incidents, Principal Blount was known to force the perpetrators to listen to the entire recitation of Jackson's maneuvers at Belleau Wood for what amounted to hours of eye-glazing detention.

A bachelor for all sorts of reasons, PFC Jackson is survived by his sister, Abigail, her husband, Bosworth, as well as his maiden sisters, Annabelle, Lillian, Gertrude, Lucille, Cassie, and Miranda Mae. He also leaves behind his niece, Regina McManis Somers, wife and business associate of the esteemed Jasper Somers of *Sunnyside Up* Enterprises; his grandnieces, Adelaide Frances and Felicity Jane Somers; and the extensive collection of bullets and WWI ammo that will decorate his headstone as specified in his Last Will and Testament.

Sunnyside Up invites the bereaved to the chapel for a military sendoff on Saturday at 9 a.m. followed by a

21-gun salute and parade around the graveyard in honor of the slain soldier. Guests are reminded to bring their own flags but leave their kids and guns at home with the pets for safety reasons.

When asked for a comment about the death of her uncle, his niece, Regina Somers stated, "Sunnyside Up isn't just an egg, it's an attitude."

NINE

ADELAIDE

Adelaide has a fitful dream that feels more like a memory. Hard to tell the difference anymore. Life comes and goes as it pleases, crossing over and under every bridge and intersection, paying no respect to time. It's flat-out impossible to follow any of it, at least not lately. It's like it's happening to someone else. Maybe it is. But in this particular dream, five-year-old Flitty looks so real and solid, Addie can almost feel the whooping she's gonna get just for dreaming it.

"Come on, Addie," says Felicity, her flaxen braids trailing down her bony back, her knees scuffed, her grass-stained floral romper torn on the right shoulder. "Mother told you to play with me. It's your job!"

"Why would I play with you?" snaps Adelaide. "Y'all are half my age." *Get lost!* She shimmies into the corner of her bed, knees up, hiding *The Ladies Home Journal* magazine she pulled from the mail pile. "Anyway, didn't I just play with y'all, for goodness sake?"

Felicity rubs her nose, thinking. "Yes, Addie, but Mother said..."

"'Mother said', 'Mother said'," mocks Adelaide in a singsong. "Mother saaaaaiiiiiid!"

Good grief, how is Adelaide ever going to get time to herself? She's ten years old, and has so much to figure out. Girls a few years older in the holler are having kids already! Why should Adelaide be stuck playing with a kindergartner? She didn't give birth to this child. It isn't her responsibility. "Go bother Cousin Edgar," she mutters."

"He's diggin'," says Felicity.

"Ok then go find Cousin Sam."

"Sam told me to go find y'all."

Adelaide buries her face in her mother's magazine—a whole section on bras and girdles that Adelaide would like to know about. *What are they?!* And an article on bad marriages, which she suspects might be the case with her parents. I mean, really, who could be married to Mother? Actually sleep in the same room with her? Please! Who?! She's a jail warden. Everybody knows it. It's not news to anyone. Adelaide spies Felicity out the corner of her eye. "Be gone," she says, shooing with her foot.

"But where shall I go?" Felicity whines. "Mother told me to stay with y'all before she left." She wags her finger in imitation. "She said, 'Stick to Adelaide like glue, you hear me?' That's exactly what she said, Addie, I swear."

Adelaide lowers the magazine. "Mother left?"

"She went to the market with Daddy. And she said ..."

"Outskirt or Louisville?"

Flitty shrugs. "Lou-ville I think."

Adelaide slaps the magazine closed. With Mother gone, she can cross the field to Belinda's house and get in some fun mischief with Belinda's brothers. But first, she has to lock Flitty up somewhere safe and inescapable. She stares out the window. *Hmmmm. Oh, I know!*

Turning back to her sister, she says, "You wanna play, is that it?"

Felicity raises her arms and jumps. "Yes'm, I do!" She claps three times. "I do; I do!"

"Ok then, what shall we play?"

Flitty frowns, thinking. "Can we jump rope?"

"No, we did that yesterday, and anyway it's rainy out there now."

"Jacks?"

"No." Adelaide places her index finger on her chin and narrows her eyes at Felicity. "I know! Let's play dead. Won't that be fun?"

Felicity scowls.

"We'll see how long you can lie there," says Adelaide. "Just lie there pretending people are coming to see your dead body, how's that? Everyone cryin' and wailin'. *All boo hoo, Felicity!* '*How could she leave us? Just disappear like she did! Holy cow, we miss her so much! What in the wide world will we ever do without Felicity! Where's my hankie?*'" She squeezes her fists against her eyeballs. "*Waaaaaaaa!*"

Felicity stares down at her dirty Keds and locks into one of her weird trances for what feels like five whole minutes, like she's viewing a movie in her head, scene by scene. Adelaide would like to smack her out of it, but she needs her sister's cooperation, so she holds back. All at once Flitty's little bow of a mouth forms a perfect O, and she gasps. "Ever'body's crying, alright, Addie," she says. "Every right one of 'em." She opens her eyes wide. "The whole town's turned inside out, but I can't see who or what. Or really, why. Mother's sad too, but also angry." She cocks her head, scratching it, and blinks hard. "Daddy's not here though. Daddy's gone." She looks up, startled. "Oh Addie, where is he? Is he dead?"

"What in the dickens you running on and on about, Felicity Jane?" Adelaide scolds. "Daddy's not dead. What gets into you, anyway? Snap out of it!"

But Felicity can't snap out of it; she's locked-in. "He's gone, Addie. I can't see him cuz he's not there."

Adelaide swipes her hand in the air. This could go on forever. "You're crazy," she says, forcing a smile. She's got to play nice if she's gonna ditch Felicity in time to get to Belinda's and back before her parents return. "Go get dressed real pretty," Adelaide says. "Put on your frock and your Mary Janes. You got to look your best if y'all expect people to really fuss at your viewing."

"What about you, Addie? Aren't y'all playing dead too?"

"Oh hell, Flitty, nobody gives a rotten egg about me. Y'all are the only one anyone cares about around here. Now go get dressed. Scat!"

As Felicity skips out the door, Adelaide flips the magazine to a story about the actress, Ingrid Bergman, in a movie about war. She studies the picture, thinking no one could be that beautiful. If someone that pretty died, it would be a terrible loss. Why, everyone the world over would grieve.

And the war is a real thing, she knows. She remembers over-hearing Mother and Daddy all upset about a giant war across two oceans on both sides of America. It has to be far away, though, because Adelaide's never even seen a real ocean. Only pictures. She can't imagine how wondrous it must be to soak your feet at the edge of an endless pool of water. Dig your toes into the wet sand! Only place she's been outside Outskirt was the Oink Auction with Uncle Stewart. Not that she's complaining. Pigs are fun.

Lost in thought, Adelaide's surprised when Felicity shows up in her pink crinoline, silver fairy crown, and Mother's scarlet lipstick spread all over her face.

"Good grief!" she says, then bursts into a helpless giggle. "Lawdy, girl, look at y'all! Ha ha! Anyone sees you in a casket looking like that won't be able to cry for laughin'!"

Felicity smiles impishly.

"Well, y'all do look mighty special, I'll say that." Adelaide scoots off the bed. "Time to have some fun for a fat change. First one to open her eyes or sit up in the coffin is the loser. You wanna be a loser, Flitty?"

Flitty shakes her head solemnly.

"Then y'all be stone quiet no matter how long you're in there, got it? Stone quiet till I say it's okay to leave. Take a nap if you have to. Whatever it takes to win. Winnin' is all that matters."

Adelaide pushes her feet into her woolen slippers and tightens the red grosgrain ribbon around her long black ponytail. Off they go through the family apartments, down the back stairs, and around into the business quarters of *Sunnyside Up.* Adelaide has snooped more than once in these offices at the risk of "severe punishment." Hell, everything she does is at the risk of severe punishment, so it doesn't mean much. You listen to Mother long enough, breathing's a risk.

Moving slowly down the dark, narrow hall, they stop short of the heavy metal doors leading to the prep room.

"Here we are," announces Adelaide. Just to be sure, she

darts to the hall window to see if Uncle Tavish's truck is there, and it isn't. Uncle Tavish is married to Aunt Mimi, Daddy's sister. He's the embalmer, which means he shoots glue and varnish into dead people to keep 'em fresh and waxy, at least that's what his sons, Edgar and Sam, say. But just in case the truck is parked somewhere else on the property, she knocks hard and listens for footsteps. She's ready to run.

No one answers, so she kicks the door hard just in case. The last thing she wants is to explain to Aunt Mimi why she's bringing Felicity into the prep room. *To teach her a lesson is why!* Plus sometimes Adelaide likes to see the dead people to make sure they're really dead. She doesn't want half-dead people wandering the halls all the sudden. Edgar showed her a comic book like that, but it wasn't funny. This here is not a hotel! She doesn't trust wacky Aunt Mimi one bit to make sure the clients are dead coming in. Mimi's a frustrated beautician who treats every corpse like a live customer. *"What shall we do today, Rosie? Hmmm? Maybe some fake lashes? A fancy upsweep for the big day? And which outfit, hmmm? Oh, I know! How 'bout we do some costume changes throughout the evening so you get to wear all y'all's favorites one last time? How's that?"* Adelaide has overheard her aunt mumbling to her clients more than once. Edgar says, what do you expect from someone who spends her life putting eyeshadow and lipstick on dead people?

"I saw Aunt Mimi leave with Uncle Tav in the truck," says Felicity.

"You did? When?"

"Before lunch." She crosses her legs tightly. "I have to pee, Addie."

"There's a bathroom inside. Just wait a minute."

"I don't wanna pee in there," Felicity whines.

"Tough noogies."

"And anyway, we're not allowed."

"Maybe y'all aren't allowed inside, but I am. I'm almost eleven years old. Soon I'll be working here like everyone else." She turns the handle, but it's locked. "Wait here."

Adelaide runs around the corner to the Right Reverend's office and retrieves a key.

Felicity is a scribble of energy, hopping on one leg then the other. She's such a pain. The only way Adelaide will ever get rid of her is by teaching her a lesson. She turns the key, opens the creaky door, and cranes her neck inside. "Hello? Anybody in here?"

Silence.

"Come on in," she orders Felicity.

"I don't wanna go in this bathroom, Addie!"

"Don't you wanna be a big girl?"

Felicity nods. "I do, but..."

"Okay then, come on through and I'll take you to the bathroom."

She pushes Flitty into the small room, nothing but a sink and a toilet, one of the only indoor bathrooms in all of Outskirt, excepting the one in the family quarters. A real luxury for these parts, minus the overwhelming odor of stinky glue and varnish from the prep.

"It smells in here," says Flitty, pinching her nose.

"You can use the outhouse if you want. I'll wait."

Felicity huffs. "Fine, I'll go here." She blows up her cheeks with air and closes the door.

"Wash your hands," Adelaide calls to her.

While Felicity is peeing, Adelaide surveys the prep room landscape. First thing she does is drag a milk crate to the far wall, stand on it, and bang open a window so she can breathe. She knows she's not allowed in here without a grownup, but who cares? This is what the grownups get for leaving her in charge of someone half her age. She counts: one, two, three, four caskets, all closed. This should teach Felicity to bother Adelaide when she's busy. She hides behind one of the larger ones.

Felicity finally flings open the door, bursting for a breath. "Where are you, Addie?" When Adelaide doesn't answer, Flitty's voice shoots up three octaves. "Where are you, Aaaaaddie?!!!!"

"That's for me to know and you to find out!" Addie shouts from behind one of the caskets.

Felicity whimpers.

"Okay fine, I'm in one of the caskets. You have to guess which one."

"No, Addie, nooooo! Please just show me!"

"If y'all cry, I won't play. This is a big girl game. Are you a big girl or not?"

In her tiniest voice, Flitty says, "I'm a big girl."

Adelaide hears Flitty's little feet scamper over the linoleum floor, and moves over on her haunches as Flitty gets closer.

"Are you in this one?" Flitty asks.

"You have to check, Felicity. You have to stand on the stepladder and open the top."

"No, Addie, no!"

"Okay, I'll take you back home and you can play alone in the furnace room."

After a long pause, Addie hears her dragging the stepladder to one of the caskets, grunting, "Uuuuhhhhhh." The hinges creak.

Adelaide hears Felicity gasp. "Oh," she says. "I didn't mean to disturb y'all, ma'am. So sorry. But why are y'all in here if you're not dead? How can you breathe?"

Just as Adelaide peeks around the corner to see who the heck Flitty thinks she's talking to, Adelaide's head swirls, the room turns, and the dream fades into the familiar milky blur of what's become her present life.

TEN

FELICITY

While Addie naps in the other room, Felicity sits alone in the kitchen. Her hands cover her ears to stop the buzzing cacophony of competing signals, including Addie's snores. It's hard to pick out one signal from the next without laser concentration, tuning her head like a radio dial to the most demanding frequency, which in this case comes from Pothead.

"Clean up the yard, for gawd sake," he demands. *"I'm a Marine! Marines need order! This cemetery is a GD slop yard. No wonder nobody wants to be buried here anymore!"*

Pothead is interrupted by Auntie

Lucille's high-pitched squeal, *"I didn't ask for geraniums! I hate geraniums! The smell is suffocating! Everyone here knows I hate geraniums, and what am I surrounded by? Geraniums!"* Followed by Granny McManis' buzzsaw of a voice, *"Tell Adelaide to throw away that jumbo sack of salted peanuts in her bedside table along with the damn donuts. I didn't pay her charm school tuition to watch her gag to death on nuts."*

Felicity's losing patience with all of them. As fond as she is of her family, their interference makes her job more difficult. And really, most of their input is more than a little one-sided. Selfish even. Felicity thought heaven would be heavenly, but who can tell from this bunch? No one. So maybe her family, fractured as they are, never landed in heaven. Maybe they landed in some kind of hellacious holding tank. So what if they did? What can she do about it? Nothing. It's not as if she has any cosmic influence. She barely knows who's who half the time on any number of planes. She barely knows herself anymore.

And anyway, why can't they just address Addie directly? Felicity's tired of being her sister's translator. It's not as if Addie believes a thing Felicity says. The spirits say Addie's thick as a brick, but Felicity's not so sure. After all Addie's got the same mile-wide stubborn streak as their ancestors. The same streak that swings through their maternal DNA like a wrecking ball. If you factor that in or out of the equation, maybe Addie's dense and maybe she's not. Maybe she's just plain pigheaded. As long as the spirits keep jabbering at Felicity and ignoring Addie, no one will ever know. Felicity's an easy mark.

All this static makes her feel more wobbly than usual. She has to protect herself to keep her head from spinning into outer space, which feels like a real possibility. But how will she do it? Just then she remembers something Mrs. Phipps told her privately after the last class.

"It's all right there for the taking," she'd said. *"As long as you're aware of your power, and execute it with confidence, you shall want for nothing. You're a special individual, Felicity Jane. You can do it! Stand in a safe place, state your intentions, reach into the Void. And retrieve!"*

"The Void?" Felicity had asked.

"Yes," she'd said kindly. *"You've already been using it subconsciously. To use it consciously is a skill of a different order. The Void is emptiness and at the same time, abundance. Purity. The Original Womb. In emptying yourself, you have access to, well…everything. You have access to bounty."*

Felicity wasn't 100% sure what Mrs. Phipps meant, but since she'd been feeling pretty empty to begin with, she accepted it without further inquiry. In Felicity's experience, questions are sometimes the weights that prevent your dreams from rising to fulfillment. *Why aren't my dreams manifesting?* Stop asking!

Maybe it really is as simple as that. Cut the strings and let the balloons rise. Release them. *Stop begging!* After all, will any of us ever understand everything? Unlikely. And really, who cares? One thing she learned after the accident is that logic isn't all it's cracked up to be. In fact, it gets in the way. Sometimes you just have to be willing to let go and see what happens.

Felicity tiptoes into the coat closet and shuts the door ever so gently to keep from disturbing Addie in the next room. The last thing she needs is somebody swatting at her good faith like a mosquito. The closet is dark, low, and full of shadows. Her head scrapes the ceiling. Her sinuses congest almost instantly in the moldy air spiked with traces of nauseating camphor. When she reaches slightly to her left, she hits the silk garment bag containing Mother and Daddy's professional wardrobe of moth-eaten funeral apparel, all black. To the right, she's able to extend her arm nearly straight out and parallel to the floor. Her outstretched fingers barely touch the dusty eyebrow window on the pitched wall above the dilapidated steamer trunk.

This closet is a tight fit for sure, but since Addie hates this closet, it's still the safest place for Felicity's experiments in the Void. To Felicity's knowledge, Addie hasn't entered this closet in ages. Maybe she's afraid of it, who knows? Maybe she senses its power. After all, this is where Felicity has been subconsciously attracting almost everything she's wished for from the past, present, and even the future. Everything from incidental knickknacks for the gravestone décor all the way to the puffy white ski jacket she conjured last week from the future. Or at least what she believes is the future. After all, where would such a shiny fabric have come from in dowdy old Outskirt? Nowhere! Felicity had never seen anything like it.

You would think Addie would become suspicious of such conjuring, but no. She expresses little interest in almost everything Felicity produces, other than the occasional appraisal of how inappropriate it is. Or appraisal of the closet in general with remarks such as, *"Clean that thing out!"* and, *"How can one closet hold all the crap you come up with!"* Addie is a disgruntled McManis through and through, not that she'd ever admit it.

But Felicity can't afford to let thoughts of Addie block her inspiration now. This is her first truly conscious encounter with the Void. "Nice to meet you," she says aloud. What will it bring? *Bounty!* Something worthy of reporting back to Mrs. Phipps, she hopes. Squeezing her eyes shut, she clenches her fists and states her intentions as clearly as she can.

"I wish to protect my head from incoming static," she says. "I wish to remain sane, grounded on this earth and available to Addie. Without me, she's alone." Felicity thinks hard, scouring every corner of her mind for even the most microscopic addition. "Oh yes," she says, "and whatever y'all provide, let it be familiar, remind me of my roots, and give me comfort."

She holds her breath, extends her right arm to the window, opens her hand, and waits. *What will it be? What will it be!* Her heart jumps like a gymnast. Within seconds she's fingering a tiny piece of metal attached to twine that's clearly attached to something else. She opens her eyes, and by the dim light of the dusty window, sees that she's holding a key strung from the ceiling. Slowly, she unties the twine, fingering the sharp edges of the key with anticipation. Her keen sensory perception leads her to the steamer trunk where she lowers herself, inserts the key, and nervously twists and turns. Her hands tremble and sweat, and she wipes them on her scratchy crinoline skirt. At last, it opens! She sits back, adjusts her eyes to the darkness inside the trunk, and stares until she is able to make out a metal hat stand upon which sits Mother's multicolor floral bathing cap.

"Mercy," she whispers reverently.

The Void has certainly outdone itself this time, she thinks. Mrs. Phipps will be proud of her. Mother's swim cap is an excellent and downright whimsical choice that Felicity would never have thought of on her own. A motorcycle helmet, yes. A safari hat, perhaps. Even a wig. But a swim cap? Never. The Void is pure genius! She wastes no time stretching it over her crown, down the back of her head and over her ears, tucking as much of her unwieldy silver hair inside as she can without tearing the aged rubber. After all, this is Mother's best cap. The one she wore in the infamous beauty contest at the Red River Pavilion in 1925. Not that she won or really, to Felicity's knowledge, even placed.

To be honest, Felicity's not sure what Mother was doing in the pageant to begin with. By all accounts, she was a bit over-sized, a bit manly even, with an impossibly ruddy complexion that turned downright prickly under stress. Plus, there was the perennial hint of a moustache that dogged her throughout her life. Mother had her attributes, but she was not pageant material. It was no doubt Granny's overzealous ambition that landed Mother in the pageant in the first place. First prize was a sizable purse back then. Granny was said to have made a career out of forcing Mother into one humiliating situation after the other. Some were painfully tight, others embarrassingly large and loose, like the Louisville Debutante Ball debacle, all to advance the McManis name in society. An unfortunate tendency that Mother perfected and tried without luck to pass along to Addie. It certainly ended with a bang when Julian came along.

Exiting the closet quietly, Felicity fastens the strap snugly under her chin, touching each of the ten colorful three-dimensional chrysanthemum appliques on the cap to make sure they're all intact. *One, two, three, four.* She doesn't want to lose any. *Five, six, seven.* Even though the flowers are fake, they have an instantaneous stabilizing effect on her psyche. They ground her. Just the *idea* of them grounds her. After all, flowers have roots. *Eight, nine, ten.* And anyway, it must be the perfect headgear, because according to Mrs. Phipps if you play by the rules with awareness, the Void does not make mistakes. Not that Felicity is a rule player in general, but who would mess with anything as daunting as the Void?

Well, Addie would, that's who.

Felicity knows darn well Addie would mess with the Void. She wouldn't think twice about it. She's never played by the rules in or out of the Void, unless the rules were concocted by her. The only thing she trusts is herself. But according to Mrs. Phipps, the Void is always listening. So if you don't learn to state your intentions in a conscious manner, sooner or later it will tune into your subconscious thoughts and desires, manifesting the garbage that preoccupies your lower mind. Like donuts and bourbon. Or death. You may access the Void, but not its bounty. You stick your hand inside only to find it full of all the offensive rot that's been littering your mind your entire life.

Felicity knows Addie's mind is a lead weight, but even so. If she would just listen to Mrs. Phipps for five minutes she could be shopping in the Void like Felicity instead of living on its leftovers. And the Void is not the only thing Phipps is trying to teach them, or more accurately, prepare them for. All her talk of thought forms and elementals, not to mention telepathy and teleportation are useless to Addie. She whistles mindlessly through it all. She knits, crochets, and horses around giggling with youngsters half her age. The truth is, Adelaide Frances Somers will do just about anything to remain right where she is. No further right nor left, north or south. Just right plop in the middle of a base world locked in a cast iron vice of unforgiving logic and sequence. Boxed in by time. Who could be satisfied living with all that restriction, Felicity wonders. Who? If she had a choice? But maybe Addie just doesn't care. And because of that, maybe Felicity will have to stop caring on her behalf.

Before Felicity leaves the house, she peeks around the corner to check on Addie. There she is, blessedly asleep on the recliner, a bag of butterscotch candies scattered haplessly across her broad bosom, rising and falling with each raspy breath.

Felicity wanders through the kitchen, out the door and down the stairs, stopping to adjust the laces of the combat boots she discovered last winter in the back of the barn. Although they're slightly large, they're comfortable as long as she stuffs the front with the old robins' nests that were abandoned right there in the boots when she found them. And even though they're heavy for her slight frame, they're perfect for working in the yard. Besides, they ground her. They do. They keep her from flying off.

She bends down to pick up a fallen magnolia blossom that she tucks into the right side of the swim cap by her ear. Sugar magnolias are her favorite flower along with lilacs and wisteria. And dogwood. And don't forget azaleas. Gardenias and hibiscus are also grand. And who could forget the many varieties of clematis? Just as lovely images of these flowers waft through her imagination, she spots the car again. The convertible driven by Julian's cousin, Thaddeus, though she has no idea how Addie knows his name or how he's related. Felicity recognizes him by the derby that sits on his bald head. She waves, because why not be friendly? He's hardly there to do harm, she thinks, in spite of Addie's neurotic fears.

He waves back.

Hmmm, she thinks, as she wanders down the slate path from the house to the gravel drive to the graveyard, where she kicks the squeaky gate until it swings. Why is that man driving through their yard all the time these days? She would think it was just 'in her head' as Addie is always proclaiming, but Addie sees him too. Well, maybe he's just trying to be friendly. In spite of his peculiar appearance, there's a light about him. A bright aura, as Phipps would call it. But that might be her imagination. And anyway, who is she to talk about peculiar appearances?

She drops her basket of gardening tools beside the flats of annuals she placed there earlier. The sun peeks out behind a dark rain cloud, and she closes her eyes in homage to the light, however faint. *It's been dark so long!* She sheds her jacket and drops to her knees in the rich soil over her mother's grave. She grabs dirt in both hands, squeezes it through her fingers, and releases it over and over again like a mantra. How she loves dirt. How she loves the cemetery. This graveyard is her life.

In the distance, she watches a little girl skip barefoot toward the copse of trees at the fence line. "Oh hello, Shelley," she calls out. "Long time no see y'all!"

She tips her finger at her blonde, blue-eyed little cousin, Shelley, smiling to see her so full of life. Shelley was ill for so long that it thrills Felicity to see her finally enjoying herself. Resurrected is what she is. Lazarus! Felicity watches Shelley climb the fence, wondering where her cousin found the flowery wrap-around skirt that used to belong to Addie. Felicity's pretty sure Addie made that skirt herself on Granny's old Singer. Why, the Void is nothing but a giant Lost & Found. Maybe Felicity's things and Addie's all landed there after the accident. Maybe the old RCA Victrola fell down there too with their favorite Roger Miller records and the old black & white Phillips TV.

"Look at me, Felicity!" says Shelley.

Felicity looks up to see Shelley gliding effortlessly along the top of the fence.

"Look what I can do!" she says.

"Why, aren't y'all the clever one!" Felicity replies.

"Want me to teach you?" says Shelley. "I can teach you. I teach lots of people to fly. I can teach you, too!"

"Maybe tomorrow," Felicity says. She imagines herself gliding, never mind flying around the house from room to room giving Addie one hemorrhage after another. Although she could certainly practice elsewhere—behind the barn, perhaps, or in the woods. She has to admit it's mighty tempting to just glide everywhere instead of plodding ahead step after tedious step, especially in Pothead's combat boots.

"Just lift your arms like this," says Shelley. "Come on, cousin!"

Shelley's too persistent to ignore, so Felicity rises from her knees and places her hands in the air, as instructed.

"And jump up!" says Shelley. "But not down," she warns. "Don't drop down. And whatever you do, don't look at the ground. Your sight determines your altitude."

"Oh for heaven's sake," says Felicity nervously. To be honest, she just wants to get back to her plantings.

Behind her, she hears Pothead and a chorus of distant cousins cheering her on. "Do it! Do it!" Followed by Granny's growl, "Don't do it, for gawd's sake," she warns Felicity. "It's just a damn trick."

Felicity pulls down her bathing cap to block the negativity.

"Okay, here goes," she says, jumping up. She does her best to look ahead at Shelley, and not at the ground. Much to her surprise, she stays above ground. "Mercy sake, I'm doing it!" she screeches. "I'm floating, y'all!"

"Now move with your eyes," says Shelley. "Decide where you want to go, and follow your eyes. Do not look down!"

Felicity freezes, worried that she's gone too far. Worried that mastering this trick will distance her even further from Addie. Distance her so far that she'd be unable to protect her ailing sister. She moves a short distance toward the fence, but looks down and falls to her knees.

"Told you," snorts Granny. "Gettin' too big fer yer britches, Flitty girl."

Felicity is relieved to be back in the dirt. She wonders, did she really fall? *Did she ever rise?* Or was it all in her head again? Shelley's gone, but their old hound, Rooster, stands in her place. Felicity can barely believe her eyes. Last time she saw Rooster he'd been laid in a deep hole, Cousin Samuel on his knees with a shovel, racked with tears. But now here he is, trotting along with half the hens behind him until he whips around, herding them back to the coop. Felicity is tickled half to death at this sight! This is where she wants to be, watching her life in rewind, her knees covered in earth, soil, loam—call it what you will. It's the one grounding element left in a world that barely contains her anymore. Other than dirt, she has no idea what's real.

All at once Pothead looms before her.

"Not now, Uncle Stewart," she says dismissively. "Can't you see I'm wearing my protective head gear?" She pulls the cap taut over her ears. Not to be rude, but she's in such a state of wonder, why ruin it with complaints? '*You're not doing enough to keep the place up! Work harder! This is our legacy!*' No thank you; she's not in the mood.

All at once she remembers an earlier lesson of Phipps' and snaps her fingers to get rid of him. Any deliberate signal would probably do, but Mrs. Phipps favors the versatile finger snap because according to her, when executed properly, its effect is as undeniable as a holy artifact. And while holy artifacts are not always available, one's fingers generally are. Looking Pothead directly in the eye, she snaps again with confidence.

He disappears.

Others pop up while she's planting, but no one helpful. She snaps again and again until they too disappear and she can resume her train of thought. Why is she in service to their lives, she wonders, and at such remove from her own? Is that why her world is mostly so bland and colorless? Why it rains all the time? Why she lives in the past? Why she's no longer saturated in the deep pigment, rich texture, pungent flavor, and intoxicating fragrance of her own life? And what happened to the fiddle? The accordion? The barn dances? The boys.

What happened to *her*?

Brain damage from the accident is the most likely answer, she knows, but she can't say for sure. She only remembers what she's heard from the ghouls. That she was driving a car.

That the car crashed. That's it. Not a word more. The start and finish of her life as she knows it. No more than a breath. Or more like a gasp. But in the end, does it matter? After all, when everything changes, you have to figure out how to change with it. The problem is, Felicity's the only one interested in adapting. Addie won't even acknowledge how weird it all is. Or maybe she doesn't notice. Or maybe she just can't see anything through the swamp of donuts and bourbon.

Felicity rolls up her sleeves and digs six inches into the mound above Mother's grave. She places the roots of a pretty raspberry petunia in the hole, and sits back, admiring its velvety red petals. She digs another hole, and another, until the entire mound is alive with pigment. Mother will be pleased when she returns from wherever she is, Felicity thinks. Or maybe she's just sleeping in. It's been so long she barely remembers what Mother looks like.

Felicity moves on to Aunt Miranda's grave, planting pink asters, followed by Cousin Hatty's grave, where she plants jade impatiens. Hatty was such a fidget, she thinks. Impatiens are perfect for her. Crawling around in her crinoline skirt on her hands and knees from this grave to that, all at once she finds herself kneeling in front of a hole. She does a triple-take, because who's been digging holes? She hasn't seen a fresh-dug grave in this cemetery in so long she can't remember. Although time is as unreliable a measure as she can think of right now. *Still.* She pulls herself up against the low hanging limb of the live oak behind her, breathing heavily. But why should it shock her that there's a hole in a cemetery of all places? Maybe Addie finally found Samuel and Edgar and put them back to work. Maybe their cousins finally showed up. Although by Felicity's reckoning, they're plenty old to be digging six-foot graves at this point. But maybe they're not.

"Hey!" says a deep voice behind her.

Startled, she turns to find a young man, covered head to toe in tattoos. She's never seen anything like him. Dense blades of hair stand up on his head like Kentucky bluegrass. He leans against a shovel buried a couple of inches in the soil from the new hole.

"Hope you don't mind me helping out," he says.

Felicity's eyelids flutter repeatedly. Unlike most of the people she talks to out here, this one looks slightly more solid. Not quite as transparent. So maybe he's real—not a figment of her accident head. It's hard to rely on sight alone in Felicity's world. But he does look familiar.

"Do I know you?" she says.

He shrugs. "I know your sister, but don't tell her I was here."

"No problem," says Felicity. To be honest, she hardly tells Addie what she sees or doesn't see, and who she talks to. Addie says they're not there anyway, so maybe they're not. But what is Felicity supposed to do? Ignore them? There are so many gaps in her memory, how is she expected to know who's who and what's what? It's so confusing—who's alive and who's dead and why it's getting so hard to bury people. To actually put them in the ground and make them stay.

"Not to be rude," she says, "but what do you want?"

He pulls a cigarette-looking thingy from his pocket and puts it in his mouth in a leisurely manner. Like he hasn't got a place to go or a worry in the world. "Just digging," he says, blowing out a small ring of smoke. "Just trying to help out is all."

"Well, who sent y'all? And why do we need help?"

"Thaddeus," he says.

She drops her trowel. "Thaddeus sent you?"

"Yes, but don't tell Adelaide. He doesn't want her to know."

"Thaddeus sent you here to dig a grave?"

"You could say that."

She looks down at her dirty combat boots, hand to chest, gulping air. "But why?" she asks, looking up. But now the boy's back is to her as he digs hard and fast, pitching heavy packed dirt across the fence line like loose sand.

Obituary for Release to:
Blue Grass Bugle &
The Louisville Gazette
Wednesday, June 30, 1946

Michelle Lynn Mcbride Dies of Broken Bone Disease
Born: January 1, 1939
Passed into eternal life: June 30, 1948

Nine-year-old Michelle Lynn McBride, known to most
as 'Shelley', beloved daughter of Travis and Mimi
McBride of Outskirt, Kentucky, finally died on Monday
after suffering her entire life with broken bone disease.
Shelley's frail bones began to break when she was just a
wee thing, and no one within a hundred miles of Outskirt
General could figure out why. Doc Witherby drove her to
Louisville and Lexington, and wrote letters to hospitals
up and down the East Coast, begging for help. But no
one in the region ever heard of it or could figure out
why it was happening. The money basket at Peabody
Baptist was passed too many times to count, which
bought Shelley a used wheel chair when she was six. No
one ever saw a more grateful child. She was something
to behold, and will be sorely missed by all, especially
her older brothers, Edgar and Samuel, currently
employees at *Sunnyside Up*. Shelley leaves behind
countless adoring aunts, uncles, and cousins, as well
as an impressive collection of glass ballerinas that will
adorn her headstone. Shelley's Pa, Travis, has been the
embalmer at *Sunnyside Up Funeral Home and Chicken*

Farm since 1935. Her Mama, Mimi Somers McBride, is the Hair and Makeup Artist at the same establishment. Shelley will be groomed by traveling professionals from Peabody Memorial who have compassionately agreed to trade services, in case you were wondering.

Sunnyside Up invites the bereaved to gather in the chapel on Friday for a tearful goodbye. Hankies will be provided, but must be laundered and returned in good condition. Assorted village dogs and chickens will be admitted with escorts only, as will Shelley's favorite pig, Presley, who will be squeezed into a pink tutu for the occasion. Afterwards, at Shelley's request, mourners are invited to travel by roller skates or pogo sticks to the Community Room for strawberry ice cream sodas, lemon meringue pie, and bubble gum. In honor of the deceased, no vegetables will be served.

When asked for a comment about the death of her niece, Regina Somers, wife and business associate of the esteemed Jasper Somers of *Sunnyside Up Enterprises*, stated, "Sunnyside Up isn't just an egg, it's an attitude."

ELEVEN

ADELAIDE

A delaide sits in the office of her shrink, Dr. Joy, whose specialty is yanking memories out of Adelaide's head like teeth. She shifts positions on the worn leather couch, tugging at the ends of her black and white checkered stretchy pants trying to cover the gap between the pants and her unraveling tube socks. Why did she leave the house in such a hurry, she wonders. Would it kill her to be late once in a while? To inconvenience someone else instead of herself? And what possessed her to wear these old pants, anyway? Who does she think she is? Felicity?

The pants hardly fit. Her thighs press

against the seams in a threatening fashion, and the half-opened waistband causes the zipper to creep steadily south. Luckily the zipper is mostly covered by her pilly purple sweater, though it keeps riding up. Thanks to her steady diet of baked goods, there's no hope of closing the gap any further. She realizes she has to get her eating under control, and she's tried, she really has. It's a goal. But considering the astronomical stress in her life right now, how will that ever happen? It could be worse, she supposes. At least she's wearing a pair of her best, clean, high-waisted rosebud underpants in case of an accident. She wouldn't be caught dead without them.

"You were saying?" says Dr. Joy from the dandelion yellow wingback chair facing Adelaide.

Adelaide scoots up attentively. She needs to get ahead of this thing. She can't be wasting entire afternoons in a shrink's office like this. It isn't how she intends to live whatever's left of her barren life. She clears her throat, and tries to sound convincing. "Well, I've been thinking that if I could get to that moment, the *exact* moment when the thing happened, I could get over it," she says. "I could put an end to all this intolerable nonsense."

Dr. Joy cocks her head. "Nonsense?" she says as if she's never heard the word before.

"Well, you know," Adelaide says. "At some point, all this…" her hand sweeps an imaginary path, "…has got to end. It's interminable! I need my life back. Don't I?" *I mean, come on!* "Felicity's gone crazy, and I'm sick of pretending it's okay. Because it isn't okay. It's an avalanche. I can't say what happens to my days anymore." She raises her chin in a lofty fashion, and sighs, "They just…vanish. Even the family doesn't visit. Except the dead ones, of course." She rolls her eyes and mutters, "Always plenty of those."

Dr. Joy's uncombed bushy eyebrows arch measurably. "The dead ones?"

"Well, you know, the figments of Felicity's fractured imagination."

Here Joy attempts to purse her thin tulip-red lips that stretch ear-to-ear across her face. Between her long linear lips and circle eyes, not to mention the scribbled brows, her features look as if they've been drawn by a child. Adelaide has the urge to stick her on the refrigerator with a magnet. Not to mention the oversized head on her stick figure body. Lawdy, she's an odd duck, thinks Adelaide. But then again, maybe all shrinks are. How would Adelaide know? This is her first. And she's not even sure how it came to this—seeing a shrink at all. Never mind this one. Advice she got from Felicity's doctor, she supposes. Back when Felicity started going crazy. But that was ages ago. So why is she still doing this?

"You're seeking a...moment," Dr. Joy reminds her.

"Oh," says Adelaide. "Right. But not just any moment. *The* moment."

"I see." Dr. Joy reaches into her alligator purse, digs deep, and retrieves a pack of Winston cigarettes. She holds it up to Adelaide. "Do you mind?" she says.

"No," says Adelaide, practically salivating. A breeze crosses the room rustling stacks of paper on the glass desk and the surface of the white alpaca rug beneath them.

Joy looks up through the tinted lenses of her crystal-studded spectacles. "Would you like one?" she asks.

Adelaide blinks repeatedly. *Is this a trick?* If she smokes in front of the shrink, will it lengthen her sentence?

But these are Winstons! Sentiment alone would dictate her right to indulge.

No, she tells herself. *No!* She will not take the bait. She remembers the smoking stick the boy gave her which seems like a good alternative. She roots through her satchel, moving aside a half-eaten box of Raisinets and the remains of a twinkie. Spotting the white cylinder beneath a snaggle of red yarn, she grabs it, twirling it between her fingers thoughtfully. She is still shocked by the boy's disappearance, if not his appearance in the first place. She must have mortified him with her flirtatiousness. Why else would he have left so abruptly?

Or like Phipps said, maybe he really disappeared.

She tries to get a hold of herself. She's not crazy. She's not Felicity! *But maybe the energies transformed him.* Ha! As if she believes Phipps' nonsense for a magical minute! As if there were such a thing as transformative energies in the first place. *Don't make me laugh!* And if there were, they would hardly pursue the likes of Dulles, a renegade tattooed outlaw. She shakes her head, amused half to death at the rollicking ridiculousness of it all. Such a sage as he walking around with chartreuse hair fuzz. *Transformed by energies!* Hahaha! *Into what?* A smoke-breathing totem pole? He already is one!

"Adelaide?" says the doctor pointedly. "Would you like a cigarette?"

"Excuse me?" she says. "Oh. No, no thanks. I think I'll have this instead."

Dr. Joy tilts her head. "What's that?"

"A cigarette," says Adelaide uncertainly. "But not really a cigarette?" She studies it with incredulity, as if she can't believe she found it. Or that it, along with the boy, ever existed in the first place. *But this is proof!* "An e-cigarette, I'm told," she says, twirling it.

"Oh? And what does the E stand for?"

"I have no idea."

All at once, remembering her flirtation, a giggle works its

way up Adelaide's throat and surfaces out her mouth. Then another. And another. She is a teenager or a toddler. She can barely talk for all the room the giggles are consuming in her mouth. "A um, hee hee hee!" She goes on like this for at least a few minutes, attempting to collect herself several times. How embarrassing. "Well, um…the truth is…hahahaha!"

"Adelaide," chides Dr. Joy, "your antics are diversionary."

Adelaide shakes out her hands and swings her head back and forth to reset herself. "Okay, sorry, well…what happened was, a handsome young hellion gave me this stick. He was smoking one, too. He said it was good for me. Or well, better than tobacco at least."

"Hmmm," says Joy. "Well, is it?"

Adelaide shrugs. "How would I know? There's nothing natural about it as far as I can tell. It's made of plastic, for one thing, and it tastes like marshmallows." She sucks hard to draw vapor like she did last night, but nothing happens. She tries again. The intake makes a whistling noise that pierces her ear, so she stops, stymied. She just can't remember how it works. He must have lit it before he gave it to her. "I guess I'm supposed to light it," she says.

"Allow me," says Dr. Joy reaching forward with her lighter.

Adelaide places the stick in her mouth and leans toward the flame, which precipitates an explosion that nearly lights her face on fire.

"Aaaaaaa," she screams, pitching the thing at the floor, where it continues to burn and pop on the alpaca rug. Adelaide jumps up, dancing frenetically, stomping around like a shaman at a healing ritual, until at last the fire is extinguished.

From her chair, Dr. Joy observes this scene with such remove it could be happening on a screen somewhere in Egypt instead of right in front of her in the flesh.

Exhausted, Adelaide leans forward, her right arm extended against Joy's desk, her left hand splayed across her hyperventilating chest. At this point her burst-open pants are practically at her hips. Noticing this, she turns discreetly toward the bookcase and hikes them up. Struggling with the zipper, she raises it slowly until it catches on her rosebud underpants. There's no way to detach it without tearing her underpants, so she tugs her pilly purple sweater down as far as it will go to cover the gap. When she turns back around, she sees the sizable burn hole the fire left in the shaggy rug.

"Good grief," she says. "Apologies." But why is she apologizing? After all, she wasn't even thinking about cigarettes until Dr. Joy taunted her with Winstons.

"Don't worry about it," says the doctor matter-of-factly. "I should have known better. Imposters show up all the time around here. Sometimes it's hard to spot them." She smashes her cigarette butt in the tray.

Adelaide isn't sure what the doctor means by *imposters*. Is she referring to the e-cigarette or to Adelaide? *Or Dulles?* Either way, she has no intention of pursuing it. There's enough going on here without starting a whole new thread of insanity. Her nerves are completely frayed; she can hardly sit still. Lowering herself back down on the couch and fidgeting demonstrably, she points to the pack of cigarettes and says, "Can you just give me..." she can't even think of the word, "...one of those..."

The doctor lights a Winston and hands it to Adelaide, then lights another for herself.

Adelaide welcomes the toxic fumes into her lungs like a faithful companion whose noble job is to usher her out of this miserable life and into the next. "Sublime," she says between hacking coughs. She should never have stopped. Why did she? She can't remember.

"Smoking can be an efficient focusing mechanism," says Dr. Joy, as if reading Adelaide's mind. She exhales a cloud that rises over her black pixie haircut and sits there like a thought bubble. "We all have our vices," she says. "Tension wires, if you will, that restrain us when we're afraid of blowing away." She peers at Adelaide meaningfully. "Attachments."

There's that word again, thinks Adelaide.

"Sometimes they ground us," says Joy.

Adelaide likes this. What a refreshing change of philosophy! "So, they're good for us?" she says, delighted. "Attachments are good for us?"

Dr. Joy shrugs. "Sandbags, let's say. Grounding us until we're ready to fly off into the yonder." She glances at her notes. "Most people have trouble releasing them is the problem. They outlive their purpose."

She shifts in her seat. "When did you start smoking, Adelaide?"

Adelaide rocks her head back and forth, thinking. "As a teenager," she says wistfully. "I smoked on the sly, of course. Behind the old shack."

Just uttering those words creates a sudden memory so granular in form and detail that Adelaide can barely drag herself back from it. In spite of her efforts to focus, her mind instead pitches a tent and moves right into the field of high grass behind the cedar shack with Julian. She sees it all. His luscious sable hair. His mesmerizing dark eyes. The careless beard. The rippling muscles.

She is all at once under him. Over him. Around him. *Ignited.* And why not? Who's around to stop her? Felicity's gone cuckoo and Julian's dead. Adelaide has to figure out how to serve the rest of her life sentence with him gone and Felicity chained to her ankle. Living in the past seems like a good way to go. And cigarettes of any kind seem like a decent way to cope while simultaneously shortening the sentence.

Adelaide tries to focus, but her thoughts are hormonal teenagers romping around drunk. All she has to do is think of Julian and he appears. It's as if he's right there waiting for her. *Julian!* She knows this is impossible, even though she sees him. Smells him. *Feels him.* But if she ever expects to get out of this office without landing in an asylum, she has to get her inner adolescent under control.

"Adelaide?" says Dr. Joy.

"Oh, yes, well, Felicity and I were at the...you know, that class I take her to? Or whatever it is. The one you recommended, where she learns about all the psycho stuff? And by the way, I don't think she's learning anything useful. I'm certainly not."

Dr. Joy removes her glasses and wipes the lenses against her leggings. "Don't wander off," she says. "Stay with your thought."

"OK," she says. "We were at the meeting, and old Phipps was going on and on about some ridiculous whatever..." Adelaide leans forward. "Honestly, if you hadn't persuaded me that my attendance there would help snap Felicity out of her wacky world, I would definitely not continue. It's completely worthless." She leans forward and taps the cigarette to loosen the ash. "But..." She hesitates.

"Don't get lost in the minutiae, Adelaide. You're there for Felicity, yes, but there's surely some value in it for you, and well, for everyone in attendance."

"I'll admit that my aha realization occurred while I was there, right after Dulles..."

"Dulles?"

"The young man who gave me the plastic cigarette."

"Go on."

"Right after he disappeared."

Dr. Joy leans forward. "Disappeared?"

"It seemed that he disappeared, yes." Adelaide crosses and uncrosses her ankles nervously. "One minute he's flirting with me, and the next he's telling me I remind him of his great granny, Emmaline…"

"Oh dear," says the doctor, wide-eyed. "Oh my!" She tucks her chin into her chest and practically guffaws.

Adelaide ignores this blatant insensitivity. After all, Joy is decades younger than Adelaide, but hardly a teenager herself.

Dr. Joy says, "Sorry. Please continue."

"And well, the next minute he disappeared. I just looked up and he was… gone."

Dr. Joy takes a luxurious drag on her cigarette, exhaling a wave of curls. "Might he have walked elsewhere without you noticing?"

Adelaide looks past the desk to the window and fixes on a vanishing point in the distance. "I suppose he must have," she says. "What other explanation is there?"

"And that's when you had your moment?"

Adelaide considers whether to go any further with this. After all, it probably means nothing, and she doesn't want to get stuck talking about it for a month or more. If she stops right now, she can pretend none of it happened. She takes a drag, and exhaling, says, "If I tell you, can I stop coming? I mean, if I identify the moment when everything changed, I should be able to figure out the rest on my own, don't you think?"

Dr. Joy straightens her back. "I won't know unless you tell me."

"Okay, well…it was the minute I realized I would have to go it alone."

"Alone?"

Adelaide nods. "And…" she can barely get it out, "I…that is…well, he…"

"Just say it," says Dr. Joy.

Blinking back tears, Adelaide says, "Go it alone without... him, I mean. Without Julian."

The doctor nods. "And when did that moment occur, Adelaide?"

"I don't know. I mean, I realized there was such a moment last night, as I said. But the actual instant of knowing is more obscure. Almost like something...that I've always known?" She shifts positions. "But how could that be? How could I have...I mean he only just died. We haven't even...he's not even..." She places her cigarette in the ashtray on the end table and rummages through her brassiere for her hanky.

Dr. Joy gives Adelaide a moment to blow her nose then says, "You've told me about the shack several times before, and the barn, of course, but that's all. What are your other memories of Julian?"

Blotting her tears, Adelaide tries to think. "I...I don't know," she says. "Right this minute I can't think of any."

"Any at all?" Dr. Joy scribbles something on her notepad.

"Not really," says Adelaide, confused. *Why can't she?*

"I see. Well, I think opening up your relationship with Julian is key to understanding your confusion right now, don't you think?"

Adelaide shrugs, tears streaming down her cheeks, plopping onto her sweater. "I didn't even know I was confused."

"The way we grieve holds clues to our healing," says Dr. Joy. "If we expect to be healthy, we have to address those clues."

"I don't know," chokes Adelaide. "Seems to me people grieve the way they grieve. It just happens. It's not planned."

"Are you sure?"

"I should know," Adelaide snivels, "shouldn't I? I work with the bereaved all the time. It's what I do."

"Well, yes, but we're all unicorns, Adelaide. There's not one of us the same. At least not on this level," she adds. "On other levels, yes, but you're not there yet." She leans back. "At least you're not aware of being there."

Adelaide's tears gather.

"Your spirit is confined." Dr. Joy blinks too many times to count. "Stuck," she adds, raising her arms above her head in a trail of smoke. "Until it's freed, you can't move on." She narrows her eyes, studying Adelaide carefully. "You're suffering, Adelaide."

Adelaide's tears unleash. She's a typhoon.

"You can't possibly progress without detaching yourself from...well, everything. Including the suffering. *Especially* the suffering. People get attached to suffering, too, you know. It can be experienced as a pious attempt at distinguishing oneself. But in truth, the release of suffering is up to us and only us. We must grow and grow until we're equal to it." She sits back in her chair, studying Adelaide. "And then we must look it in the eye and release it." She shakes her head sympathetically. "Suffering affects everything—our posture, our outlook, our sense of purpose and freedom. Our choices. Our very advancement in the infinite world. If we would just step to one side or the other long enough to let it go...why, we'd be utterly free."

For some reason, Adelaide is so upset by this, she can barely force herself to sit. Why is she letting Joy get to her like this? To have this kind of power over her? She needs an attachment, something to attach her to the chair. Something to ground her. She looks at her cigarette in the ashtray, but it's burned to the filter. She can't possibly ask for another without risking judgement. Turning away from Joy, she bends down, reaches into her purse, and stuffs the remains of the twinkie discreetly into her mouth. She chews it as quickly as possible, covering her mouth with her damp hanky. This takes more time than she'd like.

"You're very distracted today," says Dr. Joy. "Which I believe is a result of your inability to address the subject. The only way to get to the bottom of this may be through hypnosis." She tilts her head. "Are you open to hypnosis, Adelaide?"

Adelaide takes a minute to swallow the last lump of glutinous sponge cake, which lodges in her throat. Several exaggerated swallows later, she says, "I don't know. Maybe?" She shifts positions, pulling her sweater back down over her pants. "Can you hypnotize me to stop eating?"

"You'll stop overeating when you come to grips with your experience," says the doctor. "When you release your suffering."

"Well, what's *your* suffering?" asks Adelaide petulantly. "I mean, you're suffering too, wouldn't you say?" She points to the pack of cigarettes. "Or else why would you be doing that?"

Dr. Joy puckers her long thin lips into a zigzag line. "My suffering is your suffering, Adelaide. I feel the suffering of my patients in a palpable, empathic way, and reflect it back. I can't really listen to any of it effectively without grounding myself in their attachments. Your attachment is to cigarettes, among other things, like bourbon." She sighs, shaking her head sadly. "And donuts."

Adelaide shifts uncomfortably. *How does she know this?*

"Someone else's entrapments might be different. Maybe an obsession with appearance—overspending on fashion or makeup, which you clearly aren't prone to."

Adelaide ignores this vaguely insulting gobbledygook. The woman likes to smoke, and that's the end of it. And anyway, if Adelaide agrees to be hypnotized, it has to be for a good practical reason.

"If I agree to the hypnosis, can I stop coming?" she says. "I mean, I thought I was coming for Felicity. Isn't that what you told me? To learn how to deal with my crazy sister? But somehow I think all this wallowing is making me a little bit crazy too. I'm not…a wallower." She turns toward the window. "But this nonsense is making me one."

Dr. Joy makes a notation, then peeks over her crystal-studded frames. "Before I release you from therapy, Adelaide, I have to confirm that it really is Felicity who's crazy." She blinks three times. "And not you."

Adelaide grabs the arms of her chair and turns wide-eyed to the doctor. "Meeee?" she says. "How dare you suggest that I'm the crazy…" She grits her teeth. "After all this…"

"I'm not suggesting anything," says the doctor. "I'm saying it outright. Putting all the cards on the table so we can separate the aces from the jokers."

Adelaide shivers like an arctic storm. Like the north wind itself just blew through the room, capturing their very words into solid paragraphs that drop like blocks of ice onto the hard ground and shatter into shards of nonsense. But the truth is, it's hot as hell in this room. And still, she can't stop shaking.

"It's like Felicity's craziness is infectious!" she screeches in such a wild manner that even she knows it's crazy. "And I promise you one thing…I am not going where Felicity goes. Mind or body." She wags her finger threateningly. "Do you understand? Do? You? Understand?" She grabs her hanky and honks like a mating gander. "If I agree to hypnosis, I want you to know that I am in no way agreeing to wander into *that* abyss. *Felicity's* abyss." She nods emphatically. "And I won't allow you to lead me there either."

Dr. Joy nods. "I do understand," she says. "But it may be your only way out."

TWELVE

FELICITY

F ive-year-old Felicity drags the folding stool to the big wooden box that sits high on the metal stand. She climbs to the top, flings her long pigtails back, and pushes hard against the handle. All she wants is to open the top, find Addie, and slap her hard for dragging her into this creepy, stinky room in the first place. Not that she'd ever slap Addie, not really. She loves Addie, and anyway, she'd never get away with it. There'd be "conquences", as Mother says. Maybe just poke Addie in the belly instead and run fast. *So fast!* Run right out the door, down the hall, and back to the apartment like lightning.

She's never been in this part of the property before, and hopes she never will be again. She's pretty sure Mother wouldn't like it one bit if she knew.

She knows what these boxes are. They're heaven boxes. Daddy says people die and go to heaven in them, even though the boxes don't have a motor. Ludie Lindstrom went to heaven in a box, and everybody cried because they didn't want her to go. Addie said Uncle Stewart went to heaven too, and nobody cried but Granny. Felicity wasn't born yet, so she wouldn't know, but she feels like she knows him because sometimes she dreams about him. He orders her around and blows cigar smoke in her face. Granny says that's about right since he was a soldier, so he can't help bossing people around. Then she asks Felicity what she's doing dreaming about a man she never met, but Felicity doesn't know the answer.

Standing right at the heaven box now, her tummy has spiders. "Get me outta here," she whispers. *It stinks!* Her chest thumps and her hands sweat. And it really does stink! She tries to remember the smell of Granny's chocolate cake in the oven last night instead. It was so good, still steaming and almost done. The fudgy frosting all ready to spread with Granny's flat knife. Sometimes Granny lets Flitty do the spreading herself, and she sneaks a lick when Granny's back is turned. Standing here now, Flitty fills her nostrils with the imaginary cake. Juices fill her mouth. She turns her head and spits.

Eyes squeezed shut, she pushes down on the handle of the box with all her might, grunting, *uuh, uugh*. It barely opens then slams right back down. This game is no fun at all. It's a bad idea, you ask her. Terrible. Plus looking out the window she sees it's getting darker by the minute. The sun is all red and melty behind the barn, setting the blue sky on fire so bad it looks purple. It might be pretty if it weren't so scary.

All the sudden, Flitty's arms and legs get a chill that races right up her neck. Everything's purple, even her hands. This purple is more than a color. It's alive as a person. Flitty almost talks to it, but decides not to. What if Addie hears her? Or what if the purple is cross? What then? She watches the color swirl, moving up and down, inside and outside. It pops and sparkles like the worst kind of show-off. Like Buster Tweed on the playground, jumping around front and back of her, making her look at him. She stares down at her purple hands like they don't belong to her. Like they belong to her invisible friend, Celeste. Flitty wants to show the purple show-off that she doesn't care one bit about it, but that'd be a lie. She does care, but she doesn't know why. She cares, but she's also scared. All she can think is, *Where's Addie! What if Addie ran away and left her?* Her heart bounces across her chest like skipping stones. *Per-plunk. Per-plunk. Per-plunk.*

"Addie!" she hollers. "Where y'all?! Switch the lights! I can't barely see!"

No answer from Addie. Maybe she really did leave. Or maybe the purple stole her. Oh lawd, no! *It can't be true!* But it just well might.

"Switch the lights ooooon!" she yelps. "I'm purple, Addie! Everything's purple! Where are you? Come out! Are you purple? Did the purple people take you?"

Out of nowhere, Addie's voice, or someone who stole Addie's voice, says, "You got to find me, Flitty Jane! I'm not comin' out till y'all find me. It's a game, you big baby!"

The way Addie's words jump around the room, Flitty can't be sure if her sister is in this box right here or in another one. Or if it's Addie at all. She hopes Addie doesn't end up in heaven by accident, hiding in the wrong box. Maybe people games aren't games to God.

She stares hard, trying to erase the purple from her eyeballs. Trying to pretend it's a color she can see through, like yellow. She's got to open this box fast. Addie could be stuck inside! But every time she lifts the top halfway, her sweaty hands slide right off, and the box slams shut. This time she breathes from her toes, pushes against her feet, up her legs, into her belly, and straight out her arms, flinging the cover as far as she can with all her might. "*Uhhhhhh! Uuuuuuhhhh!*"

At last, the lid lifts. It rocks back and forth, teasing to shut back down. *No, you don't! No! You don't!* She keeps it open with her eyes. Just stares and stares till it settles. Till it stays open. She wipes her palms against her romper, gathering the courage to peek inside. She's never been this close to an open heaven box by herself. She holds her breath and peeks. The room's so dim and the purple's so thick she can barely figure out what all's going on inside the box. She looks so hard her eyes hurt. *Huh?* She forces herself to look again, deeper. *Addie, that you?*

Please be you.

Just then the purple stirs up like a malted shake at the Outskirt Soda Fountain, whisking like a tornado round the room and round her. This makes her eyes tear, and she rubs them hard with her fists. "Go 'way!" she orders the wind. And just like that, it obeys, surprising her. This reminds her of her dog, Rooster, when he wants a bone. *Sit!* she commands. And he sits. Then he offers his paw, drooling. When he gets the bone, he takes it behind the fence where he buries it like a secret. Like everybody doesn't know where his bones are. Everybody knows! Does the purple wind want some bones? Whose bones?

Not Addie's!

Not hers.

Felicity watches as the purple backs off, leaving behind a thin cloud of clearer air, colored softer like the spring hair ribbons

Mother bought her, lilac and lavender. Air so much clearer that she can mostly see through it, though it doesn't leave completely. She stares down through the dim darkness into the box again with all her might, trying to make sense of what she sees.

"Addie, that you?"

Nobody answers, so maybe it's not Addie. It's someone though. Or some*thing*. A doll at least, or a dummy. A likeness. Even through the lilac haze and shadow light from the setting sun, she can see it lying there real still, hands folded, playing the dead game hard, like it means to win. Who else knows about the game? Who else could it be but Addie?

"Addie come ooooon!" Flitty whines in the fast-dimming light. If she knew where the dang light switch was, she'd turn it on. "Addie, stop playin'! Stop lyin' there like that!"

Addie, is it you?

She squints harder, near nose-to-nose with what's looking less like Addie and more like the Outskirt liberrian without her spectacles. Miz Harriet Phipps right there, sure enough, lying in the box all dressed up in the same blue checkered button-down frock Flitty seen her in a hundred times. But why's she playing dead? Addie didn't say a thing about Miz Phipps playing the game. Wouldn't Addie've said?

But it's Miz Phipps alright. Flitty knows for sure when the liberrian opens her milky ole eyes, saying, "Oh hello, Felicity Jane. Nice to see you."

Flitty's hands fly right to her chest. "Miz Phipps, y'all near gave me a heart attack right there! First I thought you was Addie, and then I thought you was…dead!"

"Did your sister ever return the *Nancy Drew* books?" she says.

Felicity grits her teeth. "Um, I dunno, but maybe Mama did."

Flitty knows this is an outright fib. She's seen the Nancy Drew books under Addie's bed. But caught by surprise like she is—*who expected to see the liberrian just lyin' in a heaven box!*—a fib is all she's got.

"Those books are brand new," says the liberrian. "As is the book you took out, Felicity— *Peter Pan.* If they're not returned by Friday you'll both incur a library fee of three cents a day which will double in week number two and triple in week number three. It adds up. You should remind your mama 'bout the fines, Felicity. She's better off than most, but last I noticed there's no money tree in your backyard." She pauses and says, "But if there is, please bring me a cutting, will y'all? I could use the cash." A hardy laugh erupts from the box.

The laughter makes Flitty's eyes blink like a hummingbird. She has to say something to make it stop. "Never mind 'bout the fines," she says. "But you might well worry 'bout yourself. Mother'll be mad as all get-out she sees y'all lying 'round our property like this. Using our heaven boxes for games like y'all are. Best to stop playin' and git out now."

"Playing what, dear?" says the shriveled old lady, barely opening her eyes.

"Playing dead!"

"Ahh," she says, "Yes, well I suppose I am."

"I don't know how y'all can stand it in there," says Felicity. "It's plenty hot."

"Is it?" says the liberrian. "I hadn't noticed."

"And it stinks!" Flitty pinches her nose. "Just like Granny's lye, she cleans the kitchen."

From somewhere in the purple tornado, Addie calls out, "Mercy, Felicity, who y'all jabberin' at?"

Felicity's greatly relieved to hear her sister's voice, even full of lye such as it is. "Talkin' to Miz Harriet, Addie. Can't you hear?"

"Y'all puttin' me on?" Addie snaps.

Flitty huffs. "Don't be cross, Addie. I'm not the one who

invited her to play dead with us in the first place." She stomps her foot. "I hate this game."

A fierce rustling back in the corner shows Addie's head behind one of the fancier gold-handled boxes. "Knock it off," she says. "Ain't nobody playing dead but us, and we're not even lyin' down yet."

Just then the purple cloud wooshes right back from the edges, filling the room, settling like low fog in the holler. Even through the purple, Flitty sees Miz Phipps all comfortable on the shiny pillows, hands folded neatly like she hasn't a care. Flitty tells her sister, "You think I'm puttin' y'all on, jes come look right here. Miz Harriet Phipps playin' dead, and she jes might win."

"Swear to gawd, Felicity Jane," Addie says as she pops up, crisscrossing 'round the boxes toward her sister. "You drew me outta hiding for nothin', and I swear..."

"See for y'all's self," Flitty says, wide-eyed. She looks back down at the liberrian. "Sit on up and tell Addie what you said."

Miz Phipps says, "I can't move. I'm a bucket of cement."

Flitty says, "Hold on then. Soon's Addie gets here we'll help you on up."

Next thing Addie climbs the step stool, jumps to the kneepad and looks inside. "Good grief!" she hollers. "I didn't know Mrs. Phipps died, the old bag."

"Ask her not to call me that," snaps the old lady.

"Don't call her that," says Felicity. "Y'all hurt her feelings right fierce."

Addie grabs Flitty's fists and shakes them. The commotion jostles the stand, and all the sudden the lid of the heaven box drops back down top of Miz Phipps. *Crash!!!* Addie takes Flitty's face in her hands and oogles her eyes near out their sockets. "You insane?!" she screams. "Talkin' to a dang corpse like that! What's wrong with you?"

"What's a *corse*?" squeaks Flitty, her mouth stretched across her face so far by Addie's grip, she can barely move her lips. "That's Miz Phipps!"

"A cor-ppppp-se, you knucklehead!" shrieks Adelaide. "A dead person!"

Flitty looks right to left and back more than once. "She isn't dead, Addie. She talked to me, and I talked back. And she talked again. And I…"

"She's DEAD!"

Addie's the maddest Flitty ever seen anyone 'cept Mother, and that was only the times Mother was chasin' after Addie. Mother never got after Flitty like that. Flitty doesn't like how it feels.

Addie grabs one of Flitty's pigtails and yanks hard, yelling, "Let's get the bejesus out of here!"

Flitty couldn't agree more, but right then the door flies open and who appears but Mother, all bug-eyed and red-faced, her mouth round as Granny's embroidery hoop. Takes a minute before anybody can move a muscle; even the purple cloud freezes in place. Flitty 'bout wets her pants.

Soon enough Mother's hand points at Adelaide like a big old heavy fry pan 'bout to sail through the air. "You," she orders in her mad voice, "go straight to your room." She raises her square chin high. "Right. This. Minute."

Flitty can see how much Addie wants to be anywhere else, but to get out she's got to pass Mother, who might hurt her, because like Mother always says, Addie is one brazen cuss. "*Adelaide Frances, y'all the most brazen cuss on the face of gawd's earth!*" she always says. Flitty can't deny the truth of that.

Addie looks like she's trying to confuse Mother, inching ever so slowly 'round the box to the next box and the next, crisscrossing back and forth. Getting nowhere, she backs up; starts again. Dodges this way. That. Nowhere.

"You too, Felicity," Mother says. "Y'all are both forbidden to enter this room. Hear me?"

While Mother's eyes are on Felicity, Addie tiptoes into the corner, but soon enough her eyes are back on Addie. "You hear me, Adelaide Frances?!!!" she shrieks.

She shrieks so loud, Flitty's surprised Miz Phipps doesn't fly off to heaven right then just to get the heck out. Hell, everybody wants out. Even the purple light zooms out the window.

"I heard you," says Addie. Her eyes dart left and right, and she runs so fast and low out the door, Mother can barely clip her head on the way out. But she does.

Flitty's relieved Addie got free without more fuss. She can hear her sister's footsteps pounding down the hallway to the apartments. Maybe all the way to Lou-ville, who knows? Wherever that is. Addie talks about it enough.

Mother doesn't chase after Addie, just stands in the doorway with her arms crossed. "Come along, Flitty," she says.

Now that Addie's gone, Flitty's not so scared of Mother. She takes her time scooting down the step stool. Then she carefully folds it and puts it back where she found it. Mother likes it when Flitty puts things back where they belong. Now she skips toward the doorway, reaching out for Mother's hand. "You shouldn't leave Miz Phipps here all by herself," she says. "She's getting hot."

"Is she?" says Mother, frowning.

"And she's lonely," says Flitty, leaving out the part about the liberry fine.

"Hmmmm." Mother walks Flitty back down the hall to the apartments and up the stairs to Addie's room.

"You wait in there with Adelaide," says Mother. "Y'all might not be responsible for this travesty, but you need to learn a lesson or two yourself. When Adelaide cooks up a crazy plan, y'all got to find me and let me know straight out."

"What all's a *travitey*, Mama?"

"It's a big problem, Flitty. A great big problem. You got to find me when that happens."

"But y'all wasn't home," Felicity whispers.

"I was out the barn, young lady." She shakes her finger. "You've got to learn to listen. And when your Daddy hears about all this the roof'll blow right off the house, you hear? I must be assured that you will never DARE enter those quarters again."

"What's a *quarters, Mama?*"

"Git," she says, then closes the door and stomps down the stairs in her big tie shoes. Flitty wishes Mother'd wear prettier shoes, but they probably wouldn't fit her big feet.

Waiting on Daddy, Flitty falls asleep at the bottom of Addie's bed, Addie's warm stocking feet against her head. The purple cloud swirls back around and falls asleep with her. It turns into purple people who tell her how special she is, like Flitty's favorite faerie, Tinker Bell. Tell her how Flitty'll learn to fly one day, too. How she'll always be protected, just ask. Just say the word and they'll be there. "*You're on a journey,*" they tell her. If it's to Lou-ville, she'll have to take Addie. Addie's always wanting to run away to Lou-ville. Flitty's feeling better about everything just now, not scared like she was. The purple people have twelve heads and robes made of purple velvet, like her favorite Christmas dress with the shiny sash. Their hearts beat out their chests like bouncing balls. They're more fun than Addie.

She's fixed on their bouncing hearts when all the sudden her nose tickles. She swats it, and her eyes pop open. She smells his peppery smell before he even shows his face. "Daddy!" she croons, reaching.

"How's my girls?" he says real quiet. One heavy hand on Addie, the other right on Flitty's head.

Flitty scrambles up, while Addie grabs his arm, saying, "I didn't mean nothin' by it, Daddy. Flitty said Mother told her..."

"Shhhh," he says softly. "Come 'ere, girls."

They crawl under his big arms, one left, one right.

"Let me tell you somethin'," he says.

Flitty digs her head into his flannel chest. Smells like fresh burnt leaves in the back field.

"You did wrong," he whispers.

"But Daddy!" Addie protests. "I was just..."

He places his big finger cross her lips. "You done wrong," he repeats quietly. "But that's forgivable if you ask forgiveness, huh?" His scratchy chin bends low as he seeks their eyes. "Do you ask forgiveness, girls?"

"Uh huh," says Flitty. "I do, Daddy. I really do."

Addie nods reluctantly, but her brows are low and her eyes still full of fight.

"Okay then," he says, "y'all know what we have to do next, right?"

Addie jumps up and grabs one of her *Nancy Drew* liberry books from under her bed and puts it in her pants while Daddy removes his belt and smacks the book loud enough for Mother to hear.

"Aaaaaaaaa! Waaaaaaa!" she fake screams. "No more! Stop! Please! I'm soooooorry!"

Daddy nods, smiling, and turns to Flitty, who scuttles to the closet, uncovering *Peter Pan* behind the secret hatch. She holds it 'gainst her bum. Her good luck shield.

"Please don't hurt Tinker Bell," she whispers to him, wide-eyed.

He chucks her chin. "Lawd, child," he says, "I'd never hurt my little Tinker Bell, now, would I?" He smacks the book lightly while she screams, "Ouch ouch ooooouch!" and he nods, big finger over his lips like it's a secret nobody better leak. But who would be that dumb? Even Rooster the dog would bury that bone better.

When Daddy walks down the stairs, Mother yells up, "Girls! Get yourselves down here pronto for dinner, 'less y'all want to be put away hungry, and don't think I won't."

Addie rolls her eyes, and Flitty says, "We best go."

"Let me see that *Peter Pan* book," says Addie. "What's it doing in my closet anyway?"

Flitty grabs the book and shrugs. "I have to return it to the liberry," she says. She turns, and sees the purple cloud out the window, lit by the headlights of a passing truck. "Look at that, Addie," she says.

"Look at what?"

"The purple cloud, Addie. That must be how they get here. In a truck."

Addie drags herself off the bed and slides her feet into her slippers. "What the cripe you talkin' about, Flitty Jane?"

"The purple? Like in the room today?"

"Good grief," Addie says. She reaches for her comb on the dresser, while she looks out the window.

"Y'all don't remember the purple?" Flitty says.

Addie puts the comb down and lays her arm around Flitty, walking her out the room toward the stairs. "Y'all do right to stop making things up, Flitty Jane. Purple people, good gawd! Things are wacky enough 'round here."

"You mean like Miz Phipps playin' dead right on our property?"

Addie throws her head back and laughs. "Yeah, like that," she says. "Don't tell Mother y'all looked in that coffin, swear? She'll switch us both herself, and there won't be any books for protection."

Flitty grabs Addie's hand. "Um. Ok," she says, though she already told Mother. No sense causing more fuss around this house, no way.

Obituary for Release to:
Bluegrass Bugle &
The Louisville Gazette
Friday, October 1, 1943

Mrs. Cedric Phipps Discovered Dead in her
Empty Bathtub
Born: September 7, 1855
Passed into eternal life: September 29, 1947

Mrs. Cedric Phipps, 92, nee Harriet Corinne Walker
of the Tennessee Walker Family, died sometime
Wednesday in the widow's quarters of the Outskirt
Library, where Mrs. Phipps labored selflessly for the last
half-century or so. Inquiries as to her whereabouts were
made Thursday morning at 10:15 a.m. by two curious
patrons, Curtis Leech and Babs LaRoche.

"In all our years together she's never been late
for book group," Babs reported breathlessly. "Curtis
and me waited 15 minutes then I shooed him off to
the station to declare her missing or dead. Curtis
protested but I knew I was right; I just knew it. I have a
sixth sense about these things, don't I, Curtis? Oh, how
would you know? But I do, and I was right. I always am."
She catches her breath a minute. "Curtis, you go on and
tell her the rest." Curtis says, "Weeeellll, I ran to…" and
Babs says, "Sargant Sawyer come runnin' back with
the locksmith, but Curtis were left behind account of
his jammed toe. Me and the sarge, we busted right in,
we did, yes. Soon's Sarge seen her just stretched out in

120

the empty tub, all dressed like she's ready for tea, we wondered what happened, I can't lie. Some kinda funny business, who can tell? Sarge called the coroner and that's that. I wash my hands. It weren't me, that's alls I know." She raises her right hand. "Gawd's my witness." She shook her head back and forth sadly, adding, "She were readin' that new book, you know, *Mrs. Parkington*, opened to page 99. Scandalous! Tragedy struck before she got to finish. I'm a have to finish it fer her and educate the group."

An autopsy was performed, but the results are sketchy since the coroner hasn't done one since veterinary school.

Mrs. Cedric Phipps was the first of ten children delivered to Wilhelmina and Leonard Walker, heirs to the Walker Stud Farm in Chattanooga, Tennessee. She was educated at Vanderbilt University before eloping with Cedric Phipps, a penniless drunk, whereupon her parents promptly disinherited her. Childless, she supported Cedric for thirty years as a librarian, before he expired. Harriet moved out of their cabin and into the library apartment soon after his death. Her mourning was brief.

Mrs. Phipps is predeceased by her siblings, their spouses, and everyone but her niece, Lucinda Walker Barr, and Lucinda's twelve children. She leaves behind her poodle, Louisa May Alcott, her canary, Lord Byron, and an impressive collection of first edition books which will remain in the library as stated in her Last Will & Testament. Her headstone will be decorated with the many quills and pens that filled her desk drawers.

Sunnyside Up invites mourners to celebrate the life

and service of Mrs. Phipps in the chapel this Saturday at 11 a.m., followed by a literary luncheon for anyone who can quote a verse from any poem whatsoever, limericks excluded. When asked for a comment about the librarian's passing, Mrs. Regina Somers, wife of the esteemed Jasper Somers of *Sunnyside Up Enterprises*, stated, "Sunnyside Up isn't just an egg. It's an attitude."

THIRTEEN

ADELAIDE

After her session with Dr. Joy, Adelaide sinks into the old brown recliner, her fingers tracing strips of worn electrical tape halfway up the seat cushion where the brittle leather cracked years ago. She leans forward, straddling the footrest while reaching for her hot toddy on the tray table. All this straddling and leaning get the best of her, however, causing the snaps of her cherry-print pajama tops to burst open, spilling pools of flesh onto the cold leather.

"Brrrrr!" she says, shivering.

Hands against the cushion, she inches back up, pushes and prods herself back in, and re-snaps her PJ's. This time she reinforces her restraints with the wide collar flaps of her red terry robe. She's no exhibitionist. Not that anyone can see her or is even likely to visit. In fact, she can't remember the last time she received guests.

But let's say someone did show up, she muses, would it really matter? After all, it's her house, and she's an old woman. A biddy. A biddy for whom allowances must be made. This idea gives her a sense of satisfaction. Freedom, even. After all, biddies get to do whatever they want. Feeling smug, she secures her toddy in a tight grip and squirms carefully back to a slightly reclined position. "Ahhhhh!" she moans. *At last!* Inhaling clouds of toddy vapor, she purrs like the demon cat, Whatchamacallit, when Felicity throws him an anchovy.

Boy oh boy, she thinks. What a doozie of a day this was. Yessirree.

Adelaide doesn't like to inventory her feelings too much after a busy day of exposing her buried emotions to professional strangers like Dr. Joy. Well, maybe not so much a stranger at this point, as an acquaintance. Or a friendly spy, to be more accurate. But why borrow trouble, as Mother used to say. It isn't as if Dr. Joy is sitting in the living room of *Sunnyside Up's* residential apartment across from Adelaide right now. No one is. The only one in this living room is Adelaide herself. Felicity, the faerie gadfly, has no doubt fled to the community room to host a festive social engagement with her imagination. As crazy as that is, it sometimes serves Adelaide's purposes, like now. All by her lonesome, this living area is her safety zone. Safety from prodding professionals and lunatic relatives alike. She wiggles her toes gleefully while sipping bourbon with relish. She should stay in more often.

The luxury of this privacy and the warmth of the bourbon prompts Adelaide to view her home through a nostalgic lens.

The dark paneled room with the brown plaid couch, the slate corduroy settee, the mismatched ladderback chairs, and the scratched coffee table with the chipped stained-glass candle-holders. Everything as it was on the day...

She loses the thought. *Wait. What day?* Well, the day everyone left, she supposes. If there was such a day. Not that she can remember one offhand. But right this minute, it seems as if there might well have been a certain day when things... *when they...*

Adelaide tries to concentrate, repeatedly losing the thread of her focus like an unraveling skein of yarn. Oh, who cares?! It probably wasn't important anyway. She stares ahead at the crumbling yellowed newspapers in the basket by the brick hearth beside the kindling. Why, it's as if someone is about to enter the house to light a fire—Daddy, perhaps. How Daddy loved a fire, she thinks, smiling. But Daddy's gone, and Adelaide can't remember a fire in that hearth since...*since the day...*

Well, maybe she'll light one herself one day soon. Although after the fire in Dr. Joy's office today, she's understandably reluctant to strike a match just yet. But maybe tomorrow.

The only natural light in the living room enters through the adjacent window, which isn't illuminated now, since it's past dusk. In her recliner, which was once her father's coveted possession, she faces the hallway where the staircase ascends to the upstairs bedrooms and descends in the other direction to the long corridor ending with the guest parlors where the bereaved congregate for wakes. Or used to congregate, anyway. There hasn't been a funeral in a while, right? Well, not that she can recall this minute, but it's been a long day.

Past the hallway is the compact, linoleum-floored, floral-papered kitchen where their family of four and sometimes Uncle Tavish, Aunt Mimi, and cousins Edgar and Samuel assembled back in the day. And little Shelley before she died. How did they all fit in there? she wonders now. It's hard to imagine. She is overcome with a sudden and rare sense of appreciation for her past, and inexplicably for her life right now. For the chaos and the privacy both. But mostly, let's face it, for this toddy.

Another sip and another, and Adelaide drifts. Not in a sleepy way so much as a sentimental one. She imagines her family noisily filling the house, her cousins fighting over the Rambler wagon while young Felicity rushes about doing something domestic. Collecting eggs, perhaps, or beating butter for a cake. But where is Adelaide in this scene? She focuses hard. *Ah, there I am!* Downstairs with the Right Reverend preparing a service for the grandparent of a schoolmate. Selecting hymns and scripture passages and polishing up one of Becky's irreverent obituaries. Life was hectic back then, but full. Every resource she had at her disposal was overutilized, especially the sympathy she was expected to generate for each and every mourner. As if a specific mourner's beloved on that particular day was the only deceased they'd ever buried or ever would.

As Adelaide settles further into these memories, they become denser, and the thing she doesn't want to happen the most, happens. Julian enters the scene. But what's he doing in those clothes? she wonders. Filthy dungarees and soiled construction boots. Did he come right from the mines? She scours the corners of her memory and realizes that, no—this is the day he quit the mines, but she can't remember why. The same day her cousins dug six different graves in the rear yard and, unbeknownst to their mother, recruited Julian to dig two more while they went back to their own houses and showered for dates. Not that Adelaide can think who might have dated those two paragons of arrested development. She can't. So maybe they were just fixing to meet some girls at the bonfire parties down the road. Anyway, that was the day Julian began moonlighting as a gravedigger.

Sipping her toddy right here in this recliner, a leaden mass of flesh, Adelaide is also the lithe young woman upstairs watching Julian through the sheer curtains of her bedroom window. How she can be both of these things, she doesn't know. *But she is.* She definitely is. She sees herself part the curtains slowly, peeking out. There he is, all muddy, manly and accidentally gorgeous, tossing pine cones at her screen for attention. He sees her see him. They see each other.

She steps back.

Another hardy swallow of the hot toddy sustains the memory. Clear as daylight, she is running to the closet for her favorite navy crepe button-down dress with the pretty white lace collar, throwing it hastily over her head and down her slim hips. She fumbles with the belt, tightening it to accentuate her waist. In the silver-plated handheld mirror, she fluffs the silky black hair that frames her face as if she'd just returned from a brisk walk. As if she always dressed this glamorously. She remembers it all—the distant thunder, the sudden rain. Peeking out the window at that soggy steel god of a man, mud running joyfully down his face and limbs.

Approaching the window again, she mouths, "Come on up," motioning to the trellis. She presses a finger to her lips, not that Julian needs a warning to be quiet. He's terrified of Mother, as is everyone with the possible exception of Felicity. Her parents are overseeing the showing in the parlor on the other side of the house, but they aren't deaf. One ear of Mother's is always attuned to her children's mischief. Maternal radar of a military order. Some version of caution, however misguided or adolescent, is called for. And both she and Julian know it.

Julian climbs the trellis, slipping periodically on this loose rung and that, until finally the whole thing separates from the house and collapses on top of him. Even now, Adelaide shakes her head, chuckling. Watching it all through the safe, faceted lens of memory, she sees him splayed flat-out in the rose bed before scrambling up on all fours, attempting to patch the trellis to no avail. This is the point at which time converges, and Adelaide can no longer separate herself from this scene. No longer the old biddy in the recliner, she fully inhabits her younger self on the brink of life. It's happening now.

"Jump!" he whispers. "I'll catch you!"

"No way!" she mouths, and disappears from the window, down the stairs to the kitchen. She grabs her rainslicker from the coat rack on the way out the door. Thank goodness the apartment steps are on the opposite end of the house from the funeral parlor is all she's thinking.

They run and run in the rain, across the field, past the cemetery, leaping over the gulch. Her good patent leather flats and white anklet socks are drenched in mud. Mother will kill her, but she doesn't care. If she doesn't do this, she might as well be dead. Her hair is soaked, pasted against her head and forehead. All that matters is combustion. All that matters is running, tripping, falling, and the kind of suppressed laughter that explodes in your throat like a grenade, threatening to consume you at the same time it saves your life.

By the time they duck into the barn, Adelaide's dress, like everything else inside and out, is saturated. There's no making it to the old miner's shack this night, no way. At least not yet. Not through all that rain and mud, nor the incessant strikes of lightning, convicting them like the blades of Thor. *Sinners!* Not that they've done anything wrong yet, but they sure are thinking about it. At least Adelaide is. The barn is as far as they'll get for now. And it's well in the path of her mother's radar.

Wait, she thinks. Is that my voice? Or Mother's?

"Addie," it says. "Addie!"

Adelaide is disturbed, literally shaken from the barn. "Stop it!" she grumbles. "Leave me alone!" Her words are pebbles. How will she ever get back to Julian if someone drags her away now?

"Wake up," says the voice. "What happened to you!"

Against her will and everything she stands for, Adelaide's eyes pop wide open. She half-expects to see Mother, of all people, but instead it's Felicity. Emaciated Felicity, no less, in a plaid flannel shirt over a sheer crinoline skirt with some ridiculous flowered swim cap strapped under her chin. She's practically floating in place with that stupid cat in her arms. *Lawd have mercy!* At least it's not Mother, she thinks. Or Daddy, gawd knows. Daddy would not be happy to find Adelaide covered in mud in the barn beneath a virile young man. But in losing Mother and Daddy, it appears she has also lost the virile young man. She looks around confused. *Where am I?* She isn't in the barn anymore.

"Addie, what happened to you?" says Felicity, as she strokes the cat.

Adelaide looks down and sees that she's in the recliner in the living room she'd settled into earlier in the evening.

"You're a mess."

How can I be a mess? thinks Adelaide. I'm not wet, and I'm not in the barn. There's no mud, rain, or thunder. Just she and Felicity in the family apartment where they belong. She narrows her eyes at her sister. Why is she floating around? "Stop floating," she tells Felicity. Maybe she's still half-dreaming. Or maybe she's half-drunk.

"You're not answering my question, Addie," says Felicity. "What happened to you?"

Adelaide straightens herself on the chair, blotting the spittle on her chin with her sleeve. "I just...I don't know. I dozed off, I guess."

"I can see that much, but look at you; you're a fright!" Felicity turns to the cat, and says, "Isn't she just a fright, Marmalade? An absolute fright!" Back to Adelaide, she says, "Your hair and eyebrows are burned!" She shakes her head, "Am I going to have to hide the matches from now on, Addie?"

Adelaide straightens up, brushing the singed ends of her loosened hair behind her ears. She shakes her head, trying to remember, but all she can think of is Julian in the barn, rain teeming, thunder booming, loose hay in the back of her father's truck, and the solid weight of his body against hers.

"What am I going to do with you?" Felicity scolds. "I'm afraid to leave you alone anymore!" The cat arches his back and leaps from Felicity's arm to the recliner, where he licks the sugary remains of the spilled toddy off Adelaide's robe.

Adelaide hisses, "Scat!" which sends him running.

"Oh, I forgot to tell you, Addie, Granny asked me to convey a message."

Adelaide rolls her eyes. "Oh yeah, right. Granny."

"Yes, that's right. *Granny.*"

"I hate to break this to you, Felicity," says Adelaide, "but Granny's dead. She's been dead a good long time. Longer than Mother even."

"She may be dead, Addie, but she wants you to stop smoking."

Adelaide braces against the arms of the chair, her throat in a chokehold. "You know very well I don't smoke anymore, Felicity Jane," she lies. "I gave it up years ago."

"Don't bother telling me," says Felicity, "tell Granny. She's the one who said you were smoking today at your visit with Dr. Joy. She also wants you to stop gorging on peanuts at night. Her words, not mine." Her eyes dart up and to her right. "What's that you say?" she asks.

"I didn't say anything," says Adelaide. "And I don't smoke."

"Sorry, Addie," says Felicity. "It's Mother. She says you're not going to get anywhere until you take responsibility for what happened."

Adelaide heaves herself up and out of the chair. She's had enough. "What did you do all day, Felicity?" she says. "Follow me around? Open my bedside drawers? Peek in some windows? Your little Halloween tea parties not enough for you anymore? Now you're eavesdropping on my therapy sessions?"

Felicity frowns. "Well, no Addie," she says. "I was right here working in the yard."

Before Adelaide can respond, the hum of a loud engine outside distracts them, and they both turn. As it grows louder, Adelaide reluctantly rises. She toddles to the window, striking the swollen wooden frame with the side of her hand several times to loosen it before lifting it up. "Uhhhhh!" she grunts, heaving it upward. "Who is that? Who's there?"

In response, all she hears is the accelerated rev of the motor.

"Who is that, I say!" she hollers in her huskiest warning voice. Leaning forward at an obtuse angle, she sees the twinkle of headlights and the unmistakable buttercream flash of Julian's 1940 Chrysler convertible as it passes under the lamp post on the driveway below.

"Why, you!" says Adelaide, raising a fist.

She's outraged that Thaddeus would continue to taunt her in such a mean-spirited fashion. She leans out further just as Felicity's frenzied cat charges between her legs and sets her off-balance. Rocking precariously back and forth against the ledge for balance, she loses her footing altogether, tips over the window frame and freefalls through the brisk night air. It's a moment with a life of its own, slow and deliberate, allowing her to consider her entire empty life from beginning to end, with and without Julian. As she falls, her thoughts are accompanied by a haunting refrain, *For the love of God, let this be it. Let this be it. Let this be it.*

I just can't take anymore.

FOURTEEN

FELICITY

F elicity grasps the window sill for support as she searches wildly for any evidence of life in the garden below. "Addie! Addie! Are you okay? Answer me, Addie!" *Answer me!*

She steels herself against a steady simmer of panic, waiting for what seems an eternity for a reply. She absolutely does not want to lose composure. Felicity losing composure is Addie's number one pet peeve along with everything else about Felicity. And anyway, maybe Addie's perfectly okay. She usually is. Maybe she just needs time to catch her breath. Time to work out her feelings of anger and spite at Marmalade for precipitating the calamity.

Or even at Felicity for allowing Marmalade in the house in the first place. Not that Marmie was a stranger to Addie when he arrived. Or at least he shouldn't have been. He'd been living in the barn for years.

Felicity reprimands the cat in the same tone Daddy would when he pretended to punish his girls. Loud enough to demonstrate her support for Addie. "Naughty Marmie!" she shouts. *Or is it Izzy?* No wait, Tango, that's it. *Right?* It's hard to keep track of all the names this fierce little animal has acquired through their mutual incarnations. Each time she calls his name, she has to think—*what is he this time? Is he a cat or a dog? A bunny or a horse? Male or female? Izzy or Tango? Marmalade or Pharaoh?* When Felicity speaks with her heart, he answers to all these names. Which is the problem with Addie. Addie has forgotten that her heart has a voice. Or maybe she just never knew.

Ears piqued, Tango circles the recliner, his back arched, hissing. He isn't fooled by Felicity's duplicity. She wags her finger. "Y'all don't get a free pass for everything, Tango," she scolds gently. "Y'all aren't infallible. Animal guides make mistakes too, as you very well know." Felicity's just glad Addie can't see Tango's utterly unapologetic posture. He could not care less that Addie flew straight out the window. *Who's Addie?* Those two must have some complicated history, Felicity thinks.

She leans out the window, calling, "Addie? Addie!" waiting anxiously for a response.

At ten seconds, no reply. At fifteen, only the background chorus of chirping tree frogs and whistling whippoorwills. At twenty, nothing. No movement. No swoosh of leaves in the ground cover below. No struggle. No cry for mercy! A shudder runs through Felicity. She has to do something. But what? Terror snakes up her spine and into her brain like one of those kundalini serpents Mrs. Phipps is always talking about, and all at once she is paralyzed with fear.

"Sweet baby Jesus, Tango," she says in a gush, "what have we done?" She seeks answers beyond the window that frames the dark night, calling out helplessly, "Answer me, Addie! Answer me! I don't know what to do."

Do something!

Felicity struggles to focus. She places her right hand on the swim cap at the top of her head to hold herself down. To keep her spirit inside and low to the ground, as she's been taught, so she can focus with her lower brain, or what's left of it. Her Earth brain, as she thinks of it. Her organic brain. I can do this, she thinks. I have to do this. This is Addie!

Filled with resolve, she clenches her fists and charges head-down through the sitting room, the hallway, and the kitchen to the back door where she fumbles frantically with the handle that's become sticky with humidity. *Let me out!* She jiggles, kicks, and pulls until it finally cooperates, freeing her from the bondage of the separation she feels so intensely. As if Addie's body and hers is one and the same. And why not? They share DNA, do they not? They share a mother, a father, a home, a graveyard. A destiny! They share everything. Against all that common ownership, what difference does it make who's in the kitchen and who's knocked out in the myrtle? They both are.

Clinging to the railing, she hobbles awkwardly downward in her heavy boots. The wooden steps are slippery, and she has to ward against a fall. As she makes her slow descent, she calls again and again, "Addie! Addie! I'm coming! Hang on! I'm almost there!"

At the bottom of the stairs, she can't bear the suspense. She struggles to untie the boots, hurling them against the rose trellis beneath Addie's bedroom. She takes off running. As she moves through the wet grass, she hears Mrs. Phipps' urgent voice in her right ear, "Project yourself, Felicity. *Project!* If you project yourself as I taught you, you would not need to run through space. You would simply *be there.*"

Felicity swats at her ear. This is no time for voices, she thinks. This is time for action. Anyway, she hasn't managed to master any of the so-called gifts Mrs. Phipps claims Felicity possesses, or really, even advance to more than an intermediate level on a single one. When would she practice? Addie's always around, so what use are they? The idea of special gifts she can't even use makes her feel crazier than she already is.

As Felicity turns the corner, she spots Addie in all her half-naked glory, face-down and spread-out amidst the blooming myrtle. The tiny purple flowers pop out in the moonlight, framing her head like a garland. A chipmunk scampers across the fleshy arc of her back, pulling on the collar of her favorite cherry-print pajamas. Felicity rushes over and shoos it off. "Scat," she says. Seeing Addie like that, so still and vulnerable, completely upends Felicity just when she needs all the gounding she can get.

"Addie?" she says, trembling, "Y'all okay? Say you're okay. Addie. Okay?" Felicity's words are unintelligible. Her throat is a vacuum that sucks her words in backwards so they make no sense. Leaning over Addie, she whispers tentatively, "Are... you...? Alive?" as if she doesn't want to know the answer.

She doesn't.

Addie doesn't move.

Kneeling in the dampness, she sticks her finger under Addie's nose where she thinks she detects a slow breath. Then she places her hand on Addie's back where she feels a slight, nearly indetectable rise and fall. *Is it enough?* She tries to lift her sister's left hand, but it's too heavy, as if it gained gravity with the drop. Right hand, same. She jumps to her feet, shaking the tension out of her system by popping up and down like a pogo stick. No longer able to control herself, she screams, "Breathe, Addie! Breathe!" with each jump.

For the love of God, breathe!

She turns to her left where the driveway winds around to the front of the house, praying for a glimpse of the car and driver, someone to help her, but both are long gone. Casting her eyes past the cemetery to the night sky for inspiration, a nearly full moon streams filtered light through the tall pines.

"I've messed up this time," she tells the moon.

Following the beams to their source, she adjusts her eyes to the garish glare. Wow is it bright! She places both hands firmly on either side of her trembling head, pulling her swim cap down over her ears to keep her head from spinning off. *Sweet baby Jesus, what should I do?!* Arms outstretched to the light, she pleads, "Pleeeeaase! Somebody! Help us!"

All at once, Granny's round face appears all yellow, cratered, and swiss-cheesy like a comic-strip moon. "Help yer dang self fer gawd's sake," she says. "Do sumpin' fer once!"

"Do what?" Felicity begs. "Tell me. I'll do it!"

"Git that nitwit Barrows," says Granny. "He's the only one around who can help her."

"But it's night time, Gran, and I don't remember where Barrows lives," Felicity whimpers. "He moved years ago, didn't he?"

"He lives in the miner's cottage back of Millie's place with his skinny ole wife, Inis, 'n their chubby half-blind kid, Reginald," says the shriveled old moon face. "The one with the thick glasses; can't see his own hands."

Rubbing her sweaty palms against the scratchy crinoline of her skirt, Felicity tries hard to focus. In the end, it's up to her and no one else, not Granny or anyone. If it even is Granny, that is. She's never looked worse.

Not a day's gone by Addie hasn't tried to convince Felicity that the spirits she sees are imaginary. And who's to say they're not? One thing about Felicity, she's sane enough to know she's at least half crazy by any standard. But what does that matter now? Crazy or not, she's the only who can help Addie. She's got to pull herself together and figure out what to do. *What to do?!* She consults her lower, rational mind which is slow and out of practice, but still able to cobble some sense out of this world now and then. Her lower mind tells her it's a terrible idea to leave Addie's near lifeless body alone in the myrtle surrounded by carnivorous varmints and opportunistic spirits.

"Go git Barrows," snaps Granny. "It's the right thang to do. It's the only thang!"

"But what if they take her away from me, Granny?" Felicity says. And then all at once she's had it with Granny and her cheesy moon. She stares her in the eyes and snaps her fingers. "Go away," she says. "Y'all are not even here. Y'all are nowhere."

"Good gravy, child. Stop all that senseless snapping. Ye see me, don't ye? I'm still here." The shriveled old floating head moves forward in a threatening manner. "Well? Don't ye?"

Somewhere above and to the right side of Granny, Aunt Annabelle swings on the branch of a tall pine. "Don't listen to that old lady," she says sweetly. "She means well enough, but if ye leave Adelaide now, she's doomed."

"Shove it, Belle," Granny retorts. "Can't you see Adelaide needs help? Someone should take her to the hospital, for gawd sake. Ye never did have a lick of common sense, did ye? Pretty is as pretty does, which is pretty much nothin'."

While Granny and Annabelle duke it out, a legion of graveyard relatives rises up, all arguing the pros and cons of the situation.

Felicity is sorry she ever talked to the moon. Sorry she ever asked anyone for anything. She should have known better. As in life, so in death. Like dear Mrs. Phipps taught her, you think people magically transform the minute they die? Or even a thousand years later? Not on your life or theirs. They do not. Transcendence is a power you have to allow into your life, she says. You have to know about it. You have to *want* it. Free will prevails in every case, and most souls progress at a sloth's pace, if at all. She must be right, because none of her relatives has ever offered a speck of advice worth following. Full of malarkey is what they are. Dim bulbs in an ink black night. Follow them, and you're just another hapless critter lost in the haunted woods.

Pothead joins in and Trudie shows up, each arguing a position. As they prattle on, Felicity hears the voice of Mrs. Phipps in her right ear, "Snap like you mean it, Felicity. Snap like you believe it will send them away."

Felicity clenches her jaw and snaps with both hands. Snaps and snaps. Their faces come and go like fireflies. Like they can't believe her folly. Like she has no right to send them away because after all, they are her informants. *They own her.* They are the ones who anchor her. Who keep her low and steady where she can keep an eye on Addie. Without them, she would transcend the atmosphere.

"Ye get all high 'n mighty with that Phipps witch, 'n ye'll lose yer sister," says Pothead. "Mark my words. Y'all will never see her again."

Felicity pulls her swim cap down nice and taut, tightening the chin strap until her eyelids droop from the pressure. She will not listen to another word. She walks around the corner, collects her boots and returns to the scene, placing them on either side of Addie for protection. "Just stay right there," she tells her sister before leaving in search of overnight supplies.

In the house, she collects a few crocheted blankets and a flashlight and scuttles back down the stairs. To save time at the bottom, she raises her arms to her shoulders, locks eyes with the night sky, and levitates a foot above ground. This time she keeps her chin up, as her cousin, Shelley, taught her, and glides all the way to Addie without dropping a thing.

"Here y'all go, sweet Adelaide," she says. "Here y'all go, my darlin'. In the morning, you'll be your regular old self, I swear. I'll get up early and serve you donuts and hot chicory myself. That's a promise."

She covers Addie with a blanket, and makes a bed with another for herself right beside her, where she sits and waits. Whatever comes of this, she will not abandon her sister. She will not. She will stay right here no matter how long it takes.

"She abandoned *you*," Pothead barks from the forest. Even through the barrier of her bathing cap, she hears him. She has to look hard in the dark to find him, but there he is, a solid force in his marine uniform, arms folded resolutely, tree trunk legs daring her to challenge his muscular authority.

Granny's moon face moves from behind and smacks him right down. "Leave her alone, Stewart, fer cryin' out loud. The girl's made a decision fer once. Leave her to the consequences."

"That's the point," Pothead protests. "She doesn't deserve the consequences. Everything that's wrong with Felicity is Adelaide's fault."

Now Felicity knows for sure it's her own craziness talking. What else could it be? You could say a lot about Addie, but one thing is true—she's stuck by Felicity every day of Felicity's crazy life. The crazier Felicity gets, the closer Addie sticks. They are family, solid and true. They are one fragile thing, a partnership forged together in a changing world neither of them can make sense of. Addie would never leave Felicity. Not on her life.

"Would you, Addie?" she whispers gently, placing a string of Addie's frazzled errant hair behind her ear. *Would you?* How would she survive without Addie? She wouldn't.

Lying down beside her sister, Felicity falls into a deep abyss. As bleak as it is, the abyss is familiar. She's been here before. In the abyss, she falls and falls through the thin, chilly air until the sleeve of her wildflower dress catches on the branch of a hardy magnolia. Here, she springs up and down for a flash of a second that repeats infinitely until she doesn't remember another thing. Just rising and falling like a yoyo in the chilly night air, her arms flailing, grasping for branches and birds. Hawks taunt her, pulling streams of her dense silver hair, but for what? To keep her afloat? To make nests from her remains? It isn't clear.

As always, the experience ends there.

Felicity awakens to the rising sun streaming stripes of red rust and goldenrod across the yonder hills. It is then that she realizes she hasn't seen a sunrise in a very long time, at least not one like this. Not one so clear and definitive a herald of dawn. Of life. Every sunrise for years, it seems, has been obscured in gloom, the sky as mottled as a day-old bruise. *Now this!* It's a sign, she decides. A very good sign. She pulls herself up on her knees, brushing the dirt and leaf fragments from her crinoline skirt and flannel shirt just as Mr. Barrows drives up to the house in his colorful old milk wagon with his morning delivery.

Her heart flipflops. "Glory be!" she calls, jumping up. Her hands in the air, she runs towards the house, but Barrows ignores her. "Over here!" she calls out, waving. "Here! Help!"

Barrows frowns, cocks his head and listens hard, as if she's whispering, and she realizes he must be hard of hearing. Not to mention half blind, since even dressed as colorfully as she is, he looks right past her.

"Over here!" she screams. Her cries are drowned out by a woodpecker who decides at that very moment to sink his beak into the window frame and peck like a jackhammer. "Over here!" she shrieks, afraid to wander too far from Addie lest the woodpecker switch from the window frame to Addie's skull.

Though Barrows seems not to hear her, still, he marches slowly toward that side of the house as if following some inner guide. He's so oblivious to Felicity that she wonders how in the world he can drive. Why, he can barely see in front of him. Or hear!

But as he rounds the corner, he stops, drops his bag of groceries by the cemetery fence, and gapes. "Mmmmiss Adelaide?" he stutters.

Felicity doesn't want to startle him, so she approaches gently. In the distance, she can see his delivery of donuts already ransacked by a team of raccoon bandits.

"She fell from the second story apartment last night," Felicity says quietly, trying to keep her panic from overtaking them both.

Barrows runs to Addie's side and places his hand on her back. Satisfying himself that she's alive, it seems, he hesitates before moving briskly back to his truck.

Felicity thinks he must be fetching some first aid tools, but when he scrambles up and inside the driver's side and turns the motor, she becomes suspicious. "Wait!" she cries. "Where are you going! Help us, for pity sake! You can't leave now!"

He zooms off, the awkward multi-color truck careening on its left wheels as it screeches out the driveway.

Felicity lies down, wraps her arms around Addie, and falls asleep. She awakens to the sound of sirens wailing from a distance, and jumps to her feet. "Here! Come here!" she cries until she spots the red flashing lights at the top of the long drive. As it approaches, she sees that Barrows is seated upfront in the passenger seat.

"Over there," he calls, pointing to the patch of myrtle.

Everything after that is a blur to Felicity, a swarm of black flies smeared across her future. All she remembers is the ambulance approaching. Men jumping out. Addie hoisted on the gurney like a cadaver. The ambulance backing out.

"Take me with you!" she begs. But they ignore her, and she can't catch up. Her feet drag as if shackled to the center of the earth. No matter how hard she tries, she simply cannot move.

"Don't let her die," she whispers as they all disappear. "She's all I've got."

FIFTEEN

FELICITY

Felicity sits alone in the community room on a ladderback chair, elbows on the table, forehead against her hands, chanting, "Where have they taken Addie? Where has she gone?" And repeat. She has never felt so abysmally alone in her entire life.

She pulls the irritating bathing cap off her head and whips it across the room. A lot of good it did, she thinks. It censored no one. Granny and Pothead seem to worm their way into her head no matter what the barricade. Then again, it may have been her own fault for summoning the moon in the first place. Note

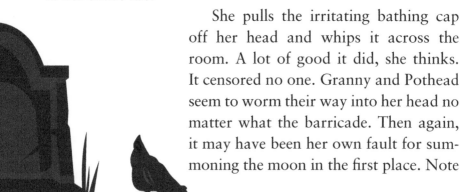

to self: do not summon the moon. Do not summon anyone or anything for that matter! *Even the truth.* If you summon the truth, you will contaminate it with your own ideas and opinions. Truth is truth only if it's free. It can't be chased. Let it come to *you.* Always.

Staring blankly ahead at the framed certificate of occupancy, now faded and yellowed, on the wall to the left of the heavy double doors, she remembers the day it was proudly hung. The day the chapel was expanded to include a gathering room for families and friends to honor the deceased with a repast after the burial. She remembers the potluck banquets—Addie greeting the mourners with hot cider, often spiked. She pictures her older sister at seventeen, already in charge of so much, yet never happy. Never. She wishes Addie had been happy.

"Addie, Addie, Addie," she whimpers helplessly, her neck bent low in remorse. "Where have you gone? Where have they taken you? I have failed you. I was supposed to protect you, and I didn't. I failed."

All at once her torment is interrupted by a familiar voice, a husky tone she can't quite place. "I'll make some tea," it says.

Felicity's head shoots up, startled. Her wild silver ringlets orbit her aching head like Medusa's snakes. Is she imagining this voice? She listens hard. *Is it Addie?* But why would it be Addie?

"Would you like some tea?" it asks.

Turning slowly, a flimsy image of someone who is not at all Addie appears in the corner of Felicity's right eye like a floater. She concentrates hard, and as she does, the image enlarges, gathers density, and takes form. It's as if Felicity herself is the projector. As if the spirit can only project itself into this world with Felicity's cooperation. With her extrasensory equipment. Felicity is the tool. She may regret it as much as she regrets summoning the moon, but she has to take this risk. This is her weakness. *She has to know.* And anyway, she didn't exactly summon this entity, did she? It came to her freely. So maybe it came to tell her the truth.

The truth about Addie.

As the image condenses and clarifies, it appears to be shaped somewhat like...*Mother?* Or at least some version of Mother, it's hard to tell. It's still only visible peripherally. Were Felicity to look at it head-on too early, she knows it could all fall apart. These things take time to develop. Fragile specters such as this aren't dense enough to withstand much scrutiny. And it's been a long time since anyone's seen a three-dimensional image of Regina McManis Somers, otherwise known as Mother. Except for the rare cameo performance in a passing dream, it's been decades at least. Since Mother's funeral, for sure. An event Felicity remembers dimly, as if she were barely there.

Like most family funerals, the service was arranged by Mother years prior and updated annually, complete with pre-arranged hymns, obituaries and eulogies to eliminate any harsh and unforgiving submissions from Daddy's second cousin once-removed, Becky Stark, who'd been drafting the obituaries for decades. Mother knew she couldn't fire Becky, on account of her status as a direct Somers relation. Instead, she near bit Becky's head off day after day to make her leave. But Becky paid her no mind. Becky stayed. *That* Mother, the one they all feared, cast an intimidating shadow a mile long and two miles wide on everyone in its path. That Mother was a gargoyle. This Mother is a cherub. If it really is Mother at all.

"Mother?" says Felicity. "Is it you?" Still looking peripherally, she narrows her eyes. "Or an imposter?"

The figure makes a vague gesture and turns to the sink, where she fills a copper kettle from the spigot and places it on the stove.

Felicity scratches her head. Well, was that a nod or wasn't it? Is this her mother or isn't it? It's all too confusing. She knows there's only one way to be sure, and that's through confrontation. How she hates confrontation! But as Mrs. Phipps counsels, beginners often accept the presence of spirits unwittingly, and even engage with them as if the spirits carry any supernatural authority whatsoever. They do not! Not even a sliver. Though they can easily fool an ingenue, as Felicity well knows. But Felicity is no longer an ingenue, and she will not be outwitted. Not this time.

Felicity has learned the hard way that other than a smattering of legitimate guides, spirits who occupy the lower realms are mostly low-awareness entities. Clenched fists of dark belief systems and bombastic egoistic opinions that stick together like Granny's pecan clusters. Belief systems that travel with them lifetime to lifetime, drawing a blackout shade on any possibility short of their own preconceived judgment. Leaving no room for forgiveness. No room for light. No possibility of ascension. This is something Felicity has trouble remembering about her own beloved family of wacky low-life's. They are not in charge of anything. They don't own her unless she allows them to.

Felicity calculates that by now the specter has most likely materialized sufficiently to withstand a direct look without disappearing. If it really is Mother, then no harm done. If it isn't, well...Felicity will snap her fingers and wish traveling mercies on its continued journey. Gathering courage, she stands, approaches the figure, and snaps her fingers in the space between them.

The image remains.

From the back, it could be anyone's mother. Her striped shirtwaist dress, her sensible oxford shoes, her softly curled chestnut hair with streaks of white. If it really is Mother, where did the demanding figure with the severe bun go—the one Addie is always trying to emulate, not that she realizes it. Where's the turnip face? The angry shapeless brows? The resolute chin? The fire-breathing mouth? The blooming rosacea? The large rectangular dresses made of scratchy black wool and course gabardine, as if she were perennially bereaved. When it came to most folks, especially Addie, that mother had a nature so icy, winter cowed in her presence. Yet now...everything about this creature, though faint, appears warm and glowing.

"Is it really you, Mother?" she entreats. "If it is, say something familiar."

The image leans forward, staring directly into Felicity's eyes. "Yes, Flitty," she says, "it really is."

Flitty!

Coming from Mother, the childhood endearment utterly disarms Felicity. She wants to sit in this mother's lap and tell her everything. She can't help herself. As the youngest, Felicity is possibly the only one who was ever on the receiving end of this mother. The kind mother. The concerned mother. This is the mother she aches for.

"I remember when I first called you that sweet name," Mother says, shaking her head softly. "Y'all flitted around the kitchen chasing that dang hound..."

"Rooster!" chirps Felicity, delighted.

"Yes, yes, that was it. Rooster. Rooster." She sighs. "So I said, 'Lawd, child, stop flittin' around after that hound,' and you pounded your chest, delighted, and said, 'Mudder, I...Flitty. Me... Flitty!' all wide-eyed and grinning. And there we were." Hand to heart she whispers, "Ahhh yes. I have missed you, my love."

Felicity drinks these words down like sweet tea. All her suppressed terror comes tumbling out in the presence of a trusted confidante. "They came and took her, Mother," she says. "Addie. They took Addie."

The figure nods plaintively. "I know, dear."

"They loaded her up in an ambulance and drove away without me." Felicity's chin trembles. "I screamed; I ran. I pounded the doors and yelled, 'Take me! Take me, too!'" She drops her head. "I couldn't get anyone to listen, or even look. They didn't care. Nobody cared. I don't even know where they took her."

"They took her to Outskirt General," says Mother.

Felicity brightens. "She's alive?"

"In a way."

"In a way?" Felicity repeats. "You mean, like me?" she says hopefully. Because even if Addie made it that far, as fragile as Felicity's existence sometimes feels, there would be hope. They could muddle through together. Felicity would care for her. She would improve.

"Not exactly." Mother turns to the counter and lifts Granny's crocheted tea cozy from the pot. She pours the steaming water from the kettle slowly over an infuser filled with loose chamomile tea.

"But how do you know where they took her?" says Felicity, perplexed. "You followed?" Phipps told her that low spirits can't travel far from the familiar. To most of the McManis and Somers clans, the only familiar place in the galaxy is the graveyard.

"Yes," says Mother, who gains confidence and density with every action, every word, as if words and movement are the glue that secure her elemental presence to this plane. "I followed her to the hospital, but after a while I turned back." She lets the tea steep, then fills a chipped porcelain cup, turns around, and offers it to Felicity.

Mesmerized by the apparent softening of this harsh creature, Felicity accepts the tea, even though she doesn't want it. "I haven't seen y'all in so long," she says. "I didn't know what happened. I thought you couldn't leave the property." She raises the cup to her lips. "The others can't leave. Or at least, they won't."

Mother pours tea for herself and sits across the table from Felicity. "I've worked hard to let the light in," she says. "That's the only way to operate independently from the others, which was my motivation. How could I bear an eternity stuck with the likes of them! When I died, I went to a place that I'd created myself, as I now know we all do. A wretched place I'd apparently been creating for a lifetime in the back of my head. A deep dark place, as you can imagine, after what happened..." She stops herself.

"After what happened?" says Felicity, puzzled.

A distant look overcomes Mother for a second, but she snaps out of it. "Anyway, it was a while before I realized I'd created it myself," she continues. "Before that I blamed everyone I could think of." She turns her head. "Everyone but myself."

"Even me?"

Mother's eyes widen. "Well, of course not you, Flitty darlin'. It was y'all..." She stops herself again, inhales deeply, and continues. "But eventually I realized I was wallowing in self-pity, like everyone else around this dang graveyard. That I alone was responsible for the insufferable forms that composed the border world between my here and my hereafter."

Felicity lays her tea cup back in its saucer. "Border world?" she says.

Mother nods. "Our border worlds are part of us, Flitty. And the last of us to die. They form our earthly context. As long as that border remains, we're pinned to godforsaken crannies between space and time. Our borders define our personas. There's no escaping them until we unclench our minds. And as long as we believe only what we see, it's impossible to see beyond them and cross over to bliss."

"So why build it in the first place?"

"Most of us don't know we build, but build we do. We build borders that help us make sense of the world, and borders that make no sense at all." She leans in passionately. "Oh Flitty, these worlds are so real it's impossible to imagine that we're making them up. We don't own our own power. It's unimaginable that my elaborate border world could be completely foreign and meaningless to you or anyone else. Invisible even! Pure illusion!" She shakes her head, sighing. "Then again, what intimidates us is personal, isn't it? What terrifies me isn't necessarily what terrifies Granny. Or Adelaide. Or Uncle Stewart"

Felicity's eyes narrow. "So border worlds are built on fear?"

"The tighter ones are," Mother says with a distant stare. "The tighter the border, the more elaborate the justification, the more secure we feel. Border worlds project our inner thoughts and feelings, our attachments and demons. Demons that have to be annihilated, or at least acknowledged, if they are ever to be conquered."

"Uncle Stewart thinks he's in a fox hole in France half the time," says Felicity. "But he isn't. He's right here."

"He's combined his borders," says Mother. "They're one and the same to him. For most of us the border is a dark and hopeless place patrolled by witless monsters. Monsters we've been feeding for a lifetime with generous helpings of our own insecurities, though we never stop wondering where they came from or how they got so big. Stewart never forgave those Germans for blowing up his friend, Bo. He's still trying to kill them."

Felicity shakes her head emphatically. "I don't want a border world," she says. "I just want to fly up and up and up." She raises her arms and flaps, and suddenly stops. "But not without Addie," she adds solemnly. "I have to wait for her."

"You could fly right now if you wanted to, Flitty, and that's the bald truth. The rest of this clan, including Adelaide, is a bunch of pigheaded cynics, myself included. But I'm working on it. We created our own damn hells, or at least fed the flames. I should have known better." She sighs with remorse. "The truth is, I did know better."

"About what exactly? About being cynical?"

After a long pause, Mother says, "About many things." She leans over and takes Felicity's hands. "That's enough for now, dear. I'm wearing myself out."

Flitty considers her mother anxiously. "But what about Daddy? I haven't seen him anywhere. Haven't even seen his…" she swallows hard. "…his grave." A big heavy tear drains out her eye and down her cheek. "I have no memory of it, Mother. No memory at all of his funeral. Or even how he died." Goodness, she had no idea how much she'd been missing Daddy all these years. *How many though?*

Mother nods. "Well, Jasper…" she says plaintively then pauses. "Jasper just…" She swipes her cheek. "Truth is I miss him too, Flitty Jane. To be honest, I never did right by him on this earth, so I should not be surprised that we were not reunited upon death. Up till recently, I built most of my border world with blame." She shakes her head. "Blame directed at your father walking out on me just when I needed him most."

Felicity's eyes widen. "Daddy walked out?"

"Wasn't his fault," says Mother. "And when he went…" she snaps her fingers, "well, he gone straight upstairs."

Felicity points. "Up there?"

"That's right."

"But, then…where's he buried?"

"Cremated," says Mother, staring at the floor. "Killed me to do it, but that's what he wanted. Signed a paper right there in the hospital front of the doctor. 'Don't let her bury me in the yard,' he said." Her throat rattles with phlegmy pain. "Like the graveyard is something to be ashamed of," she continues. "Like I didn't dedicate my lifetime to his family's business…" She lays her head in her hands.

"But, why?" says Flitty as she rises from her chair to comfort Mother. "Why in the wide world would he want to be cremated instead of buried with us all?"

She raises her head. "Well, he wanted to be…in the Gorge. Wanted your cousins to spread his remains…there."

"But why the Gorge?"

She sighs deeply. "That's a truth you'll have to discover on your own."

Mother is looking paler, and Felicity doesn't want to push her too far. Plus she's just not ready to tackle Daddy's death with her accident brain. Not yet. How will she tell Addie? she wonders. But surely Addie must know.

She sits back down in her chair across the table. "But you've returned?" she asks eagerly. "Right, Mother? Y'all will stay with me now? Help me get Addie back from the hospital and teach her about border worlds? And light? And hope?"

"Now, that will depend on Adelaide," says Mother, "won't it? Adelaide is my last stop. There's a heap of forgiveness got to travel both ways between us before we can become a family again, that's for sure."

"But you'll help me to help her? Right? You won't leave again?"

"I'll do what I can," says Mother uncertainly. "As I said, I've got my limitations. It takes more will and energy than you can imagine to project a mass dense enough to be seen by you. At least you've got the eyes to see. The others can't see me at all, no matter what I do."

"They think you're asleep in your grave."

"Yes. They're limited by what they think."

Felicity pushes up the sleeves of her flannel shirt and fidgets with a teaspoon. "The others are always complaining about Addie," she says. "You know, Pothead...I mean, Stewart and them? They say she's stubborn as a wort hog in heat. They say she sees what she wants to see, and she does not want to see any of them, is what they say. They outright resent her at times. It's exhausting."

"Adelaide gets her stubbornness from me, and I get it from Granny," says Mother. "And Granny gets it from Great Granny, and on back as far as we care to go. These parts were settled by tough women, because that's what it took to pioneer. But wherever it started makes no never mind. That's the whole point. Once it's in your lap, it's your monkey, plain and simple. Y'all got to stop it from swinging through your trees. Got to discipline that thing, not turn it into a pet or a warden, either way." She shakes her head. "No one else can do it for you."

Felicity shifts positions in the hard chair. "Well, I told the family that Addie may be stubborn, but that's not why she won't talk to them." She leans in meaningfully. "Am I right? Y'all know I'm right. Addie can't see spirits. She's earthbound, is what I tell them. Don't be expecting her to hear all y'all's nonsense, I say. I say it over and over till I can't stand myself. *Blah blah blah*. It's discouraging how often I have to say it! Not that they listen. They don't."

Mother tips her head thoughtfully. "Well dear, because of you, Addie can see some things in the nether. But she's altogether undeveloped. She sees only what the governing angels allow her to see, what they impress on her in her sleep so she can make the transition one day. And even then, who and what she sees in the beyond is flat and two-dimensional. A child's scribble. An incomplete connect-the-dots. It's the only way her brain can interpret whatever they're showing her—an image or a lesson."

Felicity frowns. "In her dreams, maybe. But I know she can't see spirits in the daylight like I do. She thinks I'm crazy as a rabid hare when she catches me at it out by the yard, and maybe I am. I hardly doubt it. I see the family in all their naked nonsense. But Addie doesn't see them." She sighs. "Because she can't."

Mother folds her arms tightly against her chest, weighing her words. Her image flutters tenuously in the glaring noon light. "You deserve the truth, so I'm going to give it to you," she says. "But I don't have much time."

Felicity nods eagerly, waiting.

"You have a border world too," says Mother.

Felicity blinks. "I do?"

"You do. It's made up of attachment and denial, like so many others."

"But..."

"Attachment to Adelaide." She gazes deeply into Felicity's eyes. "Adelaide Frances Somers is your border world."

Felicity tries to drink this in, but it makes no sense.

"Y'all have to cross over Adelaide to get where you need to go." Mother clasps her hands in an urgent plea. "Y'all need to forgive your sister, Flitty. The sooner the better, for everyone's sake."

"For everyone's sake?" Felicity repeats, confused. "But I'm the one who needs forgiving, not Addie. I didn't care for her properly..."

Mother wags her finger. "No. No. No. Y'all need no forgiving. Adelaide does; Adelaide needs the forgiveness. But you can't forgive her till you acknowledge what she did in the first place. What she did to you, and because of that, to all of us." She narrows her eyes. "And I can't forgive her till you forgive her. And Granny and Stewart and the rest can't forgive me until I've forgiven Adelaide. And lawd knows I need forgiveness. So you see the dilemma we're in. The whole family's sitting plop in the middle of our miserable border worlds waiting on you."

Felicity gulps. "But..."

"And if you don't forgive her before she dies, she'll be stuck in the graveyard like the rest of them, mark my words. And for quite some time. Maybe for all time. Somewhere in that thick head of hers she knows what she did and what she deserves. And she can't forgive herself, so she buries the mess like everyone else, only deeper. You have got to forgive her before she dies." Her mother nods resolutely. "Or not at all."

Felicity's brain is a compressed rubber ball bouncing up, down, and yonder. She can't help but wonder if this is someone else's mother after all? Or maybe her own mother lost in another lifetime? *What is she talking about!* While Felicity sits agape, scanning her mind for some long, lost horror in need of forgiveness, Mother's image flickers like the end of a silent film reel. Her image comes and goes, but she keeps on talking.

"And Adelaide can indeed see spirits," Mother continues. As her image fades, her voice becomes a distant echo somewhere between space and time. "The ones she wants to see, that is. The ones she chooses to see."

Felicity doesn't know what part of this message is more shocking. If Addie sees spirits, that's news to Felicity, and she bets it would be even bigger news to Addie. "Are you certain?"

Mother's image is no more than a sheer veil in the dissolving steam of the kettle. "I am certain," she says.

"But she doesn't let on... I mean, she's never...even once..."

"She's unaware that she sees spirits," says Mother faintly. "But she sees them."

Felicity speaks with urgency. *Mother, don't leave me now!*

"She claims not to see Granny or Pothead or Trudie, or Shelley, or anyone, really. Her head never turns when they talk; she isn't the least bit curious. She walks right on by, oblivious!" Felicity balls-up her fists in frustration. "So, who does she see?"

"You, Flitty," says a voice outside of time. "Adelaide sees you."

Obituary for Release to:
Bluegrass Bugle &
The Louisville Gazette
Sunday, July 25, 1965

Mrs. Regina Somers, 58, Dies of Resentment
Born: March 30, 1907
Passed into eternal life: July 23, 1965

Mrs. Regina Somers, widow of the esteemed Jasper
Somers of *Sunnyside Up Enterprises* in Outskirt,
Kentucky, died suddenly last Friday night while
arguing with a cantankerous customer, Wilbur B. Miles,
over the price of a decent burial. Wilbur, who has ten
kids and suffers from black lung, claimed the prices
at *Sunnyside Up* were highway robbery compared
to *Jumping Jack's* in the holler. *The Sunnyside Up*
bookkeeper/manager/services director/obituarian,
Becky Stark, said she overheard Mrs. Somers tell
Wilbur in no uncertain terms that she had no need of
his shabby business, and if it weren't for the misguided
charity of her husband, Jasper, Wilbur would never
be considered a customer in the first place. To which
Wilbur retorted, "Ever'body knows that's a dang
lie. *Sunnyside* losin' business left 'n right since the
Reverend died. Nobody wanna do business with the
likes of you."

Wilbur, who relished an argument, continued the
volley without reserve until all at once Mrs. Somers
clutched the sides of her beet red head and screamed,

"Gawddammit, Wilbur Miles, if I die right now it's on you for eternity."

Miss Stark ran to the scene just in time to witness her employer's eyes freeze, her legs collapse, and her spirit drain right out her left thumb toe.

When asked later on by this reporter how he felt about killing Mrs. Somers, Wilbur Miles shrugged and said, "Dang if I feel bad 'bout losin' a badger like her; I do not. But I do feel sorry fer her troubles. Ever'body does. Terrible what happened."

Mrs. Somers was a stern and competent businesswoman who continued her husband's business the best she could, though there was no end to her resentment. As most of Outskirt knows, Mrs. Somers' cold heart became a glacier after a series of rapid losses beginning with her mama, Granny McManis, followed by the unspeakable loss of her favorite daughter, Felicity Jane, and ending with her husband, Jasper, who she said straight-up abandoned her in her time of greatest need.

Regina Somers is survived by her eldest daughter, Adelaide, who is said to be returning to the homestead soon. It's unclear if she'll be able to stay on her own, or even if she'll get there in time to attend her mother's funeral.

The community of Outskirt is invited to honor Mrs. Somers at the *Sunnyside Up* chapel on Thursday for a formal service followed by high tea in the community room served in signature porcelain china from County Clare, Ireland to the first twenty-four guests who are formally dressed. Her extensive collection of unusual salt & pepper shakers will be on display for three days before decorating her headstone for eternity, per her Last Will and Testament.

Mourners are asked to bring their extended families, neighbors, and visitors, as Regina Somers arranged an epic finale to her miserable life, complete with violins, harpsichords, and four sopranos from Franklin Baptist. All those unable to squeeze into the community room for the repast will be moved to the grounds and served loaves and fish sticks until they're gone.

> *What once was is never more and at the same time, will always be.*

SIXTEEN

ADELAIDE

Something has happened to Adelaide, but for the life of her, she can't figure out what. She's lying on what feels like the biggest, cushiest spring-coiled mattress she's ever laid upon, which is a good thing, because she might be here for a long time. She's not sure she could leave if she wanted to. There's a soft breeze against her cheeks, the scent of rose in the air. She's a prisoner of comfort. If she's in a dream, it's the realest dream ever. Realer than real. But after a while, which seems like a very long while, absolutely nothing changes.

Everything just *IS*. And she knows she has to do something about it, because she can't just lie around and breathe roses all day. There's a funeral home to run!

She takes a deep breath and works up the courage to take the barest, teensiest peek around her. Maybe she's just in Dr. Joy's office after a disorienting session. Or on the recliner in her house after a chug or two of relaxing hooch. It's happened before. Slowly her eyes open into tiny crescent moons, just enough to see that she isn't in Joy's office at all. Or at home. Or the graveyard. *Good gravy, where is she?!*

All her milky eyes can confirm is that her chunky old hands are still attached to the end of her chunky old arms. She has a feeling she's been injured, but can't remember how or why, and she feels no pain. She squeezes her left eye shut and opens the right, trying to trick herself into not seeing anything she doesn't want to see. Anything too frightening, like a bloody puncture wound in her belly, for instance, or a raggedy hole left by a severed limb. Based on the strange way she feels right now, anything is possible.

She blinks when she sees what she sees, which is her horizontal dome of a body covered in a hospital gown made for a child, decorated with clown faces. She can't see past her vast midriff to know whether or not she still has legs. Whether she does or not, she can't feel them. Not that she can feel anything; she can't. She moves her eyes all the way left, back to center, then all the way right. The cavernous mountain appears to be composed entirely of...vapor! She opens both eyes wide to confirm. *Yes, that's right.* She's lying in a giant puffy mountain made of clouds. It's official: she's gone round the Felicity bend and lost her caboose.

What now?

Unnerved beyond measure, she swallows a primal scream lest the aliens who no doubt delivered her to this remote station on Planet Cumulous are listening. Better to play dead until she can come up with an escape plan. Though she's so agitated right now she couldn't play dead even if her life depended on it. Which, from the look of things, it might well could.

"Where am I?" she calls out from some foreign source. A source not remotely associated with her throat. This voice— this strange, otherworldly Adelaide voice—surfaces at the same time she tries to move her arms and legs and realizes…she can't. Neither can she move her head. Or really, other than limited facial expression, anything at all.

"Help! Somebody, help!" she screeches in the largest, loudest thought bubble she can conjure. The screech blasts through the cosmos, reverberating in a deafening echo that generates more fear within her than she already had. Well, good. Maybe it'll scare the aliens, too. Scare them into releasing her. Convince them that she's not worth the trouble. *She isn't.* Even she knows that.

"Heeelp!" she screams in her head. "Heeeeeellllllllp!!!!"

An expressionless technician appears at her bedside exhibiting no signs of fear or even the slightest interest in her zealous rebellion. He points some sort of radar gun at her heart. Terrified, she projects a long string of "*where am I's*" into the universe like speeding bullets. A few seconds later the radar gun beeps three times and the technician nods, "Uh huh," and disappears.

Adelaide has the very queer feeling that she could escape right here and now from her massive body if she wanted to, but is afraid to risk it just yet. After all, what if she can't re-enter? Although why would she want to re-enter this mountain of flesh? Maybe she could climb into a brand new svelte and glamorous body instead. A tempting thought. With a brand new svelte and glamorous body, she could strut shamelessly in front of that young tattooed fellow, Dulles, if she could find him. Prove to him how much more she has going on than he might have noticed in the barn the one night. Like how clever she is. Clever enough to switch bodies.

But then her brain hijacks her heart and says, *y'all wanna climb into somebody else's body!!* And boom, she's afraid of herself. Terrified. Who are you?! *Ah, so you're the alien!!* Her brain is a divided country screaming in different languages in protest of her own thoughts. A moment or two of this verbal combat, and a scaly, white-jacketed, bearded creature appears with a stethoscope around its neck. All she can think, is, *Hallelujah! The physician has finally arrived!* Although something about him is fishy.

He checks her chart. "Adelaide Frances Somers?" he says.

She forces herself to be courteous. "What's it to you?"

"Just verifying your earthly identity," he says.

Earthly identity? "Where am I?"

The doctor, although bearded, looks suspiciously like Mrs. Phipps. "You're in a transition school for now," he says neutrally, as if remarking on the mild weather.

She tries to sit up and protest, but her body won't cooperate. "What!" she says. "A what?"

"A transition…"

"I heard you," she screeches. "What's a transition school, and how long have y'all been holding me here?"

He strokes his beard thoughtfully before saying, "Long? How do you mean?"

"Good grief, how do you think I mean? I mean how many days have I been in this fog?"

The doctor nods solemnly. "There's no such measurement here," he says. "Then is now and now is then. What once was is never more and at the same time, will always be."

She glares at him. "That's the biggest plate of garbledy-gook stew anyone's ever fed me," she snaps. "And that includes

Felicity who serves up banquets of that junk food when she isn't gorging on it herself. Now march right back into the kitchen and bring me back a plate of plain damn English."

It's then she remembers she fell out a window. Lawdy, she thinks, am I dead? Not that she wants to know the answer.

"Not yet," he says.

Apparently around here, thinking is as good as speaking. "What does that mean? Am I dead or not?"

"Whether you die or not will depend on your willingness to awaken," he says.

She widens her eyes in disbelief. "I'm awake in case you haven't noticed. I'm talking to you, am I not?"

"You're sleep-talking," he says. "It's the language of the low country, the only language you know. We don't speak that language here unless we have to."

At that, a cirrhus cloud floats by, leaving behind it, a gigantic brass gong. Attached to the gong on a long rope is a mallet. "I can awaken you though, if you so will it," says the doctor. He raises the mallet, ready to strike.

"Hold on," she says. "That's a big gong, and it looks mighty loud."

"It's our loudest model," he says. "You're in a very deep sleep."

"I don't want to wake up that way," she says. "Do you have something more melodious? A flute? Or a banjo?"

"Awakening a resistant somnambulist is always difficult," he says. "I can only do it with this model and only if you agree to it."

"If I agree to it, will I get my life back?"

"Not the one you had."

"Well, whose life will I have then? Priscilla Presley's? The Queen of England's? Whose?"

"We're running out of time," he says, raising the mallet. "Let's do this."

"No!"

He puts down the mallet and approaches the bed. "Maybe this will convince you," he says, adjusting her neck with a loud crack.

"Ouch!" she protests, though secretly pleased. At least now she can move her neck sufficiently to see more of her surroundings, especially her cushy bed. Studying it for a minute, she thinks, *Huh*. Apparently this bed is the one thing on Planet Cumulous that isn't made of clouds. Well, how could it be made of clouds? It's so deeply supportive of her big lazy body, and just one more reason not to disrupt her alleged deep sleep.

"Very unusual mattress," she says, wishing she could run her immobile fingers over the shiny material. "What's it made of?"

"Snakes," he says.

What?! Desperate to lift herself up and away from the pile of what now appears to be a nest of coiled copperheads, she screams, "Good lawd, are you insane? Where did these dead snakes come from?"

"They're not dead," he says. "They're in a very deep sleep. Like you."

"Well, get me the hell out of here before they wake up!"

"They won't hurt you, Adelaide."

"How do you know?!"

"You pose no threat."

"Well, I may not pose a threat, but I have no interest in remaining on a bed of sleeping snakes!"

"Good," he says. "We're finally getting somewhere."

She heaves a long sigh. "If I agree to wake up, where will you send me?"

He points up. "You'll go there."

"To heaven?"

"Look closer."

She focuses hard. The place is far away, and its details are obscured by a bank of dark fog. As the fog slowly lifts, she says, "Wait a minute! What are all those squirmy creatures?"

"There are snakes there too," he says. "They're awake and moving, as you will also be once I sound the gong."

She is outraged at his blatant insensitivity. Why, this is outright abuse! Snakes below; snakes above. This is no choice! "Are you mad?" she says. "Why would I choose a world of slithering snakes over a world of sleeping snakes, for cripe sake? At least sleeping snakes can't hurt me!"

"Ah, but they can hurt you," he says. "And they are. They're preventing you from moving on. The awakened snakes will keep you alert, unsettled, and committed to completing your journey. You'll never get comfortable there on any level, and eventually, you'll arrive at a place equal to your value." He grabs the mallet again and raises it. "Shall we?"

"Don't you dare bang that gong!" she says. "Even you said I'm the one who gets to make this decision!"

"I am you, and you are I," he says. "We are one and inseparable. We are the same. Division is an illusion only sleepwalkers see."

"I am not you, doc," she says, outraged. "The delusion is all yours. Keep your goldarn snakes and get me out of here now. There were no snakes where I came from."

"There were and there still are."

"This is a waste of my time. I have things to do that matter!"

"Such as?"

"Such as finding Felicity, if you must know. She needs to know I'm OK before she loses what's left of her moth-eaten brain."

"But are you really OK?" he says. "Whether you are or not depends on what you mean by OK. Do you acknowledge what you've done?"

She thinks hard, concentrating on the murky events that led her here. Finally she remembers. "I haven't done anything," she says. "Not one single goldarn thing. What happened is, I was pushed out of a window by a malicious cat. I acknowledge *that*. And now I want to get up and go home to take care of my fragile sister who won't survive without me."

The doctor jots a note on Adelaide's chart and looks up. "I'm sorry, but according to this evaluation you're not ready to go home and take care of anyone."

Before she can protest, he leans forward, snaps his fingers and boom.

She's gone.

Gone to a place of unimaginable weight, physically and mentally. A place where she feels every ounce of her arms and legs which are seized with pain, not to mention the rest of her. Exiled to a place where she can barely breathe from the smell of ammonia and chloroform, and the agony of fractured vertebrae, cracked ribs, and an endless list of other injuries. A place where masked people whisper all around her. A place where she can't scream even in her head. Where her distant alien voice is strangled with layers and layers of medicated confusion.

She can't stay in this painful place long. No one could. She would give anything to be back in the clouds, snakes or no snakes. But she was admittedly so uncooperative that returning to the cloud clinic doesn't seem like a realistic possibility. Anyway, she has no idea how to get there. As her mind spins, a rush of liquid enters her right arm and she swoons into merciful nothingness before waking up in the funeral home in front of Julian's upgraded satin-padded, brass-handled, mahogany casket.

Barely covered to the knees in a short, drafty hospital gown printed with tiny clown faces, she paces back and forth in her sensible black dress pumps trying to psych herself into performing Julian's ceremony. It has to be done soon. No, wait. Not soon. *Now!* After all, what if there's an expiration date at the pearly gates? What if Julian's prevented from entering because he lingered too long in the between, unburied? She can't bear the thought of it. *She'll never see him again!* She imagines herself all dressed-up in her lacey white wedding gown, St. Peter ready to administer the marital rites to half a couple. Her alone. Solo. Abandoned at the altar by a ghost she never properly buried. It's all her fault. A ghost who roams the earth in his perfectly restored 1940 buttercream Chrysler convertible.

Wait. *What?*

This thought is a head-on collision. Her brain is an accident scene involving multiple jack-knifed images. She can't process any of it. She returns to the casket, which is finally ready. Not the plain pine box, which was obviously not right for him. It was probably the plain pine box that held up the works in the first place, come to think of it. After all, Julian deserves only the best. This casket right here is premium in every way. She strokes the pillow. Classy. Inviting even. Now that the right casket has been selected, there are no more excuses. It's time to bury Julian. *If only she could remember where she put him?* She looks around, confused. Felicity must have stored him somewhere. The walk-in, maybe. Or the barn. She'll go looking in a minute, but right now she sprays the silk padding with a fine rose mist and plumps the satin pillow. Soon the Easter lilies will be delivered, and all will proceed as planned. Finally!

Standing there, musing, she is all at once chilled to the bone. Brrrr, she thinks, this prep room is a bit cold for a hospital gown. She crosses her arms, rubbing them up and down to generate heat. And also, she is just so tired. So tired of trying to stay alive all the time, to be honest. Tired of eating and drinking and bathing and dressing and breathing. Tired of undoing everything, then doing it all over again. Then undoing it. Then doing it. *All the time.* Every day. Tired of dragging her butt from room to room in search of Felicity or whatever—Papaw's hooch, Barrow's donuts, or the Moon Pies she's been looking for since 1955. Tired of arranging her frizzy old gray hair into a smooth bun at the nape of her neck. Tired of trying to dress like a lady when she's got the body of a retired sumo wrestler.

Stepping back, she wonders what it would be like to take a little break from all this tedium and just lie in this coffin right here and close her eyes. Just pretend to be dead. For a minute. Or even to actually *be* dead. After all, she's been preparing the deceased for eternal salvation her entire life without ever sensing the spiritual superpower in that job. Taking every bit of it for granted. Lil old Adelaide Frances Somers, speaking to the Maker on behalf of those who can no longer speak for themselves. She, a rural minister, performing the sacred rituals that grant them access to eternal freedom. If she really believes all that crap. Some days she almost does.

She lays her left hand against the smooth, polished mahogany, and traces the curves of the burl all the way around, head to foot and back again. What a lovely place to rest. Why, who wouldn't want to lie here forever? She grabs one of the shining brass handles and nods rhythmically, chanting until she is nearly in a trance. Until all she hears is a hallelujah chorus, and all she smells are lilies. Until all she feels is the sleek satin bedding right up to her neck. Until all she sees is her peaceful body lying unperturbed by the piles of emotional dung associated with her family and this graveyard. Dung she has been shoveling six feet under day in and day out for decades. She stares at this image until she can't take it anymore. And then, slowly removing her sensible black pumps, one then the other, she hikes up her hospital gown, and climbs inside.

SEVENTEEN

ADELAIDE

"**I** can see what you're doing," Dr. Joy chides Adelaide. "This won't work unless you cooperate. Look at the watch, not my hand."

The antique gold pocket watch swings back and forth like the measured force of destiny. *Tick tock; tick tock.* Adelaide stares ahead, glassy-eyed, yet determined to evade it. She will not be conquered by a swinging timepiece. Not even this one, which reminds her so much of her grandfather's. Anyway, she's not the hypnotizable type. Her mind is too keen, too focused.

Tick. Tock. Tick. Tock. Tick. Tock.

The rhythm invades her brain then her soul, and all at once her eyes sink back in her head. She jolts up, opens her eyes and widens them, forcing herself to concentrate on something else in the room. Joy's scribble of a Betty Boop face, for starters, or her red high-top sneakers. Or her mesmerizing pink bubblegum ring. Or the rubber duck swim tube hanging from the ceiling. Anything but...the... *Tick. Tock.*

Before she knows what's happened or who sent her there, she's deep in the woods. Dappled sun highlights dirt paths and the hood of Julian's Chrysler like faerie lights. Everywhere are dense clusters of wild dogwood, sugar magnolia, and black walnut. The convertible top is down and they are flying along a rugged country road. She lifts her arms over her head, closes her eyes, and feels her long hair fly behind her like kite tails. She has never felt so alive.

"I think we should get back," says Julian somberly.

"Me too, Addie," echoes Felicity from the back seat. "It's getting dark."

All Adelaide can think is what is Felicity doing on a date with her and Julian? More than a date! The day he would propose, or at least the day she'd expected him to propose. Or wanted him to propose. Hoped he'd propose.

"Mother will be worried," Felicity whines.

"What?" Adelaide shrieks. "Head back home, you say? No way!" She turns around, kneeling on the weathered seat leather, feeling the crisp wind on her face. "Not on your life, toots! And anyway, Jules, we haven't even found your cousin's still!"

"I might be lost," he says. "Don't remember that last fork thar. Junior's contraption ain't nowhere near here, far's I recall."

"*Isn't,*" corrects Adelaide. "*Isn't anywhere.*"

"What?" he shouts. "Can't hear nothin' in this here wind," he says.

"*Anything,*" she yells. "Not *nothing. An-y*-thing!"

Julian gives her the sly eye, but she doesn't apologize. After all, if they're going to get married, he'll have to drop the holler slang at some point or answer to Mother. Might as well start now. Adelaide's doing him a favor. He should be grateful.

Other than his sloppy talk, hearing his voice again is too thrilling. It's as if she hasn't heard it in decades. She whips back around and drops into her seat, snuggling against his firm frame. Ahead is a tunnel.

"We shouldn't be at Nada already," he says, pointing to the tunnel. "We gone too far, I'm sure of it."

Adelaide doesn't care how far they've gone or if they ever leave. She doesn't even care if they find Junior's stash of rock gut moonshine. She's intoxicated by the wind, by the sweet grape fragrance of mountain laurel, and if she's honest, by the prospect of danger. She could live right here in this forest. Become a wood nymph. Just burrow on in and never leave. How has she survived this long surrounded by so much death? she wonders. Burying people who barely lived? When all this time, the Gorge and the forest—what feels like the very pulse of life—were practically next door?

"I'm gonna reverse," he says. "My backside's already sore from the whoopin' yer mama's fixin' to give me. It's now or never time. We got to turn this thang 'round, by gawd."

"No," she says, grabbing the wheel and turning it hard. The car spins off-road right into the side of a limestone shelter.

There's a struggle that feels like an inner struggle even though Julian's strong hands are involved. She lets go. Gives in. Or at least she feels like she gives in. Everything and every-body evaporate right then and there to a chorus of Felicity's whining soprano. Kick the baby out, is all Adelaide's thinking, as she rises above the scene. Kick her out of the car and let her walk home alone. She doesn't belong on this date anyhow. Who does she think she is?

"Adelaide?" says a voice outside of time. "That's enough for today. Good work. Relax into your chair. I'm going to count to ten and snap my fingers, and you'll awaken. Afterwards you'll remember nothing. You'll merely feel refreshed."

Obituary for Release to:
Bluegrass Bugle &
The Louisville Gazette
Wednesday, October 26, 1960

Felicity Jane Somers Left to Die
Born: November 15, 1942
Presumed date of passage into eternal life:
October 24, 1960

Felicity Jane Somers of Outskirt, Kentucky, age
seventeen, beloved daughter of Regina and Jasper
Somers of *Sunnyside Up Enterprises*, died tragically
Saturday at the Red River Gorge in Stanton, Kentucky.
The suspicious incident took place deep in the woods
outside Nada Tunnel, so no one in town could confirm or
deny or even fabricate any details of what might have
occurred, outside the funny feeling of what were she
and her sister doing that deep in the woods in the first
place? An investigation is underway, but that could take
a while since Sheriff Gibbs has the gout and his Deputy,
Leonard, is an unaccountable drunk. I should know;
I married him. A search posse has been formed by
neighborly volunteers to try and recover the body.

A private service will take place with an empty
casket at the family funeral home, where Felicity resided
with her surviving family, including her sister, Adelaide
Frances, who was injured in the same accident, but
somehow made it out alive. Hmmmm. To make matters
worse, her father, Jasper, beloved proprietor and Right

Reverend of *Sunnyside Up Enterprises*, had a heart attack shortly after hearing the news. He's laid up at Outskirt General in critical care.

When asked for comment, Regina Somers, wife and business manager at *Sunnyside Up* shook her fist and slammed the door. Even from the porch this reporter heard her scream, "For the love of gawd, mind your own dang business, Becky, you hear me? Now git." Last I knew drafting these obits was my business, since I've been doing it for 20 years, but now I'm worried.

Felicity's grave will be laid open and bare until such point as the body is recovered, if it ever is. No one can say since the water is higher and the rapids are stronger than usual this season. Felicity had no Last Will and Testament since she was only seventeen years old. Her only collections consisted of a handful of live hens, one cantankerous rooster, and a jar of fire flies, so no one knows what items will adorn her headstone if she ever has one. Mourners are advised to keep their suggestions to themselves for the time being, if you know what I mean.

Over my dead body.

EIGHTEEN

FELICITY

When Mother's specter departs, Felicity wanders the property in a mental fog which, at the moment, is as bad as any physical fog she's ever experienced. Probably because her mental body is all that's left of her, not that she's complaining. At least it's something. She could be nothing more than the whispering wind or a drop of glistening dew on a prickly thistle, or some other such impossible-to-decipher sign from the natural world or God himself. How would anyone as dense as Addie ever decipher clues as ambiguous as those? At least Felicity's got something to work with. She has a body. Or more accurately, according to Mrs. Phipps, a *subtle body*. A body of the same template composed of energy that simply manifests at a higher frequency than the dense physical body she left behind.

Left behind?

She shudders at the thought of leaving such a huge piece of herself behind. Not a thumbprint or a lock of hair. Her entire body! How careless. After all, it wasn't intentional. She didn't mean to leave it behind. And where did she leave it? Other than possibly the so-called accident Addie's always referring to, that is. Not that there were any details. She's never seen her own headstone. Does she even have one? Doesn't know the year or the circumstance of her demise. Didn't even know she was dead!

As she stands on the slate path, a distant diffuse light slowly penetrates her fog, and she reflexively shields her translucent eyes from its glare. She seeks answers; she does. There's no hiding from any of this. She's already dead. But how will she find answers when Addie, her most likely source of information, is so compromised? And according to Mother, not just her source, her entire world! Or more accurately, her border world.

All at once, Felicity's spine jerks and her brain is a live wire. She scours the fog for evidence of lightning or some other source of electricity, but detects none. She moves forward guided by a force of direction she doesn't recognize, a force of confidence. A powerful and focused force designed to guide her specifically, she feels. Designed to split open the secrets of the universe like raw eggs fresh from the hen house cracked high over a hot skillet. What will she find in the center? A double yolk? A stagnant yolk? Or the beginnings of life?

Or maybe she'll find what Phipps has been trying to tell her all along—that there are no secrets. That the center of everything is the same. That everything within is simultaneously projected without. That there's no such thing as within. Every passing thought is an elemental that gains form with repetition until eventually, it becomes as solid as destiny. A feature film projected on a cosmic screen. Even when you're not the author or actor, you're likely running the projector or buying the tickets or selling the popcorn. Movies don't make themselves.

As her inner radar sheds light on these mysteries, the fog thins and her path becomes more visible. At least now she can see her hands. She can almost see her feet. Slowly rounding the bend of the garden path, she finds herself in the myrtle patch where Addie landed yesterday when she fell out the window. *Was it just yesterday?!* She forces herself not to surrender to the crush of despair that threatens to reduce her visibility all over again. And if it limits her, will it not also limit Addie? Weaken her? Even kill her? Kill her before she has a chance to be forgiven for whatever the heck she did? *What did she do?!!* That part of the path is a low-lying cloud.

Felicity quickens her pace to cross the myrtle as fast as she can. It's only her mind that limits her now. And limit it does, because clearly her mental body is still earthbound. Still sequential. Still one foot in front of the other, stuck in the momentum of unnecessary physical law. It's hard to get used to a boundless nature when you've been grounded for so long. But she's determined to do it. Not just do it, but master it. She pushes her mind hard to move past yesterday into today. And from there, who knows? *Eternity?* Not that she's in a hurry. Before she can get to eternity, she has to pass through the myrtle patch where Addie fell, swing around the cemetery, and arrive at the ridge where she can get some perspective. She tries to pick up her pace, but her legs are stiff. *Come on now! You can do it! Move!* Her only transportation is the power of her immobile will.

At the end of the myrtle patch, she arrives at the cemetery, another scene that sticks to the past like molasses. She cuts a wide berth round the rundown picket fence that surrounds the yard, head down, determined. *Keep on going! Don't look up!* All around her, whispers and echoes fly like bats at twilight. *"Felicity, get over here right now! Felicity, tend to my petunias! Felicity, tell Stewart to mind his own dang beeswax! Felicity, don't get too big for your britches—you belong to us!"* Felicity! *Felicity! Felicity!* She refuses to engage with any of them. They will only drive her to despair. And not her despair—*theirs!* She can't take them on. She won't. After all, if their dim spirits can project a movie of ego and despair, can her willing spirit not project selfless compassion and healing? And *light!* Isn't that what she was made for? A movie of joy?

No sooner does she think it than the power of joy germinates within her like a vine of purple morning glory climbing up her legs into her torso. Nestling in her heart. Causing her heart to open and bloom. Creating joy itself. At the same time her heart blooms, the fog lifts from her personal surroundings, replaced by rays of radiant light. She stops to take it in, warmed by the heat. Stunned by the clarity. Why, she hasn't seen sunlight like this since she can remember! *Since she died?* Hand to heart, she jumps the culvert, crosses the hillock, and climbs the crumbling stone steps to the top of Somer's Ridge.

At the overlook now, she absorbs the dome of expansive azure sky pulsating with life. A sky that invites her to live as the sky itself has always lived, openly and fearlessly with nothing to hide. Every action displayed in the theater of the sky an unabashed, bold reflection of its eternal nature. Life-affirming sunshine. Wisps of vapor. Menacing clouds. Threatening thunder. Reckless twisters. Promising rainbows. Free performances all. No charge; no withholding. What you see is what you get.

You get it all.

Sitting on the chipped gray bench on the ridge, she releases her mind with all its snapshots and random scrapbook contents to the sky. She is as much a witness as a participant in this movie that begins with blurry vignettes on scratched film, featuring award-winning actresses, Felicity Jane Somers and Adelaide Frances Somers. Did she become an actor in Addie's movie, or did Addie become an actor in hers? Or did they write this screenplay together? She leans back and watches the scenes unfold.

Scene One opens with Addie commanding 13-year-old Felicity to lie to their parents about an outing with some miner boy from the holler. Felicity's never seen the boy before. He's handsome enough with a cool junky car that runs its noisy motor right outside the long drive at the end of their property. Motor so loud the corpses are complaining, so Flitty's not sure who's going to believe her lie. She'll think of something. Luckily cousin Becky stops her parents outside the chapel to argue about somebody or other's obituary. Becky presses to tell it like she sees it, as usual, and Mother scolds her as she always does.

"This is a professional business, Rebecca," says Mother. "Not some slapdash amateur operation where you can say whatever the devil you want. We are not in the business of publishing undignified drafts. Polish your work or I'll do it myself!" Turning to leave, she adds, "Lie if you have to."

Anybody at *Sunnyside Up* could write this script. Like Mother and Addie, Becky is nothing if not stubborn. She says what good's an obit if it's nothin' but a lie? This tussle keeps the three of them congregated on the sidewalk, backs to Felicity till the miner boy's car finally speeds off in a cloud of cheap gas with Addie inside. Becky stomps off in the other direction, and Mother, halfway up the path coming toward Felicity, says, "Where's your sister, Felicity Jane? Tell the truth, now. Did she just leave in that car?"

Felicity shrugs. "I dunno."

"Of course you know, Felicity," she says. "Don't you let your lying sister drag y'all into her web." She taps her foot expectantly.

Felicity looks down, tracing circles in the dirt with her bare toe, thinking hard.

"Well?" says Mother in her warning voice. "Did Adelaide take off in that car? "

"She might've needed to go to town for something, I guess." Felicity pretends to draw lipstick on her lips, making like Addie's out buying makeup, which maybe she is. She can't honestly say what the heck Addie's doing. One way or the other, her big sister's likely to get whooped. And maybe Felicity too, for lying. She might as well make the lie believable.

"I told that girl she is not allowed to wear lipstick in this house or anywhere else!" says Mother through clenched teeth.

Daddy overhears, catches up to Mother, and in defense of Addie, says, "Now, Regina, she's a girl after all. Girls like to look pretty."

Fists all balled-up on her hips, Mother says, "That right there's the dilemma, Jasper, is it not? Just what kind of girl is she? Wearing lipstick behind our backs. Driving in cars with delinquents for gawd's sake. She's defiant, is what she is. Defiant and maybe loose."

Before Felicity can hear Daddy's answer, the scene vanishes like a gust of hot air, Scene Two in random order fast on its heels. This time, Mother and Daddy are standing in the back of the chapel, Felicity behind the trough of blessed water, hiding. She doesn't know why she's hiding, just that hiding was a sure reflex for her in those days. A safety instinct.

"That boy is trouble," Mother says, pointing outside to someone Felicity can't see.

"Oh for worry sake, Regina, he's just a boy wants more from life than he got."

"More from Adelaide you mean," she snaps.

As the funeral recession moves ahead of them and out the door, Mother stomps her clunky-heeled tie shoe on the vestibule stone and says, "Jasper, this is the LAST of their sort I'll have you tending to in this chapel. Y'all hear me? I have had it with those people. No good can come of this mingling. They don't even pay their way!" Her face blooms like a field of poppies. Mother never was able to hide her mad.

"They're people like us, Gina," says Daddy, shaking his sorrowful Jimmy Stewart head. "Wherever they come from, so do we. Can't you see? The only difference between us is circumstance, and lawd knows, that can change in a flash."

"How can you say that?" Mother seethes, her mouth tightening. "Do you want our girls to end up like... them? After all we've done?"

Daddy shakes his head and says, "We all end up in a box."

"How dare you!" she whisper-shrieks. "I worked my butt off to get out of that place! I will not be pushed back down that high hill to the holler because you wish to do someone a reckless favor. Why don't y'all think of your own family for once."

Just as soon as that scene delivers a case of the chills straight down Felicity's spine, it disappears, followed swiftly by Scene Three. She watches from high up the sugar magnolia beside the house, peeping through its velvety petals. Down below, Mother bull-charges Julian's car from ten feet away with a fireplace poker, as he wildly tries to restart his engine. *Vroom! Vroom! Vroooooom!!!* Finally, he takes off, just in time, Adelaide weeping behind him on the driveway in a cloud of exhaust, "Come baaaaack!"

When the dust settles, Mother turns around to face Addie

in what seems like slow motion. "Go to your room, young lady." The way she says it, all low and mean, sends even the sunning salamanders back under the safety of their hot rocks.

Addie screams, "I won't let you ruin my gawddamn life!"

"I won't have to," says Mother all snake-eyed. "Y'all keep going like this, you'll ruin it all by yourself. That boy's got no future. You hear me? None."

Enter Daddy from the barn, a shovel in his hand. "Strong boy like him wants a better life," he says. "It's only natural. Let him work here, Gina. We've got plenty digging for starters. Eddie and Sam'll be moving on soon. I could use the help."

"Over my dead body," she spits. "You got that, Jasper?" She leans her square torso so far forward she nearly lands on her head. "Over. My. Dead. Body."

Felicity watches the sky-screen flicker and fade in smoky spurts, the projector of the universal mind burned out, at least for now. Not that Felicity's sorry to see it end; she isn't. For all its unpleasantness, it hasn't shed a spark of light on whatever hateful deed Addie might have committed to warp her own destiny, as she clearly did. All Felicity remembers is how much she admired Addie for standing up to Mother back then. For creating her own movie from scratch—nobody's storyline but hers. She remembers thinking that she, too, would like to create her own story. This admiration of Addie makes the idea of her sister committing an unforgiveable act even harder to conjure. Only her will to save her sister from a sequel worse than her original drama gives Felicity the courage to pursue this mystery.

But then she thinks, If I have trouble remembering a misdeed of Addie's in the first place, is it even worthy of conviction? If she doesn't feel injured, was there ever an injury to begin with?

She stares more deeply into the theater's azure dome, and with her inner radar, opens her lens further, and further again, inviting one last scene.

Scene Four is a red tail hawk, its scaly curled claws grabbing her by the back of her neck, flying high and dropping her on her knees in the open field deep below the ridge. She scrambles up, finding herself standing in a field of incandescent yellow blooms lit from on high by a tangerine sun, her hands ablaze with luminous backlight. Every color is radiant, unearthly— citrine, amber, aquamarine, opal. She is nearly blinded by the radiance. It's too much, she thinks. *What have I done?*

If I rise too soon, I'll ruin everything.

Off in the distance stands the haloed outline of a rugged figure. She draws closer, studying the sturdy profile of his square chin, his sculpted body, his thick head of windblown hair. All at once her belly transforms into a pond of jumping frogs, her brain a hive of frantic bees. She is chaos itself. *But why?* Moving closer, she follows his eyes up the sandy cliff that leads to the abandoned Diamondback mine above the town and the surrounding fields. Why is the mine abandoned? She can't remember. *Did she ever know?* That was the town's only real industry. Every other enterprise in town supported the people who worked there. And last she knew, it was bustling with activity.

The longer Felicity studies the scene, the more she is drawn to its witness down below. Near-blinded as she is...still she knows it's him. Julian. She can read his energy. The usual clear light around him, muddied. He's distressed, deeply sad, but knowing. He is no country bumpkin. He's a candle in the darkness from a place of light. Like her, maybe. It's hard to figure. In spite of Mother's constant harping about his sloppy appearance and ignorant dialect, Felicity can see he's elevated.

His energy is bright, dynamic. And kind. Daddy was right about him. Mother was wrong. Something happened to him, too, she realizes. *But what?* If Addie is Felicity's border world, then Julian is surely Addie's. And maybe a little bit hers. And finally, she gets it.

To understand Julian is to understand them all.

Obituary for Release to:
Bluegrass Bugle &
The Louisville Gazette
Sunday, October 30, 1960

Rev. Jasper Lewis Somers Dies of a Broken Heart
Born: February 1, 1905
Passed into eternal life: Friday October 28, 1960

Rev. Jasper Lewis Somers, age 55, esteemed owner,
Right Reverend, and Funeral Director of *Sunnyside Up
Enterprises*, a lifetime resident of Outskirt, Kentucky, was
delivered via the back of Barrows & Co. milk truck to
Outskirt General on Thursday afternoon after learning
of the likely death of his daughter, Felicity Jane, at the
Red River Gorge in Stanton. According to the young
truck proprietor, Lionel Barrows, the usually dignified
reverend kept banging the truck, screaming, "Hurry
up! My daughters need me!" At the time, seventeen-
year-old Felicity Jane was missing at the Gorge, while
her sister, twenty-two-year-old Adelaide Frances,
had been delivered to critical care in the arms of an
unidentified frantic interloper from the holler. According
to Barrows and another witness, the interloper was later
arrested by security personnel and locked up tight
since nobody could vouch for his innocence.

Upon seeing the sorry condition of his eldest
daughter, Adelaide, and hearing of the near certain
death of his then-missing daughter, Felicity, Reverend
Somers crumbled helplessly to the floor. He was finally

lifted onto a gurney and rolled straight to critical care where he lasted a few hours insisting the whole time that he be cremated upon death and sprinkled over the Gorge. A document was drawn up and executed before relinquishing his spirit to the Lord. "Felicity Jane, here I come," he said with a smile on his face, according to a nurse's aide. "Adelaide Frances, may your life continue to bless us all."

No one from the extended Somers family was reachable for a comment that made any sense, so I asked the truck proprietor, Lionel Barrows, who stated, "The Somers are royalty to us village folk. I'd do just 'bout an'thang fer any member that family 'cept the wife and mother, who's a pill if I ever choked on one. Rev. Somers buried my sweet mama hisself in the side garden at midnight; never told the wife. All along he knew I couldn't pay him a dang penny." At that, Barrows held his hand up, sniffling. "All I can say is I'll continue to deliver free milk, donuts, cheese and whatnot to the Somers family, long as I live, no matter what I think of the wife. I owe it to the Reverend." He shook his head sadly. "That's all. I can't say no more, Rebecca. Leave me be."

As of this morning, no information about Rev. Somers' funeral or burial plans was provided by the family or management of *Sunnyside Up Enterprises,* by which I mean Regina. The phone just rang and rang. I finally gave up. After all, Uncle Jasper stood up for all of us, including me. Without him, I'm just one more sitting duck like the rest of them.

NINETEEN

ADELAIDE

B efore Adelaide knows what's happening, she's yanked from her hospital bed, stuffed into a cannon and shot backwards into a wide upholstered armchair in the office of her shrink, Dr. Joy. The sturdy chair rocks precariously on its back legs, barely containing her momentum as it knocks into the bookcase behind her, spilling its contents in slow motion—*The Nursery Rhymes of Mother Goose; Grimm Brothers' Fairy Tales; A Tree Grows in Brooklyn; The Seven Sleuths' Club: A Mystery;* every *Nancy Drew* book ever published; *The Unabridged Encyclopedia of Mortuary Terms;* and a loose-leaf binder marked *Obituary Drafts from Sunnyside Up*. She reaches up and out in all directions, but can't seem to catch anything as the books crash around her. Broken spines, bent pages, ripped illustrations—the pages of her life torn asunder.

Her back to Adelaide, Dr. Joy taps her right foot as she stares out the opposite window into the courtyard at what look to be frolicking dogs made of purple pipe cleaners with crepe paper tails. "You're late again, Adelaide," is all she says.

Adelaide tucks the ends of her clown-print hospital gown beneath her spreading buttocks to cover that which must never be seen. She barely remembers who she is, where she came from, or who loaded her into the cannon in the first place, but she remembers her dignity. "Do you have a blanket?" she asks.

Without even turning around, Dr. Joy grabs a throw made of chicken feathers from a bouncy marshmallow couch and tosses it behind her in Adelaide's direction. "Did you forget our appointment again, Adelaide? Is that what happened?"

Adelaide shimmies backwards into the chair, busily covering herself with the throw.

"Well? What do you have to say for yourself?"

Adelaide ignores the insolence. The woman is lucky she comes to these useless sessions at all. If it weren't for the cigarettes, she wouldn't bother.

Barely visible in her cellophane jumpsuit, Joy turns slowly. Her face is a poorly drawn circle, her hair a pile of green macaroni stuck together with clumps of dried mucilage. When she sees Addie, her corkscrew eyes nearly hit the lenses of her black licorice-framed glasses. "Whoa! What happened to you?" she asks.

Chin down, Adelaide peeks down at her hospital gown covered in iodine stains, dancing clowns, and dried blood. Luckily the chicken feathers cover the worst. "You should talk," she says. "You look like you were thrown together by a committee of drunken one-year-olds."

"I look exactly as you allow me to look, Adelaide," says Dr. Joy. "It has always been thus. I am a precise reflection of the maturity of your psyche and spiritual consciousness. You'd think you would know that by now."

Adelaide's blood rushes. She wants to scream, but it's difficult with a tube down her throat. "I did not come all the way here to see a reflection of my own psyche," she whispers hoarsely. "I came here to talk to somebody who knows something about anything at all. Someone who can help me." She lowers her bruised lip in a pout. "How dare you!"

"Ah, but you did come here to see yourself," says Joy as she pulls the antique gold pocket watch slowly out of her plastic apron, poorly stitched with red yarn. "It might be scary, but it's the most worthwhile journey you'll ever take. Shall we begin?"

The chair's brocade upholstery is itchy against Adelaide's bare butt, and she twitches uncomfortably. "Just...do you think I could...maybe smoke one Winston....before..."

The clock swings. *Tick. Tock.*

"Don't fight it, Adelaide. You've made very little progress on our task, and you're running out of time. The consequences of all your avoidance over all these years could be, well... catastrophic."

Tick. Tock. Tick. Tock. Tick. Tock.

Adelaide tries to look away, but the glint of the gold arrests her. A cigarette would surely help her to resist. She wants to insist on one, but all she can manage are fragments, *"Can I..."* And then, *"Just one..."* The words drool out of her mouth.

"There's no avoiding this task, Adelaide. It's now or never."

Tick. Tock.

Tick.

Tock.

Adelaide's eyes roll around in her head like the Magic 8-Ball Felicity had as a kid. She's in danger of losing her concentration. Losing *herself*. "What...what...task are you...are we...?"

"The task before us is the transposition of the entire trajectory of your eternal life," says Joy in what is surely a deliberately hypnotic drone. "That's it in a nutshell."

Adelaide can't hear her anymore because she's busy rocking at the edge of a second story window.

"Where are you now, Adelaide?" says Joy. "Where have you gone and how did you get there? Tell me what's happening. Tell me everything."

Adelaide drops from the ledge, spinning through space. Spinning and spinning in a deep empty vortex. Teetering. Plunging. It is seemingly bottomless, and then.

Smack.

Her head aches and her body breaks in too many places to count. She lies motionless, wishing for it all to end. All of it. *Everything.* All the pain of all the years. All the nonsense. All the tears. "Just let me go," she moans. "Let this be...it. Oh, please."

But it isn't. *It isn't it.* And it doesn't go away. Instead, her broken mess of a body is flipped over like a sloppy egg, arms and legs dangling. Once flipped it's lifted onto a stretcher into an ambulance and whisked off to a hospital in the clouds.

"Tell me where you are now."

Adelaide, her mouth full of dry cotton, mumbles "Clouds. Cloud doctors."

"What are they telling you?" asks Joy who sounds as if she's yelling into a jar. "Tell me everything."

"They say, well...that time is meaningless."

"Was there ever a time that was meaningful, Adelaide?" says Joy. "Meaningful to you?"

A ray of light pierces the cloud, and Adelaide is struck by a bolt of clarity. "There was a time when I was becoming myself," she says. "It was just...well, glorious." In spite of her catastrophic circumstance, she grins at the memory of such a time.

"And then?"

Darkness descends, a storm approaches, and Adelaide is suddenly frantic, desperate, flailing. "Where is she?" she cries. "Where did she go?"

"Who, Adelaide? Where did who go?"

"Felicity. You were looking right at her. She was just here. She'll never find me now." Her eyes moisten and a tornado spins at her feet. The tornado bifurcates, rushing up each leg through her torso, rejoining in her neck. Rain rolls down her face and she is racked with grief. "I've lost her," she sobs. "She's gone. I've really done it this time." As wind gusts storm her lungs and lightning strikes her heart, she fights back with all she's got. It couldn't have been Adelaide who caused all this pain. *It couldn't have!* It must have been someone else.

But who?

A soft voice reaches through the storm with a blanket and an umbrella. "That's enough for today," it says. "Good work, Adelaide. Relax into your chair now. I'm going to count to ten. When I snap my fingers, you'll awaken. Afterwards you'll remember nothing. You'll merely feel refreshed."

TWENTY

FELICITY

The image of Julian in the field vaporizes, and Felicity finds herself back in the community room, wondering how she got here. She is so stunned by the entire experience that the rising pool of sparkling lilac mist surrounding her ankles barely registers at first. She blinks repeatedly as the mist pulses and hums, billowing outward and upward, rising to the level of her knees, her waist, her shoulders, gradually filling every corner of the room. The longer she watches, the more it intensifies in form and pigment, deepening into a rich and familiar amethyst. She is reminded of a recurrent dream

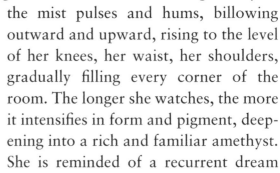

she had as a child. Not that it felt like a dream at the time. It didn't.

Neither does this.

Through the haze, Felicity sees Adelaide spread out on her belly in the myrtle, and then again on her back in a sterile hospital room, near lifeless. She extends her arms to help her sister, but can't penetrate the mist. Frustrated, she reaches out desperately, overcome with regret while vaguely remembering that Addie was the single solitary soul on the face of the Earth she was ever entrusted with. And look what happened.

But who entrusted Addie to her in the first place? she wonders. She can't remember. After all, Addie is her older sister. Shouldn't it have been the reverse? Shouldn't Felicity have been entrusted to her? She squints hard trying to access the truth, to mine any logic at all from her short life. All she comes up with is a big gummy tar ball of people and circumstances, dates and times, stuck to the dirt wall of her decaying memory. She can't sort any of it out. Does accident brain remain with a person after death? she wonders. Maybe so. Or maybe she's not really dead at all. Maybe she's just crazy. After all, where's the grave?

As if eavesdropping on her musings, the purple vapor reacts frenetically in dashes, dots, and whorls like a strange language Felicity was born knowing. *"It was Us,"* it signals. "We are the ones who entrusted Adelaide to you."

"Us?" says Felicity half to herself. *But who is Us?* She can't recall that either. She dives deeper and deeper into collapsed caves of repressed memory as confusing as the milieu that envelopes her. The deeper she dives, the more the vapor gathers in density, breaks apart, and forms into twelve faceless figures. She studies them carefully and then incredulously as her memory crystallizes. *"Ohhhhh,"* she whispers. *"Us is you!"*

"It is," they signal, pleased.

At that, a skein of distant memory slowly unwinds revealing Felicity's struggle with the disparity between her own deep inner life and the very surface lives of most of her family members. Never was it better illustrated than in this moment right here, right now. '*Us*', better known to Felicity in her girlhood as *The Purple People*, are the very entities she was forbidden to acknowledge by everyone but her father.

"But they're my friends!" she would insist as Addie mocked relentlessly. As Mother, bending down on wide dimpled knees, looked Felicity straight in the eye, and said, "Y'all listen to me now, Felicity Jane. You're old enough to know those purple devils are *not* real. They're in your head, you hear me?" Face all pinched and finger wagging, she wouldn't stop. "And if y'all ever want to have real friends, never mind a real husband, you will not speak of this again. To anyone!"

Following that memory, a later one surfaces of Mrs. Phipps in the barn trying to teach a class of mostly glazed-over half-dead hooligans about *The Purple Order of the Sacred Light*. "The highest order of governing energies manifest on this plane," she said. "At least for now." According to Phipps, new orders of light are always poised to enter when the time is right. "When people are ready," she added. "When enough people have shed the many layers of scaly darkness they've acquired over lifetimes to reveal even the slightest degree of their core brilliance." And then more dramatically, "When they have manifested light dense enough to withstand the intensity of new, more radiant energy...*without burning up*." She'd emphasized the words, *burning up*, nearly bug-eyed, to get their attention. Before this, the only place Felicity ever thought of as being that dangerous was hell. But maybe that's what hell is. Maybe she had it wrong all along.

Even now, recalling the details of that lesson, Felicity

shivers. She'd always thought of hell as a place of exile for evil-doers, not a simple matter of standing in place as her own dim light is consumed by a much greater light. Burning her up! Not because she did something bad, but because her flame didn't have enough oxygen to burn on its own. Because she depended on others for light. Because she didn't bother to grow.

Shouldn't life come with a warning? she thinks. Or at least a few instructions? Or maybe it does. Maybe people tear them off like mattress labels, or simply disregard them in the first place thinking they have it all figured out. After all, the rules are simple and people are not.

"It's important to enhance the density of light throughout your life with acts of love and contemplation," Phipps continued. "Wandering through the world of separation as we do, our light becomes porous, our spirits weak and unprotected. In the end, light is our only currency. Light is meant to be shared, not hoarded in misguided acts of ego and celebrity. The more light we share, the more light we generate, you see? It's a never-ending loop until we've generated enough light to sit down with a big old glass of sweet tea before the blinding face of the Godhead without so much as a parasol." Tapping her pointer on the podium, she says, "Am I making myself clear?"

It was clear to Felicity, but she may have been the only one. Addie and the other rowdy troublemakers were either asleep or otherwise engaged.

"Did I make myself clear!" Phipps repeated at a resounding volume that echoed throughout the barn. Frustrated by the lack of response, she reached beneath her podium producing a floodlight which she held over the head of Earl Brinker, one of the dimmer students in the front row. She held it over his head until he complained about how bright it was. How hot!

Shielding his eyes, he said, "I dint do it, Miz Phipps! I dint steal that money and I dint bury it in Vern's side yard, swear to gawd."

"No one said anything about stealing money," said Phipps as she brought the floodlight closer. "But where does Vern live?"

"Get that thang 'way from me," hollered Earl, flailing. "I can't see nothin'!" Rocking his chair on its back legs to get away from the light, he tipped over backwards.

Phipps bent down, holding the light closer to him.

"Ouch! Yer burnin' m' hair! Turn that thang off 'fore I report y'all to the authorities," he threatened.

"I am the authority!" said Phipps. "And for your information, Earl Brinker, this light is on the lowest possible setting. You are living in the cold dark cellar of life, boy. You need to make your way out the hatch and get some sunlight before you die of spiritual fungus."

Hands protecting his face, he cried, "Ok I did it! I did it! I buried the dang money, but not in Vern's side yard. In Rupert Cuttyback's septic field. Rupert made me do it. Held his rifle to my head till I were done. Now git that blasted light 'way from me! Ain't I been through 'nuff?"

Phipps shook her head. "Mr. Brinker, you have got some work to do!" she warned. "And it does not involve digging. It involves climbing." Shutting off the floodlight, she scanned the room mercilessly, "And by God, you're not the only one."

Once the room cleared that night, Felicity remained for her solo lesson. It was then that an exhausted Phipps explained to her that *The Purple Order* were Felicity's governing energies. That they had guided her throughout her life, and would be with her always. That they would never desert her. Recalling this now, Felicity wonders if this current haze of purple light— the imaginary friends of her childhood—are also the governing energies Phipps had mentioned so many years ago. Could *Us* be them? More than childhood friends? Lifetime guides? She hasn't seen them since she was ten years old. They'd faded into the muted memory of her childhood along with Tinker Bell, Glinda, and the tooth fairy. Although come to think of it, there was the one time at the Gorge, but she can't be sure about that. The Gorge is a blur in general ever since... She shakes her head, searching.

Ever since what, Felicity?

Ever since whatever. The accident, probably. Not that she remembers anything about the accident. Honestly, all she can focus on is the penetrating light right here in the community room right now. She's dumbstruck at the ombre ebb and flow—the lavender deepening to magenta, to berry, and finally to a rich incandescent amethyst light of the sort that could blind a seeing person or conversely, give sight to the blind. It's all Felicity can do not to rise off the chair and blend into its consuming wisdom. Surrender herself. Become it.

She watches awestruck as the mist separates like the Red Sea revealing an exquisite lady with the delicate features of a goddess dressed in a sparkling lavender robe with an elaborate headpiece of orbiting planets. "Remember me?" she says as she floats toward Felicity.

It takes a minute, but soon Felicity's eyes widen in recognition. *No! It can't be!*

"And yet," says the lady, curtsying, "it is."

"Celeste?" Felicity whispers with reverence. No sooner does she utter the name than the word itself is inexplicably sucked back into her mouth, swallowed whole, and lodged in her bones like marrow. "Is it really you?"

"It is," she says.

Felicity shakes her head in amazement. "Y'all have really grown up!"

"With you, Felicity," she says, nodding. "I've grown with you."

"Well, not exactly *with* me," says Felicity. "You've turned out far more beautiful than anyone could've predicted from that scrawny li'l girl..." She freezes at this unkind slip. The last thing she wants is to offend Celeste. "Sorry," she says shyly.

Celeste chuckles. "You see me as I see you, Felicity. That's all. There's no difference between us."

"Impossible." Felicity picks at a piece of her skeletal, liver-spotted arm as proof. "Unlike you, I stayed scrawny and grew plenty old."

"You aged by Earth years," says Celeste. She cocks her head. "But you didn't have to."

"I didn't?" This is news.

"Of course not." Celeste sweeps the length of her own transcendent image with her elegant hand. "It's all a matter of becoming. You haven't become yet. That's the only difference. Other than that, we're the same."

All Felicity thinks right now is that her brain feels like an undercooked biscuit. Rubbing her tired eyes, she says, "You sure I'm not making you up? I'm good at making things up, just ask Addie."

Celeste shakes her head no.

"You're really real?"

"I am."

"But Addie said...and Mother..."

"Their feet are bound to dirt. Yours to sky." Celeste leans forward, beckoning. "Come with me, Felicity. With *Us*. You're ready now."

"I really am dead then?"

"Your heart is open," says Celeste. "You're alive in the only sense that matters."

Felicity wants to go; she does. It takes all her strength to resist. To remain in the community room where Addie can find her.

"Addie, too," she bargains. "We'll go together."

"Adelaide is far from ready."

"How long before she's ready?"

"Maybe lifetimes." Celeste shakes her head sadly. "Maybe never."

"Never?!"

"It isn't up to us," says Celeste. "It's up to Adelaide, and Adelaide refuses to learn."

"I'll teach her," Felicity says. "She'll learn now, in this lifetime. From me."

"Teaching is different from being," says Celeste. "You have much to learn of your own gifts before you teach them, especially to one as resistant as your sister. You must *become* before you teach or your teaching is an empty chalice. Come with us and we will show you the way."

"I want to," says Felicity, "more than anything. I do. But I can't abandon Addie. I just can't. And anyway, you entrusted her to me!"

"We entrusted her to you for a lifetime, not an eternity," signal the twelve. "We are always sending guides to work with her, but she refuses to acknowledge them. She remains utterly undeveloped—your darker aspect. Your fundamental entanglement with her on the quantum level complicates our options. If she continues to resist growth, there is nothing you can do but absorb whatever light that remains of her and move on."

Felicity grips the table to keep her head from spinning off. "Absorb? Addie? I can't *absorb* Addie! Addie is Addie. I can't annihilate her!"

"She's annihilating herself."

Felicity's stomach turns. She wants to run away, but she has to see this through. "Addie's ornery," she manages to say, "but there's so much to love about her still. So much worth saving."

The twelve deepen to a solemn violet. "Name one thing."

"Why, there's…" Felicity is unexpectedly stumped. "And then…" She attempts to conjure her sister's many attributes. Or several attributes. Or one. She digs deep to plead her case. "Addie tries; she really does! And she's challenged, as you must know!" She says this even though her own challenges would certainly seem to eclipse any Addie may have. After all, Felicity is brain damaged. And apparently also…*dead!*

Celeste and her cohorts tighten into a huddle then expand, surrounding Felicity in a ring. "Listen to us carefully," they say. "Adelaide is the one thing holding your story to this lifetime. If she dies before all is resolved, and you refuse to absorb her, she will be yours to deal with for eternity. Your story and hers will fracture into hundreds of fragments, each of which will take hundreds of lifetimes to resolve. And only then if new stories with new consequences don't interfere and take priority. Which they most certainly will."

The figures flicker and pop with frustration. As Phipps instructed Felicity early on, the Spirits of all realms can persuade, but not command. They can issue guidelines, but not orders. The one irrevocable law of the universe is the free will of humankind. The will to determine their own destinies for better or worse. To return freely to the Godhead. Or not at all.

"This is your only chance to resolve all debt," they insist. "To carry whatever light that remains in her within your own heart and leave the darkness behind. In that sense she'll continue, and in the best possible way. The minute your sister dies without the awareness of what she did, that opportunity is buried. She will be lost, and if you don't rise now, you will be left to live out her story, regardless of your own enlightenment."

"Addie loves me," says Felicity with a degree of doubt, because...*does she?* She's beginning to question everything.

"She loves you in the way of attachment. In the way of not knowing how to operate without you. That's all."

"How we love each other shouldn't matter," Felicity replies. "The fact is, we do." She shakes her head with resolve. "No. I won't leave her, whatever the reason."

"Adelaide can't rise until the darkness between you is resolved. And you must face the darkness if you want her with you, Felicity. You have to forgive her."

"I already forgive her."

"You don't know what she did."

"I don't care what she did."

"You can't look away," says Celeste firmly. "If you choose this road, you must descend into her darkness yourself. You must truly *see* it. See how it moves and what moves with it. You have to acknowledge it. Accept it. Darkness only dissolves in the light."

The twelve huddle again and disperse. "It will take work for you to stay low," they signal. "You're rising already. It's the nature of light."

"I can do it. I can stay low," she insists, but her resolve is weakening.

"To stay with her you will have to focus with intent on the shoddy man-made illusions and false systems that comprise the Earth plane, or you will drift from her. These are not your systems or your illusions. You will have to work hard to stay low enough to interact with her. To cooperate with the laws of gravity. To wait for her." All nod in unison.

"It will not be easy," warns Celeste. "There is risk."

"But if I'm already dead," says Felicity. "Isn't that what I've been doing all along? Staying low?"

"Yes, but you've been doing it without awareness," she says. "Now that you know what you've been doing, everything is changed. Your light is already transforming you from within. Your glorified body is struggling to burst through the carapace of time-worn decay. Once it reveals itself fully, you cannot remain low. You will move instantly at the speed of light across all time and all realms, filling all space with radiance."

Felicity's heart flutters at the thought of such freedom. She aches to go with them. To move at the speed of light. To be everywhere at once. To leave this crazy place and go where life makes sense to her, as it most surely has not for too many years to count. "I want to go with y'all," she says, tearfully. "I really do." Her chin drops. "But I can't."

The figures blend and move like the valley hawks, swirling and whooshing in the canyon swales. "Your deep attachment to Adelaide will keep you low enough for now," says Celeste. "But one day you will find it's not enough. It can happen at any time, with or without Adelaide. Light rises, Felicity. It can't be held down for long."

"I can do it," she says. *But can she?*

As the figures converge and rise, and the deep pigment fades into a flume of pale lilac, Felicity hears their distant voices. "We will continue to send her teachers," they say. "But it's up to her to open her mind and heart. We can't do it for her. And neither can you. It's a choice. Her choice."

"She'll do it," says Felicity. "I'll see to it."

In an echoing contrail from somewhere in deep space, Felicity's ears burn with their warning: *Be aware of the risk.*

Aware of the risk.

Aware of the risk.

TWENTY-ONE

FELICITY

O nce *Us* is gone, Felicity's head spins on more than one axis. She tries to rein it in, but it isn't working. She's more wobbly than ever. Holding onto the back of the chair, she manages to stand up just as a penetrating radiant heat gathers in her feet. It's as if she's standing on hot coals. To cool down, she pulls off her boots, instantly noticing a warm, near-blinding golden light rising from her ankles to her calves. *Oh no!* Isn't this exactly what she can't allow?

Attempting to drain the rising light from her legs, she stomps her right foot hard against the slate floor, then her left.

The light drops, pools at her ankles, but doesn't disappear. Panic consumes her. What will she do? She has to stay low. *Light rises!* She rushes out of the community room through the long hallway, into the apartment and up the stairs to her bedroom. Winded, she roots through her drawers for an old pair of Daddy's thick woolen work socks. Since the elastic is long worn, she wraps the socks in tight rubber bands to cut-off circulation to the light. She can't let it gain an inch. She has to stay low and dim. *She has to.* She has too much to do.

For starters, she has to clear up the confusion about life versus death and how similar they really are. How one is simply an extension of the other. How they can't be separated. How life never ends. How you can feel alive or at least half-alive when you've been dead for...well, how long exactly? She has no idea. She's lost all sense of time. Or maybe she's lost all sense.

As she lingers in the swoon of *Us*, she thinks she should keep her death a secret, at least from Addie. At least for a while, considering Addie's fragile state. Not that Addie would believe her anyway. Addie would no doubt mock her relentlessly, because that's what Addie does when she doesn't understand something. For Addie to believe that Felicity is dead would require a massive leap in awareness, a leap that Felicity doesn't know whether to hope for or not. After all, in Addie's current condition, such a leap might provoke a fatal stroke or a heart attack before Addie has a chance to figure out what in the world she did, never mind apologize for. Addie could slip through a cosmic crack and be lost for eternity. Anything could happen in a world without physical limits. With no beginning or end. With no boundaries at all. And then what would become of them both? If Felicity loses Addie from her border world, how will they ever find each other again? If there even is an Addie to find. Felicity is just not ready to take that risk. Who knew death would be more complicated than life?

Or maybe Addie could find out about Felicity's death a different way. Maybe the graveyard rascals could find a way to make Felicity's death known to Addie little by little in a gentle and discreet fashion. She shakes her head. As if that crew could do anything in a gentle and discreet fashion. Still, they must already have a clue about her death, what with all their constant busybody chatter. Somebody must have noticed *something!* Although it's also true that with few exceptions, every last one of them is too self-absorbed to notice even the most obvious situations concerning anyone else. It's never been clearer to Felicity that, with the exception of Mother and Daddy, her family is shackled to a stagnant existence that ended ages ago. An existence fueled solely by memory. A deep groove in the record of time.

"Sound familiar, Felicity?" calls a distant voice, like Phipps or even Mother.

Or maybe the voice is her own. The one deep within her that is just now yawning and stretching on the horizon of a scarlet dawn. After all, Felicity knows that she's likely been shackled to Earth for quite some time without so much as the fundamental benefit of a body. But unlike the graveyard spooks, she did not even know she was dead. She still doesn't know how it happened or when. No matter how hard she tries, she remembers nothing. Her eternal mind contains no snapshot of her final Earthly vision, no drawing of her last physical breath or final exhalation. No awareness of a transformation from the solid physical world to a world of pure energy and light. Nothing. It's as if the single most anti-climactic event of her entire life was her own death.

And now here she is, suddenly eternal, released into a

boundless wilderness of who knows what. A world where she's only as limited as she allows herself to be. A world unconfined by space and time where the past is as real as the present, and the future has already occurred. This will take some getting used to.

Surrounded by this indigestible glut of awareness, Felicity wonders if it isn't more the future she's been living in than the past. A future that never happened, though she never stopped trying to live it. A future she may have had a claim on at one time, but somehow lost. Ever since whatever happened happened.

What happened?!

Well, she could get caught in the grip of this seemingly unsolvable mystery or she could begin the process of solving it by hightailing over to Outskirt General to find Addie. Just the desire to do this causes her arms to rise. As her arms rise, her body magically follows. Like a cold engine, though, her movement stutters and stops. She doesn't let the hesitation discourage her. She's determined to succeed at something. *Focus!* She will see her sister one way or the other. She will see her today, or soon—or whatever the word is for no time at all. *Now,* she thinks. *The word is Now.*

Thoughts of Addie are her only compass.

"Addie is your border world…your border world," Mother echoes from somewhere. *"She's never far from you. Far from you. Far…from…you."*

"Focus," calls Phipps from another direction. *"Picture where you want to be and you'll get there."*

Forming a mental picture of Addie laid out like a mound on a skimpy hospital bed, Felicity is able to rise above the house and then the tree line, her etheric body a faint shadow against the billowing clouds. Almost giddily, she glides over the graveyard and its low-lying ghosts. *Wheee!* The deep grave she saw the young man digging yesterday is still there, she notes. How long has it been there? Had she just not seen it? *Is it hers?*

Not ready to know, she focuses again on Addie, shifting her head instinctively to the west. Her arms in front of her, she leans slightly and glides over the barn, the culvert, the rusted old electric fence into the adjacent property and eventually over the whole abandoned town. Over the emerald hills and valleys of her beloved Kentucky home. Over the broken bridges and collapsed coal mine. She hesitates. *Wait. What?!*

Since when did the mine collapse! How could she have missed such a literally earth-shattering event? It must have passed her and Addie right on by like so many other things. She is torn apart just thinking about what such a catastrophe would have meant to so many neighbors and friends. How many must have died! No matter how hard she tries to concentrate on Addie, this distraction causes her movement to dip, stutter, and drop into a spiral of grief and turmoil that spins her like a whirligig.

Round and round she goes. She is so dizzy she can't remember who she is or why she was flying around in the sky to begin with. There is no air in the center of this funnel; her lungs are sucked dry. She squeezes her temples between her hands to stabilize her spinning head, but it doesn't seem to work. Nothing works.

"*Get control of yourself!!*" commands her mother from somewhere outside.

"I'm...try...ing!"

"*Discipline your mind!*" Mother shrieks, which does nothing to help Felicity to discipline anything.

As she spins out of control, a wad the size of a lifetime forms in her throat. Her stomach lurches and her throat gags. She wants nothing more than to retch and retch until the whole confusing corpse of her life is expelled into the valley beneath her. Until she is free of it all. Free to walk away. Free to flee into the embrace of *Us*.

Enough of this crazy godforsaken world!

At this, Phipps calls out in her deepest, most authoritative voice, *"Felicity Jane, y'all listen to me now and listen good. You are not what you think you are. Not right now, you're not. Right now, you're a puffy white cotton cloud warmed by the hot sun over a still mountain lake. You hear me? A cloud. Visualize it. NOW! This instant! Feeeeel it. BE IT! You are a cloud."*

Phipps' voice penetrates Felicity's panic like a hypodermic needle, and suddenly she is able to listen. She takes a deep etheric breath. She concentrates. *She is a cloud.* It all makes sense. She is a cloud and beneath her is a lake. *Right down there; see it?* Yes, she sees it. All silvery blue and glassy. *And still.* The sun above her is a banquet of heat and light. She uses the heat for consolation. She uses the light to cast out the friction, confusion, and burning emotional debris kicked up by the twister. She casts out the debris without naming it, without assigning it any meaning or priority. Without judging it. Without worrying that she may need it one day. She is only a cloud. A big fluffy cloud unburdened by thought or purpose. Unburdened by motive, hers or anyone else's. Just one high cloud over a serene mountain lake, home to warblers, loons, and rainbow trout. On its surface floats a single meandering sailboat. Tree frogs chirp in the towering pines. On its southern beach, a child dumps a bucket of sand on her mother's toes, giggling. Nothing is in a hurry. The only destination is now.

A passing breeze creates a pocket of peace, and in it, Felicity is able to return to the purpose of her trip. "Addie," she whispers, and whispers again. She repeats the name like a prayer, "Addie. Addie. Addie."

No longer a cloud, Felicity lifts her arms and rises on a gentle thermal above the placid lake which shortly transforms into a smattering of tenement houses on the west side of Outskirt. She is back on track, aloft in a field of cyan. Beneath her lay piles of rusted metal, abandoned vehicles of every size, and the occasional lost soul staggering down the street from the only open saloon in town. She sees the rain water rushing down the gulley in Mulligan Holler and the fat raccoon behind the dump, his head stuck in a discarded jar. She glides over the temporary miners' housing, the remains of apartments, and the one general store, its creaky door swinging open and shut in the wind. Beyond all that on the far side of the town limits, she spots the once bustling hospital, its parking lot sparsely occupied with the cars of what appear to be the only employed citizens in the entire town.

Here, she hovers uncertainly, unsure of her next step. Where in that large building is Addie, she wonders. Which window? Which room? *How will I find her?*

"Lower your frequency," says Mother, *"and you will locate her instantly."*

"Energy vibrates faster than mass," adds Phipps. *"To contact anyone down there, you have to slow yourself down. Control your breath!"*

Felicity obeys. Deeeeep inhale, slooooow exhale. And again. Yet again. One more time. As her frequency lowers, she feels herself gain mass. Gain gravity. *Inhale. Exhale. And Again.* Looking deep into the hospital corridors with x-ray vision, she attunes herself to Addie. She locates an unpleasant buzz that feels like a distress signal. It's Addie's signal, she knows. It has to be. She feels her sister's desperation, but tries hard not to get trapped in it. She has learned her lesson. Just listen and follow, she tells herself. Listen and follow. *Bzzz bzzz bzzz. Bzzz*

bzzz bzzz. She picks up the rhythm of the buzz, and before she knows it, she's inside the hospital's Critical Care Unit looking down at disheveled old Mr. Barrows in the corridor talking to a man in a white coat with a stethoscope around his neck.

She hovers near the ceiling at a careful distance. Not that they would see her, but you never know. She checks to make sure the light has stayed below her ankles. So far so good. These new rules of engagement are a mystery. She doesn't know what she doesn't know. Everything is a lesson, and the consequences are unclear. The only consequence she's not prepared to accept is the loss of Addie.

"She lives alone," Barrows tells the doctor in a nervous, high-pitched tone. Baseball cap in hand, spare gray tufts of hair dot his scalp like clover. He shifts right foot to left, back and forth in a constant two-step shuffle. "Me and my wife, Inis, we clean-up 'round her. Bring her food ever' day," he says. "Inis draw her a bath ever' day. Help her in; help her out. Tries help her with her hair 'n such, ye know. Stays overnight at times. But lately she don't know who Inis is half the time. She's mostly confused, mean as a mink, 'n losing her mind by the minute." He rubs the thumbs and forefingers of both hands together repeatedly.

"I see," says the doctor. "And other than you, she's completely alone?"

"Might as well be," says Barrows. His bushy gray eyebrows twitch madly. "She got a cat just as bristly as her. Scratched me up good one time." Almost as an afterthought he adds, "She calls the cat Felicity after her late sister. When I visit, all's I hear is '*Felicity this*' 'n '*Felicity that.*'"

Felicity gasps, reflexively covering her mouth, though she realizes it's unlikely anyone could hear her. Barrows, at least, doesn't strike her as a man in possession of extrasensory gifts, but you never know.

"One time she go 'n throw a jelly roll at Inis on account of Inis dint shake the damn cat's paw," Barrows continues. "'That's my sister!' Miz Adelaide say to Inis. 'Y'all acknowledge my sister when you're in her presence. She deserves your respect!' Well, Inis won't offend a dead gnat, so she chase that feline all over the kitchen, callin' *Felicity! Felicity!* tryin' shake its paw, ye know. Make Miz Adelaide happy. That critter run straight out the house into the wild yonder, Inis right behind. Sprained her ankle, Inis did. Near 'bout broke her neck."

Barrows takes a deep breath. "Can't even check on her by phone, Doc. Keeps yankin' the cord out like she don't know what's it there fer. Can't teach her to use a cell phone neither. She's hopeless, I'm tellin' ye. Should of been in a home long time ago, but I couldn't git her on board. Couldn't git her to the dentist fer cryin' out loud."

The doctor frowns. "So, she never goes out?" he asks.

Barrows scratches his head. "She wanders off, yessir. Few times, I found her stumblin' through town on her way to some class, she say, up the barn with Felicity. But what's a cat doin' in school?" Barrows shakes his head. "Miz Adelaide say she hates the classes, but her sister won't let her cut. Felicity needs the company, she say. I just say, 'Yeah, yeah, yeah,'—no sense tryin' make sense of it. Ever' time's the same thang. Me 'n m' son, Reginald, we pick her up in the truck when we see her. She tells us it ain't a truck, it's a bus fulla crazy people, 'n neither one a us knows how to drive it. We're a danger to society, she say. We should take drivin' lessons. Git a license, she say, like we ain't got 'em already.

"Jes to keep her calm, we drive her wherever she say the classes are, usually that barn built into the hill outside town. Ye know that barn, Doc? It's hidden. But not always the barn, sometimes downstairs the library we go. Sometimes the ole mine. We wait while she gits out, looks 'round. Mumbles to herself. Me and Reggie, we can't make nothin' out. When she's done, we drop her back the house, help her on up the stairs. Soon's she's inside, she looks back out the screen door like we a pair of polka dot wort hogs shot out the tail of a comet. 'What all y'all's doin' at my house this hour?' she say all the sudden."

The doctor pulls absently on his stethoscope, sighing heavily. "Ok, well if she makes it through this episode, we'll have to find her a home somewhere. There might be a place in *The Gulch*. I could try to pull some strings."

"I owe the family," says Barrows. "If *The Gulch* won't have her, Inis and me, we'll take her in, gawd help us." He blesses himself three times in rapid succession as if to ward off the curse of his offer. "*The Gulch* is a better bet though, trust me. Inis and I gittin' old ourselfs."

Felicity's becoming agitated. From what she remembers, *The Gulch* is a nearly abandoned institution for old, discarded people without teeth or brains. Addie still has her teeth; she would hate it there.

The doctor thanks Barrows who says he'll stop by tomorrow to see if there's anything else he can do. Felicity had no idea how loyal Barrows really was, in spite of his resentment—catering to Addie the way he has and all. How had they taken his frequent comings and goings for granted? Still. Whether Addie ends up at *The Gulch* or living with Barrows and Inis, the result would be the same. Addie living anywhere but *Sunnyside Up* puts Felicity right out of the picture. There would be no communication between them with a bunch of flesh and bone people walking around listening in on every conversation. Convincing Addie she was talking to ghosts. Medicating her to block her so-called delusions. If Addie were removed from *Sunnyside Up*, she would likely be too confused to ever see the light and reckon her past. *To save herself!* And beyond Addie, what would happen to their homestead? To Granny and Pothead and the rest? Who would tend their gravestones? Polish their trinkets? Tell their stories? Would their entire history be lost?

Still unsure of barriers like walls and doors, Felicity waits for the doctor to open the door to Addie's room, and glides right in alongside him. What she sees makes her gasp all over again. Not just Addie, who lies motionless under a tent, tubes running up her arms and legs and down her throat. Horrifying as that is, the most shocking thing is Thaddeus, suited-up in his familiar tweed ensemble, black bow-tie at the neck, sitting at the end of the hospital bed, derby in hand. She is shocked by the force of her reaction. Why, the nerve of that old man!

"What are you doing here?" she says.

He blinks.

She tries again. "You know very well that if it weren't for y'all driving through our private property at night, Addie would never have fallen out that window and landed in this horrible place," she says. "Just look at her! It's all y'all's fault, and you darn well know it." Her blood is hot and getting hotter. It's like she's channeling Addie. She can't remember the last time she felt this mad. If ever. All she can think is that this man is a wildcard whose recklessness could change Addie's eternal destiny, and in so doing, Felicity's destiny as well. What does he want?!

Thaddeus tilts his head as if he hears something, then reaches into his ear and adjusts a small device. Well, he must hear something, she thinks. For the first time she notices what a wrinkly old codger he is, and older than he should be, considering. Oh, who knows how old anybody is anymore? This whole thing about living outside of time is throwing her completely off.

The doctor who's been examining Addie under the tent,

slips outside of it and nods at Thaddeus. "Are you the husband?" he asks sympathetically.

Thaddeus adjusts his spectacles and shakes his head, no. "She never married," he says quietly.

"So...you're what? A brother?"

He shakes his shiny bald head again, "No sir," he says, standing. "Just a ole friend is all. And, em, well...landlord of sorts."

"So, you own the house she lives in?"

He weighs his words. "Ye could say that."

At this, Felicity's vision blurs and she falls from the ceiling with a thud. *What?????!!!!* Thaddeus owns *Sunnyside Up?!* Weightless as she is, the tumble leaves her entire body sore and disoriented. Death isn't all it's cracked up to be, evidently. Signals break up; energy gets distorted. It's just pain of a different frequency.

While Felicity scrambles to recover, Thaddeus is looking up, down, and all around like he just heard something drop from the ceiling with a thud.

"Are you here collecting rent?" says the doctor suspiciously. "Can't be collecting rent in my ICU."

"No sir," says Thaddeus. "Jes dropt by make sure she's okay." He swallows a lump of words and coughs them back up with phlegm. "Saw the ambulance 'n followed it on over is all." He reaches into his pocket for a handkerchief and wipes his mouth.

"Only relatives allowed in my ICU," says the doctor. He twitches his lips. "Though she doesn't seem to have any."

"None livin'," says Thaddeus, spinning the derby in his hands. "She ain't been right fer..." he lowers his head, "too many years to count. I try to help, but she don't recognize me." He shrugs. "I pay the caretaker 'n his wife to bring provisions fer her 'n her cat." He shrugs. "Cook, clean. Personals, too, lately—she's absent-minded 'bout that. House 'n property, too."

The doctor nods. "Well, I guess it won't do much harm to have you visit then. Looking after her like that."

"Thanks, doc."

The doctor wags his finger threateningly. "But no collecting rent!"

"No sir," says Thaddeus quietly. "Okay then. See y'all tomorrow." He shuffles out the room, head low.

Once Thaddeus leaves, Felicity quick slips under the oxygen tent and kisses Addie's forehead. "I'm here," she whispers. "Anytime you need me, just think of me and I'll be right here." She doesn't linger as she does not want to startle Addie awake. Addie needs her rest. She needs to heal. Not to mention that Felicity has to catch up to Thaddeus before he has a chance to escape. *Where does he come from? What does he want?* Felicity aims to find out.

She spots him in the lobby, raises her arms, and glides behind him at a safe distance. He will not get away from her, no. He won't. Felicity will solve the mystery of this conniving interloper once and for all. What does he know about Addie and Felicity? *And Julian?* To unnerve him the slightest bit, she lowers herself discreetly and blows on his shiny head as he rushes through the hospital's revolving door into the still autumn day.

Invisibility is a lonely affair.

TWENTY-TWO

FELICITY

S truggling through the stubborn revolving doors of the hospital lobby, Thaddeus exits into a whirling wind tunnel. Felicity watches as he carefully sets his cane against a nook in the red brick exterior and catches his breath. Head erect, he grabs the rim of his derby firmly with both hands and yanks it down almost to his ears. He buttons his tweed jacket to the neck, retrieves his cane, and proceeds uncertainly through the parking lot. Felicity follows closely.

Thinking about what he's said and what he's done, she doesn't care about protecting her invisibility anymore. She hardly recognizes her rage. It's as if it comes from the outside in. From her border world. *From Addie.* The man stole *Sunnyside Up* right out from under their vintage tea set! How long had he been waiting for just the right moment? Did Addie forget to pay the taxes? Did he steal a bill from their mailbox and tear it up? Commit forgery? Take out a mortgage? How dare he take advantage of two doddering old women like that! Well, really one doddering old woman, which is even worse.

As she follows him through the parking lot, Felicity whips up a mighty froth of righteous rage against this unconscionable thug on account of Addie. On account of Addie not being able to defend herself. How dare this no-good carpet-bagging scallywag rob them of their livelihood! Their entire legacy! *Who is he?* How long has he owned their property? Was it even for sale? Certainly not that Felicity knew, or Addie let on. Or Granny. Or Pothead. Or even Mother, who would most certainly have come unglued by such a development. Then again, since her death, Mother's agenda has certainly changed significantly if not entirely, leaving only Felicity to seek justice. And she will seek justice; she must. She has to find a way to get *Sunnyside Up* back before Addie discovers the theft and loses her mind all over again. Addie is no one without *Sunnyside Up.* Neither is Felicity, if she's honest. In spite of its ancestral challenges, it's the backdrop of her entire physical existence, not to mention her death up to this point. How can a complete stranger rob her and her family of all that?

This in mind, her agitation gets the best of her. She glides close enough to Thaddeus to spark static in the narrow field between them. The discordance is uncomfortable, but she doesn't care. She can deal with the friction, but can he? She backs up and moves in again. And again. She is scorched with static, but all he does is rub his left ear and keep going. Nothing stops him. She moves in again, even closer, snapping, *"who are you?"*, whirling like a dervish at his front, back and sides. She wants to throw him off balance. Confuse him into tendering a confession. *"Whoooo are youuuu?!!"*

He blocks his ear with his left hand, and picks up his pace. She is not getting through to him. She inhales deeply, gathering steam, then screams at the top of her lungs, permeating all the filters of all the layers of all the planes between them. "And why are you stalking my sisterrrrr?"

At this, Thaddeus stops abruptly. He tugs the lobe of his left ear and frantically scans his surroundings. She knows he hears her. Senses her presence. Feels the friction! She will persist until she finds answers. For Addie's sake! Her lips practically inside his ear drum now, she buzzes, "Whooooo are you, old man?" like a hive of killer bees.

He removes his derby, swatting his ear. "Why I'm...I'm Thaddeus," he says hesitantly, as if he can't believe he's talking to himself.

"Well, Thaddeus, why are you bothering Addie? Hmmm? Addie didn't even know Julian had a Cousin Thaddeus. Or Uncle, which is it?" She flits around to his right ear. "And how did you manage to steal her inheritance? And not just her inheritance, but our family's entire ancestral history?" She blows on his bald head until he shudders, replacing his hat. "And why?" she adds. "Why?"

The old man grips his cane tightly and restarts his journey at an impressive clip. His right leg increasingly rounds at the hip socket in an exaggerated limp as he struggles to escape Felicity's torture. She thinks he's talking out loud until she realizes his lips aren't moving. She's reading his mind.

Git me outta here. Somethin's wrong. Somethin's very, very wrong, yessir. Yes, it is. No question. Gotta go. Gotta git outta here now.

"Who are you really?" she says in the lowest growl she can conjure. *Who are you? Who are you? Who. Are. You?!!*

At this, the old man stops in his tracks, looks around then pokes his cane into the air, jabbing left, right, and center until it lands directly at Felicity's abdomen. "Who's thar?" he says aloud. "Someone thar? Leave me alone, dangit!" He pulls his glasses off and wipes them against his jacket, returns them to his eyes and peers through them, squinting.

Does he see her? He sees something.

But maybe not. He limps another 100 feet along the patched asphalt, stopping at the classic 1940 buttercream convertible he stole from his dead cousin. He unlocks the door, turns around and drops backwards into the driver's seat. Slowly lifting one leg inside and then the other, he pulls the door closed and lays his head against the wheel, panting. Hand to chest, he remains in this position until his breathing normalizes.

Felicity feels no pity for his obvious physical handicaps. He's lucky to have a body at all, is what she thinks. A body that can eat and drink and pretend to be somebody it's not. A body that can steal other people's property, not that he'll get away with it. Not if she can help it. She'll track him day and night until she gets some answers, yes, she will. She just prays Addie doesn't need her in the meantime. Life is tricky enough right now without figuring out how to be in two places at once.

"When you need to multi-locate, you will," Phipps once told her. "All you have to do is give 100% of your attention to all locations at the same time."

Wait. *What?*

Felicity hoped this math would make more sense to her when the time came, but it didn't then and it doesn't now. Not that she's a math genius, but maybe that's the problem. She's still trying to solve an infinite equation with finite math using the Earth brain she deserted some time ago. It doesn't add up.

Once Thaddeus is in the car, Felicity knows she's supposed to glide alongside him to get where she wants, if not spontaneously appear wherever her intentions take her. But all this new movement is taking its toll. Her mental body is downright exhausted, its energy leaking like a punctured balloon, tiny little pinhole dots all over the membrane. She can see the leaks! On top of that, the sight and proximity of Julian's car creates an inexplicable storm within her that surges head to toe, taxing her mental body even further. Why in the wide world the Chrysler has this kind of impact on her, she can't say. Maybe because it's been a very long time since she's driven in the old heap? Well, not so much a heap anymore as a first-class vintage vehicle, it's true. Which makes it all the more tantalizing to take a deep breath, relax, and reconsider. Put her resentment aside for a minute, and give herself a break. Hop right on in. For old time sake. For Addie.

She rises above the door, and once inside, slowly settles into the butter soft leather of the front passenger seat, nearly purring. *Mmmmmm!* She grins with pleasure in spite of the fact that she's seated alongside a thief. Not only a thief of *Sunnyside Up,* she reminds herself, but a car thief as well. Because if anyone has a right to this vehicle, it's Addie. Whether she was ever able to drive it or not is irrelevant. Barrows could have been chauffeuring her all this time. Felicity's quite sure Barrows would have enjoyed driving a convertible quite a lot more than driving his beat-up old jalopy of a psychedelic milk truck. Especially since, as far as she can remember, he stopped delivering milk to everyone but Addie when the Piggly Wiggly opened years ago.

Traveling up and down the crayola patchwork of autumn

hills and dales, Felicity's heart trembles with nostalgia just before it busts wide open. She feels like she's moving through a time warp that whitewashes her with hope, generously returning her to a brief youth she barely remembers. A cool easterly wind ripples through her long silky hair, waving it like a pennant behind her.

As she shields her eyes from the glare of the low sun, she notices her leather-gloved hands, and does a doubletake. Why, these are the coveted gloves Addie ordered all by herself from the fat Montgomery Ward Catalogue the first year after high school when she apprenticed at *Sunnyside Up*. How proud Addie was of these gloves! How she showed them off everywhere! So, what are they doing on Felicity's hands? And wouldn't Addie just kill her if she knew? An adolescent thrill runs up Felicity's spine just thinking about it. Clearly, she's not as innocent as she remembers. But then again, they're just gloves.

She clasps her exquisitely gloved hands tightly in her lap, resting them against the sweater-coat Addie knitted a few years back. Another great borrow, apparently. The lovely wide-cable knit is made of opal mohair with a shawl collar that shows off Felicity's slim neck and ivory complexion. Peeking under the coat, she's relieved to see Aunt Lillian's silky wildflower dress, Felicity's favorite, even though it's more of a summer frock. But, so what? She was never one to care about seasonal fashion rules anyway. And now that she's dead, she cares even less. She'll wear anything she can conjure any time, no matter the season or expense. Although it seems to her there's a particular reason, however mysterious, that she's wearing this dress right now, right here. It's not like she chose it. It just happened! Not to mention these borrowed gloves and sweater coat. But she doesn't know what the reason is. She can't get to it. It feels more like a trick than a memory.

The further they get from the hospital, the more relaxed Thaddeus gets, until eventually he starts whistling something reminiscent of *"Oh, ma darlin', oh ma darlin', oh ma darlin' Clementine..."* Even though it's embarrassingly off-key, something about it lifts Felicity spirits. Reminds her of something good. She glances expectantly from his saggy profile to the powder blue sky to her floral-clothed lap and down to the expertly carpeted buttercream floor of her luxury ride. What does it all mean? she wonders.

Her narrow feet wiggle in the pearly white patent leather sandals that she most certainly also borrowed from someone. Mother would never have allowed her to wear these shoes, even though many of the girls Felicity's age in the holler are already married and wear whatever they please. Not that Felicity is allowed to consort with those girls; she isn't. Lawd forbid she should be influenced by their hand-me-downs or, in Mother's words, "...their predictable list of ignorant choices." There are no fashion rules in the holler, it's true. Life is harder than that down there. But as Mother always reminds her, Felicity was not raised in the holler. Mother, however, was. Though no one dared mention it.

She flips down the visor, startling Thaddeus, which nearly causes another accident as he veers off-road, braking inches short of a massive bur oak. Felicity wishes he would calm down. She only flipped the visor to look in the mirror, is all. It's been ages since she's had a look at herself. And since she feels so youthful, she wants to see if all this vitality is reflected in her face. *She wants to remember!* In a selfish way, she wishes Thaddeus could admire her, too. Or anyone! Invisibility has its advantages, but it's a lonely affair.

They wind down a steep hairpin into a deep, familiar holler. Felicity's belly jumps with recognition, though she can't pin it down. Something familiar that only her belly recalls. Or maybe not so much familiar as long-anticipated. She doesn't know which. The brakes squeak and squeal as they curve down the rocky road, which she notices has no large stones or fencing on the periphery to break a fall. She would certainly not want to be riding down this road in a storm, she thinks. Or sitting beside a wild driver. She'd best keep still for now.

At the end of the road, the landscape flattens into a broad valley that terminates at a small cabin, its side yard bursting with old barrels, broken machinery, and three-legged chairs. Thaddeus pulls right up to the rickety porch and turns the key. The engine stutters briefly before surrendering fully to the robust treble of warblers and wood thrush and the distant bass of threatening thunder.

It takes Thaddeus forever to open the car door, move his ancient body around and up, and close the door behind him. Felicity rises out of her seat and into the yard, watching as he opens the trunk, retrieves a canvas tarp, covers the car right to the ground, and weighs the corners down with cement blocks. Seemingly satisfied, he hobbles down the cracked cement path with Felicity in tow. Best not to get ahead of herself here. He seems to tune into her signal naturally, and after all, wasn't he present at every one of Julian's aborted funerals? And once there, didn't he stare at her good and hard? Or maybe it was just a blank stare, hard to tell. It was before she knew she was dead. She remembers handing him a program. She remembers locking eyes with him as he took the program in his hand. And didn't he say hello to her once in the yard? Or at least wave? Good grief, the man waved to a ghost. As far as she can tell, he's no spiritual rookie. So why doesn't he see her now?

"Because you don't want him to," says a voice in her ear that sounds like Phipps.

"Now that you're awake you have a different vibration," says Dr. Joy. *"He has to adjust his vision to see you."*

Up the cement steps he limps, Felicity at his heels. He the decrepit codger, she the honey-haired youthful innocent in the dazzling silk dress and sandals. The turmoil in her belly persists, but why? What possible danger could she be in? She can leave whenever she wants. She's an invisible specter with magical powers who can supposedly project herself anywhere, as long as she can concentrate. Why should she be afraid of a stodgy old man who isn't even dead? Whose perimeters are solid and predictably slow-moving? Maybe she just doesn't trust him. Or maybe he has powers too.

Inside, she backs into a corner of the dingy mudroom, watching as he rests his cane against the wall and sits on the bench to untie his polished leather shoes. He removes them one after the other, pushing his feet into a pair of worn moccasins. After hanging his tweed jacket on a hook, he reclaims his cane and taps his way through the dimly lit hall up a small cement stoop into what appears to be the living space. As they enter the dark, low-ceilinged room, she catches a permeating acrid odor she can't quite place. Burnt wood, perhaps. Dampened by rain.

After a bit, he feels the wall for the chain of a sconce which he yanks. A low light illuminates the space, and further down he lights another sconce, and another. By the time the third is lit, her hand flies to her mouth to squelch a scream or any other indication of her presence. But how will she manage to contain her surprise? The walls on either side of the narrow hallway feature pictures of her, Felicity. Pictures of Felicity in the same dress she's wearing now. Swinging from the low branch of the bur oak whose much broader trunk they nearly ran into earlier. Stretched out on the rusty, pocked hood of

Julian's beat-up convertible, grinning. Another from the back, her voluminous gold curls flying recklessly in the air, her head turned to the side, chin tucked flirtatiously into her shoulder. From the looks of her clothing and the chalk blue sky beyond, it was all photographed on the same day.

She is stunned. Who took these pictures? *Is this really her? It must be.* But how did Thaddeus get them? *Does Addie know about them?*

More than stunned, her belly roils with a deep sense of betrayal which she isn't sure springs from her own spirit or from Addie's spirit in her border world. Is she channeling Addie this time, or is the outrage her own? All she knows is she has to leave. She lifts her arms, and just as she begins to glide, the old man leans reverently over a small dish, lighting a chunk of frankincense, which he gently blows until it smokes.

She hesitates, transfixed, as he touches the photo where her chin nestles her neck. Slowly, he traces the outline of her shoulders, her hair, and the curve of her back. Then, head down, he wanders slowly through the corridor and out of sight.

TWENTY-THREE

ADELAIDE

Adelaide can't bring herself to climb out of the casket, but why should she? She's never felt better. She shimmies deeper into the lush satin bed as blood-red rose petals float from the ceiling, surrounding her in a benediction of fragrance. She is peaceful, yet somehow filled with anticipation.

If this is death, bring it on.

After all the time she's spent overseeing the eternal runway—the painstaking selection of scripture, hairstyles, makeup, jewelry, and wardrobe—she wonders how she ever missed this fundamental truth. That outside the casket, life makes sense. Haircuts make sense. Makeup makes sense. Ice cream sundaes make complete sense. Outside the casket, people age predictably from short to tall, small to large, young to old. Outside the casket, Adelaide, like most people, has progressed from a helpless infant to the arthritic old snapping turtle she is today—irritated by all and loved only by Felicity. Inside the casket, however, she is neither old nor arthritic, and is in fact rapidly reverting to a version of herself she genuinely enjoyed.

The twenty-one-year-old version. At least she feels twenty-one. She sits up to verify.

Oh yes, she is definitely twenty-one! Only a twenty-something could be the proud custodian of the long, slim, supple-skinned, curvaceous legs stretched out in front of her right now. Not to mention the thick, loose, shiny waist-length raven hair draped across her shoulders. And just the strength of the sturdy abdominal muscles that allow her to sit up so effortlessly in the first place. Outside the casket she is lifeless. Inside, she is life itself.

She raises herself at the waist and reclines back down several times to reinforce the experience. To prove she's strong enough to do more than one sit-up. Up and down she goes, up and down, convincing herself it's really real. *It really is!* Or at least it appears to be real. She folds her arms easily across her perky bosom and clasps her long piano fingers right on top, a simple act she hasn't been able to execute in as long as she can remember because of the great, aging mounds of mammary girth that prevented it. She's surprised she remembers how. Just bring your hands together like so. And clasp. Easy! So easy.

If only she could begin again, she thinks. Start right over right now at the age of twenty-one. Just swing out of this magic casket on springy knees. Land on a pair of strong, bare, bunionless feet against the cold stone floor without ripping tendons or fracturing bones. Without flat out crippling herself. And after that, run right out and greet Julian in a wild embrace at the end of the gravel drive. No one the wiser.

Just Adelaide and Jules. No parents. No rules. Just the two of them escaping in his dilapidated Chrysler without a care in the wide world. Without a care for his social status, or lack thereof. Without a care for Mother's consent or Granny's. For Adelaide's obligations at *Sunnyside Up* or his obligations at the mine. For Felicity's irritating clinginess or the disingenuous sulking that inevitably got her handed off to Adelaide at the most inconvenient times. That is, just when Adelaide had arranged to sneak off with Julian. *Every. Single. Time.* As if Felicity were Adelaide's child. As if Adelaide were responsible for her sister's gawky adolescent petulance in the first place. As if Adelaide should be putting Felicity's happiness before her own just because Felicity was a few years younger. Not to mention wacky and unstable, which is putting it mildly.

Lying here in the coffin now, Adelaide stares up at the old oak beams of the pitched ceiling at the same time she wiggles deeper into the cushiony layers. It's amazing to lie in a sumptuous bed of white satin like this! Why has she never done it before? What's wrong with her? Like Sleeping Beauty, she closes her luxurious Maybelline-lashed lids, and before she can remember her name or where she was born, she's whisked through some sort of super-charged pneumatic tube like the one she saw at a bank in Louisville that time, right to...

Good grief, where is she? What's going on?

Why, it looks like...

In what feels alternately like the length of a morning or a lifetime, the world has sucked her up and spit her out plop in the middle of *Sunnyside Up*. In the family graveyard, of all dang places. At least she's above ground. But after all that glorious daydreaming about youth and life, the graveyard isn't exactly where she dreamed of landing. Then again, why should she be different than everyone else? After all, wasn't she just lying in a coffin? Next logical step is a graveyard, right? Not that she's dead, or even planning to be dead. She isn't. *Or is she?* More likely she's here to do her job—to manage the business of someone else's demise. *But whose?*

When the sun stops spinning a salad of amber hayfields, rust-red barn silos, and whatever else the wizard tossed into this tornado, she finds herself standing upright in a refreshing autumn breeze that surprises her. After all, it was springtime last she checked. Wasn't it? But just now, tiny little whorls of crackling gold and crimson leaves swirl at her ankles. The clean, crisp air against her face incites unexpected euphoria, and she has to force herself not to grin. Grinning is painful for Adelaide, as it always has been. Although she can't remember when that became true or why. Maybe when she started caring for Felicity after the accident? Yes, that must be it. After all, as much as she loves her sister, nothing about Felicity's unhinged behavior has ever been the least bit easy.

Rubbing her hands briskly together for warmth, twenty-one-year-old Adelaide wanders up the gravel path, curiosity piqued. The graveyard with all its quirky paraphernalia is laid out before her like an Alfred Hitchcock movie set. Why had she never noticed how spooky it was before? The feathery willow branches tickle the edges of Granny McManis' stone in the breeze, and all Adelaide can think is how much Granny would hate that. No one despised all those icky willow bugs more than Granny did. Adelaide's skin crawls just thinking about how irritated Granny would be. At the same time she knows she should trim those willow branches, she knows she never will.

Just accept it, she tells herself. Stop trying to change things all the time. Stop trying to make things right for everybody. All it ends up doing is making Adelaide miserable. It's not like Granny knows the gawdforsaken difference. *She's dead!* Dead is dead; isn't it? Minus the magic casket she's in right now, that is. Other than that, there's no coming back from death.

Wandering slowly up the gentle incline to the rundown picket fence she never got around to repairing, or rather, Barrows never got around to repairing, Adelaide spots something puzzling in the distance. She steps a little closer. *What's that?!* Well, if it doesn't look like a dang six-foot hole, she thinks. Fresh dug, at that. She can smell the loamy soil. There's only one explanation for a hole this size in a graveyard, she knows. Someone somewhere dropped dead. Someone familiar, since it's a local graveyard. Or at least a selective one. After all, Mother did make exceptions—like Sheriff Gibbs and his whole weird family. Why she allowed that bumpkin in is a mystery they'll solve right after they catch the Loch Ness Monster. But as far as Adelaide knows, no one around here's died in a while. At least no one she cared about. And then it hits her.

Julian.

She makes her way slowly up the path, thinking the hole must be for her beloved. And although this thought squeezes her lungs like an accordion, she doesn't scream or go entirely berserk as she has in the past. She doesn't fall apart, storm the heavens as she has all the times she tried to bury him from outside the casket. Right now, she isn't outside. She's inside. The inside affords her an entirely different perspective. She sees things differently in here. From inside the casket her gasps don't spring from grief, but from what actually feels a lot like...*relief.* How surprising. Relief is something she hasn't felt in a dog's age. Here she is burying the man she loves, and all she can think is—it's about damn time. The nightmare that has haunted her entire life will soon be over. Julian will be buried.

And Adelaide will be able to move on.

It occurs to her that perhaps she crawled into the coffin and regressed in years specifically to do this deed at the very time it should have been done in the first place. How about that? Wouldn't Dr. Joy be proud of her for figuring this out? And really, who needs a therapist when you can just lie in a coffin and travel back in time to complete a karmic task? She feels so dolgarn good about all this she's actually motivated to execute the burial even though Felicity isn't present. After all, maybe Felicity isn't present for a reason. Maybe Adelaide's been waiting this whole time for Felicity to disappear. Maybe Felicity's the one who's been holding Adelaide back all along, and not the reverse.

It's all beginning to make sense.

It was Felicity, not Adelaide, who couldn't bury Julian. Felicity could have helped Adelaide bury him if she'd wanted to. She could have even done it all by herself, considering the obvious emotional toll the task would extract from Adelaide, the almost-widow. Felicity could have made it easier, but she didn't. She made it harder. *But why?*

All at once a gummy lump the size of God's honest truth forms in Adelaide's throat. Felicity made it harder to bury Julian because Felicity loved him too. At least this is what Adelaide's heart is whispering to her right now. This is the feeling bubbling up. And it's not a good feeling. It's a sickening feeling, in fact. A feeling of betrayal. A feeling Adelaide would rather not feel at all. *Where did it come from?* But the thought and the feeling keep hammering at her, and she can't ignore it. It's relentless. Felicity loved Julian. Felicity loved Julian.

And Julian loved her.

The bastard.

Adelaide stops to acknowledge this excruciating moment of unrelenting honesty with a keening cry of grief and rage, "*Aaaaaaaaaaaaaa!!!!!!!!!!!!*" she wails. "Aaaaaaaaaaaaaaa!!!!!!!"

The wail echoes on and on and on, reverberating through time. "When will it end?"

"*When you forgive your sister,*" calls a familiar voice from the bottom of somewhere deep and distant like the Gorge.

Adelaide nods in recognition. *Aha!* So, this is the carnivorous truth that's been devouring my broken heart all these years. Julian did not love me. At least not as much as he loved Felicity. Or as much as I loved him. *Well, screw him!* This time Adelaide won't back off. This time she'll bury the two-timing turd on his head if she has to. She'll commit him to the slime from whence he rose. He will not escape from this betrayal no way, no how. She is so done with this. So very, very, *very* done.

Shielding her eyes from the glare of the low autumn sun, she looks around and spots the glimmer of tarnished metal by the back fence. She stares at it until the shape makes sense. A shovel! As she marches resolutely toward it, she spots a pair of work boots caked with mud standing behind it. Work boots leading to denim britches leading to...*good gravy!* If it isn't Julian T. Buck himself!

Staring at him now after missing him all these decades, her rage diminishes from boil to simmer in an instant. Hands on hips, she shakes her head, "Would you just look at that man," she mutters to herself. *Lawdy lawd!* She hasn't seen him in so long, she barely remembers how solid he was. How freaking handsome with that Viking jaw and scandalous Cherokee cheekbones. That pile of shiny sable hair. *Those eyes—each its own deep sea of obsidian.* She would gladly dive in if only she could remember how to keep from drowning. But she's no lifeguard. She never even learned to float.

Back in the day he seemed like a giant to her, a regular Paul Bunyan. She sees now that he isn't as tall as she remembered, though what he lacks in height he surely makes up for in muscle. In spite of herself, she smiles a wide, toothy grin. She's speechless! The man's a Roman deity. How is she expected to resist? A Roman deity whose perfect features could turn Shakespeare into a blathering idiot. Just rip the poetry right out of his driveling brain. "To be or not to...*what?*"

Adelaide rubs her eyes to make sure he's not a mirage, then reopens them only to see him standing there like he never left. Like all this time he's just been waiting to wrestle with her in the hay—*what took y'all so long, Adelaide?* Just standing right there in his old Wrangler dungarees, a blue flannel shirt half-tucked, a jaunty cap atop his messy crown of soft curls. His perfectly straight ivory teeth sparkling in the sunlight, melting faeries in the dew left and right.

"Well, hell," he says, "it's about time y'all showed up, now ain't it?"

Glancing down timidly, she sees she's wearing the same flouncy fern green skirt and white lace peasant blouse she was wearing that day...*what day was it?* She narrows her eyes, thinking hard because she wants to remember every last detail. *Oh. Right.* Why it was the last day she saw him, she believes. The day she thought she was getting engaged. The day they went for a ride in the Chrysler over by the Gorge. She tilts her head, frowning. She wants to remember, but really, who has time to think about a dumb gorge right now? Her brain is a fiery volcano spitting passion like molten lava.

Slowly, she approaches him. At first, she feels so buoyant she might just rise like a hot air balloon right into the clouds before she can get to him. Just rise right up into the crisp, clean air and vanish into the sky, empty arms outstretched like a risen saint. But the image of the buoyant balloon explodes in a deadly blast as she recalls she's not here to mingle with this deity in a hayloft, or even to admire him from a distance. She's here to cover him with dirt.

They meet up beside the hole.

"Been diggin' fer days," he says, sweat dripping from his temples. "M'nephew before me." He pitches the spear end of the shovel into the pile of soil at the base of the gravesite, and leans against the handle. Removing his cap, he says, "I'm so sorry, Adelaide. Honest to gawd. But we both know who's responsible fer this here tragedy, 'n it ain't me."

"Isn't," she corrects him. "Isn't me."

He shakes his head. "What?"

"Never mind."

It wunt of worked out anyways," he says. "Y'all know we wasn't suited fer ch'other."

"Weren't," she snaps. "Weren't suited." She raises her faux patrician chin in the uppity manner of her mother. *Why is she becoming her mother? She hated her mother!* "And anyway, what are you insinuating, Jules? That I was responsible?" She reaches out and jerks the pole of the shovel from his hand. "And by the way, responsible for what?"

He jerks the shovel back.

She lunges forward again and yanks it from his hand. He regains possession, and so forth and so on in a tiresome tug of turf war.

"Whatcha doin'?" he finally says. "Fer gawd sake, Addie, I got to bury her. I owe her that much, as do you."

Adelaide flinches. "*Her?*" she says. "What?"

He nods emphatically. "Yeah, Addie. *Her.*"

Adelaide jams her fists into her hips, leans forward and narrows her eyes. "Oh, no you don't," she says. "Y'all are not faking me out. Not again. The only one getting buried here is you, and it's about dang time."

She jumps to the other side of him and tries to push him into the hole. He ducks under her arm and swings around, grabbing her by the wrists.

"What in the jiminy ye doin'?" he says. "Y'all can't bury me! I'm alive, dang it!"

"If only that were true," she says, and reaches behind her for the fallen shovel. What does she have to do to complete her Christian duty? Whack him upside the head and knock him into the freaking hole? Is that what she has to do for cripe sake? This is way harder than it should be. No wonder it's taken so long.

He shakes his head in wonderment. "Have y'all gone cuckoo, Adelaide Frances? I ain't the one dead. Look at me! I'm livin' 'n breathin' sure as I'm standin' here!"

Pointing at the hole, she says, "Get in there, Jules. Jump in. *Now!* I can't take much more of this crap. I've spent most of my sorry life trying to bury you, and I've about had it."

The next thing she knows, Julian pulls Felicity's limp body out of the thin air, places it gently into an intricately carved sarcophagus straight out of a museum in Egypt, and lays it all down on two boards across the six-foot hole before grabbing the end of a rope to lower it.

"What the bloody hell are you dooooiiiiiing!" she screeches till her throat nearly ruptures. "Don't you dare bury Flitty! Flitty's not dead! Flitty's all I've got! You're the dead one, Julian T. Buck! *You are! The dead one!* Stop messing with my head! Let my sister out of that fancy box!" She drops to her knees, distraught. Decimated.

And then, right through the sarcophagus, she hears Felicity say, "Don't worry, Addie! I'll be alright, I will. I won't leave y'all, I promise. In fact, you'll barely notice I'm gone, I swear."

What?

"No!" Adelaide rasps with her ruptured throat. She reaches for her sister, reaches so very far, and yet is unable to stop the casket from free-falling into the hole in the slowest motion she's ever witnessed. Slower than all these years she's suffered without Julian put together. Slower than her entire agonizing life. As she leans over the hole to get Flitty back to rectify this monumental mistake, she's pulled back. Off in the corner stands her steely-eyed mother, arms crossed, the expression on her broad face so sharp Addie has to back up a foot just to keep from getting harpooned.

"I have to take you somewhere," she says ominously.

"Oh no you don't," says Adelaide. "I have to bury Julian."

"That can wait," she says.

"No! No! I'm finally doing it…"

Mother grabs her, and *boom!*

Adelaide's the size of a humpback whale back in a bare hospital room, hot lights overhead, attendants bent over her arms, sticking her with needles and cold instruments. She's a mass of density, ancient as Deuteronomy, filled with confusion about her life—the lies and the truth of it. Where had she just gone? Hadn't Julian been there? Instead of the familiar longing though, this time her heart aches with an unsettling mixture of remorse, and…betrayal? But the betrayal is an illusion. It's unreal; it has to be. After all, Julian loved her. *He loved her!* They were to be joined in holy matrimony as soon as he proposed. *He was about to propose!*

"We have to move her to Lexington, I'm afraid," she hears someone tell someone else. "Her intracranial pressure is increasing. If we don't move her, we'll lose her."

She squirms and struggles. "NO!" she screams in her head. *Don't do it! Don't send me to Lexington! Felicity will never find me there!* Where's my sister? Someone please find Felicity! She's the only one who can stop this insanity. "The crazies are trying to bury me, Flitty," she cries out. "Bury me and bury you!"

Bury us alive.

TWENTY-FOUR

FELICITY

Felicity's spirit is so scattered, she barely knows where she is. She knows she's at Addie's bedside, but she also feels as if a piece of her is wandering around Thaddeus' junkyard wondering why he has pictures of her everywhere. At the very same time she's with Addie and Thaddeus, she's also sitting in a folding chair in the cavernous barn on the outskirts of Outskirt, watching Mrs. Phipps pace thoughtfully back and forth.

Death is exhausting.

She tries to gather herself into a focal point, but it's not easy. If bilocation is tricky, she thinks, try omni-location, or whatever it's called when you're everywhere at the same time. This new trick of being all over the place in a tumbleweed of time is difficult to manage, never mind master. Wherever her mind travels, her energy follows, even if it's in four places at once. It's too much. She has to figure out how to discipline her thoughts so she doesn't scatter herself across the universe like space dust and get lost in the process. After all, how many places can a person be at the same time and still remember why she's there?

Back in the barn in Outskirt, Phipps says, "Remember your lessons, Felicity! You have three bodies. Your physical body obscures your emotional body. Once you have surrendered your physical body, your emotional body is visible to anyone at the same energetic level or higher." She nods at Felicity. "Are you with me?"

Felicity's head is a pile of dried-up leaves in a wind storm. "Not really."

Phipps steps to the side and points at a diagram on the chalkboard beside her. "Your emotional body is a reflection of your mental/emotional health, which is a reflection of your attachments."

"So, it looks like Addie?"

"No," says Phipps. "It looks like you—your body template, only darker or lighter depending on the strength and force of your passions. Your fears and desires."

Felicity sits back thoughtfully. "Granny and Pothead still look like themselves," she says.

"Yes," says Phipps. "They have gained no ground. Their light is dim, and their focus is fixed. They identify with their material bodies, as you have for all these years. The truth is, they could appear any age they wish—15 or 50. Nothing in that realm is fixed unless you think it is, and time only has the influence you assign it."

As if to underscore the point, Felicity suddenly finds herself gliding through the back woods at Thaddeus' house, a little lost or maybe just confused. The roar of an engine startles her and she spins around, only to find her younger self stretched out on the hood of the Chrysler, laughing. That version of herself slides off the hood and pops easily into the front seat. Drops a tube of Addie's lipstick into Addie's raglan satchel and ties a colorful kerchief under her own neck.

Just as quickly, her thoughts return to the barn, and there she is back in the dim shadows, faint streaks of light leaking from the spaces between the roof slats. She wonders if she's moving too quickly. If her storm of unhinged thoughts and emotions are preventing her from focusing on staying low. She has to focus. *She has to!* If she can't, she'll lose everything she cares about. She'll lose Addie.

She leans down to peek under her thick socks to see if the light is still low. It's becoming such an effort to hide it she can barely stand the pressure. She stomps twice on each foot to shake it down, and once again for good measure.

"You don't have to hide your light here," says Phipps. "In fact, you can't."

"I can't?" Felicity nearly faints with relief. Permission from Phipps is all it takes for the pooled light at her ankles to shoot up the legs and torso of her lithe young body. She is electric. The unbridled light burns up and through her in the most inexplicably satisfying way. Up her chest to her shoulders and down her arms it spreads. She raises her arms and hands, astonished at their opalescence. "Why, this is…" She can barely speak. "…thrilling!" She blinks from the sunspots created by her own radiance. "The light is blinding!"

"In some places," says Phipps. "But you haven't checked your heart, Felicity. All that really matters is what you see when you look into your heart."

Felicity tucks her chin into her chest to view her heart, which looks okay except for a single black spot the size of a nail head. "Not too bad," she says. "Except for this speck." The more she concentrates on the speck, the more she feels it.

The more it hurts.

"Your third body is your body of thought," says Phipps, "otherwise known as your noetical body. It's eternal. Even a speck of darkness in your emotional body is enough to hide your eternal body, which will prevent you from ascending. Every mote of darkness must be released to manifest the kind of radiance you will require to survive the unimaginable intensity of the higher realms. The last speck is the hardest."

"But Celeste told me I was ready," says Felicity. "That I could go with her any time."

"It's true," says Phipps. "Just say the word, and you can release that darkness. You have control over your bondage. But willful bondage is the hardest to release."

Felicity trembles with agitation. "The Spirits told me if I lose my lower bodies, I'll lose my connection to Addie. I can't do that," she tells Phipps. "The speck will stay."

"Only if Adelaide dies without awareness," says Phipps. "And she's learning things now she couldn't learn before."

"How can she be learning? She's in a coma!"

"That's how."

Felicity can't process Phipps' comment because the speck in her heart suddenly consumes all her attention. It beats to its own discordant rhythm: *ba boom ba be boom ba be ba BOOM!* She lays her hand over it, feeling the increasing pressure. The escalating heat. "Ouch!" she blurts inadvertently, and all at once she realizes she can't tolerate the pain for long. "How long have I lived with this?" she asks.

"You tell me," says Phipps.

Confused, Felicity says, "But why hasn't it hurt me until now?"

"It has always hurt you," says Phipps. "But you attributed it to other irritants."

"Like what?"

"Like Uncle Stewart and Granny."

"Oh."

"But now you're aware of the true source."

It's a red-hot coal in her chest burning hotter by the minute. "It's an attachment?" she asks.

"All unresolved issues pin us to our border worlds," says Phipps. "We can't overlook anything. All must be resolved to ascend."

"Even a speck?" says Felicity.

"Can you live with the pain?" says Phipps. "For eternity?"

As much as Felicity would rather live with the pain than address wherever it came from, she knows she can't. "No," she says. "It's killing me."

"Well, then," says Phipps as she fades into the slate gray walls of the weathered barn. "You'll have to face it, won't you?"

If I knew you were coming,
I'd have baked the cake.

TWENTY-FIVE

ADELAIDE

Adelaide lies motionless on a lavish purple Edwardian chaise in Dr. Joy's office. How did she land in this office again? she wonders. Is life outside the coffin nothing but the same old crap on endless, nauseating repeat? Didn't she convince Joy she was above this hog-wash? She tries to escape, but she can't feel her arms, and her legs won't move.

"What do you value about yourself?" asks Joy in a no-nonsense manner.

"What kind of a question is that?" asks Adelaide.

Joy narrows her eyes. "The most important question of all."

Adelaide gazes up, as if there's a cheat sheet on the ceiling. "What do I value? About myself?"

"Yes, Adelaide, what are your qualities?"

Adelaide has to think. Hard. "Well, I guess you could say I'm solid?"

"Are you asking me or telling me?"

"I'm telling you," says Adelaide easily, since she feels like a pile of rocks right now. "I'm solid."

"Okay good. Solid. Anything else?"

Adelaide purses her lips. "Solid and hardworking," she says. "And reliable."

Dr. Joy nods. "Okay. And what about Felicity?"

"What about Felicity?"

"What are her attributes?"

"She...I don't know. Why don't you ask her? Why me?"

"To help you differentiate from your sister," says Joy. "To prepare you for independence."

"I already am independent," says Adelaide.

"You're not."

Adelaide huffs. "Felicity's the dependent one. Even she knows that."

"You're both dependent, Adelaide."

All Adelaide can think is: the world is afloat in psychobabble. But what's new about that? She employs every physical and mental effort she can think of to make herself get up and walk out, but nothing works. The only thing she can move are the features on her face, which are puckered with frustration.

Joy checks her watch. "I'm waiting," she says. "What are Felicity's attributes?"

"I don't know. Let me think." Adelaide scours her brain for answers. "She can be kind, I guess, but so can I. So that doesn't differentiate either one of us."

Joy's eyebrows rise so high they almost detach from her head. "You think of yourself as kind, Adelaide?"

Adelaide is affronted by Joy's surprise. "I've taken Felicity in, haven't I? Housed her. Fed her. Cared for her all these years. It hasn't been easy."

Joy settles back in her chair. "Okay then. What else about Felicity?"

Honestly, Adelaide can't think of a single thing. She just can't. How does one separate two long lives that are this enmeshed? Why, Felicity is the only one in the world who knows...who can understand what happens when... "Felicity and I are all mixed up," she blurts. "We're not a bunch of ingredients; we're a cake! Stop trying to separate us. Where is she going, anyway?"

"Angel's food or devil's food?" says Dr. Joy.

"What? Neither!"

"Okay then, what flavor?"

Adelaide blinks. "Banana. We're a banana cake."

"Uh huh, okay. Banana. That's something. And which ingredients do you contribute to this cake, Adelaide?"

Adelaide realizes her only way out is to answer. She wants out. She answers, "Flour."

Joy adjusts her position on the high ladderback chair. "Why flour?"

"I don't know. Flour holds the cake together, I suppose. Gives it weight. Shape."

"And Felicity? Which ingredients is she?"

"Isn't it obvious? Bananas!"

Ignoring the inference, Joy says, "Flavor then. Felicity provides flavor."

Adelaide sighs. "Sure. Why not? Felicity provides flavor."

"And maybe a little baking powder, hmmm? Or soda?"

"That's about right," says Adelaide. "A few scant teaspoons to the cupsful of flour I supply."

Joy makes a notation on her pad. "Flour is important, Adelaide," she says. "But what good is a cake that has no flavor and doesn't rise?"

"This is ridiculous!"

Dr. Joy taps her fingers on the armrest. "I know it makes you uncomfortable, but why is it ridiculous?"

"Because we're not really a cake! We're people!" She sighs long and slow. "And anyway, if we were a cake, we'd be half-baked."

Joy leans forward, pointing her pen at Adelaide. "Which is why I'm about to turn on the heat." She promptly stands, reaches into her pocket and produces a brilliant crystal pendant that she swings seductively back and forth. *Left, right. Right, left.* And repeat. This little trinket generates scorching heat.

"Open your eyes, Adelaide," she commands. "Look at the crystal."

Adelaide doesn't want to look. She won't be drawn in again. She just won't. Her only recourse, however, is to roll her eyes so far back she can barely see the periwinkle glint of the crystal as it swings left. But on the return sweep, it catches the rays of the mango sun through the skylight and explodes into a million fractals of unimaginable color all over the room. The scope and intensity are irresistible. One look and it's over.

One look and she's sitting in the passenger seat of Julian's convertible, top down, on the finest autumn day she's ever known. Her shiny hair flies gleefully around her face. She grabs a thick handful of it and holds it in her fist. She doesn't want it to knot up. She wants Julian to run his fingers through it later when he asks her to marry him.

"You okay back there?" Julian calls out.

Adelaide thinks, huh? *Who's back there?*

"Right as a stuffed turkey on Thanksgiving!" calls a squeaky voice from behind.

Adelaide whips around. *Good gravy, what is she doing here!*

Oh yeah, right. Mother and Daddy left for a wedding in Bush Hill, making Adelaide promise to take Felicity with her to Penelope Wiggins' fake shower.

"You'll have fun," Mother demanded in her sour manner, which made it sound like no fun at all. As if taking Felicity anywhere could be fun in the first place. As if it weren't the lamest, least fun idea in the universe. How will Jules ever ask her to marry him with a big whiney baby in the backseat? Which was probably the point.

"Felicity's not invited," Adelaide told her mother.

"Well, then I'll call Penelope myself and ask her," Mother said slyly, like she knew it was all a sham to begin with.

Adelaide huffed. "Fine. She can come."

"Y'all take care of your sister," Mother warned. "She's the only one you've got, and she's a vat of sugar sweeter than you ever were, that's for sure. You could learn a thing or two from her if you bothered to spend the time."

Adelaide seethed, but what could she do? And here she is now in the front seat of a convertible beside the finest looking dude in the county. Or maybe the world. Her simple-minded little sister installed right in the backseat.

"I gotta stop fer a sec," says Jules, who turns around and winks at Felicity.

Adelaide swings around to find Felicity grinning coquettishly. Adelaide spits flames of envy as Jules merrily walks to their left, disappearing behind a holly bush in the thicket to relieve himself.

But here the story fractures into a million shards like the

crystal that brought her here, progressing from blue to violet, eventually revealing a vein of deep red. The red hemorrhages until all that's left is a pool of blood and the sound of her own voice demanding that Felicity, "Get out! Get out of this car and leave us alone."

Adelaide can't make heads or tails of the scene unfolding from that point on. The view is obstructed by a struggle that shoves the gearshift whatever which way. A door opens. Flashes of autumn golds, scarlet, and burnt orange fly by as they careen down the canyon road with no apparent way to stop.

Her head wrenched back on her neck looking skyward, she sees Julian's irresistibly rugged face floating above her in a cloud. She extends her long youthful arms, reaching for him. "Save me," she wails.

"Save yerself," he says, not unkindly. "Ain't no one else can do it for ye this time."

"You can!" she cries. *You can!*

He shakes his head. "I already tried," he says. "Tried my best."

Find the air holes or die.

TWENTY-SIX

THADDEUS

Thaddeus tries to tighten his loose suspenders with one hand as he makes his way slowly up the cracked cement path him and his cousin, Rasmus, poured fer Uncle Thad the one time, 70 years ago the least. They poured real good. Real careful. But while the cement were still wet, they got good and silly. Threw anything within reach right at it— nettles, twigs, acorns, and some wild ass mulberries for color. They walked the hounds through it, back the forth, thinking this here's the funniest. The chickens too, till one the hens got stuck and they had to cut her out. No telling what was in thar thick skulls that time 'sides moonshine from Ras' brother's still.

When they seen what they done, him and Ras made like it were fine art. Like they messed it up on purpose fer a school project. Like the holler school taught art! Hell, it hardly taught reading. Not to him or Ras at least, but his sister, Dolly, were a different story. Not that him and Ras went to class half the time. They was needed in the mine—the old Diamondback side the holler. Not that Thaddeus went to the mine half the time neither. He hated mining something fierce. Hated it more than school. He didn't have a heart fer tight spots, dark tunnels, burning eyes, or the rattling grip of the coffin chest the men got later on like they called it. Enough coffins in Thaddeus' life last him the end of time.

But one day he come to realize that sometimes the darkest holes hide the only treasure worth digging up. Treasure ye can't barely see in daylight with all its shimmering trickery. All its distractions. Ye go deep and dark enough though, ye might just find yerself a diamond the size he found in Section 3 with his pickaxe the one day. '*Holy shit! What's this?!*' *i*s what he were thinking. Couldn't get her loose right off, but thar she were right in the wall sticking out. He seen it clear as a 1,000-watt bulb. "Come look!" he called out. "We're all rich!" He were willing to share it. Willing to give it away, he had to. Could of been anyone found it. Fair is fair.

"What we lookin' at, junior?" they all laughed, huddling round his treasure.

"This here diamond!" he say, spitting the top and cleaning the grit so they could see it real good in the shadows. It were a big old thing. Who could miss it? They could.

"Keep tellin' yerself it's a diamond," say Raymond, the top man. "Diamonds don't grow in coal mines, boy. That's a wives' tale. What ye lookin' at here's nothin' but a cheap piece of quartz, if that." He waved his hand. "It's all yers, kid. What'd anyone want with that ole rock? Git back to work 'fore I fire yer ass."

Rest of them rolling laughing.

All's he could think were, this stone's mine. None the others could even make out where the wall ended. Where the stone began. Quartz my ass, he thought then, still thinks. This here's a diamond, he ever seen one. Not that he seen a lot of 'em. But he seen enough pictures to know. He picked and picked at the wall with his knife till she come loose. Popped her in his pocket and carried on. Diamonds might not usually show up in coal mines, genius, but this here diamond did. *Open yer eyes to the treasure!* Thaddeus never went back the mine after that. No need. Found his treasure already. Zipped it in his pocket till it disappeared the one day. Where'd she go? Had hisself a dream the night before it disappeared. In the dream it slipped from his pocket right into his heart and burrowed deep. Not that it felt like a dream. It didn't. Ask his heart; it's still thar.

Thaddeus had no soul fer mining, no sir, but he sure had a soul fer beauty. Still does. Has a heart fer gems and jewels. Paint and color. Big puffy clouds, fresh air, a raptor's view of the Red River and the big wide valley it feeds. A heart fer streams of gold light cutting paths through thick, dark clouds. A heart fer light, period. Fer purity, ye could say. A field of sunflowers 'neath a pool blue sky like to turn him into a weeping willow, by gawd. A big old human willow. Just big old branches of tears weeping right out his eyeballs straight into a fire opal of a gurgling brook filled with rainbow trout. Just thinking about all this chokes him right up, right now. No room fer art in a coal town, though. No sir. No room fer artists, free-thinkers, neither. No room fer innocence. No wonder he wanted more. But he reached too high.

His pa dang near killed him the once with the wet cement shenanigans, and probably should of. Thaddeus shakes his head, chuckling at the memory of his gentle Pa so fierce and angry the once. "Look what y'all done to yer Uncle Thad's walk!" he hollered. "Not jes the walk, but ye done in the hen, by gawd. Y'all happy now? I bet y'are. Bet yer thrilled! No more eggs fer y'all, sonny boy. That were yer hen. She's gone."

Bent forward, finger wagging at him, then Ras. "Wipe that smile off yer face, Rasmus, 'fore I call yer pa. Y'all think he'll tolerate yer disrespect? Huh? He bloody hell won't, I guarantee it. Neither will I."

Whole time, old Uncle Thad rocking top the porch, squinting through thick spectacles, muttering, "Chicken fer dinner, yessir. Fry 'er up. Love me some chicken legs. Git her in the fryer. Thankee boys!"

Ma paying no mind at all—just, "Kids is kids, Pa. Least they ain't out gittin' drunk."

Those was the days, all right. Riots of mischievous hilarity right here in the holler. Thaddeus should of stuck with his own kind. Should of known better than chasing after folks he didn't belong with. He should of listened to Pa. Respected his elders. But he didn't.

Those was the days, and these here are not the days, Thaddeus knows. These days a struggle. But so what? Today's a day without a jumpsuit or a ball and chain, so he'll take the struggle. Every day he spends a free man 'neath the open sky's good enough, yessir. This rickety old life weren't nothing he could of predicted. The troubles started when he got all full of hisself at Auntie's funeral, thinking he could take up with that flirting belle, Adelaide Somers. Man, she were something to look at back then fer sure. Got a lot worse the day his heart hurtled through the atmosphere like a guided missile at the sister. But who could blame him? He shakes his head. No one. No one could.

Turned out Adelaide were a cranky old sow of a demanding wench. Fun at first, but then. All she wanted were the diamond in his pocket, not his heart. Not that she could see it, but it's like she knew it were there. Wanted the rock, not him. Wanted light, but not her own. Weren't willing to dig that deep, or dig at all. Just hitched herself to his star or anyone's, really. But he were the one right thar in front of her, and she were all over him, yes she were. Thank the lawd he didn't give in to her, not that it weren't tempting at times. It were, lawd help him. But that weren't the way to do right by anyone. He knew that much. But that's all.

Making his way up the steps through the sticky old door, he sighs out loud thinking about Flitty. She's close; he feels it. Not that she knows who he is, but she will. One day she will. This life or the next, what's it to him? Time's a disappearing act. It ain't real. Put it in a box, cover it with a black silk scarf, tap it twice. *Presto!* It's another year. Tap it again, it's altogether gone. Flitty don't live inside a magic box, no sir. She lives on high. Pure as the alabaster feathers of angel wings, she is. He taps his heart. She buried right here, she is. Right side the diamond, nice and deep. Protected.

Which is why he still keeps check on the old sourpuss, Adelaide, every single day. Flitty would of wanted that. He does it fer her. Fer Flitty. Not that Addie ain't more than paid fer her sins, ye ask him. She paid too much. Her life's just one more collapsed mine in a ghost town. A dark space she never searched, just circled blind till the landslide took her down. Thaddeus got a soft spot for a suffering dame, he does. Even her. He wishes he could just shake her hand in forgiveness. Start over as friends. Say, "How do ye do? Name's Thaddeus now." Start fresh.

But by the time he were released from the *Castle* in Eddyville,

otherwise known as the state penitentiary, Addie's brain weren't
working too good. And he, well, he didn't look nothing like
the stud she fell fer back the day, neither. He were just a blob
of wrinkled old putty by then. Assigned the kitchen instead the
yard, he were soft, round and bald. Unrecognizable fer sure.
Not that she looked like herself neither. Y'all kidding? He'd of
seen her somewhere besides *Sunnyside Up*, he'd of never figured
out who she were. Life beat the shit outta both of 'em.

Inside his cabin, Thaddeus removes the derby from his
itchy bald head, resting it on a hook in the dark entry hall. He
squirms out the tweed jacket Dolly bought him back the day.
She believed in him, Dolly; she did. She really did. No matter
what. Never stopped. Dolly finished school, went some more,
became a teacher, married rich. Later on, she had a boy named
Dulles, but that's another story.

Just before Thaddeus were released from the Castle, Dolly
sent him this same wool suit from the haberdasher. He never seen
nothing like it. Brown tweed lined with something smooth and
shiny against his legs. Looked good; still does. Changed everything. Funny what clothes can do. That day on, he never dressed
like a holler kid again, no sir. That suit changed his life. All dressed
up in his new tweed suit out the gates of prison, head still low.
Dolly shows up back seat of a chauffeured limo, good gawd.

"I'm taking you to see Pa," she say. "He's a dying man,
brother. Needs to see his only son."

Tweed suit or no tweed suit, Thaddeus can't look her in the
eye. "He meant to raise a gentleman, sis," he say. "I ain't no
gentleman. Let him die in peace."

"Nonsense!" Dolly say. "There's no peace for Pa without
seeing you, and that's the truest thing I'll ever say. Y'all are
more than a gentleman, brother. Y'all are a hero!"

On and on she gone in her fancy English like she grew up

the city. On and on about all the sacrifices her brother made and all the good he done, all the way to Pa's. She didn't stop till he believed her.

This memory reminds Thaddeus he's more than a ex-con. He's a do-gooder. A do-gooder who served time fer others, deserving or not, who's to say? Do-gooder who carried the weight of the law fer a prominent family about drowned in grief. A family, near he could tell, who appreciated nothing. Who haunted his midnight slumber and midday meanderings his entire life. Still do. Family who follows him around his mind so often he could almost touch 'em. See 'em. Walk amongst 'em. Thar his whole world. His destiny, ye could say.

He hobbles cane-first down the narrow hall of his cottage, stopping to brush Felicity's cheek in the photo where she's spread across the hood of his broken-down jalopy. The one he restored with the fortune Dolly left him when she passed. "Fix your car," Dolly say before she died. "If you won't do it for yourself, do it for me."

Weren't nothing Thaddeus wouldn't do for Dolly. Name it; he'll do it. Always that way. So, day and night he worked the Chrysler in Dolly's barn before he sold her whole estate, like she wanted. Replaced the engine, he did. The transmission too. The whole works, one bolt the time. Drove to Lexington in Dolly's truck and ordered the leather. Cut the patterns real clean. Stitched 'em hisself. He had an eye fer beauty, precision. Hammered out the hood. The fenders. Everything. All fer Dolly. Not that Dolly lived to see it, or anyone else, neither. Dulles were dead by then. Dolly's husband, Langley, long gone. Except fer Dolly, the whole dang family, not to mention the whole town, disappeared while Thaddeus dished up slop at the state penitentiary. Only Thaddeus left now. Like he even wants to be here. Thaddeus, the ex-con, only heir to a fortune earned by a big-time lawyer, of all folks. A lawyer with a Medal of Honor, for gawd sake.

Justice a funny thing.

This Chrysler here, he thinks, looking at the picture, is more than a vehicle. This Chrysler's Dolly herself. It's Dolly and also Flitty in that old-time dress, not to mention his entire self-worth all jacked up on wheels. It's the thing that doomed his life and saved it. He drives it everywhere now, even in winter with the canvas top, but not in snow. Up and down the hills to the market he drives. Through the holler and up the piedmont to *Sunnyside Up* where he shows it to his angel, Flitty Jane, near daily. Shows her how he turned a piece of shit jalopy into a collector's piece. Drives right by her open plot and all around in circles to get her attention. *Look what I done, Flitty!* Not that she's thar, but that's where she should of been. Every day, *honk! honk!* To prove he's worthy. Dependable. Somebody with decent skills who could of taken care of her. If she hadn't of died.

Standing front her picture, he whispers, "I s'pose y'all weren't built to last long in such a harsh family, were ye, angel? Minus yer daddy, that is. Him 'n me could of been good friends with half the chance."

All the sudden, thoughts of Flitty set fire to his chest like they do, flaming like a cow pie in a field fire. The flames fill his lungs. It's too much. He gasps to release the scorching heat. But it'll never release; he knows. Course he knows. He were a fool to let hisself fall fer either one of 'em. Addie and Flitty one inseparable thing. Light and dark sides the same planet. Even now. Still. Always. One thing; two bodies. Hell, maybe we all are. Maybe there's no dang difference between a one of us and the other. The dark; the light. Older Thaddeus gets, clearer this is. Addie didn't stand a chance without Flitty. Without Flitty, she rotted faster than a crop of pumpkins in an early freeze.

Deep sigh travels from his toes right on up his bent back to his tired neck till his head hangs. Times he thinks he messed with fate. Like what if he'd of married his neighbor, Edith Taylor, the way his parents thought he would. Like he thought hisself before the one funeral at *Sunnyside Up* changed his whole dang life. He and Edith a had twenty kids by now. Forty grandkids. Enough to repopulate the whole empty town. Just pop 'em out left and right, they would of. Plus, he'd of been spoilt to death by her poke pie. Every kind a poke pie every dang night, he'd of had. Raspberry, chocolate, pumpkin, and shoofly, just name it. There were no end to Edith's poke pies. Poke pie instead of puke pie at the slammer like he had. Ah, but the heart wants what the heart wants. Yes, it does. Ye can't tame a wild heart, no sir. Anyways, Edith married Fred, and they both died in the landslide after the collapse.

In the kitchen, he stumbles on a tacky corner of rotten linoleum, lurching forward to the sink. He grabs the faucet to keep hisself from falling. Falling could be the end of him, what with no phone and no neighbors since the collapse. The Diamondback collapsed while he were in the Castle. He'd of not been in the Castle, he'd of been buried in that mine hisself like everyone else. Buried in the mine or buried in the land- slide. Buried on the way to the mine or buried at the breakfast table or buried at the school. Buried in piles of coal waste and all the rocks, trees and rooftops it took along with it. That's the one thing he owes Flitty's rattlesnake of a mama. It's no small thing, no sir. It's big. Throwing him in prison when she did, saved his life. Spared him on the way to killing him off. Not that she meant to save his life. But that's what she done.

Hanging over the sink right now like he is, he about chokes on some pissy sulfur smell rising up the drain like a death cloud. This hut smells like a skunk, all right, but it's all he's got, and he ain't moving till Addie's gone. Once Addie's gone, he'll clean up the *Sunnyside* homestead and make something of it for history sake. Lotsa history in that house before the states took up arms against tharselves. Lotsa history after. Folks it lodged up top and folks it hid down low. Folks it sacrificed and folks it saved. He been looking into it. Wants to do right by the old reverend—by all the old reverends! Wants to do right by Flitty and Adelaide. Wants to get rid the guilt that snaps his heart like a dry twig every day.

Not guilt fer no crime, no sir, just guilt fer circumstance. Guilt fer just being thar. Unless ye call loving Flitty a crime, which maybe it were back then. Sure did feel like a crime. Felt dangerous, it did. To love Flitty, he had to figure out how to wiggle loose of Addie. Convince Addie they didn't fit, him and her. *They didn't!* Convince her that him and Flitty was a truer match. *They was!* He knew Addie cared about him in her own bossy way, so he had to let her down easy. Open the gate real gentle and let her tear into the meadow like a pissed-off filly. Give her time to get over herself. He didn't count on getting rid of Addie the way it happened though. He ain't no monster. He shakes his head side to side. He sure as hell didn't plan on losing 'em both that same day, no sir. But he did.

He opens the old cooler, pulls out a lager, pops the tab and chugs. He'd of rather drunk water, but the water stinks, so. As he peers out the back window past the rushing stream into the purple wisteria blooming past season, he realizes he's half in half outta life, or what's left of it anyways. He ain't sure when it started, but he sees stuff. *Sees it.* Like a gypsy, he sees. Can't deny it, no sir. Stuff no one else sees, lawd help him. Right into the beyond. Into the nether. Either that, or someone lit his brain on fire, left him to die. He should be so lucky.

Darn if he don't see Flitty time to time right thar in the

beyond. Long curls of silver hair. Bewitching eyes. Not just see her, but *feel* her presence, yessir. Half-expect her to hop right up the polished hood of his shiny new vehicle and lean into the pose that near made him lose his mind the first place, innocent as it all were. Him tooling up the long drive to her house. Him inquiring about Addie was all. Running into Flitty at the cemetery gate like he did. He's replayed this scene near a million times.

"Addie's not home," sang the angel, pausing to pull a long strand of gossamer hair off her rosebud lips. "She's running errands for the Campbell service tomorrow."

"Oh yeah?" His heart pounded like a jackhammer for reasons not yet clear to him. "What 'bout you?" he say. "Near as I see, yer home."

"That I am," she giggled, those cat eyes catching sunlight like they did. Pair of tourmalines they was.

"So, hop on in," he say, leaning over to flip the handle. "I'm teachin' myself how to use my pa's camera. Need me a model."

It's like he's snapping the photo now, yessir. Framing it right in his brain. Flitty deciding whether to go with him or stay. The skirt of her flower dress rustling in the breeze like a flag. Finger on her chin. Brushing a ringlet of hair behind her ear. Eyes shifting side to side, considering what all might happen. Or not happen. Then finally, the verdict.

"Well, I guess I'm a model then!" she say, grinning.

And that were that. Seemed so right and so wrong the same time, he could barely catch his breath. Miles of dirt road down the holler, her hair whipping. Both of them singing, *"Oh ma darlin'; oh ma darlin'; oh ma darlin' Clementine!"* Singing and laughing, all natural, easy, meant-to-be. Nothing between 'em but bright light and sheer joy. Then at the cabin, messing with that old camera his pa got from his boss. Trying learn about shutter speeds, he were. About light and dark. About shadows. Trying to figure out what to do with his life. Like maybe he could of been some kind of magazine photographer. Could of traveled the wide world! He had an eye, he did. His mama say so. An eye fer beauty, lawd help him. Maybe he could of snapped pictures stead of slopping mush in a prison. Maybe he could of painted scenes of ice-capped mountains or turquoise oceans. But no sense dwelling. Life's a coal mine. That's the truth. Dig just so, ye get a twelve-sided diamond fits right in yer heart. Dig too deep, the mine collapses. Ye gotta find the air holes or die.

All roads lead to reckoning.

TWENTY-SEVEN

THADDEUS

Thaddeus cracks open the sticky cabinet door to see what sort of supper might be possible. Shelves full of kidney beans, pinto beans, black-eyed peas and white beans. Beans, beans, beans. If he could muster the oxygen, he'd get hisself to the store fer a can of sardines or spam. But darn if life don't suck the air right outta him time to time. Just *whoooosh*. Like a hoover. Don't matter anyhow. Store's closed.

He reaches way back the cabinet on his tiptoes fer the last can of BBQ baked beans, which might contain a lick of bacon, he's lucky. He'd love hisself a big slab of bacon or a hunk of ham hock,

but there ain't any. He ate better at the Castle some days. Just lazy is what he is. Not enough gumption to stay alive at times. He sets the can on the stained counter and looks all around fer his jackknife. *Thar 'tis.* He grabs it from the window sill. Jabs the can till it hisses.

This day here been coming fer some time. The day Adelaide's restless soul departs the world fer good maybe, as it near about has. Can't be long now. Like his dreams been telling him fer years—all roads lead to reckoning. Reckon away! His life ain't amounted to much anyhow. Why's he still here? He don't know. Once Addie's gone, all's left of his life on Earth is him, his car, *Sunnyside Up,* and this here tiny cottage down the holler. Funky old shack untouched by the landslide—pure luck, that. No one seen it coming. Uncle Thad weren't no gypsy.

Yes sir, Uncle Thad built this shack hisself back the day. Everybody say, *"Why you livin' so far out? Build closer to the mine! Closer to work 'n family! Don't y'all love us?!"* But all old Thaddeus wanted were peace, a forest, and a decent shotgun to catch hisself some quail time to time. Quail and rattlesnake or both the one time the rattler ate the quail. Quail still moving inside when the rattler were shot, so he swore.

Poor Uncle Thaddeus escaped the landslide just to die of black lung a month on. Whole time, Julian's behind bars, no help to anyone. Can't even visit. Soon's he got free, though, he took over Uncle's house. Took his house and took his name. Weren't no use for Julian no more, no sir. The name or the man. *Who's Julian?* Just a fool served thirty years fer a crime he didn't commit. Cost Dolly plenty to get him out, too. Lawyer after fancy lawyer to dig up the truth that Regina Somers buried soul-deep. Son of a bitch. Aw hell, don't matter now. Julian were a fool. Fool fer love, but still. A fool. Anyways, with Flitty gone so sudden, didn't matter much to him where he lived. *If* he lived. Or how. Prison were good as anywhere. His heart good and locked-up in solitary anyways. He were good as dead.

Thaddeus pries the can of beans open, digging in with a bent spoon. Why he still feels responsible fer both girls is beyond him. All the dreams, probly. Him burying the girls; girls burying him. Night after night, him digging graves by moonlight. Day after day watching his own funeral like he done. His coffin rocking and rolling down the aisle willy nilly. Him in the chapel dressed in his tweed suit waiting on his own coffin. Him, too, inside the coffin starved for light, craving air. Craving indigo sky, rainbows, fields of scarlet poppies reaching fer the sun. Both gals trying to put him in the ground time after time. Trying do right by him, he s'poses. Though they never really did. How could they? He's still alive. But they tried.

He shovels a couple more spoonfuls of beans in his trap, throws back his head and chugs some brew to warsh 'em down. Beans get stuck time to time. He's so tuckered out dealing with Adelaide in the hospital today, he can barely swallow. End of a era, 'tis. Almost, but not quite. She ain't dead far as he knows. He glances at the clock. But maybe now she is.

He wanders 'cross the room, turning left to where the bed fills the alcove. Crawls up the sour mattress with the brew in his grip, turns on his back, drifting into one them comas he has near every night now. Where he sees the world naked, not dressed in lies, like it mostly is. Sometimes naked's pretty, but sometimes it ain't. Sometimes it's ugly as sin, he's honest. But something inside him knows, pretty or ugly, what he sees is plenty real. Bare as bones, real as skin. Not one of 'em is in the ground yet—not him, Flitty, or Adelaide. So what got buried in all that dirt? He sighs heavy. Truth is what. Truth got buried deep.

His left arm hanging off the metal bed frame goes limp; his

eyes slam shut. Can of brew drops on the old plank floor. He hears the *PLUNK!*, tries to open his eyes. But he can't. The dream's a diamondback snake or a rattler, swallows him whole like the quail, him still squirming inside, but it ain't no use. The beer mess'll have to wait till the snake spits him out the morning. Or never. Never's okay. Never's good a time as any to clean up a mess this big.

Deep in the dream stands the old barn outside Outskirt. Barn got buried in the slide. Last time he were in this dream the barn were dim as a mine shaft and full of fools. Fools in carnival costumes taught by a half-dead instructor talking in tongues. Gobbledygook to most folks, but Thaddeus picked up a thing or two, truly he did. He picked up the thing about darkness and the thing about light. The thing about how the world works inside and out, both at once. Above and below. He picked up the thing about timelines, too. What don't happen here might well happen thar. Things get reckoned somehow; they do. Might end up in murder or marriage, can't say. Just got to wait and see. It all made sense to him then. Makes sense now. Life ain't one thing. Ye got to watch yer back and watch yer front. Watch yerself inside and out. Be on yer toes. Figure out the shape of the dark. Just like crawling out the coal mine, ye ask him. Coal mine collapsing behind, ye got half the chance. But sometimes it caves up front.

This here tonight's a different quality of light altogether. Different light, different colors. Tiny blinking moonstones and big orchid lanterns strung from the roof. Periwinkle sparklers leaking through the slats. Thaddeus never seen nothing like this here. Shades of purple everywhere. Color of majesty, he thinks. Color of Spirit.

All lit up like she is, the teacher don't look like a dried-up stick of beef jerky this time. Same librarian used to give him hell back the day—Miz Phipps. Harriet Phipps. But right here she's looking like her best day. Lit up like a sparkler, unearthly. Radiant. Hair piled up her head like a crown of lilacs. The lilacs smell so good everywhere, even sitting way back the room like he is. Smell good and look good. Hard to take his eyes off old Phipps, he's honest. How weird.

Sometime later, hard to say how long, Thaddeus' sight drifts elsewhere. Pretty soon his tired old eyes do a double-take. Tripletake. He pulls off his spectacles and rubs his eyes hard. Squints real tight. *Can it be?* Sure enough, Adelaide Frances' laid right out front of everybody in indecent a gown as Thaddeus ever seen on a female. Like to make him blush. Her loosely tied gown spread halfway to her dimpled knees, all covered in sad clown faces. Same gown she were wearing at the hospital today, come to think on it, but good and shrunk. Least it seems shrunk. Maybe because she's so high up whilst he's sitting back at just the wrong angle. *The wrongest angle!* He can't keep looking. *Stop looking!* He looks away.

Straining his neck, he checks the whole barn real careful to see who else might be in attendance. The more he looks, the more he notices. This character here and that one thar. The old sheriff to his right, back straight as a pole, hands cuffed to a post. Over thar's his warden locked up in the horse stall, shaking the iron bars real hard trying to free hisself. *Lemme out! Lemme out!* Floating heads and faces everywhere, looks like. No end to it. Prisoners from the yard all lined up, large to small. Big ones beat him up pretty good stand right in front. Same ones stole Dolly's confections way back. Course, he'd of rather been beaten up any day than lose a single square of Dolly's peanut butter marshmallow fudge, he's honest. That fudge fed his dreams. Kept him alive. Just thinking on it, chocolate coats his tongue, oh boy.

The rich flavor spikes then fades and Thaddeus looks up. *Well, lookee thar!* Cousin Rasmus, long gone in the collapse, lying sideways up the rafter. Looking down, grinning. Looking for mischief, what else? Not just Ras, but everyone Thaddeus ever tangoed with in this barn right here, seems. Folks who done him right and folks who done him wrong. Folks who done him so wrong changed his whole life, like Miz Somers, standing thar next to Addie, arms folded, looking fierce. Fierce, but altogether younger and more fit than he ever seen the old cow. Near human, ye could say.

He continues searching the room left, right, center, back, and then…he stops. Catches his breath. *Mercy!* Will he ever get used to it? he wonders. The feast when she shows up? The famine when she disappears? He rubs his eyes twice and again. Can't get all worked up fer nothing, no. Can't afford no foolishness at his age. Got to conserve every heartbeat, every breath. He blinks like a broken light to clear his cataracts, but no. It's her just the same. *Jasus J., whar's the oxygen?* He's breathing fumes.

Leaning closer now, he can see Flitty's looking a tad weathered tonight, poor thing. Not that he cares. Why, he's a wrinkled wreck hisself. But dang if she don't light up the room no matter what. Especially wearing that same flowery dress like she is. That dress stands out to him as the dress she wore…*that day.* The last thing anyone saw her in, far's he knows. He weren't allowed at the funeral, not that they could bury her. They couldn't find her! But that didn't stop him from digging the grave. A place to rest when they do find her is what he were thinking. Whenever that may be. When she comes home. All night long under the harvest moon, all by hisself, he dug. Dug straight down to China, he did. Squared it out, four corners, 90 degrees measured. Labor of love. He'd of dug ten if she needed them. He couldn't stop till they cuffed his wrists.

"Welcome," say the bright young librarian from the podium. "I'm Mrs. Phipps, and this is my assistant, Dr. Joy."

Dr. Joy looks just like the gypsy down the holler owned the flower shop uptown. She's all lit inside out like one of them see-through candles. Lit up same as the librarian, just as radiant. Both of them younger than Thaddeus by a mile, even though they was both middle-aged when he were a kid. Light streams from their fingers like they working miracles.

All the way from the back, he hears Addie holler, "Get me out of heeeeeeere!" Her deep crackle echoes off the barn walls, eerie as a wolf in a full snow moon.

Flitty jumps at her sister, "NO!" she say, firmer than Thaddeus ever heard her. "It wasn't easy getting you here, Addie. In fact, it was nearly impossible. Y'all are going nowhere till we allow it. Till we say it's time. Y'all are listening to what we have to say."

At this, Adelaide's entire body trembles, shaking the dirt floor like a avalanche. Thaddeus' wood chair near falls apart spindle by spindle.

Without moving her lips, Addie wails, "Fliiiiitttttty! Is that really you? Where'd y'all come from? Oh, my lawd, you can't believe what I've been through, sister. Don't let them take me back to the hospital! Bring me home to *Sunnyside Up* right now! Rescue me!" She starts bawling. "I'm begging you, Flitty!"

"We'll see about that later," Flitty say more softly, angel hair flying in all directions. "First there's work to be done. Lots of it."

"Promise me, Flitty!" screams Addie. "Promise me!"

Thaddeus can tell that If Adelaide could, she'd of strangled a promise outta Flitty and left her deader than she already is. Only thing Addie can move is her mind though. And even that's half-stuck.

"We're here to learn about reckoning," say Phipps.

Flitty raises her hand. The delicate movement overwhelms Thaddeus. He jumps from his chair to rush up the aisle, but someone pulls him back.

"Hey," he say. "Leggo me."

"It's for your own good," say a familiar voice. "Your turn will come."

Thaddeus whips around just to find hisself staring open-mouth at a tall fit young man in fancy a white suit as he ever seen. Takes him a minute.

"Dulles?!" he say, shaking his bald head. "That you?"

The young man nods.

"Last dream I seen ye in, ye was a smart aleck junkie fulla crack cocaine," say Thaddeus. "Why, y'all look angelic now. Ye go steal a angel's costume, boy? That's low."

His nephew grins wide. "No sir, I'm a helper. I've seen the light."

Thaddeus grabs Dulles' hands eagerly. "Ye done good, boy."

"Thanks!"

Thaddeus sighs. "Y'all tortured yer mama, ye know."

"But we're good now, me and Ma," he say.

Thaddeus eyes light up. "Whar is she, boy? Whar's Dolly?"

Without even looking, Dulles reaches unnaturally high right through the gaps in the barn roof into the starlit sky where he plucks a shooting star out of thin air. Admires it fer a minute, he does, then drops it into Thaddeus' shirt pocket like a gumdrop. "Right there," he say. "Keep her safe."

Thaddeus' right eye drops a tear as Dolly's star burns a hole in his pocket. Burns through his skin like shrapnel. Slides into the right side of his heart, finds a home in his diamond. Wiggles in. Stays.

Phipps taps her pointer on the floor to command attention

then points to a string of violet lights up the rafters. "When one of these lights goes out," she say, "it puts pressure on the others to compensate. To bear more light."

Right then, one light after the other goes dark except one.

She points around the room. "Y'all are a string of lights connected in your border worlds, whether you know it or not." She raises her chin importantly. "One of you is about to go dark."

Hush all around.

"One of you has too little light, and one of you has too much. That is, one of you can't light a single bulb, and the other has enough light to blow the entire transformer with a wish."

She pauses, letting it all sink into their tiny brains what that might mean. Thaddeus' head throbs. He feels it all. He really does.

"The overabundant light is transformative in nature," continues Phipps. "It cannot be contained or diminished. It's the light of completion. All this good soul wants is to distribute this bountiful energy generously among you, so you can all rise together." She shakes her head, sighing. "To do that, however, we have to expand your capacity." She points around again, one head the time. "Your capacity and yours. And yours. To expand anyone's capacity, though, we have to reckon the past."

Thaddeus' just sitting there wondering who it might be, all juiced up with light like Phipps say, but he should of known. His jaw drops as he watches Flitty's dark little wrinkled body light up, flicker, dim, and dance around like the one bare bulb in his shack. Young, all the sudden, like a teenage girl. Like to explode with light, she is. Trying everything to hide her glory, but she can't. Sparks fly. Light beams shoot like rockets up her arms and legs. Only one can't see what's happening is Adelaide, eyes sealed shut. Open 'em and she'll go blind. She's a shadow, he ever seen one.

"Get me out of here!" Addie screams even with her mouth shut tight. "I did not agree to any of this!"

Miz Phipps, only half as bright as Flitty now, bounces her pointer straight off Adelaide's belly. "Careful what you ask for," she warns. "Your request affects everyone in this room. If it's granted prematurely, it may very well be the last request you make."

Flitty presses her white-hot hands into Addie's shoulders. "Y'all are staying right here until you wake up, sister."

"Ouch!" complains Adelaide, flinching. "Your hands are hot rods!"

Flitty removes her hands, but lowers her face close enough to Adelaide's to light her up. "Wake! Up!"

"Good grief!" Addie whines. "How do you expect me to do that? I'm in a coma for gawd sake! I can't wake up!"

"Maybe not," say Dr. Joy. "It's an advanced technique. But you owe it to us all to try."

Obituary for Release to:
Bluegrass Bugle &
The Louisville Gazette
Friday, April 3, 1964

Miss Jolene Oakley Young Slain by the Ten of Swords
Born: April 1, 1886
Passed into eternal life: April 1, 1964

Seventy-eight-year-old Jolene Oakley Young of Outskirt
Hollow, stepsister of Sheriff Lloyd Gibbs, shuffled her
last deck of tarot cards on Wednesday after scaring the
hell out of the Sheriff's wife, Dottie, with an ominous
reading. According to Dottie, "The Ten of Swords, the
Death card, and the Five of Pentacles showed up three
times in a row. I thought it were fer me, but I were wrong.
When Jolene figgered out it were fer her, she turned
pasty white, excused herself fer a nap back The Little
Shoppe of Flowers, whar she lives, ye see. Well, course
ye do, y'all been thar yerself." Dottie pulled a tissue
from her sleeve, mopped her perspiring forehead, and
continued. "Whilst Jolene slept, I tended to a customer
upfront, then walked on back to check on Jolene..."

The interview paused while I went and got Dottie a
cup of hot tea so I could milk the rest out of her before
she melted right down the floor and out the door.

"Thank ye," Dottie said about the tea. "Whar was I?"
She took a long sip. "Oh yes. When I went back to ask
Jolene if I should accept another one of Berle Addison's
bad checks, I could not rouse her one bit. 'Jolene!' I say.

'Jolene!' But nothin'." Dottie put her hands up high and shook her head, trying to gain composure (I guess). But nothing she added after that made a lick of sense.

Jolene Oakley Young, known to customers by her initials, JOY, got herself a mail-order doctorate in occult arts from the Esoteric Temple of the Lower Ozarks, which I would've called for a comment if they had a phone, but that's not how they communicate. Dr. Joy, as she liked to be called, ran the Little Shoppe of Flowers as a front for her popular tarot-shuffling, tea leaf-reading, séance-hosting professional life Mondays and Wednesdays 3 to 5. Half the wives in Outskirt attended regularly, though they'll never admit it to their husbands. Don't worry, y'all, Dottie swears she burned the customer files. Your secrets are dead and soon to be buried at *Sunnyside Up*.

Dr. Joy Young never married. No one knows why, but they have hunches. She leaves behind her thirteen black cats: Mel, Belle, Marvel, Merlin, Bealzie, Magic, Abra, Cadabra, Wiz, Glinda, Elpha, Circe, and Hydra. She is survived by her step-brother and sister-in-law, Lloyd and Dorothea (Dottie) Gibbs, and their six children of assorted names and ages. Her gravestone will be decorated with her collection of miniature porcelain tea cups from the Winn-Dixie.

Mourners are invited to join the Gibbs at *Sunnyside Up* on Monday at the chapel, followed by a gypsy-themed tambourine farewell on Tuesday from 1-3. When asked how a holler-born practitioner of the dark arts was able to get serviced and buried at uppity *Sunnyside Up*, Mrs. Regina Somers, Owner and Manager of the esteemed enterprise waved her hand dismissively and hustled off.

TWENTY-EIGHT

ADELAIDE

Everything that's happening to Adelaide in the barn right now is worse than anything that's happened to her before, unless she counts Julian's death. Not that she remembers how Julian died; she doesn't. Half the time she can't even remember he's dead. All she remembers is Mother telling her he died and that he would not be buried at *Sunnyside Up* under any circumstances. That he died in the woods *that day*. That Adelaide would never see him again. She remembers how smug Mother was when she said it, like it made her happy. Like he got what was coming to him. Maybe he did.

That was the day life took a hairpin turn down a steep and unforgiving mountain pass without guardrails. Adelaide doesn't remember a single detail of the actual event except being deliriously happy one minute, and just plain delirious the next. The rest of her life is a hole as deep and raw as the Red River Gorge. Jagged, bottomless and irretrievable. It's as if someone ripped that day out of her head and gave it to someone else. Someone completely unreliable, like Felicity.

All she remembers is that one minute she was young, in love, and driving through the brilliant autumn woods with her lover, and the next minute, she was a baggy-skinned waddling old spinster wondering what happened. A cranky old spinster subsisting in a dismal ghost town with her crazy spinster sister. What a pair! Oh, she remembers scattered details from the past, alright. Most of them unsavory. Like being shipped off to Mother's cousin Hyacinth's house for rest and recuperation. From what though? She can't even remember how long she was at Hyacinth's, or really, anything else about it. Just that she was finally allowed to leave at some point after Mother's funeral, whenever that was. Time is a blender.

But that was then and this is now. And what's happening now is worse than being subjected to Mother's forked tongue or Felicity's insanity as much as she misses Felicity. It's worse than all the other visits to the barn put together. This is because the edges of her hospital gown are splitting apart and she can't endure the humiliation. She can't fix it because she can't move. She might be paralyzed; how would she know? No one tells her anything. You'd think someone would help her out, get her a larger gown at least, but no. She's on her own. Story of her life.

On a normal night in the barn, people would hardly notice this indignity. But the barn's all lit up for once, and here she lies, hot as hell in a hospital bed with a shrinking gown under a dome of penetrating light. How many indignities must she suffer at once? Is it a spy light? Is she under investigation? It sure seems that way. Big oversized spy faces with exaggerated features penetrate her closed eyes. Burn right through her eyelids into her retinas and out the back of her head. The spy faces are inescapable. They want her to stay. They are all mumbling orders in a confusing chorus.

"You *must* stay," says one more adamantly than the rest.

Adelaide tries, but she can't move her neck to see who this tyrant might be. If it weren't for the resoluteness of the command, she would swear the voice belonged to Felicity. Is she hearing things? *Flitty, is it you?!*

As the voice gets closer, Adelaide makes out the unmistakably narrow silhouette of her sister. Feels the magnetic heat of her body. Smells the familiar lilac fragrance. It's Flitty, alright. At first she's ecstatic to be in Flitty's presence again. *Save me, sister! Bring me home! I miss you more than I could ever admit!* After all, isn't that why Felicity came? To rescue Adelaide after the repeated times Adelaide rescued Felicity from...well, everything? From her blatant dereliction of duties at *Sunnyside Up*. From her delusional tea parties with spooks. From sheer homelessness! Wasn't it Adelaide who provided Felicity with a roof over her loopy head? Fed her? Tolerated her homicidal cat? Anyone could see if it weren't for Adelaide, Felicity would have been institutionalized by now—half out of her mind, drugged-up and force-fed strained peas through a straw. Why, there's no end to what Adelaide spared her sister by watching over her.

"Y'all are going *NOWHERE*," Felicity commands in a new, no-nonsense voice from the nearby planets of shame and humiliation.

Hearing her sister's complicity with the devil, Adelaide's mushy brain spins with confusion. Is this the thanks she gets?

Really?! Felicity ordering her to remain the object of ridicule, spinning through yet another, more infernal circle of hell? Where's the justice in any of this?

Felicity's isn't the only traitorous face looming over her. Some kinder alien version of Mrs. Phipps' bulging eyes and sharp little pointy features stare straight into Adelaide's brain, dissecting it with laser vision.

"Jutht relax," she keeps repeating. "Jutht relax, Adelaide. Let go."

The old prune must've taken a shower, Adelaide thinks. Or pulled her skin back with a clamp. Adelaide only recognizes her because of the lithp.

And right next to Phipps is the face of another traitor, Dr. Joy, the one who lured her here in the first place with her evil crystal. "Come along, Adelaide," she said. "We're going on a little expedition to save your eternal life." She and her skinny old squiggly cartoon body has hijacked Adelaide from one nasty situation to another. And now they expect her to cooperate? And just stay? *Till they see fit to let her go?*

"I won't staaaaaay!" she mysteriously screams into the cavernous room without so much as opening her mouth. "You can't make me!"

Although to be honest, she has no idea how she's going to escape. Her arms are like lead pipes, and she can't even feel her legs. Unless a choir of angels assume her into heaven, she's not sure how she'll get out.

"Who's restraining me?" she yells.

"Yourthelf," says Mrs. Phipps.

"You think I'm paralyzing my own legs? If I could get up and walk out, don't you think I would?"

"Free will is always in play," says Dr. Joy, nodding in the most irritating manner. "You know that, Adelaide. It was our first lesson. Some fundamental piece of you simply does not want to learn." She leans in closer. "Or leave."

Adelaide squeezes her mind like a sponge. "I want to leave," she begs. "I damn well *do* want to leave."

"Then get up," they seem to all say at once.

Adelaide struggles. *She'll show them!* But how? She can't move. She really can't. "Somebody must've drugged me," she says.

"That'th an excuthe," says Phipps, shaking her crooked little witch's finger.

The unimaginable heat of the search light stimulates Adelaide's pores, and she begins to sweat like a team of swine. There's so much sweat in what seems like five minutes that she slides right off the bed onto the dirt floor, landing on her belly, eyes wide-open. She sees this as her one opportunity to escape. She can't blow it. She concentrates hard, *so hard*, gathering every available ounce of will power to rise up on all fours. *She succeeds!* Her bare butt is sticking out of the shrinking gown, but that's the least of her worries. What's important is that she's no longer paralyzed. She can move her arms and legs. They said she'd be able to leave if she really wanted to. She really wants to.

Down here on the dirt floor, it's darker and cooler, but more confusing. No bright light to blind her or even to point the way. She searches for a space large enough to squeeze her cumbersome body between all the skinny legs. She spots an escape route to the left and moves in that direction. Just as she's making progress, she hears Felicity's voice.

"Don't do it, Addie! I'm begging y'all! You hear me? If you do it, you'll go completely dark. You'll lose us forever, and worse...we'll lose you!"

Except for Felicity, what's it to Adelaide if she loses them all? The loss of Phipps and Joy would only improve her life.

But Flitty, well. Flitty's kin. What would she do without Flitty to care for?

"You won't just lose *us*," says Joy, as if eavesdropping on Adelaide's thoughts. "You'll lose your*self.*"

"Don't make me laugh," says Adelaide, laughing.

Just then her left knee lands on a stone, and she collapses in pain. "Aaaaa! Ugh."

"It's true," says Felicity in earnest. "Listen to us! If you move only in the shadows and refuse the light, y'all will disappear altogether, Addie. There will be nothing to sustain you. This is not the same as the material world. Where we are now, and where we're headed, light is not a luxury. It's oxygen."

Adelaide picks the stone out of her knee, tosses it, and resumes her escape. "It's a cult, Flitty. Get out while you can."

"It's not a cult," says Felicity. "It's truth. You can't run from it. Truth casts no shadow."

Still trying to push her way through the jungle of legs, Adelaide says, "Did it ever occur to y'all that maybe I want to disappear? Have you seen what I'm wearing!"

"You won't just disappear from the barn," says Phipps. "You'll return to the hospital room and disappear forever. Your vitals are diminishing fast."

Adelaide stops for a second and tries to clean out her ear with her finger. What happened to Phipps' lisp? If she's starting to understand Phipps, she's in real trouble. She's got to get out fast before they convert her.

Phipps continues, "Felicity will have to absorb what tiny little specks of light you still have into her greater light." Her voice drops an octave. "Your persona will break apart, unindividuated, and vanish into the shadows."

Adelaide pounds the dirt floor with her fist. *Felicity will absorb my light? Into her greater light?* Ha! It's all she can do not to convulse laughing. "As if Felicity has any light what-soever to spare," she says. "As if she's the least bit functional on her own. For your information, Felicity can't do anything without me! Right, Flitty? You tell them! I keep you going! Right?!"

"What can we do to get through to her!" says Dr. Joy despairingly. "Time is running out. Her kidneys are failing!"

"We have to do something!" cries Felicity. "I can't lose her this way! I can't!"

Adelaide sees this crazy talk as a bargaining chip. Crawling around on the floor in a circle doesn't seem to be getting her anywhere anyway. "You want to know what to do?" she says. "Get me a big bag of praline and a bottle of bourbon, and throw in a barrel of fun. Remember fun? And a few cigarettes wouldn't hurt anyone." She takes a deep breath. "Then we can talk."

Joy doesn't hesitate. "Give her what she wants. We're running out of time."

Phipps clears her throat, considering. "If we do as you ask, Adelaide, do you promise to cooperate of your own free will?"

"Sure," says Adelaide. "I'll promise. None of you could recognize a barrel of fun if it rolled over you anyway. What have I got to lose?"

"Is that a yes?" says Phipps.

"Yes. There. How's that? *Yes.*"

Just then Adelaide makes it through one pair of legs and onto the next before she's stopped by a barricade of solid, white linen-covered calves. One of the calves kicks command-ingly out to her left to stop her from moving in that direction. When she pivots, the other calf blocks her from the right. She reaches out to evaluate its strength. Can't be a woman. Way too strong to be Felicity or Phipps, and lawd knows, Dr. Joy's legs are a pair of pickup stix.

"Hey now," calls the owner of these calves in a familiar baritone. "Watcha doing down there?"

She can't quite place the voice, so she cranes her neck to get a look. Well hell, if it isn't the boy. *What's his name?* She can't remember his name.

"Dulles," he says smiling down. "I can read thoughts now."

A fever of humiliation paints her cheeks scarlet, and she sits back on her rickety knees to cover her bare butt. *I gotta get out of here and change my clothes,* is all she's thinking.

Dulles crosses his Hercules arms across his Thor chest. "Please don't leave," he says.

"I can't stand it here," she pleads. "And anyway, you should talk. Didn't y'all disappear on me once already?"

He winks, cocking his head. His garden of short-clipped, grass-green hair barely moves. "How 'bout we disappear together this time?"

She grins. *Is she dreaming!* "Now *that* sounds like fun!"

"You're gonna need some clothes where I'm taking you," he says.

Before she can think, she's standing in the middle of the barn in a ruffled white lace blouse, a flirty fern green skirt, and fine strappy sandals. The whole ensemble fits her figure, suddenly fit and trim, in a familiar way. *She's worn this before, but where?* Shiny black hair falls across her shoulders and down her back like a silk cascade. She twirls. Why this is exactly the way she wants him to see her! All young and revved up for a party and that's not all.

"Sure do look pretty," he says, grinning.

"Y'all got that right," she replies, batting her lashes. She sticks out her hip and piles her hair on her head. "Who's your granny now?"

"Definitely not you," he says, and grabs her hand. Twirls

her. "Now stand right here with me till the light comes to get us. Just be a minute."

"The what?"

"The light."

She jerks her hand away. "The only lights I have any intention of disappearing into are disco lights. I've had just about enough of this dead seriousness."

He retrieves her hand. "Here it comes," he says into the glare. "Will you accompany me, yes or no? I can't take you against your will."

She sighs, thinking. *On the other hand...*

"Don't be afraid," he says with a tenderness she can't resist.

I'm all yours, her heart says, but before she can form the words, she's near blinded, confused, and spun dizzy in a cyclone of light. She knew this kid was dangerous, but if she's honest, that's her type. Always has been. And dang if he doesn't remind her of Jules. Not the face, but just the feeling. The countenance. If you're going to do something risky, she thinks, make sure you pick the right person to do it with. And anyway, whatever this crazy light is about, it's a hell of a lot more fun than the hospital. Or crawling around naked on the barn floor in an ambush. *"You can't leave,"* my ass, she thinks. *Oh really?* Watch me. *Poof!*

I'm gone.

*Light accrues in the cracks
that ego abandons.*

TWENTY-NINE

FELICITY

"O h no!" cries Felicity. She backs into a folding chair and sits down, trembling. "Where's Addie? Where did she go!" She prays Mrs. Phipps and Dr. Joy know what they're doing. Addie turned into a teenager and disappeared with a young man. Anyone who knows anything about Addie knows they'll never get her back now. She's good as gone.

"It's okay, dear," says Phipps. "It's Dulles."

"Dulles?" she says, confused.

"The young man," says Phipps. "His name is Dulles."

"Y'all know him?"

"We do," says Phipps kindly. "He's a helper."

Felicity places a hand on either side of her head to keep it from spinning. "A helper?" she squeaks.

Phipps draws a chair beside Felicity and takes her hands. "A helper is a person who assists lost souls in other realms."

Felicity nods uncertainly. "An angel then?"

"No," says Joy. "Angels have never led human lives, but helpers have. Many helpers have been lost themselves and been helped by others. It's their wish to return the favor. Mrs. Phipps and I are helpers."

"You?"

"That's right," says Phipps. "We help people to accept their circumstances, rise above them, and awaken, just as others have helped us do the same. Help is best provided by souls familiar to those lost."

Felicity shakes her head, astonished. "I should have known."

"People often become confused when they pass over," Phipps adds. "It's almost never what they've been taught to expect."

"Either they expect nothing at all," adds Joy, "or they expect to become instantly enlightened vessels of universal knowledge. But how could that be if they were close-minded to begin with? Rigid belief systems don't automatically expire at death. They reside in the mental realm. The mental realm continues. Death is a passage, that's all. A door. All that's lost is the physical body. The mind with its rigid belief systems carries on in those who are still attached."

Phipps nods. "The mental body has the same form as the physical body. It's composed of light at a higher frequency, that's all. Its light varies in density depending on the awareness of the individual. People with elevated sensitivities like yours are able to see the projections of others even in the material world."

"Spirits, you mean," says Felicity.

"Indeed," says Joy. "And elementals."

Felicity squints. "What's that?"

"Elementals are thought forms projected from those still on Earth, as well as some near-solid ones that have been left behind."

"The mental body," says Phipps, "has a transient existence that expires upon the second death."

Felicity chokes. "The what?!"

"The second death," Phipps repeats evenly.

Joy spreads her arms in a broad circle. "The release of your final confinement, dear. Your mental limitations."

"The death of your attachments," adds Phipps.

Felicity leans forward. "Then I'm not really dead after all," she says. "Am I?"

"Not entirely, no," says Joy. "Not until your mental body has released its physical context and all obstacles to freedom."

"Think of it this way," says Phipps. "If a person is enraged and unforgiving when she dies, she'll remain enraged and unforgiving until she releases her attachment to victimhood and the objects of her rage. Until she identifies life from a celestial perspective. A higher order."

"Addie's enraged and unforgiving," says Felicity sadly.

"Not just Addie," says Joy. "The ego in general fights relentlessly to survive. When it makes it through the first death intact, it often acquires a sense of immortality, and digs in all the deeper. The mental realm abounds with these types. When the ego rules the spirit, and not the reverse, the spirit remains dark and low. Beware of low-lying entities."

Felicity sighs. "Granny and Pothead."

"I'm afraid so," says Joy.

Dr. Joy paces thoughtfully. "The single common currency

of all realms is light, Felicity. That's all you really need to know. Light accrues naturally in all the cracks that ego abandons. The nature of light is to rise."

"And light is a byproduct of love," says Phipps.

Felicity wells up. "So, Addie…"

"You can't control Adelaide," Phipps warns. "You may as well concentrate on yourself."

"Yes," agrees Joy. "Complete your own work. It's all connected anyway. As for Mrs. Phipps and myself, our job is clear. We must tightly coordinate actions to release the black spot from your heart at the same time Adelaide awakens."

"*If* she awakens," says Phipps.

Felicity's attention is drawn downward to her pulsating wound. All at once the area around her speck is festering with inflammation. "Ouch!" she cries. "Can't we pull it out? It's killing me!"

"You have to release it yourself," says Joy. "No one can do it for you."

Felicity fumbles to grasp it between her fingers, but the spot eludes her, wiggling left or right just as she attempts the opposite. "I can't grab it," she complains. "It keeps moving."

"It can't happen until you've forgiven Adelaide," says Phipps.

"But there's nothing…"

"No more time for questions or protests," says Joy. "Adelaide's time is at hand. Do exactly as we say."

"Close your eyes," they say in unison.

Felicity shuts her eyes tightly, her legs quaking. She reaches up for the shower cap she got earlier from the Void, but the cap is gone. She panics. The cap was her protection. How will she survive? This thought is obscured by a dense cloud of frankincense that surrounds her, and beyond the cloud, a glaring light. She chokes on the incense and squirms as the light, exponentially brighter than her own, approaches. "It's so hot!" she complains. "So intense."

"Growth is uncomfortable," says Joy. "It is best born with faith and dignity."

Phipps grips her hand. "Find your center," she says, "and stay there until we arrive."

"Arrive?" says Felicity. "Arrive where?"

Before Phipps can answer, a deep hum gathers around them and builds like a planet of bees. The approaching light intensifies in waves of deep violet, acquiring density and radiance. It hovers at a courteous distance as if asking permission to move forward.

"It's you," Felicity whispers with the only breath she can muster.

"Yessssss," hum the Spirits. "It is us and it is time."

No sooner does Felicity nod consent than she is dropped into a dark shaft that feels like a deep crack between worlds. As she descends, she gains weight and definition at an alarming rate.

After what seems an uncomfortable lifetime, the sense of motion ceases, and the Spirits signal, "This is your first stop, Felicity. We'll leave you here for now."

No wait! she thinks. *Don't leave me here!*

But the heat diminishes rapidly, and she is cooled by a deliciously spicy autumn breeze.

"You can open your eyes, dear," says Phipps.

Felicity is relieved to be flanked by her helpers as she slowly opens her eyes to a familiar scene in her distant memory. She's at the Gorge, but this time she isn't standing on the edge. This time she's somehow hovering above. The majesty of nature from this new perspective is frightening and invigorating at once. She is awestruck. "I'm floating!" she says.

"The trick is to float without us," says Phipps, "but that will take time."

"And confidence," adds Joy.

Felicity glances right to left, assuring herself of her guardians' presence. "Please don't leave me," she says. "Please."

"Don't worry, dear," they say in unison. "Even when you don't see us, we'll be here."

The scene plays out in a thousand ways. It's hard to keep track of whose head she's in, whose perspective she's experiencing from this dizzying height. First there's Julian's convertible in the distance, Julian driving, Addie leaning against him, her long lean legs crossed at the ankles and resting against the passenger door.

Julian stops the car, confused. "I don't know where I am," is the thought she plucks right out of his head.

Addie persists, "I don't care where we are!" But it's hard for Felicity to know if it's a comment or a thought.

In the back seat sits some version of Felicity. It's undeniably her, and yet how can she be in two places at once? And why is she on a date with Julian and Addie in the first place? Way up high as she is, her head splits with a cacophony of mixed signals. She can't take anymore. *What's happening?*

Instantly, Phipps and Joy transport her from the scene.

"I can see you're not prepared for this," says Joy enroute. "Let's try it in reverse."

"But..."

"If it shocks your system too much," says Phipps, "you'll freeze."

"Yes," says Joy. "We certainly can't afford a time freeze at this point. We'll lose all our progress."

Escorted back to the shaft, they are dropped again, this time into a walled campus topped with barbed wire. Again, she floats above, listening to a familiar voice somewhere inside.

Somehow aware that her presence is tenuous, she whispers, "Where are we? Whose voice...?"

But her words return in an empty echo. She is alone.

Everyone knows ghosts aren't real.

THIRTY

ADELAIDE

Adelaide clutches Dulles' cast iron bicep and tries to keep up with him. It's not as if they have a deadline. They're just having fun! She can't move too fast in these strappy sandals with their sexy kitten heels. They're as impractical as they are pretty. And she's out of practice!

Then there's the shimmery silk half-slip that caresses her firm thighs. She guesses it arrived in her most recent Sears & Roebuck mail order. She wishes she could remember ordering all of this, but she's been gone so long. From where she isn't sure.

"From that timeline," says Dulles.

"Well dang if y'all don't eavesdrop on every little thought in my head," she says peevishly.

"Better be careful then," he warns with a chuckle.

Attempting to match his stride, she stumbles on a piece of buckled pavement. "Y'all are walking too fast!" she says. "What's the hurry and where's my whiskey?"

"Ha," he says, grinning. "Good one."

She stomps in protest. "No, really! We're supposed to be having fun."

"Well, what do you call that cyclone ride I just treated you to, pretty lady? If that wasn't fun, what is?"

She giggles. Anywhere with Dulles is fun, to be honest. But she doesn't want him to know that yet. *'Play hard to get and let him sweat'* is her new philosophy. She spent too many years chasing after things too slippery to catch.

"I admit that was a heck of a wind tunnel," she says, "and don't make me do it again." She grabs a handful of her tangled hair and combs her fingers carefully through the matted ends. "At least not without a beauty parlor."

"Better find a beauty parlor then," he says, patting her hand. "I bought a round trip ticket."

"What?! Round trip from where? Y'all are not taking me back to that godforsaken barn, I can tell you that. Or that big ole body! Don't even consider it. Or back to those ladies, either! A bunch of busy bodies, you ask me."

He arches his brow. "Even Felicity?"

"Well, we'll see about Felicity. We might have to rescue her from that cult, I don't know. The poor thing wasn't born with a discriminating cell in her entire body, not to mention that sketchy mind of hers." She pouts. "But enough about Felicity."

Dulles pauses for a second, surveilling their surroundings. Addie thinks he's probably lost, who knows. *Who cares?!* She has no intention whatsoever of returning to her previous old, broken-down life. He can take his sweet time finding whatever he's after. A saloon, hopefully.

Waiting on him to collect his bearings, she points her right foot in front of her, admiring her lovely new sandals all over again. She puts her right foot back and points her left foot forward. Then her right. Then her left. She can't stop looking. The best she can recollect, these shoes along with the rest of her hard-earned wardrobe disappeared around the time she was shipped off to cousin Hyacinth's for R&R. Or whatever she was shipped off to Hyacinth's for.

All at once a burst of intense light strikes Adelaide's field of vision. Squinting, she looks up slowly, shielding her eyes from the noonday sun. As she surveys her surroundings, she and Dulles are standing in a cement courtyard scattered with men in striped uniforms wandering around aimlessly. Her stomach sinks.

"This place doesn't look like any fun at all!" she whines. "We must've taken a wrong turn. Where the heck are we?"

Leaning down, he chucks her chin. "I'm sorry, Adelaide," he says. "No wrong turn. You and I are done for now, but I'll be back, I swear."

"What! No! You're not abandoning me again! Not here you're not!"

"Not abandoning you at all, sugar."

"Don't sugar me, you cad! I should have known it was too good to be true, y'all running off with me like that." She stomps her foot. "What a joke!"

"I swear I'll be back," he says fading rapidly. "You can count on it, Adelaide. I'm a new man. I keep my promises now."

She reaches out desperately. "No!" she wails. "Don't leave me here alone! In a prison yard, for cripe sake! I won't survive!"

No matter how much she protests, he continues to fade. His disappearance is no act. She is utterly alone in a prison yard dressed in a frilly frock, a string of pearls, and kitten heels. What is she supposed to do now?

A familiar androgenous voice interrupts her panic, "Don't be afraid, Adelaide," it says. "You're not alone."

She turns, and wide-eyed, jumps back from the vision. She must be seeing things. *Or...maybe it's really a ghost?* But everyone knows ghosts aren't real! *This one sure looks real.* Why, the whole world is turned inside out. Adelaide's beginning to feel like Felicity, and she doesn't like the feeling.

"Go away," she commands the specter. What else can she do? The thing's just hanging there, staring. It doesn't leave.

It may not be a ghost, she thinks, but dang if something about it doesn't smack of her mother. Her very dead mother. She points at it. "Things are bad enough without you here to..." her eyes widen in horror, "...to do what?" The words get sucked back into her throat like splintered bones. She chokes. "To stick me in...in jail?" she coughs. "Is that why we're in a prison yard? So you can finally get rid of me like y'all probably wanted to do my whole life?"

Adelaide's lungs tighten and her legs stiffen. She feels like she did in the barn—paralyzed. She can't let this happen again. She can't get stuck in a prison yard with her mother's ghost. Not even Dulles to protect her.

Dr. Joy's words bombard her ear, *"If you want to leave you will."*

Well, she's never wanted to leave anywhere more. Or faster! She forces herself to drag one foot in front of the other, arms stuck at her sides like a wooden soldier. She wants to run, but she can't. She just...*why can't she?!*

The filmy specter glides in front of her. "Of course, I don't want to put you in prison, dear," it says in a fake voice ripped right out the throat of the good witch Glinda. A voice no doubt designed to trick Adelaide into believing her mother's outright lies. "I'm only here to help you," it says.

This makes Adelaide laugh out loud in spite of her predicament.

The ghost tilts its head in a fake attempt at empathy. "It's true, dear," it says, moving forward. Reaching.

Adelaide steps back. Turns. Moves forward. Steps to the side. Wherever she goes, the thing blocks her path. Impossible to avoid, Adelaide finally yields, staring right into her mother's mysteriously youthful face. A face so young she doesn't remember it. A face backlit in soft light. A face without the familiar harsh features and severely pinned-back hair. Without a perennially angry expression etched deeply into her baggy eyes and famously tight-lipped mouth. Without the resolute chin that dared Adelaide *or anyone at all* to defy her. Nothing about this imposter rings true. *Who is it? Really?* At this point, Adelaide's too smart to trust anyone or anything. She will not cave in to this delusion!

"Dulles!!!!!" she screams. "Get your ass back here now!!!"

"He can't," says the imposter quietly. "Not yet."

Adelaide's gut wrenches. She searches everywhere for Dulles but sees only the distant lumbering bodies of men in stripes. An alarm rings, and the men assemble slowly, marching into the cement block building, heads hung low. Adelaide can't deny it; she's relieved that they're going inside, that they didn't attack her. Though some piece of her wouldn't mind if they forced this version of Mother into a striped uniform of her own, and locked her up for good.

"What can I do to prove to you that I'm your mother?" begs the imposter.

"Stop being a ghost," says Adelaide, like that was possible.

Like her real mother could just appear out of nowhere. Like Adelaide would even remotely want her to. Although at this point, almost anyone who could get her out of this prison yard would do.

The image strengthens. Gains density and form. As it gains form, it ages familiarly. Back is the sturdy frame, the rounded back, the broad shoulders, the tightly pulled hair. *The square jaw, the severe features, the angry eyes.* The plain black shirt-waist dress buttoned to the neck. The block shoes.

"Is this better?" says the woman angrily.

Adelaide's eyes open to the size of quarters. She is gobsmacked. This is by far the most hideous nightmare she has ever suffered. Almost as scary as life with Mother. Life as Adelaide knew it. Almost anything would be better than this.

"What are you doing here?" she says, confused. "How did you materialize out of nowhere like that?" Her voice is steady, but her legs quake.

"We're in a different timeline," says Mother.

"What? Why? Why you?"

The angry face softens. She reaches forward for Adelaide's hands. "I come to beg your forgiveness."

Adelaide cackles. "So, clearly you're not my real mother. My real mother would never..."

"I need your forgiveness," the woman whispers plaintively. "I can't move ahead without it." And slowly, she transforms back to the young, gentle creature who first appeared.

"Forgiveness for w-w-w-what?" Adelaide stammers. The mother she knew was a dictator who wouldn't have apologized for gutting a family pet. This has to be a hoax. *Unless.*

"Come with me," says the woman. "I'll show you."

THIRTY-ONE

THADDEUS

Thaddeus' dream takes a nosedive. He struggles to punch his way out the top, but it ain't working. He can't break surface. One minute he's in the barn all googly-eyed over Flitty while checking out a gallery of most every person he knew his entire life—ones done him right and ones done him wrong. Next thing he's headed straight fer a cement-block cell. How the hell did he land back in prison? Is this here a trick? Didn't he serve his time? Well, sure he did!

Or maybe his brain's just woozy from all the old faces he seen, can't say. One thing's sure, these blood-pumping dreams ain't dreams, no sir. Not the way they make him feel inside and out. The way his heart beats like a jackhammer the sight of Flitty. The way the autumn wind rustles his suddenly thick hair like a field of high grass. The way fresh-cut spruce from yonder woods peppers the air. The way the crows caw 'cross the prison yard fer a mate, like they do. Like most his dreams, this here seems just one more crazy ass version of real life. A life he'd rather ferget.

He sees now this struggle ain't so much with his jailor this time as his young dumb self. A guy named Julian. *Remember him?* All too well. The last thing Thaddeus wants is to be stuck in the Atlas body of his derelict youth. He'd rather be old, bald and resigned. He'd rather be bent over crippled. He'd rather be anything else than who he were then, but no. In this here not-so-dreamy-dream he's a pissed-off pile of confusion on his way back to the slammer. Just dumb old Julian trying to do right by everyone but hisself. Doomed to relive the worst of his life over and over. That's why everyone's always trying to bury Julian, he reckons. Even Jules tries to bury hisself under Thaddeus. He'd love to bury that dumbass Jules fer good, he's honest. But the colt keeps popping up. Someone please throw a heap a dirt top that boy and keep him down. Throw another one and another. Keep him from wrecking what good might be left of a sorry life. Problem is, it don't work. Jules keeps coming up for air. Maybe he's just got to live with this boy. Figure out who he was and still might be. That's the hardest thing by far.

Thaddeus tries resisting whatever supernatural force trying work him back to Julian. He can't tell where the force begins or ends. He can't see it so he can't dodge it. It's everywhere— front, back, in, out, up, and down. Pushing him deeper and deeper into this timeline till he can't remember how else or who else to be. How to get away. How to float. No. He's weighed down like a barbell, pinned to the earth by gravity. Real flesh, real bone, muscles popping out everywhere. Too many dumb muscles to count. Old man Thaddeus' gone. Bald head, soft belly, spectacles—gone. He pinches hisself. *Ouch!* He's here alright—a twenty-eight-year-old convicted criminal named Julian T. Buck decked out in stripes. Thaddeus just an old uncle lives out the holler by the crick.

The guard shoves Julian's ass into an open cell down the hall from solitary and locks him up tight. "Murderer," he spits through the gap in his front teeth. "Rapist."

Jules knows this guard. Not personally, he don't, but who he is deep down. Where he comes from. How he thinks. Jules and this guard come from the same place. Different hollers, different mines is all. Only thing puts 'em opposite sides of these bars here is the love of different women. That and the brains to protect yerself, which Julian lost somewhere in the Gorge that day. Or maybe never had.

In the cell, he drops to the cot and lays flat out, thinking on all this. Thinking—how'd he get back to prison? How many times this loop gonna replay? He got to get his mind on something sane fast. He got to focus. He got to get out. He rubs his face with his sweaty sleeve and heaves a sigh of despair. He ain't no raping murderer, but he's good as one here. Branded fer life. He covers his face with his hands. Being honest right now, he could figure out how to hang hisself he'd do it. He really would. But he can't.

He struggles off the cot, dragging hisself to the bars, gripping them like they might melt in his hot fists and set him free. It's then he spots two familiar figures strutting down the dark hall, no guard, nothing. Just walking on down like it ain't nighttime in lockdown. Like it's some kind of museum. He sees the shadows first. How'd *they* get in? They might be ghosts or he might be crazy. Maybe both. Likely both. One's looking just like Adelaide before the accident. Pretty enough to snatch James Dean hisself right off the pick list. James Dean or some rich boy from the city—lawyer, maybe, or doctor. Someone to make her mama proud, but no. She sets her sights on a dumb miner boy from the holler. She sets her sights on Julian. By her side is what looks to him like a younger, gentler version of the battle axe mama. They stop at his cell and stare right at him. Or through him, more like. Right through him like they watching some kind of gangster flick on a screen.

"What the hell?" say Adelaide, wide-eyed.

It's really her all right. No mistaking that cranky whine.

"How'd ye get in here?" he say.

Like she can't hear him, Addie does a doubletake from him to her mother and back. "What are we doing here?" she say. "This can't be real." She squints hard. "But it sure looks real."

"It is real," say her mama in the unrecognizable voice of a decent human. She nods at him. "Hello, Julian," she say real somber.

"Ye can see me?" he whispers. "Hear me?"

"I can, but Adelaide can't hear you. Not yet. She's too unformed on this timeline." She shakes her head. "Or really, almost any timeline. But her guardians are helping."

"Helpin' her see me?"

The woman nods slowly. "And hear you. May take a minute or two."

He might be hallucinating, but he can't keep his voice down. He wants to scream so bad, it's like he swallowed a screech owl. He feels fierce. *Crazy.* But he controls hisself. Last thing he needs is more trouble. "Y'all dare come here?" he say a tone or two up. "Of all people?"

"I have no choice," replies the old, young-looking witch.

All the sudden Adelaide's eyes go bonkers and she starts to tune in. "What the cripe?!" she keeps repeating.

Julian's not sure what to do. *Are they here to release him?* Looking at Adelaide he say, "I thought ye were, ye know... unfit, I was told." Should he say these things? He shrugs. Who cares? What's to lose that ain't long gone?

"Unfit...what?" She turns to her mama. "Did he say *unfit?*"

Her mama nods. "I'm sorry, Adelaide. You were never right after the accident."

Addie screws her face up like she can't remember.

"At the Gorge, dear."

All this matter-of-fact calmness getting to him. "What's going on here?" he demands. "Y'all come to tell the truth or what? Y'all come to spring me loose?" He squints. "Or triple the torture?"

"Shut up, ye fuckin' lunatic!" screams the guy from the next cell.

Julian lays his head against the bars. The guy's right. He is a lunatic; he knows it. These folks ain't real. Figments of his exhaustion. He squeezes his arm through the bars to try and touch Addie, but he can't reach far enough. "Come 'ere," he say. "Come closer." He wants to touch her. Wants to pinch her skin between his fingers. Wants to make her feel what he feels.

He thinks she wants to come closer. She looks like she does, all doe-eyed and such. But she don't move. It's like they're reaching out from different worlds. He can see them there, both of them. *Right there!* But. *No.*

"So Julian's not dead?" say Adelaide to her mother like she's staring at a likeness.

Her mama shakes her head slowly. "That's right."

"But...we buried him." She pauses. "Didn't we?"

"In a way."

Their figures move backwards into the cement walls like a movie Jules once seen in Louville with Uncle Thaddeus—*Topper* or something. Ghosts.

"Why's he in prison?" asks Addie, her voice fading.

He watches dumbstruck as they flicker on and off till they disappear.

The now invisible mama say, "Because I put him there, Adelaide. I did it."

"What! Why? What'd he do?"

"He threatened my family," she say.

"With what?" shrieks Adelaide. "With a pickaxe? A rifle? What?!"

"With his ignorance. With his sorry social status and his weak genes. I blamed him for all of it. For everything. For his ability to trick you with his decency and his charm. Blamed him for reminding me where I came from. Not a place for my daughters, no. No way in hell."

He strains his ears, but he can't hear nothing else. They're gone.

Flat as he feels in this moment, he knows she's right, that mama. She were just protecting her own from a sorry boy born to a sorry place. Who can argue with that?

THIRTY-TWO

REGINA

Regina waits for the energies to enfold them and usher her and Adelaide to the next timeline, but the guardians are lollygagging somewhere in infinite space, leaving her to her own negligible devices. She supposes she deserves this. Let's face it, her earthly persona was a vindictive bitch and Adelaide, her natural-born target.

Not that she had any of these insights when she walked the Earth. She emphatically did not. She was too consumed with her own pain to notice anyone else's. Too determined to right the wrong inflicted on her from conception. The wrong of sending her down the wrong birth canal into the arms of exactly the wrong mother—crazy Abigail McManis. Not just crazy, but dirt poor and hopeless to boot. The catastrophic trifecta of a doomed childhood.

At least Regina didn't duplicate the trifecta in her own family. Not that anyone noticed or gave her credit. She was smart and ambitious enough to marry into the Somers clan and work hard at the funeral home and chicken farm. She toiled day and night collecting eggs, learning to fry them to perfection without a single punctured yolk. Wringing necks and burying bodies. Reading books. Educating herself. Why, she single-handedly converted *Sunnyside Up* from a charity into a bona fide business. A business of honor and prestige envied throughout the county.

There were those who thought her ruthless. Maybe she was. But it was that very ruthlessness that elevated her own social status and the status of her children. She would have done anything for them. She provided them with a degree of financial security that she never knew as a child. Security enough to be hopeful about their own futures. Security enough to focus on improving themselves even more. But it's a world of opposites. How does one understand hope without despair? Impossible. You have to know both to understand either. Her girls didn't know despair. How could they possibly appreciate the value of hope?

Well, Adelaide couldn't. Always the entitled one, she was. Regina tries not to dwell on this, but it's difficult, even now. Back in this timeline, her Earth brain reconnects to circumstances and emotions she has to work hard to detach from— the same circumstances and emotions that form the border world she is desperate to escape. One thing Regina has learned the hard way is this—you can't take grudges to heaven. They weigh you down. A grudge is nothing but a free pass to the lowest state of consciousness, a dark and unwelcoming cave of subsistence. A cave Regina knew so well she could walk it blindfolded. When she walked the Earth, her natural habitat was a cave.

She focuses deeply. Focuses deeply and reaches high to remember who she is outside space and time. To reconnect to *that* light, her guiding light. She almost gets there, but dang if Adelaide, screaming and squirming right there on the ground of the prison yard, doesn't drag her right back down. Regina knows she can't get where she needs to go without accepting Adelaide. Accepting her completely without holding their opposing selves within her as one complete thing. But standing here watching Adelaide pitch a fit the likes of which only Regina's mama, Abigail McManis, could have matched, turns Regina's blood cold. What is she to do when every unforgivable, godawful reason she couldn't deal with this child in the first place plays out right in front of her all over again? She grits her teeth, telling herself, *let go of this fight!*

Breathing deeply, she forces herself to say, "Adelaide dear, I'm sorry; I truly am. Please believe me." She wants her words to be true. She will say them until they are.

Adelaide, her cheeks stained with mascara, glares at Regina through a toxic haze of rage and confusion. "You locked him UP?"

Regina searches frantically for the guardians to support her. *Where are they? They said they were coming!* "I did," she says with genuine contrition. "I hated him then."

Adelaide grabs a stone from the prison yard and raises it threateningly.

Regina winces in anticipation. "Go ahead, throw it," she says. "Get it over with."

Adelaide doesn't hesitate. She pulls her arm back and pitches the stone right at Regina's face. It strikes her in the chin, and Regina feels it in a shockingly physical way. Gasping at the unexpected pain—*it's been so long!*—she touches her wound. The bump is already large and round. It feels like real flesh. It has a life of its own.

"Why?!" rages Adelaide. "How could you?!"

Regina meets her daughter eye-to-eye. "I blamed him for what happened, Adelaide. I couldn't accept it."

Adelaide's eyes widen. "I'll tell you what happened! Felicity and I have been running around trying to bury that man our entire adult lives, that's what happened! It's practically all we can think about. *When do we bury Julian? How will we bury Julian?* And do you know why?"

Regina lowers her eyes.

"Because we thought he was dead!" she says, collapsing on her knees. "I was told that the love of my life *died*. That he died and my own mother wouldn't bury him in our cemetery because he wasn't good enough. All I wanted was to make things right."

"It was too late to make things right," Regina says softly. "Flitty was gone, and y'all were, well—you were half-gone." She shivers at the visceral memory.

"Flitty never left my side," says Adelaide. "The only one gone was you. Gone right out of your mind, apparently. Julian was...he was..." She cocks her head and frowns. "He was... serving time? For what? Serving time for the unforgiveable crime of pissing you off?"

At that the Spirits gather in form and density, enfolding them in heat and light. Regina has never been more grateful to be rescued. The grief of the encounter with Adelaide drags her down like a ton of regret. Another minute and she'd gladly sink straight to the eternal bottom just to end the pain.

The guardians lift Adelaide's crying heap, moving her to the portal. Regina follows, her grand lightness of being turning swiftly to an ungodly weight. Her emotional body is heavier than her physical body ever was. But maybe that's the way it's always been. She just hadn't understood.

"Where are we going?" Adelaide screams. "What's happening? Where's Dulles? "Dulles!" she screams. "Dul-lllllles!"

The portal opens and there stands Dulles, slick in his white linen suit. A fresh white gardenia in the button hole of his jacket. A grin on his handsome angular face. Regina watches as he embraces her daughter.

"I'm right here," he says. "I told you I'd return."

Looking up, Adelaide is sucked like a magnet into his embrace.

Regina glides forward to join them. "Do you forgive me, Adelaide? Please?! Without your mercy I have nowhere to go. I'm stuck in between for eternity."

Adelaide turns around slowly, raising her fist. "Hell no!" she says. "Y'all ruined my life. Tell me how in the hell I can forgive that."

As the door closes between them, Regina hears Dulles say, "Ah, but you must forgive her, Adelaide."

"Never!"

"If you don't, Flitty won't be able to forgive you."

"For what?!" Adelaide shrieks. "Good lawd, the whole world's gone mad!"

THIRTY-THREE

FELICITY

F elicity tugs on Phipps' robe. "I can't watch anymore," she says. "I can't bear their pain."

"Ahh, so you see it then?" says Phipps. "The pain? How it all travels back and forth multiplying times seven every time it's returned?"

"I see it, yes." Felicity looks down. "But worse, I feel it." She grips her chest. "I am the pain."

Dr. Joy waves her hand over Felicity's head. "I'll adjust your antennae," she says. "There's a tendency to be too empathic on this level." She makes adjustments in Felicity's field. Satisfied, she nods. "That's better."

If you ask Felicity, it's too late for a technical adjustment. At this point, there is no separation between her and the others. They are one thing, antennae and all. The more desperate Mother is, the more restrictive Addie becomes. The more restrictive Addie becomes, the more pain Felicity suffers. The wound in her heart bleeds and pulsates. She drops to her knees. "If Addie could just feel Mother's pain, she might at least try to forgive her," she tells her helpers. "Can't you make her feel it as I do? Good God, it's unbearable!"

Phipps shakes her head. "That's a matter of consciousness, dear. She doesn't feel your mother's pain, just as your mother couldn't feel Granny's. And on and on as far back as you care to look. All of these women have been too blinded by their own pain to access the compassion that would have released it."

Felicity blinks. "I do understand their pain," she says, "but not what happened. What in the world is Julian doing in jail? And why is Mother responsible?"

"You'll see dear," says Phipps. "You'll see."

With that, Felicity is dropped back into the slender temple of her fleeting youth. While Julian is off in the woods, she leans forward from the backseat of his convertible, urging Adelaide to let him drive them home. "We're a long way from *Sunnyside Up*," she says anxiously. "And it's getting dark. Mother and Daddy will be looking for us."

Adelaide turns to face her, infuriated, her temper escalating with the whirling wind. Her long black hair whips around in every direction, and to Felicity she appears as a dark faerie queen.

"You're ruining my...LIFE!" Addie screams at her.

"And you're ruining mine," Felicity mutters.

"What did you say!!" Addie screeches.

"Nothing," says Felicity.

"What are you even doing here?" Addie screams into the wind. "You're a bloody nuisance is what you are!"

Felicity knows she shouldn't, but life is already risky, so really, what's there to lose? "You're just jealous," she snaps.

Addie's eyes practically pop out of their sockets. "What did you say?"

"Nothing." Felicity stares at her lap.

Addie points her finger accusingly. "Say it, or you're never going home."

Felicity leans forward and screams, "Okay I'll say it! YOU'RE! JUST! JEALOUS!" Her words are cannonballs. Releasing them, she suffers the recoil.

Addie's features tighten. "About what?!" She leans forward. "Exactly what am I jealous of, Felicity Jane? Your utter immature childishness?"

Felicity raises her chin. "Take me home," she says.

"Not on your LIFE, sister! Not until you tell me why in the wide world I would possibly be jealous of your skinny butt."

At this, Felicity turns sideways, staring out at the high brush that Julian disappeared into. "Jealous that he photographed me," she says.

"Whhaaaaat?!"

"Uh oh." She bites her bottom lip.

"Photographed you?"

Felicity nods uneasily. Too late to go back now. What's said is said. "Yes," she mutters. "Julian asked me to wait until he tells you, so I hope you're proud that you got me to break my promise."

"He photographed *you*?"

She nods at the floor.

"When?"

"Last week."

"Where?"

"At his, um, house."

Addie screams into the wind. "Aaaaaaaaaaaaaaaa!!!"

"I'm sorry, Addie," Felicity says and repeats. "I really am. I honestly didn't think you would care this much." From the looks of it, though, she doubts Addie can hear her through the escalating maelstrom of wind and debris.

Felicity watches all this from above at the same time she engages from below. She is there but not there, at least not attached. She watches as Addie climbs awkwardly over the gearshift to the driver's seat. Suspended over the console, her right leg catches in the loose hem of her skirt. She yanks madly to free it, and in the process, accidentally shifts gears. A pile of squirming limbs, she emerges upright, facing backwards, her long arms hailing the past. "Jules!" she screams, but he's nowhere to be seen.

The car moves steadily ahead.

"Oh no, Addie!" says Felicity. "Turn around and stop the car!"

Adelaide tries to twist back around, but she can't. The car picks up speed and from above, Felicity can feel the moving landscape disorienting them both, but especially her sister. Terrified, Addie screams at Felicity, "Now look what you've done!"

"Turn around," Felicity shouts. "You've got to turn yourself around and grab the wheel. The brake!"

Addie's only instinct is to scream. "You've ruined my life!" she shrieks. "This is just one more thing! He was going to ask me to marry him today!"

The car bounces over ruts, stones, and branches, careening off exposed tree roots on its now steep, downward course. With great difficulty, Addie manages to twist around on her knees against the momentum. She reaches for the wheel, but is thrown back and forth repeatedly by the car's unpredictable obstacle course. "Aaaaaaaaa!" she screams over and over. "Aaaaaaaaa!"

Things are moving so quickly, Felicity's brain is bound and gagged. She is only what she sees and hears: a whorl of wind, a screeching raven, a branch of orange sumac tearing through her hair.

"Julian, heeeelp!" Addie yells into the wind, arms flailing. "Heeeellllp!"

Pinned to her seat as if by destiny, Felicity wonders if she and Addie will ever see Julian again. Or their family. Or anyone. We won't, she thinks. *Knows.* We are too far gone. She watches dispassionately from above as her frantic sister tries to stand, but is dropped squarely onto the driver's seat by sheer force. The car careens down the sloped path, picking up speed.

"The brake, Addie! The brake!" Felicity screams just as she is tossed forward like a sack of flour into the back of the passenger seat. Her voice cracks like an egg.

She's had enough.

Willing her spirit up and out of the car, she separates herself from the scene. "I can't take anymore," she tells her mentors, breathless. "Whatever happened, it's over. I'm done with it. I don't care what happens next. I forgive her."

"Ah, but you do care," says Phipps. "And you will see it through."

"No," she whimpers. "I can't."

"You must."

Felicity turns beseechingly to Joy. "Please?"

"I'm sorry," says Joy. "Not only must you watch, you must reenter your body in a conscious state. You must do this scene over with singular awareness."

Phipps takes Felicity's hand. "It's true," she says. "You must reenter. But you don't have to do it now."

THIRTY-FOUR

ADELAIDE

Adelaide purrs with delight as Dulles lifts her onto a gold velvet barstool and takes his seat beside her. Ahead are mirrored shelves stocked with glittering crystal bottles of every imaginable pigment. Prisms of aqua, magenta, emerald, ruby, and rich caramel are projected onto the clear glass countertop, the venetian glass walls, and the expansive skylights. As she is busy being dazzled by all the sparkling color, Dulles forms a fist and pounds the countertop with an air of authority that melts her spine.

"Time for a beverage!" he declares.

"You can say that again!" she says,

chuckling with relief. "I was beginning to wonder about your idea of a good time."

"Don't be fooled," he warns. "This is a rest stop, not a destination."

Addie leans forward to debate his mistaken viewpoint, but he places his finger against her lips. "No objections," he says firmly. "You have to trust me on this. Your life depends on it."

She opens her mouth to nibble his finger and he pulls it back, ignoring the invitation. Still playing the gentleman, she supposes. Well, two can play that game, but not for long. At least not after the dreamy cocktails they're about to order. And while they're at it, maybe a cigarette or too. Why not? Moments like this cry out for indulgence.

No sooner does Adelaide visualize a cigarette at her lips than Dulles tells the bartender, "I'll take one of those slim cigs for the lady."

She grins broadly. All this mindreading is so convenient. She just wishes it worked both ways. She would love to know his intentions. Maybe it's not too late for her to be a devoted wife after all.

His back to the counter, the bartender opens a drawer under the mirrored wall and produces a long slim cigarette, exactly as described. He inserts it carefully into an opera-length Tiffany cigarette holder, turns around and offers it to Adelaide on a silver tray.

"Ooooo," she coos. "Fancy!"

When she places it between her lips, she feels like Audrey Hepburn or Hedy Lamarr, or really, any glamorous leading lady from the silver screen she could name. The man leans forward to offer her a light, and her eyes widen in recognition. Why, minus the handlebar moustache, the silk vest and stylish gabardine trousers, this gentleman could be Barrows' twin brother. As foreign as this place is, it's also somehow familiar.

"Say, are you related to Lionel Barrows?" she asks.

The bartender leans forward and lights her cigarette, ignoring the question. Huh, well. She must be seeing things. She draws the smoke deeply into her throat, pursing her mouth and exhaling it in little puffy clouds of contentment. All she needs now is a double bourbon.

"Coming right up," says the psychic bartender.

The Barrows' lookalike grabs the neck of a tall green bottle off the mirrored wall of glass shelves and pours two crystal tumblers half-full of the smoothest Kentucky bourbon ever to waft up Adelaide's eager nostrils. She's practically drooling. Life has certainly become more meaningful lately, she thinks, her chin raised, puffing thoughtfully. Just proves you should never give up. At some point, just when you're about to surrender, the world suddenly lines up behind your righteousness and produces a glimmer of justice. She exhales the smoke in a long thin philosophical stream this time, thinking that just when everything is freefalling to hell in a broken mine shaft, heaven shows up in a blaze of glory, escorting you to one of its many celestial saloons. Who knew? At least she hopes it's one of many saloons. Not that she's in heaven but...where is she? She shakes her head. Who cares.

The barkeep slides the tumblers of glistening bourbon across the countertop like shuffleboard discs. "Here y'all go," he says. "Drink up."

"Oooo," she says, giddily. "You can bet on that!"

Dulles reaches for his wallet.

"No sir," says Barrows' twin, holding up his hand. "It's on the house."

"Well, isn't that nice," Adelaide chirps, hoping that this is also the first of many experiences "on the house" with Dulles. In spite of his tacky, hidden tattoos, he's probably rich and influential, she thinks. Probably inherited millions from his banker daddy. Or lawyer daddy, or whatever. Probably so full of cashola he can buy her anything she wants. One sip and she's already dreaming of the second drink and the third. Maybe she'll have a mint julep next. Or a whiskey sour, or both. It's all she can do not to chug this one right down to get to the next one to make up for lost time. But that would be so Outskirt of her. And the truth is, Outskirt and she were never a good fit.

She taps the lengthening cigarette ash in a ladylike manner on the edge of a crystal ashtray trying not to think anything at all, anything that could be mindread, that is. But it isn't working. She doesn't want Dulles to know how anxious she is to experience everything in this candyland. She doesn't want him to know how desperate she is for fun. Crazy unabandoned fun! Nothing measured or rule-based or in any way attached to consequences of a negative nature.

For example, to her far right sits a romantic couple in a booth feeding each other dainty little spoonsful of caviar. Not that she's ever had caviar, but she knows what it is. She isn't ignorant. She doesn't even care what it tastes like or how slimy it looks, she wants Dulles to feed it to her, just like that, one dainty spoonful at a time. She wants to feed him back. She wants cocktails and mixed nuts at the bar followed by a five-course meal beginning with a bucket of caviar followed by a white linen dinner composed of duck instead of pigeon, or really, any refined foreign cuisine worthy of her new life. Her new self! She tries to imagine the waiter taking a torch to one of those dramatic desserts she saw on TV the one time. Something to do with mounds of burnt white fluff and Alaska. She wants that. Something elegant and wild. Something on fire. Like her.

Her fantasy meal is only the beginning of a decadent evening in a luxurious resort. A honeymoon, if you will. A honeymoon followed by numerous extended holidays on ocean liners across the Atlantic. And the Pacific, why not? And every other ocean, not that she can think of any. Her imagination is going insane packing trunks of couture fashion for the trip. The world is opening up at last! She was right to wait for Dulles. *Or maybe Dulles waited for her!* Julian would never have been able to afford her exquisite taste in, well...everything! Bless his little holler heart.

She swirls the luscious amber liquid in the glass round and round. "I do love a fine bourbon," she says, practically drunk just looking at it.

Dulles leans in so close she nearly licks his neck. "It isn't bourbon," he whispers.

She smiles dreamily. "Whatever you say, sailor! Whiskey it is."

"It isn't whiskey either, Adelaide."

She bats her heavy lashes. "Oh really? What is it then, a magic potion?"

He stares at her so deeply, his eyes pierce the back of her brain. "It's courage, Adelaide," he says. "The only kind of courage you'd ever understand."

"Why Rhett," she trills in her best Scarlet O'Hara, "why ever would I be needing that?"

Without taking her eyes off him, she upends the glass of whatever he wants to call it—*she calls it fun!*—and knocks it straight down her grateful throat. *Life is so good; don't wreck it!* From there it sizzles its way slowly through her warm chest, her happy belly, down her long, grateful legs, straight into her insanely appreciative feet until her toes curl.

It's about time she gave herself permission to do whatever she wants. *Deserves!* Permission to tear right through every stop sign that stands in her way like a freight train at a thousand miles an hour. *Wooo hooo!* Whatever. Wherever.

Whenever. Courage to stop everybody everywhere from slamming the brakes on her party train like they've been doing since day one. Dodging Mother left and right straight out of the birth canal. Losing Jules in the prime of his life and hers. Burying him every time she turns around. Or at least trying to bury him. Caring for Flitty all these broken-down years, as much as she loves Flitty. Still. Year upon endless year of selfless sacrifice. Make that decades. *Without love!* Without so much as an ounce of romance to make the tedium bearable.

Her throat burns and her head spins as the fancy bourbon swirls through her system with a life of its own. Before she knows what's happening it curdles in her tummy, transforming into something else. Something altogether different. Something crass and vulgar. Something akin to Papaw's 80 proof hooch from the backyard still. Or worse.

Hey! What's happening!

All at once her fancy velvet barstool drops her like an anchor through a long tunnel into a runaway convertible on a dirt road in a forest so dark and dense she'll never find her way out. Pungent bursts of aromatic pine and sweet laurel tickle her nose and grip her throat as she descends. It takes her a minute to acclimate, but once she does, the wildfire in her heart ignites, shooting flames up her throat and out her mouth like dragon breath. She has no idea what she's saying until it's said.

But then it all comes back.

"I hate you!" she screams at Felicity who's bouncing around helter-skelter behind her. The wind is as furious as Adelaide's tongue. "You steal everything of mine! My time! My clothes! And now my fiancé! What next? My life?!"

"He's not your fiancé," Felicity shouts back, practically swallowing the wind. "And I didn't steal him! I just posed for some lousy pictures! You weren't available. I was trying to do you a favor." Long thick strands of her hair whip into her mouth while she's yelling. She gags on a mouthful, coughing and spitting it out then twisting a handful like a life rope just as the car spikes left, first knocking Adelaide against the steering wheel then sideways against the door. She jams her shoulder and wrenches her neck. Her eyes snap shut but she forces them open.

The slope steepens and the runaway car picks-up speed. Adelaide looks up only to see gangly trees overlooking a vast open space. And then she sees Felicity, against all forces of gravity and nature struggling over the seatback trying to get into the front of the car.

"What are you doing?!!" Adelaide screams at the same time she thinks—is Felicity looking for a fight? Because Adelaide can't handle a fight right now. Right now she needs all the energy she can muster just to turn this car around. In spite of her awkward position against the door, she raises her foot, strikes Felicity in the chin, and knocks her back.

But Felicity recovers and climbs back up, lunging forward and tumbling onto the passenger side of the front seat. Adelaide is pinned to the door, immobilized by the car's momentum, but Felicity's strength appears nearly superhuman. Laying back on her elbows, Felicity stretches her long legs over Adelaide as far as they'll go and flicks her foot against the door again and again until the handle gives and the door flies open. The wind on her head, Adelaide hangs onto the wheel for dear life, praying her long hair doesn't get caught under a tire and pull her out of the car. She tries to bite Felicity's leg, but before she can get a grip, Felicity curls her legs up tight and releases them in a firm kick that sends Adelaide straight out of the moving car.

As she flies backwards, Adelaide screams, "I hope you die! I hope you diiiiiiiiie!"

Almost instantly, the small of her back strikes something

solid and unforgiving—a boulder or a tree trunk. Her back spasms. Her neck whiplashes so hard it feels like it's snapping off. Her eyes slam shut, and then, for a merciful moment, she feels nothing at all.

She is set adrift in a deep dark nothingness. Before long she feels like she's drowning. Like she's casting about in an underwater cave, gulping for oxygen, her lungs on the verge of collapse. She flails about in the cave for a while as the mysterious sea rises from her ankles to her knees to her waist to her shoulders and on to her chin. Get it over with, she thinks. *Take me now.* But just before it swallows her up in its cold wet throat, she surfaces upright on her gold velvet barstool, blinking like a broken light as the barkeep slides another bourbon her way.

"Another cigarette, Mademoiselle?" he adds.

Staring ahead, stunned, she shakes her head no and breaks into a cold sweat.

"You might need it," says Dulles gently.

She turns toward him, desperate. "Don't send me back," she begs. "She tried to kill me."

"That's not exactly accurate," he says.

"I'm in no mood to explain," she whimpers. "Don't take her side. If y'all had been there you'd know." She sucks a deep breath. "I can't go back."

"Ah, but you can," he says.

She knocks back the bourbon. "What good will it do? I already know what happens."

"You don't."

"I do."

Meeting her stare, he says, "You don't, but you're about to find out."

She drops her head in her hands. "This isn't heaven, is it?"

"No," he says. "But it's the only road left."

THIRTY-FIVE

ADELAIDE

A boulder sits on Adelaide's chest and no matter how hard she pushes, it won't budge. The constant *beep beep, beep* of a nearby machine alarms her, and she succeeds against the unbearable forces of an increasingly unpredictable universe to open her eyes a sliver to see what's going on. Her eyes are sticky and her vision blurred, but at least she isn't completely blind. All she really wants to know is where Dulles went and what he did with her bourbon. The back of what feels like her ten-ton head is pinned to the bed, and there's a contraption over her mouth, so it's not like she could drink the bourbon even if she had it.

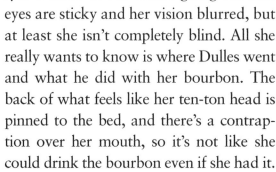

Or even hold the glass, since she can't seem to locate her hands
through all the instruments and tubes. Every inch of her body
aches, though, and bourbon would really help. Or whiskey. Or
courage if you ask Dulles. Whatever you want to call it she needs
it now. If she could just locate Barrows' twin, she could psychi-
cally convince him to deliver it through one of these tubes. Her
eyes scan the room for him or Dulles or really, anyone at all.

Just as she's sending these wishes to the mindreading barkeep, she spots an awkward willowy character in the corner
who looks more like the real Barrows himself, badly dressed in
a pair of overalls, his wispy white hair blown every which way.
From another direction she hears a weirdly familiar voice over
the staccato beeps and general hum of machinery.

"Hey! She opened her eyes!" cries the overenthusiastic
voice. "Anyone out thar hear me? She opened her eyes!"

Adelaide can't figure out who the voice belongs to or why
it cares that she opened her red-hot burning eyes. They were
better off closed. She slowly scans far left to far right and somewhere on the second go-round she spots that creep Thaddeus
in his usual tweed costume. Good lawd, she thinks, isn't he
the reason she fell out the window in the first place? Driving
Julian's stolen car through their property in the moonlight?
Will this nightmare ever end?!

"Go away," she grunts.

"She's tryin' to talk!" he cries. "Nurse! Come quick; she's
tryin' to talk!"

Moments later, a nurse appears, and he pleads, "Can't y'all
jes remove the oxygen fer a second so's we can hear what she's
tryin' to say? Likely her final words, I'd guess."

Frowning, the nurse considers this. "I don't know, sir," she
says. "The doctor's not available at the moment, and removal
of the mask could be detrimental."

"No more detrimental than death," he insists, "which is comin' with or without the lady's final words."

"Death?" Adelaide grunts under the mask.

"See?!" he says, pointing. "She wants to talk. Let her have her say."

"Well, uh, I suppose," says the nurse. She moves in reluctantly, rearranging some equipment and finally lifting the apparatus from Adelaide's mouth. "But just for a second or two. Any distress and it's right back on."

As the nurse holds the equipment at a distance, Thaddeus moves so close to Adelaide's face she can smell his breakfast sausage. She's got to get this over with as quickly as possible.

"Who...you?" she mumbles. *Why doesn't her tongue work?!* "Why you...here?" Her mouth is so dry she can barely form the words.

The man takes her hand tenderly, squeezing it between his own sweaty mitts. "Who am I, ye ask?" he says, smiling warmly.

Something about him strikes a deadly chord in Adelaide's sorry heart.

He bows his head. "Why, it's Julian T. Buck at yer service, Ma'am."

Her lungs contract; she gasps for air. Her chest pressure increases from the weight of a boulder to a small mountain. The impact of his words catapults her into a long dark tunnel of subterranean consciousness. Feet first and arms up, she races down the tunnel's mind-bending twists and turns until finally she is dropped back into the deep forest in a cold wet huddle pressed against a rough, snake-crawling tree trunk. Or at least it's the kind of place snakes would naturally gather to see what's on the menu. Her temples pound like a pair of knockout punches. She struggles to remember what happened. What landed her here. She can't get to it. So close, and yet. No.

After a time, no saying how much, her memory begins to regurgitate huge, indigestible chunks of experience. Oh yes, that's right, she remembers—Felicity tried to do her in. Her own sister! The pain of this awareness is suffocating. But maybe she has it wrong. She must have it wrong. *Right?* Because how could her very own baby sister have attempted to murder her? It makes no sense at all. The sister she jumped rope with, played coffin hide & seek with, and practically raised when you think about it. But the reality of it all is an unstoppable storm, easily collapsing her fragile wall of doubt. And then it's clear; it really is. Her own sister shoved her out of a runaway car. Left her to rot on the forest floor to be devoured by snakes. Lawd have mercy.

Her hand moves reflexively to her chest, shielding her outraged heart from this infamy. *I hate her!* Like Julian's abandonment wasn't enough, she thinks, her own sister was complicit. Beyond complicit. Her own sister attempted to murder her! And where is the little felon now, she wonders. Has she run off with Julian to some romantic hideaway? Was this their plan all along? To find a Justice of the Peace and get hitched? *Is Felicity pregnant?* Adelaide hates them both. She hates them irreversibly. And if she finds them, well, they'll be as sorry a pair as ever roamed the Earth. Why, she'll run them both right over the edge of this gorge into the cold abyss of unforgivable betrayal where they belong.

But it's Felicity!

Still.

She stole your man!

She's my sister.

And left you to rot!

As her eyes adjust to the near moonless night, Adelaide spots a shadow ahead. A shadow amongst shadows that stands out for some reason. It could be her imagination or it could be a bear. Boy oh boy, it's dark. Could it be any darker? No. This kind of darkness should be locked up in solitary for life. She shivers from the damp chill and the relentless fear that makes her hate Felicity even more if that's possible. She has to get out of here. She has to. She has to survive in spite of them. *Because of them!* She pushes her aching body upward against the snake-ridden tree trunk and steps painstakingly forward over splintered branches and wet leaves, mindful of every breath. She mustn't be seen or heard by the opportunistic residents of these carnivorous woods. As she approaches the shadow, she narrows her eyes for focus. Is it a bear or isn't it? She tiptoes a few steps further and holds her breath. A few more steps, and then, her frantic heart pounding against her chest, she leans in.

Ah, no. No, it's not a bear.

She exhales slowly. It's lower and longer and…why it's…it's a car. Yes, that's what it is. It's hard and made of metal. There are tires and wheels. And what she thought might be the head of the bear appears to be a popped trunk. Is it Julian's car? It might be. Her head and neck hurt so much she can barely think. Well, if it's Julian's car, where's Felicity? And where's Julian? Where did they go and how did they get there? By horse? Of course, how ingenious. She'll have to search for tracks in the morning.

She inches to the left, stumbling on a branch then catching herself against the side of the car. The contour of the trim is familiar. Considering what to do next, she tunes into the sound of an animal moaning some 100 feet in the distance. A bear, no doubt. It sounds like a bear. Or a mountain lion or a bobcat. Or a coyote. Or a pack of coyotes! Her gut tells her to get the hell out, but it's too dark and too dangerous to do anything but stay put until she's been found. If she ever is found. If she isn't eaten limb by limb.

She works her way slowly around the front of the car, trying not to attract any attention. The hood, still warm, is smashed against a giant boulder. Sensing her way back along its edge to see what's on the other side, she freezes. What's on the other side is...nothing. Nothing at all. A deep empty cavern of darkness. In other words, the Gorge. Well, at least the car was stopped by the boulder, she thinks. Not that she cares. Well, maybe she cares a little. She wraps her arms around herself wishing she were anywhere but here.

The moaning returns, louder. She looks around slowly. Could be anything. An injured animal or its half-eaten dinner. She inches back and looks inside the car. "Flitty, you in there?" she whispers. And what if she is? If she is, Adelaide has a good mind to steer the car a few feet to the right, slide it into neutral and send it flying off the edge. But anyway, she can't see Flitty. Flitty isn't there.

"Uhhhhh," cries a voice so faint, Adelaide thinks she's hearing things.

"Help me!" cries something in the air. Something in Adelaide's head, is all. She can't think straight. Tremors run up and down her spine. How will she survive all this, and what will be left of her life if she does? She follows the sound up and to her left, where she makes out what looks like a slim shadow, half-dressed, clinging to a branch. A crack of moonlight leaks through a bank of dark clouds. It might be Flitty. Flitty all torn up.

"Flitty, that you?" Adelaide says half to herself.

"It is," says the voice in Adelaide's head.

"Well, look at that," says Adelaide to the shadow as if it's anything at all. As if she isn't seeing things. "Sad to see me alive?"

"I can't hang on. I'm...I'm falling."

Addie knows she's hearing things. Seeing things. Her brain is shrapnel. She looks back at the car, stares blankly ahead for a minute, then inches down past the open door and climbs inside. Her sore hip hits the driver's wheel and she winces, collapsing across the cushioned seat, her skull pressed against the passenger door. Whoever's whimpering out there will have to help herself. Or call Julian, how about that? Or just die.

"Help me!" persists the voice in Adelaide's head. *Or not in her head?* Her head is a ruptured piñata spilling voices into the air.

Her mother's voice: "See what you've done!"

Granny's voice: "Save yer sister for gawd sake, child!"

Flitty's voice: "Don't leave me, Addie! I'm so scared!"

And even if it really is Flitty, so what? After what she's done to Adelaide, doesn't she deserve to hang from a tree until morning at least? And how'd she get up that tree in the first place? Did she find herself in a tough position and climb? Rabid raccoons at her ankles? Or maybe Julian left her too. Well, hell, that's not Adelaide's problem. None of this is. If there's a victim here, it's hardly Felicity. Felicity tried to kill her!

"Heeeelp!" cries the voice in her head louder. "Heeeelp!"

Her lips pressed hard against the seat, saliva leaking out the corners, Adelaide mutters, "If that's you, Felicity Jane, you can just stay up there a while longer. How's that for justice? Ponder your sins until you drop…"

Before she can finish the thought, a searing jolt shoots up her neck, pierces her eyes like an electrical current, thrusting her into the deepest sleep of her life. A sleep darker and denser than the forest that claims her. Darker than anything she's ever known. If she ever wakes up, the first thing she'll do is wring Felicity's neck.

THIRTY-SIX

CHORUS

"**D**id you hear that, Felicity Jane?" coos the grave-yard chorus. "That girl wanted you to hang until you dropped."

Felicity, perched on the branch of the same sugar magnolia that held her so precariously over the Gorge that night, whispers, "I heard her, but she didn't mean it."

"Oh, she meant it alright," mumbles Granny. She leans forward on her rocking chair cloud. "Adelaide never did care much about any of us. Ain't talked to me in decades."

Pothead cocks the hammer of his pistol and assumes a ready position. "Somethin'

wrong with that gal," he says. "Always was. Came out mean like her mother."

"Put that pistol down, you moron," scolds Trudie. "One of these days y'all gonna kill one of us with that dang weapon."

Felicity slaps her hands over her ears, wishing she could find the bathing cap from the Void, the one that blocks the voices. "Get out of my head!" she cries.

Mother reaches down from a higher branch to hand her the cap. "Here you go, dear. Not that you need it."

Felicity accepts it gratefully. "I certainly do need it," she says. "I can't think straight! They're drowning me out."

"Out of what?" prods Phipps from a floating podium.

Felicity shrugs as she stretches the cap over her morass of tangled hair. "I don't know. Out of everything, I guess. My own thoughts."

Joy, lounging elbow-up on a puffy white couch, says, "Go on."

"They make me wonder," says Felicity hesitantly.

"About what?" asks Joy.

"About something I would never consider," says Felicity. Tears pool in her eyes, collect on her lashes, and spill down her face. "About whether Addie really did want me dead."

No sooner are the words uttered than Felicity's chest convulses with pain. The wound in her heart is a stick of dynamite, and Addie holds the match. "I shouldn't have told you," she says, clutching her chest. "The idea is monstrous, and I gave it power."

"To the contrary," says Joy. "That which is spoken yields less damage than that which is unspoken. The unspoken takes root in fear and grows unchecked until it chokes us."

"So my words are true?" asks Felicity between sobs. "Addie really did wish me dead?" From the passenger seat of a newly restored Chrysler buttercream convertible parked at the far edge of the woods, a youthful, well-dressed Adelaide bellows, "Me wish you dead? *Ha!* You're the one who kicked me out of a moving car! That's a crime that'll put you in the electric chair, not me." Leaning against Dulles, who sits coolly behind the wheel, she disappears below the dashboard, emerging with a bottle of whiskey that she upends in her mouth. After a long, audible glug, she wipes her chin with her sleeve and says, "Don't talk to me about death wishes, sis."

As soon as Addie says this, a realization strikes Felicity like a blast of winter wind, nearly knocking her off the branch. "Adelaide Somers, y'all are here!" she proclaims joyously. "That's all that matters! Y'all are here and willing to deal with this." Hands clasped over her pulsing wound, Felicity sighs, "You showed up!"

Adelaide burps. "Not that I want to be here! I was tricked, by gawd. And what do I learn for all my effort? That my own sister tried to do me in!"

Dulles swipes the bottle from Adelaide's grip. "Enough of that," he says. "You have to confront this with full awareness or not at all."

Addie pouts. "And you're the one who tricked me," she tells Dulles. "Glass of courage, my eye!"

Pondering Addie's previous accusation, Felicity frowns with confusion. "Why in the wide world did I push you…"

"That's right!" Adelaide cries, pointing accusingly. "The sister I fed…and housed…all these years!" Hesitating, she scratches her head. "But if you left me to die, how did I feed you…and house you…"

"Did you really want me dead, Addie?" asks Felicity. "I know that can't be true. But I heard you say…"

Adelaide raises a fist. "You stole my man! My entire future!"

Her echo reverberates throughout the canyon. "You ran off with the love of my life...*life, life, life, life.*" She taps Dulles on the shoulder. "No offense, sweetie," she says. "I didn't know you then."

"None taken," Dulles assures her.

"I didn't run off with Julian," says Felicity. She blinks at Dr. Joy. "I didn't, right? I don't remember doing that, but I..."

Dr. Joy and her cloud podium advance quickly toward Adelaide. "Do you forgive Felicity for pushing you out of the car?" she asks.

Adelaide folds her arms tightly across her chest. "Why should I? She practically killed me." She pinches her left arm. "But I survived, right? Yes indeed, I did. I survived! No thanks to her." She whispers in Dulles' ear. "Just one more swig, I swear."

"Absolutely not."

"I remember now," says Felicity thoughtfully. "I *had* to push you out."

"That's ridiculous," says Addie.

"It might be ridiculous, Addie, but it's all I could think to do."

Adelaide puckers her lips to imitate Felicity, "It's all I could think to doooo!" she singsongs. "I couldn't think of a single other thing to do but shove you out of the car like picnic trash! Deliver you to certain dooooom." She rolls her eyes. "Now I've heard everything!"

Bits and pieces of memory falling in line, Felicity sputters, "To...to save you, Addie! It's all I could think to do to save you."

Adelaide climbs up on her knees raising her fists. "Save me from what?" she cries. "From marrying Julian? From living my intended *life.*"

"Why, I...I really don't know what I was saving you from,"

says Felicity, puzzled. "What could it have been? What...what happened next?"

Mother hops down a branch to sit beside her. "It's time to show you what you spared Adelaide, my darling. Time to bury our grievances so we can all move on."

THIRTY-SEVEN

FELICITY

One minute Felicity is staring into Mother's resolute eyes, the next she is dropped like an anchor into full flesh and bone in the back seat of a beat-up Chrysler convertible. There is no time to acclimate. The instant she registers what's happening, her eyes pop; her heart races. The low autumn light dims to lead. Clouds obscure the slender curl of rising moon as the runaway car resumes its destiny and hers, bouncing this way and that over rocks, branches, dense brush and night creatures. Naked autumn branches reach out in the darkness like starvelings. Everything about this experience seems doomed.

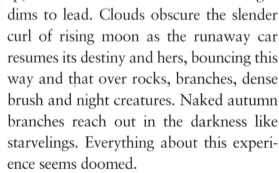

Felicity has only been to this forest once before with Daddy when she was twelve. It was a trip they made in full daylight, so the spellbinding view is emblazoned in her memory. She knows what comes next. The cliffs come next. Cliffs so high she got vertigo then, lost her balance, and would probably have fallen had Daddy not pulled her back. And just beyond the cliffs lies the deep, deep gorge. Infinitely, unimaginably deep. And below the gorge, the river. A river now swollen to its gills after a season of unprecedented rain.

Right now, coursing toward the cliffs as they are, it's obvious that Addie is too confused to stop the car. Too confused to correct their course or save their lives. And Julian is too far behind to save them. Julian is the past. Ripped-up pages of an expired calendar. Whatever the future holds is up to them. Or really, up to Felicity, who makes a split-second decision to climb in front where she hopes to grab the wheel from Addie and slam her foot on the brake. She crawls up the back of the passenger seat, situating her right leg on top of the door at just the right angle to jump over. Just as she does this, Addie leans back and kicks indiscriminately. Kicks the seat, the dashboard, and finally, Felicity so hard in the face she lands all the way back where she started. Gutted from the blow, she nevertheless manages to scream into the wild wind, "Addie, stop kicking! Let me help!"

But Addie's panic is a reckless passenger with a mind of its own. Felicity has to figure out a way to stop her. She has to. She gathers enough strength against the car's momentum to raise herself on her haunches. From there, she vaults headfirst into the front of the moving car before her sister can retaliate. As she tumbles forward onto the seat, her skirt flies up. She struggles to turn around in a web of crinoline. She does all this at the same time she defends herself against Addie's incessant assault.

The car picks up speed.

Emerging upright and clearing her sight, Felicity is treated to a terrifying view of fate just 300 feet ahead. Even as the sky blackens, she can't miss the unmistakable outline of occasional trees on the cliff's' ledge followed by the abyss of certain death. All she knows is it's too late to stop this car. She's in a position to jump out if she acts quickly. But Addie, in her prone position, is not. There's no way for Addie to turn around in time. If Felicity saves herself, Addie dies.

200 feet…

Addie grabs the wheel for ballast as she blindly kicks Felicity and everything else in the way of her stockinged feet.

150 feet…

Adrenaline rushing, Felicity lays on her back, swings her legs over Addie's torso, and kicks the handle of the driver's door repeatedly. She strikes it above and below, at every angle she can manage until finally, it releases, nearly flying off its hinges in the westerly wind. And then, against all the resistance from her frantic opponent and the elements at large, she pulls her legs into a tight ball and thrusts them so hard against Addie's hip that she flies right out of the car into the deep woods, missing the car door by a fraction.

100 feet…

Door open, car bouncing, the cliffs draw closer. Rising up on her elbows, Felicity angles herself toward the brakes, but everything—wind, acceleration, and sheer exhaustion—conspire against her. She manages to manipulate her feet under the wheel, pivoting her pelvis up and around so she can at least steer. She operates on instinct. She has never driven before. Feeling for the brake, she strikes the accelerator instead. Her tummy turns and her head spins. She is utterly disoriented. As she tries frantically to correct her mistake, a blinding light draws her attention just beyond the cliffs. Right hand reflexively off the wheel, she shields her eyes, transfixed, as the light approaches, opens like a whale's maw, and swallows time. Everything.

Stops.

Felicity has no memory of the moment's inception and can't fathom its end. There is no end. The moment contains time or rather, is time itself. She is transfixed. Everything else, even the car and its perilous path, are incidental. Is the car even moving? Felicity can't say. It doesn't matter. All that matters is this radiant vapor glowing before her in a spectrum of violet, fuchsia and iris light. There is nothing else. But this.

In this same moment the light advances, expanding in height and length, depth and breadth. It continues to expand in detail and sheer architectural complexity until its scope is palatial. A glistening castle that constructs a path of marbled lavender from its imposing arched doors straight to the hood of Felicity's deathtrap. Out of the castle, befitting its elegance, emerges a queen. More than a queen, a goddess, really. A goddess whose radiance illuminates the charcoal sky in a brilliant aurora of pigment so rich and rare it exists nowhere but here. No time but now. As the color spreads, familiarity and grace warm Felicity to the marrow. She knows who this is. It's Celeste, of course. Celeste emerging from a stream of near-blinding light flanked by twelve powerful escorts armed with glinting swords. The *Purple People* as Felicity once knew them. Celeste's guardians.

And hers.

The goddess smiles sweetly, beckoning. "Come with Us, love," she says. "It's time."

Panic races up Felicity's spine like mercury. "No!" she protests.

"Please," Celeste bids. "Reconsider."

"I can't abandon Addie. You know I can't. Not here. Not now."

Celeste extends her arm gracefully. "Of course, you can,

dear. This is not about Addie. This is about you. About your life. Your destiny."

Felicity chokes up. "Addie's no good on her own. I won't do it."

The goddess raises her arm in surrender and the light recedes.

Withdrawn from the expanded moment, Felicity is disoriented again. Before she knows where she is or why, she experiences a belly-dropping sense of acceleration followed by a cataclysmic slam. *Is this really happening?* At first it feels as if it's happening to someone else, but then the collision launches her skyward like an awkward bird, a species of neither land nor air. Seconds later her flight is intercepted by the high branch of a leafless magnolia that catches the back of her dress, suspending her precariously over the massive ridge. She is terrified as she and the branch dip up and down repeatedly in a perilous dance over an infinite abyss.

Celeste reappears, arms extended. Felicity's heart cracks with grief. "I never meant it to end like this," Felicity whimpers. "To abandon her so soon."

"It's not soon," says Celeste. "It only appears that way through your narrow human lens. But really, it's the perfect time." She smiles serenely. "It always is."

"The perfect time for me, maybe, but not for Addie. She's not ready."

"She's never ready," says Celeste. "She's a shadow. Shadows disappear in the light."

At that, the wind generates a wild gale and the branch sways up and down, back and forth, testing its strength against Felicity's shifting weight. She holds her breath anticipating the inevitable. The unimaginable. The inescapable end.

"I can't stop it now," Celeste says softly. "But if you take my hand, I can end the fear."

"If I take your hand, it's over."

"You belong with me," Celeste says. "I'm your highest aspect."

"I belong with Addie," Felicity whimpers. "Shadows can't move without light. Can't even be seen."

"Shadows are Earth dwellers."

"Not Addie. Addie's different."

"If you choose to stay, your life will be profoundly difficult," Celeste warns as she recedes into the darkness. "Difficult and confusing. You will be forced into the shadows with her."

"Difficult for me, maybe," says Felicity. "But without me, Addie's life won't be possible at all."

The branch dips progressively lower, and Felicity thinks if she can just wiggle out of her dress, she can possibly trick fate. Just drop to a lower branch and crawl to safety. It's her only option; she must try. The buttons of her dress are stretched too tightly against the branch to unbutton, but how else will she slip out of this dress to free herself? Arms at her sides, she gathers the skirt slowly into her cold stiff hands, raising it inch by inch with great care. All the while, the wind screeches, the tree creaks, her weight and the trajectory of the branch shift ever lower. Her slim legs whip around in the wind like kite tails. She can't do this much longer, and she doubts she can do it alone. She needs help.

"Celeste," she moans, but Celeste and her kingdom of light are nowhere to be seen. *Were they ever here?*

She hears a rustling in the woods behind her and calls out, just in case. Her voice is thin, she knows, and can't travel far. "Addie," she moans, terrified. "Addie, help me." Her position is so precarious, she dare not call out too loudly lest the vibration from the soundwaves alone send her falling. "Addieeeee," she mouths as evenly as she can, but hears nothing in return.

The skirt of her dress balled-up side-to-side in both fists, she moves with economy. Every movement, every breath, measured. Reaching up, she clutches the branch with her left hand, raises the dress slowly against her torso with her right, then delicately slips out of the sleeve. So far so good. Slowly switching arms, she dips her head ever so gently to free the left side. She is nearly there. *Stay with it! You can do it!* With enough faith, even fate can be tricked!

"Addie, please help me!" she cries, more loudly than she dares. The only response she hears is, "I hope you die."

Hearing this, an unbearable pain strikes Felicity's heart like a venomous dart. Tears stream down her cheeks, blurring her vision. "You hope I die?" she keens. "You hope I...die?" Her stomach lurches, her chest heaves, and her dress tears. The branch snaps. Her shoes drop. Her hands slip. Clinging only to the skirt of the torn dress, she drops to a lower branch that swings up and down with the force of her weight like a seesaw.

And then it, too, snaps.

Mid-air, Felicity rides the branch between her legs like Pegasus, clutching it with her thighs until, together, they scrape the sides of the rapier-sharp sandstone, peeling the skin off her back like bark. The pain is immediate and unbearable. The branch falls in one direction, Felicity in another. Falling. Freefalling. Falling.

Free.

A body of pain coursing like a comet to its certain demise.

"Come to me," Celeste chants through the darkness. "*Come to meeeee.*"

"No," Felicity says, or thinks she says. "Save me so I can save Addie."

Her body plunges without restraint until finally it smacks the raging water, crashing into a succession of unyielding rocks, dizzying whirlpools, and whiplashing rapids. Whatever awareness is left of her now knows nothing will ever be the same. This is it. The end. It has to be.

And yet, it's not.

Not really, no. Oddly, unexpectedly, it's as if she once lived here in this place, this body, but also elsewhere. As if her consciousness is a fickle vagabond with more homes than it can count. Too many homes to be homeless. Too many for life to truly cease, at least not yet. There she is, ravaged by the river, but also perched far above in the very same, though unbroken, magnolia branch with Mother, witnessing her own end. Her material body far below is nothing—a snail's shell abandoned. Mindless matter carried along the aimless current like a hollow log. From her psychical home on the cliff's edge, she watches undisturbed as her body slams into rocks, tree trunks, and beaver dams, no longer hers. Released to the river. The river is its home.

From above, she watches—they all watch—as the river delivers her flayed flesh and broken bones to an embankment at the woods' edge where it's caught in a tidal pool, slapping back and forth, lifeless. On the horizon, dawn cracks like an egg, its marbleized yolk spilling streams of goldenrod across the canyon, illuminating a spectral image emerging from the wreckage. The image rises out of its shell, crosses rock after slippery rock, crawling to shore. The image is faint, badly damaged, and not fully conscious.

But the image survives.

As its body is swept away in the rapid downstream current, the image stands, brushes itself off, and slips into the woods without looking back.

THIRTY-EIGHT

ADELAIDE

Witnessing Felicity's perilous fall, Adelaide grips Dulles' right forearm till it bleeds. Just before her sister strikes the surface of the raging river, she covers her eyes with her other hand, slowly opening her fingers in time to see a spectral image skulk into the woods. "Well look at that," she says. "Flitty survived after all. Of course she did. How else could I have been taking care of her all these years?"

"An element of her survived," says Dulles. "But that's not the point. The point is, she kicked you out of the car to spare your life." He shakes her off his forearm and stares at her meaningfully. "Do you forgive her for throwing you out of the car?"

"Why should I?" she pouts. "Felicity made it out just fine. How can I forgive her if I don't even know what happened to me?"

"Very well then," says Phipps. "Let's take a look, shall we?"

"Just tell me what happened!" Addie protests. "I don't need to relive every scorching minute of hell just to forgive someone!"

"So you're saying you forgive her?" says Dulles. "If so, say it clearly. We're running out of time."

Adelaide rocks her head back and forth. "I don't know. I mean, are we absolutely sure she didn't..."

Before she can finish the sentence, she's back in the convertible, splayed belly-down over the front seat, her head an exploding grenade. She can't speak, but she can hear.

"She's in the car," says a familiar voice. *Julian's voice?* "I couldn't try 'n start the car less I moved her, 'n it worried me to do it."

"So, you walked all the way back, son?" asks the sheriff.

"Yessir, I did. To get help."

"And where's the sister?"

Julian chokes up. "All I could find..."

Adelaide tries to listen, but she can't make sense of the conversation. After all, Felicity survived. Everyone saw it. Adelaide is the injured party.

"I see, well let's load Miss Adelaide on the board then, shall we? Give her half a chance."

"But she might of broke..."

"Don't matter, boy. Gotta git her to the hospital fast if it ain't too late already. There's more to worry 'bout here than a few broke bones."

What little consciousness Adelaide was able to muster through all the torment disappears graciously as they transfer her to the stretcher. She blacks out and wakes up several times, the last time in a hospital bed, a mess of confusion, her head bandaged, her body in traction, her daddy clutching his chest.

"Listen up," she hears him tell someone, "if this is my time, you make sure I'm cremated and scattered in the river with my daughter, you hear? I don't care what the missus says, you got that?"

"Yes, sir."

"Not at the house, you understand? Not in the yard."

Adelaide thinks she must be hallucinating. "Daddy," she groans in a gibber. "I'm not in the river! I'm right here..." Her unintelligible words run backward down her throat as she watches them lay Daddy out on a gurney and wheel him off.

With Dulles' help, Adelaide shifts her consciousness back to the convertible at the edge of the woods and says to her mother, "I always wondered what happened to Daddy. Seems like I woke up one day and he was gone."

"What about me?" asks Regina. "Did you ever wonder what happened to me?"

Adelaide shrugs. Does she really have to wonder what happened to everybody? "Not really."

Regina winces. "I'm your mother, Adelaide. One would think..."

"One would think that one's mother would be loving and supportive," Adelaide snaps.

Regina raises her chin. "I'm sorry for that, Adelaide. I really am. There was something about our natures that repelled each other. Like-on-like, I suppose. I was the adult; I take responsibility for that. But honestly, I don't know how many ways I can apologize."

A dam bursts in Adelaide's head. "You refused to bury Julian at *Sunnyside Up*," she says, glaring. "That's all I know."

"I lied," said Regina. "Not that I would or wouldn't bury him at *Sunnyside Up*, but that he was dead at all."

"Julian isn't dead?" she asks, puzzled.

"You already know that, Adelaide. You just can't accept it."

A righteous rage boils up Adelaide's marrow at the same time her heart inexplicably seizes in her throat, squirting tears out her eyes. How many opposing things can a person feel at once? she thinks. She's a fireball of anger, grief, and confusion. She sputters and coughs, choking on her tears until she can finally speak, "I forgive Felicity," she whispers, surprising herself. "She was just a bratty little kid who didn't know any better. Didn't understand her own charms." She takes a minute to let this truth settle into her bones. "She was a dumb little tease is all she was." She gasps at the force of this understanding. But why is that? Did anyone really believe she could hate Felicity?

"It's true," says Regina. "She meant no harm."

Rising up out of her seat, Adelaide shakes her fist at her mother. "But I'll never forgive you."

"Wait!" screeches Felicity from the magnolia branch above. She raises her arms victoriously. "You forgive me?! You do?! Oh Addie, I knew you would! I forgive you too!" She looks around. "Did everyone hear that? We forgive each other. Now we can all move on!"

Dr. Joy flicks the ash of a Winston from her floating couch. "Not so fast," she says.

Pointing to her heart, Felicity says, "But look, my wound is healing!"

"It's not red anymore, Felicity, but if you look more closely, you still have a black spot," says Phipps.

"A black spot in the shape of an anchor, kind of," says Joy, studying Felicity's wound. She inhales slowly, then exhales a stream of little heart-shaped puffs. "How curious."

Tantalized by the cigarette, Adelaide reaches up. "Toss me a cigarette, Doc!"

Regina jumps down from the branch and floats over to Adelaide's side of the car. "Forget about the cigarettes, Adelaide. You'll never forgive me for *what*?" She leans closer, eye-to-eye, "Specifically."

Adelaide looks away. "I forgive Felicity, isn't that enough for one day?"

"Not if it's your final day, daughter. And it may well be."

"My final day?!" Addie looks around frantically. "My *final* day?" she screeches to Joy then Phipps then Dulles.

"Don't get distracted," says Mother. She turns Adelaide's chin toward her direct gaze. "You'll never forgive me for *what*? Focus. Your answer may lead us to an understanding."

Adelaide swats her away. "For being the meanest rottenest mother ever," she says. "Isn't it obvious? For doing everything you could to withhold love from me. Even Julian's love."

"Do you want the truth, Adelaide?"

"I want a cigarette."

From her perch on the magnolia branch, Felicity says, "Cigarettes are transient, Addie. Say yes to the truth. Truth is permanent. Mother needs to tell you the rest; she really does. And fast."

"If I say yes to that, can I have a Winston?" asks Adelaide. She turns to Dulles, pleading. "Or one of those long slim smokes in that glamorous Tiffany cigarette holder? Please? And a crystal glass filled with bourbon in the sparkly bar with the velvet stools?" She bats her lashes and tucks her chin flirtatiously into her shoulder. "A girl's got to have something to look forward to."

Dulles looks up, consulting Dr. Joy and Mrs. Phipps for a consensus. They nod.

"Ok," he says. "We can go back there for a nightcap, but not until you pay witness."

Adelaide scowls. "Witness to what?"

"To this," he says, and before Adelaide can object, he spins the car in a cloud of dirt, spitting spirals of colorful autumn leaves over the hood and windshield. They travel at the speed of light through the dense, glistening forest into the wide-open hills and valleys all the way back to *Sunnyside Up.*

Parked beside a still flourishing blue hydrangea bush behind the cemetery, Adelaide catches her breath. This is all too much, she thinks. Way too much, and what's the hurry? Up ahead she spots Mother against the fence huddled in conference with Sheriff Gibbs. To Adelaide this scene reeks of hypocrisy already since the sheriff is a man for whom Mother held nothing but contempt. One of a dozen boys in a family of ne'er-do-wells from the holler, Lloyd Gibbs was the only one who picked the right side of the law. Not that he couldn't be compromised; he could. He and his wife, Dottie, were as desperate for respectability as Regina once was, even if it came in unrespectable packages. But Mother was against giving anyone a leg up lest the very association cling to her reputation like coal dust. "Let them figure it out themselves like I did," she'd say to Daddy. She wanted nothing to do with anyone or anything that reminded her of her derelict upbringing.

"I want you to arrest that boy," she demands.

The sheriff removes his hat and scratches his head. "Arrest him?"

"You heard me."

"Ma'am, he hiked all the way through that forest to find your gals, then all the way back to Outskirt to git me."

"Don't you tell me what that rapscallion did, Sheriff! He killed Felicity and maimed Adelaide for life is what he did. And now, even my husband is dead." She grips the fence. "How much is a lady to bear?"

Back in the car, Adelaide gasps, turning to Dulles. "I was maimed for life?" she squeaks.

"Pretty much," he says.

The sheriff lowers his head. "May Reverend Somers rest in peace," he says. "So sorry for your losses, Ma'am."

"Don't you pity me!" says Mother, wagging her finger. "Y'all are the one to be pitied. You and your kind." She pokes the sheriff in the chest. "Y'all want respect and acceptance for your family?" she says. "Well, do you?"

He wrinkles his forehead, confused. "Is this a trick question, Ma'am?"

"Answer me!" she demands. "Do you want respect for your family or not?"

He nods hesitantly. "Dottie does," he says. "And I want it fer her; I do." He kicks dirt with the toe of his scuffed leather boot. "But what does that have to do…"

"I'll tell you what!" Mother shrieks so loud he jumps back. "I am in possession of the only thing this side of death that can bring you and your hopeless family the respect you want."

"Ma'am?"

"The deed to a family plot here at *Sunnyside Up.*"

His eyes widen. "Y'all'd do that?"

"Soon's you throw that scoundrel behind bars, I will." She juts her big square chin forward. "For the rest of his pathetic life." She stomps her foot. "Not one day less."

"Well now, I ain't sure…"

"For. Life!" she spits. "Understood? Or longer if he raped

one of them or both, which I guarantee you he did. I don't need to remind you that Felicity is under age."

"You don't think…"

"Damn if I don't," she seethes. "Now what'll it be?" She folds her arms across her broad chest and stares the man down. "And if the answer isn't yes, Sheriff, just know that your life is about to be a lot more hellish than mine."

"Well now," he says, nodding up and down, back and forth, considering. "Never did like that family much. Never tried to make nothin' of theirselves worth admirin'."

"*Themselves*," corrects Mother. "Never tried to make *anything* of *themselves.*"

"Ma'am?" he says, squinting. "Believe I said that, yep."

"You want to associate with respectable folks, Lloyd Gibbs, you've got to speak respectably. Get a dictionary and learn some English. No one's going to learn it for you."

Back at the hydrangea bush, Adelaide is so agitated she jumps up on the seat. "See why I can't forgive her, Dulles?" she says. "She's downright indecent is what she is."

"She had her reasons," he says. "And you've got to admit that some of her characteristics were passed along to someone you know pretty well."

Adelaide blinks, surprised. "Felicity?" she says. "I never thought of Felicity…"

"Not Felicity."

"Then who?"

But before Dulles can answer, her brain fogs, her mother disappears, and she's all the way back at Outskirt General. Her big old aching mass of flesh is laid out on a skimpy hospital bed talking to an irritating old man named Thaddeus who just claimed to be Julian.

"Do ye fergive yer mama?" the man asks searchingly with his sorry eyes. "We're all called to fergive, Adelaide."

"Do I...forgive her?" she squeaks between short painful breaths. "What about...you? She stole...your...life."

"Oh hell, that day tore yer life 'n Flitty's asunder lot more 'n mine," he says. "I got by. I always do."

"Did you...love...Flitty?" Adelaide asks, not that she cares anymore. I mean, look at him.

A deep blush creeps up his neck to his sunken cheeks till his whole head is near about beet red. "My feelin' fer Flitty took me by surprise. Weren't earthbound." His arm sweeps the room. "Came from heaven on a highway of light straight to my heart in a split second." He shakes his head. "I jes dint have the nerve to face y'all 'bout it yet. But I intended to. Then...well, ye know what all happened next." He looks down. "She were an angel, that one." He looks Adelaide in the eye. "Can ye fergive an ole man?"

Adelaide doesn't feel like forgiving anyone for anything, but has the feeling it's the only way out of this nightmare. "I did love you, but. Well. If I'm honest, y'all weren't...weren't right for me anyway."

And just like that, Flitty's old dried-up shadow of a body shows up at the foot of Adelaide's bed in a ridiculous bathing cap accompanied by the younger, ghostly version of Mother.

"What's...hap-happening?" Adelaide stutters.

The nurse approaches with Addie's oxygen mask in hand. "It's time to put this back on," she says.

Julian holds up a finger. "Jes one more thang, nurse, I swear."

"That's it," she says, lips pursed.

Julian takes Adelaide's hand. "Yer mama saved m' life," he says tearfully.

Adelaide blinks repeatedly. "What...."

He turns to Regina. "Thank ye fer savin' m' life, Miz Somers. I'm sorry 'bout yer daughters."

Regina's eyes widen. "You can see me in this timeline?"

"Who you talking to, sir?" asks the nurse.

"Seen a lot in m' time, Ma'am," Julian says to Regina. "Folks on all levels I seen."

"You're...all along you were...advanced?" Regina says. "And I...I demeaned you."

"Ye saved m' life," he says.

"I saved nothing," she says plaintively. "I ruined your life. I'm so...so very sorry."

He shakes his head. "If I hadn't of been in the prison when I were, I'd of been wiped out with the family in the big slide."

"What?" says Felicity. "What slide?"

Julian turns to Felicity. "Some 20 years ago or so the ole Diamondback collapsed in the weeks long storm. Like Noah's Ark it were. Seconds after the collapse, giant tips of coal waste up top shook hard 'n slid down the whole town. Buried half the village, it did. Left us a ghost town."

Felicity sits on the bed beside Adelaide. "So that's where they all went, Addie," she says. "I told y'all something weird was going on."

Things a lot weirder than that going on right in this room, thinks Adelaide.

"I don't know what's happening here," the nurse says to Julian. "Y'all might need a psych evaluation, sir, but you're not the patient and that's not my specialty. Right now, this mask is going back on Miss Somers."

Julian leans in and whispers in Adelaide's ear. "Fergive yer mama," he says. "Now."

Adelaide's eyes widen as the room fills with her family. Daddy tickles her toes, Granny stands next to Pothead with her fists against her hips, saying, "It's all a trick."

Mrs. Phipps and Dr. Joy float on the ceiling, wringing their hands, waiting.

"Where's...Dulles?" Adelaide whispers into the mask, fogging it up.

"Right here," he says from somewhere behind her.

She's about to ask him for a ride to the celestial saloon when the grenade in her head explodes for good, setting off beeps and blips, code blues and whatnot all over hell and back. Another piece of her just sitting back watching it all, says, "Flitty, where are you?"

"I'm here, Addie, I'm right here."

Adelaide can hear her, but can't see her. "Meet me at the ridge," she says.

"Okay, I'll bring Mother..."

"Just you, Flitty," she says. "Just you."

Obituary for Release to:
Bluegrass Bugle &
The Louisville Gazette
Thursday, April 30, 1970

Diamondback Mine Collapses, Killing 361,
Obliterating Entire Town

Wednesday's catastrophe at the Diamondback Mine
just outside the small town of Outskirt, Kentucky
tragically claimed 361 victims so far, including town
administrators, townsfolk, and students ages 6-14 at
the St. Jude Grammar School down the hill in Outskirt
Hollow. According to Mayor Melvin "Bones" Hodges, IV,
"…after a long spring of unprecedented rain, piles of
coal waste known as *tips,* became too high and unwieldy,
and at approximately 9:00 a.m. Tuesday started to
shift and slide with the high winds and torrential rains.
"Shouldn't have been collecting that waste there so
long," he said. "Shouldn't have been that big, no sir, no
way. Like a mountain it was, plus there were six of 'em.
But anyhow, like I was sayin', the unprecedented heavy
rains all season long was a factor. The tips could not be
easily transported elsewhere in that weather. But we
should've done it anyhow," he said, choking up. "We
damn well should've seen to it. At least tried."
    Mayor Bones says the sixth tip slid forward so fast
they couldn't sound the school alarm before it slid right
down the hill, crushing the school's roof and tragically,
everyone and everything inside. The mine collapsed at

351

about the same time the landslide started, entrapping 45 brave souls inside for what might just be an eternity. Investigators don't yet know if the mine collapse triggered the landslide or the reverse. A thorough investigation will take place as soon as it stops raining. The recovery site runs from Diamondback Hill north of the mine where the tips were located all the way to the old equine center a mile away and everything in between, including the Outskirt mercantile and Piggly Wiggly, God bless their cashiers, patrons and cart boys.

The incorporated town of Outskirt and unincorporated village of Outskirt Hollow included 556 residents more or less, with fourteen young ones on the way. Minus the presumed total of 361 victims, the town is left with fewer than 200 citizens to carry on. Survivors are encouraged to move. When asked how the town will possibly recover, Sadie Jefferson, the town secretary, reported, "I had a funny feeling in my heart. I dint send my kids to school that day. Called in sick to work." She shook her head. "I knew somethin' was up. Sometimes ye just know."

The only two funeral services in the area are the historic *Sunnyside Up Funeral Home & Chicken Farm* which has been closed for service since its owner, Mrs. Jasper Somers, passed away a few years back, and *Jumping Jack's Funeral Home* south of the Diamondback. Ironically, *Jumping Jack's* is currently buried under 6' of sludge and in no shape to accept new customers. Recovered bodies from the catastrophe will be transported to nearby Clearville for burial.

Kentucky Governor Louie Nunn has deployed the state's National Guard to assist in the recovery effort.

THIRTY-NINE

SISTERS

Dressed in a white eyelet-lace dress, shimmering pearl summer sandals, a garland of fragrant gardenias in her hair, Felicity has never felt brighter. It's as if this is the wedding day she never had. But who will she marry? And who will unite them? Her voluminous gold locks stream behind her as she floats easily toward the bench at the edge of the barely sunlit ridge behind the cemetery where Addie waits.

Staring down at the rolling valley, Addie says, "Thanks for coming."

In contrast to Felicity, Addie's dressed as she was the day that ended it all—torn skirt, muddied face, bloodied blouse. Her long hair is matted and uncombed. It's as if she just crawled through a treacherous forest and landed on this bench, waiting.

On the horizon, the raspberry sky melts over the creamy orange sun like a bowl of peach melba. Felicity can't tell if the sun's trying to rise or set. Maybe it's up to her and Addie. Shielding her eyes from the brilliance, she slips beside Addie on the bench. Addie seems unaware of the illumination at first. Then her face suddenly brightens. "Wasn't that fun, Flitty?" she says with a slow grin.

Taken aback, Felicity says, "Fun? You mean...?"

"The whole jolly ride is what I mean!" Addie says, clapping her hands. "You and me and that weird old Thaddeus, good grief! I almost forgot about it until..." she scratches her head, "...I don't know, a dream or something reminded me."

Felicity doesn't know how to respond. Is Addie talking about their...life? Does she really think that was fun? Do they share that little in common? Addie feels distant to Felicity somehow. Uniquely distant, as if she's not quite there. As if she's slipping away. As if their common borders have been breached, and they are no longer related.

"And wasn't that quite the spectacle at the Gorge that night back when?" Addie says excitedly. "You shoving me out of the car and then flying through the air..." She nods repetitively, recalling. "What an adventure! Right? Not to mention all the confusion of trying to bury Julian, and those crazy barn lessons! Eegadz!" She places her hands on either side of her head as if to keep her brain from leaking out her ears. "Who thought of all that, Flitty? Was it you?"

"No, not me, Addie. And I wouldn't call it fun exactly."

Addie grabs Felicity's hands. "Let's do it again! Come on! One more time, what do you say? This time Julian's all yours. I'm holding out for Dulles."

"Dulles is Julian's nephew, Addie. He's from another timeline."

"Who cares about timelines?" Addie says. "We can all return together. There's no end to the fun we could have!"

Felicity sighs. "This was our last chance," she says soberly. "You knew that going in, Addie, but somehow you forgot, as souls do. And you were the one who wouldn't cooperate, not me." She shakes her head. "I'm afraid we're out of time."

Addie screws her features into a confused snarl.

"I'm sorry, Addie, truly," says Felicity. "But the truth is that with every incarnation my light gets brighter, and yours fades. Recedes into oblivion. Why wouldn't you grow with me? Why wouldn't *you* cooperate? All you had to do was forgive Mother and we could be together."

"She didn't deserve it."

"Addie…"

"I'm just being honest, Felicity. Do you want me to lie?"

Felicity scans the horizon for an alternate course, but knows there isn't one. "Addie, your future…is not bright."

Addie folds her arms across her chest protectively. "I'm a shadow; I was made for the dark. I like it. After all our lifetimes, you'd think you would know that by now."

"Shadows are cast by light," says Felicity. "When the light is highest, the shadows disappear." The words catch in her throat. "You should be more than my shadow, Addie. You have the potential for more. You were offered more."

Addie's silhouette becomes paler and paler against the shrinking sun, and Felicity panics. "Addie, you're disappearing! Maybe I can talk to Celeste. Maybe she can give you another chance to forgive Mother. There's such a thing as mercy if you ask for it. If you show you care even the least bit. And you do care, don't you?"

Addie shakes her head. "Not really, no. I want to care. I do. To make you happy. But the truth is, I just…don't."

"Look me in the eye and say that."

As Addie turns to face her, Felicity can't look into her dark, empty eyes. Her vision is drawn to a piercing light shimmering through Addie's bloodied blouse. "Look, Addie, you do have light," she says, leaning in to study it. "It's small, but intense. Powerful." She nods thoughtfully. "Just enough to work with, I think."

Addie blinks from the glare of the slim shaft of light rising in her chest. Where it came from, she has no idea, but it's giving her a headache. "I told you I don't care, Flitty," she says. "Take the light if you like it so much. It's all yours."

"But it's the only light left in your entire body," says Felicity. "Without it…"

Just looking at it, though, Felicity craves it fiercely. Yearns for it like nothing she's yearned for in her entire life or more. It's as if she can't survive without it. As it pulses in Addie's chest, her own chest becomes drawn and heavy, and she gasps for it.

"Just take it," says Addie. "I can see you want it."

Felicity's eyes widen in horror at her own greed. "No. I can't. I won't."

"I have no use for it whatsoever, believe me. It's yours."

Felicity tries to turn away, but she can't.

"Good grief," says Addie, wincing as she grasps the end of the blade and yanks until it slides out of her chest. "Just take it. The dang thing's burning my chest, my hands. It's ruining my life. Causing me to want things that weren't meant for me."

Felicity opens her hands to accept the light, weeping at her own desperation as well as Addie's certain demise. "How I'd hoped…"

Addie points to the black spot in Felicity's chest. "It belongs right there," she says. "Same shape. Like an anchor. Slip it in."

"Oh my God, Addie, you were my anchor." Her eyes moisten. "All this time it was you who anchored me to Earth."

"Y'all were good company, Flitty," she says. "But you were pretty crazy and hard to look at most of the time."

Leaning in meaningfully, Felicity says, "The minute that light fills this hole I'm gone."

"I always knew I would never go with you," Addie whispers." You knew it too. I don't belong wherever you're going. I belong right here."

Felicity nods sorrowfully. "We were a good team, though, Addie, weren't we?"

Addie's eyes slowly widen. "You were my light, Flitty. You really were."

Felicity's heart swells. "Where will you go?"

Addie tips her head toward the cemetery. "They could use some supervision," she says.

Felicity chuckles. "They could."

As the sisters sit in silence, the horizon bleeds streams of scarlet and purple light.

After a minute, Addie says, "I never listened to a single thing old Phipps had to say. Now I wish I had."

Staring at the light in her palms, Felicity says. "What do you want to know?"

"I want to know what a ghost is," Addie says. She looks at Felicity eagerly. "What is it really?" She blinks. "What am I?"

"A ghost is a memory, Addie. A lingering memory of a life on Earth. Strong ones have density and form."

Addie smiles. "I'll be your memory, Flitty. No one will be able to think of me without thinking of you."

In that moment, the light slides from Felicity's hand into her chest, almost of its own will, filling the black hole where her wound once bled.

No sooner is the hole filled and sealed than Celeste and her consorts arrive in a flash of amethyst. "I've come to claim my lower aspect," she says joyfully, and without hesitation, Felicity rises like the sun, merging with Celeste in a grand spectacle of light. A meteoric explosion. A Christmas Star.

And just like that, it's over.

Adelaide watches, transfixed. The minute the light recedes, she blinks trying to remember. But she can't. *What just happened?* She doesn't know. Feeling around in the empty darkness, she panics. I'm not ready to be alone, she thinks. "Dulles," she calls out. "Where's my bourbon? You promised!"

Obituary for Release to:
Bluegrass Bugle &
The Louisville Gazette
Friday June 19, 2020

Miss Adelaide Frances Somers of Outskirt Dies at Last
Born: May 16, 1937
Passed into eternal life: June 17, 2020

Adelaide Frances Somers, last of the once esteemed
Somers family of Outskirt, Kentucky, died Wednesday
at the age of 83 at the Outskirt Hospital and Craft
Center. Causes of death include but are not limited to:
senility, obesity, cirrhosis, emphysema, heart failure,
kidney disease, osteoarthritis, and a 12' fall from
her living room window into a patch of pachysandra,
although there were no eyewitnesses. According to
her caretakers, Mr. Lionel Barrows and his wife, Inis,
"It were a miracle she lasted this long. We couldn't
take much more." When further pressed, Mr. Barrows
irritably stated that Adelaide "suffered a hairball of
ailments. Her death were a mercy. She babbled all day
long to her dead sister, which might of been senility,
but could of been the hooch, who's to say? She were
a drinker. I have no idea where she hid the booze.
More 'n once I found her staggerin' off the property in
search of enlightenment and a man named Dulles. By
the time she died, me 'n Inis was wrung out and hung
to dry."

Adelaide Somers sustained head injuries in an

infamous car accident in 1960 at the Red River Gorge in which her sister, Felicity, was suspiciously thrown from an open Chrysler convertible owned by Mr. Julian T. Buck of Outskirt Hollow. The body of Felicity Somers was never recovered and presumed to have been catapulted into the air, landing in the Gorge, and carried by the Red River into the deep woods. In spite of a weak defense from the usually aggressive Calvin Gibbs, Esq., brother of Lloyd Gibbs, Sheriff of Outskirt County at the time, Mr. Buck was convicted of a series of crimes, including kidnapping a minor, rape, and manslaughter. Buck served nearly thirty years at the state prison until declared innocent. He was released in 1989, and no one's heard from him since. There are some who say he's living in the forest with Felicity and the seven dwarfs, which if it's true, would mean Felicity is still alive and the dwarfs are real.

Ms. Somers is survived by one relative, a second cousin and distinguished journalist, Rebecca Stark. Ms. Stark moved to Arkansas in 1975 with her fourth husband, and still writes obituaries from time to time when her hand can hold a pen. Adelaide Somers left no assets this reporter could find, as the property was apparently bought back from the bank by Mr. Thaddeus Buck, presumed relative of Julian T. Buck, in 1980. Mr. Buck allowed Ms. Somers "to live and die in the dignity she deserved" according to a statement overheard by Inis Barrows. Mr. Buck himself declined to comment directly for fear of digging up forgotten publicity regarding false accusations and convictions of kidnap, rape, and manslaughter. While some say he should've been left in prison, this reporter will refrain from subjective opinions, because that's a journalist's job. But he sure was handsome.

Ms. Somers will be buried in the family cemetery near the site of her sister, Felicity Jane, and next to her nasty mother, who took the cake. The ashes of her father, the always distinguished Jasper Somers, were scattered in the Gorge after his death in 1960. Adelaide's gravestone will not feature any of the usual knick-knacks Outskirt graves are known for. A private service and burial were held almost immediately at *Sunnyside Up*. No one was invited or even knew about it. When asked why, Lionel Barrows said, "Oh for gawd's sake, Becky, let it go."

FORTY

JULIAN

Arriving at the old chicken farm and cemetery, Jules parks the Chrysler in the circle drive front the house, easing out the door with his cane. Stands slow. Walks real careful on the gravel, one step the time. One step then the other till he gets behind the car, nice and slow. Pops the trunk and lifts the brown paper package tied with old twine; holds it close to his broke heart. This right here's his treasure. All he cares about. This here's how he does right by Flitty. He searches the yard for the rusty red wagon he spots up the house, then lays his cane side the car and walks up slow, taking time. What's the

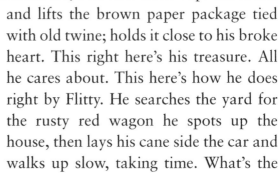

hurry? Drink it all in with a glad heart, is all he knows. Done is done. Appreciate everything. That's how ye make something new outta something wrinkly and old.

Walking slow, he admires the overgrown grass Barrows ain't got around to mowing. Greenest grass he ever seen this time year, except the autumn he lost Flitty. Just as green then it were, same thing. But right now, tufts of wild Kentucky blue run longside the beat-up slate, buttons of blooming chive push through the cracks like tiny lollerpops. Scarlet maple leaves, too. Scarlet maple and gold oak scattered all the way to the old hammock next the woods. He chuckles at the hammock; can't help hisself. Some good times on that thing, yessir. Can't think on that now though. Indecent to try. Up the walk he fetches the wagon, rests his package neatly inside, just so. Rolls the wagon up the cemetery path real slow. He could of drove, but no. Feels right to walk the path. Feels right to touch the earth with his own two feet. Walk the path Flitty and Adelaide walked every day they was alive. But now they're not.

Halfway up, he scratches at the collar where his bowtie's strung too tight. Not the best outfit fer a warm day, no, but then again he's burying a friend. Two friends, really. More like one friend and an angel. He tried to bury Flitty's things so many times, he sure did. More times than Flitty and Adelaide tried to bury him, that's possible. But he didn't have the heart to set her down. Couldn't let go the sweetness of carrying her personal things above ground, keeping her alive that way. Building an altar to her beauty, yessir. Plus burying one gal without the other made no sense. Addie and Flitty two sides the door. One coming, one going. Oh hell, we all one thing, Jules knows. Every last human a grand idea carried in the hearts of others we can't name. All carrying each other, we are.

Dragging the wagon slowly up the walk, he sees old Barrows

ahead leaning against the fence post puffing a stogie. His boy Reggie's digging up a sweat right beside him.

"Ahoy!" Julian hollers as he gets closer.

Barrows raises his arm. "Hey boss! Reggie just finishin' up. Ready fer ye now."

Same time Inis wanders up the back path by the old flower beds, arms full of hydrangeas. "Only bushes still bloomin'," she calls out. "Gotta have flowers."

Julian pats his heart. "'True words, Mrs. Barrows," he hollers.

Just out the fence, he sets the wagon against a rock and pulls apart the brown paper package, long wrapped. Setting his sore eyes upon what all's inside, he draws a breath so deep, near turns him inside out. Not that he didn't know what was in there, but it's been some time he seen it. Some time he touched it. Flitty's sandals lie right the top. Pretty pearl sandals dropped off her pretty feet by the ridge that night. Dropped right the edge against a rock. Hadn't been for the rock they'd of rolled right down the cliff, lost. Lost like Flitty. He sucks back a noseful of regret, turns his head and hocks it up. Day's long; can't get emotional yet. But he is.

Moving the shoes aside, he lifts the torn-up dress, all stiff and yellered. Crackling like parchment. It's the dress she wore on doomsday, but also the one she wore that day in the sun alone with Jules. That day surprised 'em both, yes it did. Flitty all stretched out the hood of his car like a faerie sylph, she were. One those creatures ye see then ye don't see. Like it's all in yer head. Like he made it up good. But he didn't. He knows he didn't cuz he snapped a photograph with his pa's camera. Framed it too. *Dang!* He got to hold back a dam of tears right about now, yessir. Should of opened this package at home's what he should of done. Should of reckoned his heart there. But he didn't.

No sooner he steps past the fence to the graveyard with his package than the hearse appears down the drive. Undertaker and his assistant open up the back, slide the slick mahogany coffin onto a bier and wheel her up the walk to the gravesite next Adelaide's mama, Regina. Not that Adelaide would appreciate her mama's company much, especially for all time, but what the heck. They got eternity to reconcile their differences. Close quarters might get 'em started.

Two fellers from the parlor plus Barrows and Reggie all lift the coffin off the bier and set it longside the grave. Then the two men head down the path fer the second box, wheel it on up, open the lid. Box's empty like Jules ordered. Empty but lined in padded pink satin with a frilly pillow like Flitty deserves. He would of got her a coffin of pure gold, he could of, if anyone made 'em in gold. But they don't.

Looking at all that pink inside, he wishes he could lay her silky flax-haired head down the pillow. Kiss her pretty forehead right there. But she's a piece of nature now, already. A rich patch of purple wood phlox, maybe, or some wild flame-red autumn dogwood all alone back the woods. Or both. He wishes he could touch what she turned into. Water it. Sit in her shade. Lean against her slender trunk. Pick her flowers; smell her perfume. No end to what nature can do with beauty like hers. Anything. Anything at all. He wishes he could see it though. See it and touch it. Hang it on a wall. Bend his neck and pray.

Feeling like he just might cry hisself dry, Jules presses the dress to his face. "See ye soon, angel," he whispers. "Till then, y'all light up the skies. Jes light 'em right up till we can't see no more. Till we all go blind."

He drops her things back the coffin, steps aside respectful. The men close the lid, slide straps under Adelaide's casket, then

Flitty's. Inis grabs Julian's hand for courage as the other four men, biceps straining, lower the coffins into open graves. Jules don't see death though, not at all. Jules sees life. Sees hisself, a strong teen, running cross the field with Adelaide then falling right on his dumb, thick-haired skull for Flitty. But she didn't fall for him, not really. She were just a filly. Couldn't see in herself what he saw yet. All the light. The rainbow arc all around her, protecting her. Don't matter. Jules were there to appreciate her, that's all. To see the promise. Witness it. See it rise.

How curious at first, watching the sisters try and bury him. "What's goin' on here?!" he'd say to the movie in his head. But then he knew. They was trying to bury him. They didn't know what gone wrong that night back the Gorge. They blocked it good. They didn't know Flitty passed over then crept on back through the nether. They didn't know Adelaide were half-dead herself, all sense shook out the one ear then the other. Still, they worried about Jules. Tried burying Jules. Tried and tried again. Tried do right by him. He scratches his chin. Now he's burying them.

All the sudden Inis jolts him sideways squeaking some offkey hymn Jules can't make sense of. Something about wild bees stinging sinners to make honey fer the Lawd. Something about going back the hive, going Home. Home sounds nice. Flitty's Home, rest her soul. But Jules knows Adelaide ain't Home yet. Hell, Adelaide ain't even around the corner from Home. She stuck deep in the nether's where she is. Jules wish her luck, he does, but he can't help her no more. She got to empty herself to find her way, but that ain't how she works. She like to fill herself up with anything handy. Anything make her forget who she really is fer the next five minutes.

Next, Barrows say a quick prayer. Undertaker sprinkles blest water. Choking tears, Jules throws a handful of dirt in each grave, one right one left, then he turns around and keeps on going. Just him and his cane. Don't look back. Him and his cane wandering back the house while the men fill the graves. Can't watch. They want him to. But he can't.

Back the house, Jules nibbles a baloney sandwich Inis left him, best meal he's ate in weeks. Finishing the crust, he knocks something beneath the kitchen table with his foot, leans down and catches sight of an old clay jug. *Jumpin' Jasus, that a jug a hooch?* he thinks. Sure could use a shot a hooch about now. He hooks the handle with his cane, drags it close, reaches out and hauls it on up at such an angle, near breaks his back. Hobbles around and finds hisself a good size glass and pours. Splashes her around and around, he does, sniffs the fumes, say a prayer and shoot her right on down the throat. Numb the mind. Kill the pain.

Whew! Whoa! Turns out this hooch burns bad's Ras' hooch back the day. Might just be one the same. Where else'd Adelaide get herself hooch? Inis ain't delivering hooch! Inis don't drink at all. But who cares where it come from? Hooch is hooch. Pours hisself another glass, he does. This time he sips it real slow whilst gazing out the kitchen window watching the blazing sunset gild the fields. Gild the fields and gild the slate walk. Gild the fence and gild the graveyard, too. He lifts his eyes, watching the hearse drive away. Then watching Barrows, Inis, and Reggie climb in the milk truck and take right off. What a day! Heavy sigh whistles right out his mouth whilst he waits. Waits some more. Waits till he's sure no one's coming back. Then he grabs his cane and steps careful down the stairs, holding the rail, one step the time. One step the time then the other. Outta breath the bottom, he rests a minute. Then wanders out the cemetery alone.

Poking the gate with his cane, Jules steps inside the dark

eerie yard real careful till he gets to Flitty's grave. Right there he steadies hisself in the spilt moonlight till the wood thrush quiets and the tree frogs hush. Give it time. Then real careful he gets down his cricky knees, turns over real delicate and drops top the mound of fresh-turned dirt. Lying there a time, he listens. Waits. No telling how long, he feels Flitty's warm heart heating up his chilled back, he does. Feels it good. Feels Flitty's heat and hears Adelaide giggling off the nether with his nephew, Dulles. Hears her begging, then hears Dulles say g'bye, so long. Addie squealing like she don't like it, but that don't matter. Time's up. Time now for Dulles move around the nether to help other folks. Folks who'll listen. Folks who care about waking up. Next thing, Jules spies two figures in the shadows by the willow tree, one lit, one dim. He knows who they are, he does. He buried them longside each other this very day to make things right. All he could do. Up to them now. Jules' job's done.

FORTY-ONE

REGINA

Regina waits anxiously on the old cedar bench that's wrapped halfway around the willow tree. She wants to be discreet. Doesn't want to wake up the sleepwalking relatives, or Julian who's lying on top of Felicity's grave around the corner. She doesn't want to scare Adelaide away. After all, her daughter's already scared to death. Regina remembers what it's like to lose the weight of material deceit. To find herself suddenly unhitched from the earthly persona that gave cause and purpose, however false. To find herself exposed, disarmed, and bodiless. To find herself defenseless, when defense was the only impulse she knew.

She spots Adelaide hovering above her own grave as shades often do, especially at first. Regina dims her own light and rushes to her daughter's side. Once there, she collects Adelaide's disparate energy, consolidates it, and moves them both back to the willow tree.

"What's happening?" says Adelaide. "Why am I moving? Who's there? What's going on?"

"It is I," says Regina softly. "Your mother."

Adelaide's energy stiffens.

"Please don't," begs Regina. "I've come to help."

"You can't help," says Adelaide. "Hasn't anyone told you? It's over. There's nothing to work with. What little I had I gave to Felicity."

"Because you loved her?"

"Because it scorched me."

"It scorched you because it was Felicity's light to begin with," says Regina. "She loaned it to you to get you by. But you have your own light, daughter. You're just hiding it."

Adelaide bristles, putting distance between them. "I'm not your daughter anymore. And I told you…whatever light I had I gave to Felicity. There's none left anywhere. It's over. Go away. Git."

"You borrowed Felicity's light because you couldn't access your own," says Regina.

Adelaide doesn't answer right away. "Why couldn't I?"

"It was hidden too deep."

"Hidden where?"

"Under shrouds of falsehoods," says Regina. She lowers her head. "Like mine once was."

"Since when did you have light?"

"We all have light, Adelaide. We're made of light. Everything is made of light."

"If you were made of light, I would be able to see you."

Regina brightens herself the slightest bit. "Like this?"

Shielding her eyes, Adelaide says. "Where did you get that light? Who did you steal it from?" She hesitates. "From Flitty?"

"There's a piece of each of us that's incorruptible, Adelaide. Eternal. Get in touch with that, and you'll have more light than you can imagine." She takes Adelaide's hand. "You'll shine."

"Shine?"

"And rise."

"Like Felicity?"

Regina nods. "Like Felicity when she released her human identity to complete her higher aspect."

"Celeste."

"That's right. You have a higher aspect as well. We all do."

Adelaide's energy combusts with chaos. "I doubt that, 'Mother'," she says sarcastically. "A higher aspect would be looking out for me. No one's looking out for me. Not a soul. No one ever has. I'm cold and dark." She shivers. "And scared," she adds in a thin voice.

Regina turns up her light and heat to warm Adelaide from a distance. "Hate is cold," she says. "Hate is cold and dark and scared. Hate obscures all possibility."

"You should know."

Regina fights to keep her energy cohesive in the face of attack. She hasn't mastered anything, not yet. She has to fight to stay neutral. "I still get angry," she says, "but I no longer hate. I got rid of hate." She sighs. "It was the most difficult adjustment of all."

Sensing a source of heat, Adelaide moves closer to Regina. "How can I get rid of it?"

"By holding my hand," says Regina, reaching.

Slowly, Adelaide moves closer. When their energy connects,

a new warmth kindles between them, a warmth of their own making, and she knows Adelaide feels it too. "As long as you hold my hand, hate can't endure," says Regina quietly.

Adelaide cowers.

Regina tightens her grip on Adelaide, and a deep current of possibility pulses from one to the other and back.

"It's dark," says Adelaide. "I thought I would like it, but I don't."

"It won't be dark forever."

"What if it is?"

"I'll share my light with you until you find your own."

"For how long?"

"As long as it takes."

Obituary for Release to:
Bluegrass Bugle &
The Louisville Gazette
Wednesday, January 6, 2021

Mr. Julian T. Buck Dies a Wealthy Man
Born: January 3, 1935
Passed into eternal life: January 3, 2021

86-year-old Julian T. Buck, aka Thaddeus Buck, as he
was later known, died of unknown causes at his home
in Outskirt, Kentucky. His body was discovered in bed
by his caretakers, Lionel and Inis Barrows and their
son, Reginald, when he failed to come downstairs for
his customary sunnyside up eggs and bacon. "We was
shocked," said Reginald. "Just yesterday he gave me the
keys to his vintage Chrysler convertible, and say, 'It's all
yers, Reggie!' 'Fer good?' I say, grabbin' the keys. 'That's
right, son,' he say. 'Fer good.'" Reginald mopped a tear.
"Truth be told, the man were a saint. He were as kind
and generous a man as ever walked the earth."

To the contrary, there are those who still blame Julian
T. Buck for his role in the 1960 incident at The Red River
Gorge in which 17-year-old Felicity Somers presumably
died, and her older sister, Adelaide, sustained brain
damage she never overcame. Buck served 30 years
in state prison for the conviction which was later
overturned. "He weren't bitter," said Lionel Barrows.
"Never bitter 'bout an'thang. He came into some money
'n bought *Sunnyside Up* to keep the bank from dislocatin'

Miz Adelaide. He paid all expenses, includin' a generous salary to me and m'family to watch over her." He patted his chest. "We all relied on him."

Inis nodded tearfully. "We really did," she said.

In his Last Will & Testament, Mr. Buck bequeathed *Sunnyside Up,* the ramshackle landmark once run as a funeral parlor and burial ground, to The Historic Society of Kentucky. Mrs. Burton Bridges of the Society claimed, "Mr. Buck uncovered papers in the basement of the original house revealing that it had operated as part of the Underground Railroad between 1861 and 1865. The Underground Railroad was a network of trains, meeting places and safe houses for escaped slaves on their way to Canada.

"That would be just like the Reverend Ebenezer Somers, alrighty," remarked Lionel Barrows. "He were the original godly Somers gent of the many godly sons that followed." He scratched his neck. "Some of the women was another story."

The Sunnyside Up Funeral Home & Chicken Farm served as a bed and breakfast originally, gradually evolving into a distinguished funeral and burial enterprise that served the finer citizens of the village of Outskirt and a few outcasts no one can account for, but there are stories.

With the exception of his sister, Dolly Buck Pearce, and her husband, the distinguished Langley Pearce of Alexandria, VA, the deceased lost all his kin in the great disaster of 1970 at the Diamondback Mine while he was imprisoned. "Prison saved m'life," he told the Barrows family more than once. "I'll always be grateful for the humility and long life it provided."

Both Mr. and Mrs. Langley Pearce predeceased Julian, as did their only child, Dulles, Buck's nephew, who died in 2008 of an opioid overdose at the age of 36 following a serious injury at the family's equestrian center in Middleburg, VA.

Buck will be buried at the *Sunnyside Up* family graveyard in a site he selected last year in front of Felicity Jane Somers, the daughter who was lost in the Gorge. Though Felicity's body is presumed lost somewhere in the Red River, her grave reportedly contains personal items collected at the site of the accident. "He were devoted to her memory," said Inis. "He framed every photo of her. It were touching."

Services will be held in the chapel on Friday at noon. According to his Last Will & Testament, a dozen doves will be released into the sky because "thar wings remind me of angels, which reminds me of a lost love that weren't really lost at all. Love never is."

ACKNOWLEDGEMENTS

G ratitude to my early readers: Mary Lou Alter, Kathy Baughman Lynch, Leslie Wolfe, and Marian Schumer. To my family for their support, especially my chief cheerleader, bartender, and builder of dream houses and cars, Tom Martin. Special thanks to Robin Gregory for her early review and to Victoria Colotta for her genius artwork throughout these pages.

ABOUT THE AUTHOR

R ea Nolan Martin is the award-winning author of *The Sublime Transformation Of Vera Wright* (2009); *Mystic Tea* (2014); *The Anesthesia Game* (2015); *Walking on Water—A Path to Empowerment* (2016); and *Sunnyside Up*; as well as essays, short stories and poetry published in anthologies and literary magazines. Her work has garnered over a dozen national awards. Readers can access author info, blogs, discussion questions, book signings and other inquiries, such as requests for signed copies at www.reanolanmartin.com.